PRAISE F

7¹/2

'Rejecting the rage of contemporary politics for a tender celebration of sensuality, nature, memory and love, 7½ makes a defiant claim: that even now, as the world burns, beauty is worth our attention. In this thrilling mashup of autobiography, homage, film and fiction, Tsiolkas presents a rebellious paean to joy and artistic freedom. I've admired the risk and power of all his novels, but this might be riskiest of all—so personal, so delicate and true—and I love it.' —Charlotte Wood, Stella Prize-winning author of *The Natural Way of Things* and *The Weekend*

'Powered by his electric, at times fevered intelligence and through his pushing of the English language to the point it is almost overloaded, Christos Tsiolkas offers his many readers a multi-layered novel that refuses to be categorised . . . The audacity of Tsiolkas is still a thrill. And, dare one say it, necessary.' —Nigel Featherstone, *Canberra Times*

'Expansive and effusive in its glorification of the natural world.' —*Good Reading*

'Full of lavish and finely detailed descriptions . . . this ever-present physicality, this sense of liveliness in and alertness to the world is the biggest pleasure of the book—it is sumptuous and evocative, beautiful—a celebration.' —*The Guardian*

'Tsiolkas writes with heady sensuality, overlaying the thick swathes of tastes, smells, sights and sounds onto the page . . . this is a vulnerable admission of how much of themselves writers put into their work.' —*Readings*

'A sprawling, rambling, glorious book, supremely confident in its structure and understanding . . . The world Tsiolkas creates is so well-drawn that the reader inhabits it, in all its grime, grief, corruption and misery. I cannot recommend this extraordinary novel highly enough.' —*Canberra Times*

'Visceral, muscular and relentless . . . Tsiolkas has proved himself a heroic writer, ready to enter the fray and wrestle with intractable moral and political questions. A powerful parable of our times.' —*Saturday Paper*

'Every time I was 10 pages in a new book, I thought, "It's not *Damascus*", and put it aside for another day . . . What struck me, with incredible power, was how Tsiolkas renders as ordinary people the names we know as gods, saints, demons, provocateurs, persecutors and protectors.' —Stephen Romei, *Weekend Australian*

'A narrative of shock and awe, fear and trembling, so large in ambition it will probably be the book for which [Tsiolkas] is best remembered.' —Geordie Williamson, *Weekend Australian*

'I learned more about Christianity in two days devouring *Damascus* than I did in five years at Catholic school . . . Tsiolkas may be most famous for writing *The Slap*, a very modern novel, but this latest release confirms his ability to identify and describe both the best and the worst of us humans, whether we wear sandals or sneakers.' —Bri Lee, *Good Weekend*

'A knockout novel . . . this exploration of faith, power, compassion and hope is as contemporary as it is ancient. A stunning piece of work from one of Australia's boldest literary voices.' —*Readings Monthly*

'Compelling . . . the mirror through which [Tsiolkas] shows this drama of the origin of Christianity is as dark and distorting as you could wish for. The work of a real writer.' —*Sydney Morning Herald/The Age*

'*Damascus* is ambitious . . . dripping with blood and sweat and reek of humanity, such is the violence and poverty of the era, which Tsiolkas skilfully and vividly renders.' —*Weekly Times*

'It's all as far from a sedate, hymn-singing Sunday morning in the suburbs as you are likely to get and it's staggeringly, illuminatingly alive. For a Christian reader, Tsiolkas gives faith a heft and an immediacy that is as shaming as it is exhilarating.' —*SA Advertiser*

'A brutal but riveting read, created by one of Australia's greatest literary talents.' —*The Age*

'Once in a while a novel comes along that reminds me why I love to read: *The Slap* is such a book . . . Tsiolkas throws open the window on society, picks apart its flaws, embraces its contradictions and recognises its beauty, all the time asking the reader, Whose side are you on? Honestly, one of the three or four truly great novels of the new millennium.' —John Boyne, author of *The Boy in the Striped Pyjamas*

'*The Slap* is nothing short of a tour de force, and it confirms Christos Tsiolkas's reputation as one of the most significant contemporary storytellers at work today . . . Here is a novel of immense power and scope.' —Colm Tóibín, author of *Brooklyn*

'Brilliant, beautiful, shockingly lucid and real, this is a novel as big as life built from small, secret, closely observed beats of the human heart. A cool, calm, irresistible masterpiece.' —Chris Cleave, author of *The Other Hand*

'A novel of great emotional complexity; as the narrative unfolds, it becomes clear that Tsiolkas has a rare ability to inhabit his characters' inner worlds. *The Slap* places family life under the microscope, and the outcome is nothing less than a modern masterpiece.' —*The Times*

'The Book of the Summer. Now and again a book comes along that defines a summer. This year that book is *The Slap* . . . *The Slap* has one elusive, rare quality: it appeals to both genders . . . The ideal summer read: escapist, funny and clever writing by a brilliant Australian novelist.' —*Telegraph* (UK)

'Strikingly tender . . . It claws into you with its freshness and truth.' —*Sydney Morning Herald*

'It's often said that the best politicians are those who can instinctively divine the zeitgeist of their country's centre. For the ones who can't, I would place *The Slap* as mandatory bedside table reading. It's a perfect social document of what Australia is today. More importantly, it's also one hell of a read.' —Venero Armanno, *The Australian*

'Tsiolkas is a hard-edged, powerful writer, but glowing at the heart of all the anger among these feuding families are sparks of understanding, resignation and even love . . . The novel transcends both suburban Melbourne and the Australian continent, leaving us exhausted but gasping with admiration.' —*Washington Post*

'Think Tom Wolfe meets Philip Roth. Or *The Sopranos* meets *The Real Housewives of Orange County*.' —*LA Times*

'Fond, fractious, lit from within by flashes of casual lust and malice, it's like *Neighbours* as Philip Roth might have written it.' —*The Sunday Times*

'This ingenious and passionate book is a wonderful dissection of suburban Australian living . . . this is a beautifully structured and executed examination of the complexity of modern living;

a compelling journey into the darkness of suburbia.' —*Independent on Sunday*

'A "way we live now" novel . . . riveting from beginning to end.' —Jane Smiley, *Guardian*

'An ambitious, state-of-the-nation novel of John Howard's post-9/11 Australia. Tsiolkas manages to add winding complexities to each of the inner portraits—which might have spiralled out of control in the hands of a less-deft writer. Tsiolkas's remarkable narrative fluidity proves that a fabulous page-turner can also contain great emotional power and intelligence.' —*Independent*

'A rich, provocative and poignant examination, exploring such themes as loyalty, friendship and marriage, class, gender politics, generation gaps, Aboriginal assimilation, immigrant identity and, of course, corporal punishment. It's an ambitious agenda, but nothing ever feels shoehorned in, and that's down to the even-handed skill with which he draws his characters. No clear lines of morality are drawn, and that's *The Slap*'s greatest strength.' —*National Post*

'Tsiolkas achieves an unusual double vision that both drives the story forward at speed and generates much of its pathos. We are presented with a cast of characters whose situation reflects the affluent, insecure, globalised Australia of the early twenty-first century. Yet this also makes the novel transportable into other cultures; it is at once quintessentially Australian, and a story that resonates in our own brittle and commercialised culture.' —*Times Literary Supplement*

'*The Slap* could well be one of the most successful state-of-the-nation novels of our times . . . A genuinely important, edgy, urgent book that hunts big game. Nothing escapes Tsiolkas's lacerating gaze . . . The novel keeps readers constantly on their toes, pushing boundaries, questioning lazy assumptions, provoking and, above all, smuggling in unease under the guileful blanket of a gripping read.' —*Telegraph*

'With *The Slap* Tsiolkas secures his place as one of our most important novelists . . . By painting an Australia we can recognise in language so good you don't notice it, Tsiolkas has written an absolute ripper.' —*The Age*

'A blistering portrait of domestic life. Tsiolkas dissects the psyche of each character with surgical precision.' —*Sun-Herald*

'One of the most astute chroniclers and critics of our age and culture, Tsiolkas is a passionate, poetic, political polemicist, but his critiques take the form of enthralling stories that are peopled with characters that bounce off the page.' —*Adelaide Advertiser*

The In-Between

Christos Tsiolkas is the author of eight novels, including *Loaded*, which was made into the feature film *Head-On*, *The Jesus Man* and *Dead Europe*, which won the 2006 Age Fiction Prize and the 2006 Melbourne Best Writing Award, as well as being made into a feature film. His fourth novel, the international bestseller *The Slap*, won Overall Best Book in the Commonwealth Writers' Prize 2009, was shortlisted for the 2009 Miles Franklin Literary Award, longlisted for the 2010 Man Booker Prize and won the Australian Literary Society Gold, and was also named Book of the Year for 2009 by the Australian Booksellers Association and the Australian Book Industry Awards.

Christos's fifth novel *Barracuda* was shortlisted for the ALS Gold Medal and the inaugural Voss Literary Prize. *The Slap* and *Barracuda* were both adapted into celebrated television series. Christos's acclaimed collection of short stories, *Merciless Gods*, was published in 2014 and his critical literary study *On Patrick White* came out in 2018. His sixth novel, *Damascus*, was published in 2019 and won the 2019 Victorian Premier's Literary Award for Fiction. *7½* was published in 2021. In the same year, Christos won the Melbourne Prize for Literature. Christos is also a playwright, essayist and screen writer. He lives in Melbourne.

Christos Tsiolkas
The In-Between

ALLEN&UNWIN
SYDNEY · MELBOURNE · AUCKLAND · LONDON

First published in 2023

Allen & Unwin
Cammeraygal Country
83 Alexander Street
Crows Nest NSW 2065
Australia
Phone: (61 2) 8425 0100
Email: info@allenandunwin.com
Web: www.allenandunwin.com

Allen & Unwin acknowledges the Traditional Owners of the Country on which we live and work. We pay our respects to all Aboriginal and Torres Strait Islander Elders, past and present.

 A catalogue record for this book is available from the National Library of Australia

ISBN 978 1 76147 001 1

Set in 12.75/18.75 pt Adobe Garamond Pro by Bookhouse, Australia
Printed and bound in Australia by the Opus Group

10 9 8 7 6 5 4 3 2 1

For Chris Brophy

'Two people do not lose themselves at the identical moment, or else they might find each other, and be saved. It is not as simple as that.'

Patrick White, *The Tree of Man*

1

He's fumbling, his heart is beating too fast; he has to sit on the bed. With a deep breath, he comes to. It is just the adrenaline. 'Concentrate! You're being a dickhead!' he tells himself: he has spoken the command in French, cursed himself in Greek. He gets up and returns to the open wardrobe.

A multitude of ties dangle over a wooden coathanger at one end of the wardrobe, coils of rayon and wool and cotton and linen. Perry marvels at how he has amassed such a collection over the years. He lifts a silk blade, feeling its sleekness. Where had he bought that tie? The memory is lost. Yet in trying to remember he glimpses a ghost of one of his former lives, a young man barely into adulthood, wearing a white dress shirt and black trousers made of fine wool, part of a suit that Perry's father had brought over on the ship from Alexandria to Fremantle. The memory of his much younger self has quietened the anxiety he'd been feeling, bringing with it a wave of pleasure almost euphoric in its intensity: he is in a dark subterranean club, and there is dance music blaring—that time when disco was mutating into house, with the percussive kinesis of post-punk being the trigger for the transformation. And he is wearing the tie that he holds now, as a much older man. The scarlet and white diamond pattern, the black sheen of the lining. He wore it regularly in the mid-1980s. He can't recall when he last put it on, or where he got it, but it has stayed with him through all the following decades, across oceans, from Melbourne to Athens to Rouen to Amsterdam to Tokyo and back to Melbourne.

Perry shakes his head. He hardly ever wears a suit; rare is the occasion that requires a tie. So why has he kept this collection? It seems almost mad. He runs his fingers over the seductive smoothness of the silk. It won't do—too formal, too elaborate. He sees one in simple dark blue linen, not too wide nor too thin. He has chosen to wear a simple cornflower blue shirt tonight. That tie will do.

Perry is going on a date. The word itself strikes him as ridiculous, inappropriate for a man of his age. But if he were not to call it a *date*, then what the hell was it? The struggle to find a word that can adequately describe the night's forthcoming adventure proves a calming diversion.

He lays the outfit on the bed: black denim jeans beside the shirt. He glances at the digital clock on the bureau beside the bed. He has an hour and a half before he has to be at the restaurant, before he meets Ivan.

No, that's not right either, he thinks, as he walks down the corridor to the bathroom. It's not a meeting. Is it an assignation? He likes the old-fashioned charm of that word.

After his shower, he wipes the condensation off the bathroom mirror, and looks at his reflection. He wants this self-examination to be ruthless, yet his eyes slide away as soon as they settle on his image. He breathes deeply and steadies his gaze, noticing gratefully that both eyes are remarkably clear, marked only by the faintest red lines. It has been a long time since he has indulged himself in the vanity of such an assessment. His irises are the colour of light grey slate; he is the only member of his immediate family with such pale eyes. His sister, Cleo, still teases him that some Celtic sailor or mercenary—a red-headed Belgian working on the docks of ancient Constantinople, perhaps, or an Irishman cajoled into joining the Crusades—had swept through an ancestral village and seduced and impregnated their young great-great-great-grandmother. That joke had long become family lore, so when Perry came back to Australia after twenty years, he discovered that even Cleo's children believed in the veracity of that myth—her youngest, Cerese, claimed that she too had 'Celtic eyes'.

He looks younger than his fifty-three years. And with that thought, he hears the words: 'You will always look younger than your age—it's because you don't have children.' Gerard had spoken them on Perry's forty-ninth birthday, over dinner at that small Neapolitan café near the university in Rouen. He had been pissed off then, had taken Gerard's observation as a slight, a cruel reminder to Perry that Gerard's connection to his children would always overshadow the love between them. But now, looking at his body in the mirror, at the sly silvering of his chest hair, at the paunch gathering at his waist, he realises that Gerard was probably preoccupied only with the inescapable fact of his own ageing. He had been sixty-three when Perry had turned forty-nine.

Perry turns, critically assessing his body; the protuberant belly button he has always hated, the short droop of his cock. He turns further to see whether the hair across his lower back is spreading. He has never been particularly hirsute, yet the last few years he has on occasion been reminded of the wanton-ness of hair growth on the middle-aged male body, of how it suddenly appears in the very places it is least welcome: on the shoulders, on the back.

With a shake of his head he collects himself and turns away from the mirror. Earlier in the week he'd had a haircut. He has trimmed his nails, has brushed his teeth three times today, and he shaved that morning. A shadow of bristle is already appearing across his chin and cheeks but he decides that it accentuates the golden tint of his skin tone. He opens the cabinet and splashes a few drops of cologne across his face, shakes a few more into his armpits. He combs his hair flat across his scalp. He will style it when he has finished dressing.

He is whistling as he walks back to the bedroom, pleased to feel his anxiety dissipating. He is comforted, as well, that thinking about Gerard has not resulted in the expected pain that has wearied him over the last few years. He is sad, yes, and maybe that unhappiness will be forever yoked with his memories of Gerard, but he is not gutted. He continues whistling as he gets dressed.

He has decided against cabbing it into town. Instead, he walks the short distance to the railway station. Though daylight savings is to end that coming weekend, there is no premonition of winter in the weather. Even with the day's fading, the breeze is soft and warm, and Perry carries his linen jacket over his arm. He walks at a steady pace. He knows that the shirt he is wearing looks good on him—he has been told that approvingly by friends—yet he is conscious of its light colour and the delicacy of the material, and doesn't want perspiration to darken the fabric.

On the platform, the sun is dropping into the western horizon, but the remaining light is still gently radiant. He regrets not taking his sunglasses. He moves further up to escape the sun's glare. Further along still there is a family of five. The grandmother is short, with a wizened, ancient face and bright, suspicious eyes. She sees Perry looking at them and frowns, turning away and pulling her purple sari more tightly around her body. The man—her son? her son-in-law?—is wearing an ill-fitting navy suit over a white shirt unbuttoned at the collar. He is carrying a large present wrapped in sparkling rainbow-coloured paper. The younger woman, slender and in high-heeled white shoes that elevate her to the same height as her husband, is looking down at her daughters, both dressed in identical white dresses with ballooning tulle skirts. The youngest, still with the chubby calves of an infant, is asking when the train will be coming. The oldest points to the electronic board: 'It's two minutes away.' The smallest child frowns. 'Two minutes!' she wails. Though their mother is wearing large dark sunglasses that completely screen her eyes, the smile on her lips suggests both bemusement and pride.

A disembodied mechanical voice announces the arrival of the city-bound train. It isn't too crowded in the front carriage and Perry finds a seat. As he does so, he catches the ghost of his reflection in the window. Maybe it's pompous to wear a tie? He sits straight-backed, absent-mindedly focusing on the blue and green swirls of the fabric on the seat opposite. His mind, however, is a whirl of feverish activity. Should he loosen the tie, take it off? He thinks back to the young father on the platform, at the appealing insouciance of the man's unbuttoned collar. Perry's right hand rises to his throat. Then another, more stinging thought: that man is at least twenty years younger than him. He doesn't want to look slovenly. He wants to show that he is taking this—this date? this assignation?—that he is taking it seriously.

He takes his phone out of his pocket, taps the screen, and quickly logs on to the dating site. He clicks on a thumbnail icon. Ivan's face flares across the screen.

A broad brow and high, sharp cheekbones suggest the Slavic heritage of the man as much as his surname does. His head has been completely shaved, the scalp glistening, and it is impossible to tell if he is naturally bald. His eyes are guarded, his mouth neither smiling nor stern. There is a saturnine aspect to him, undeniably so; and also, a surprising intimation of vitality. Though it is only a headshot, Perry can see that he is wearing a white shirt whose open collar is expertly ironed. His face is cleanly shaven. These last two factors made Perry decide that dressing up would be appropriate.

Ivan is attractive, almost brutally handsome. The curt biography stated that he was two years older than Perry. That, too, had been appealing: to converse with a man of a similar age and circumstances to his own. The initial messages they had sent each other were brief, hesitant, and then when Perry had sent him his number and Ivan had called, the details of where and when to meet for dinner had been canvassed quickly, the conversation lasting only a few minutes. Ivan's voice had been seductive, with a rolling cadence to his speech that elongated his vowels. The accent had been stridently Australian. Only a certain brittleness in his tone had bared his nervousness.

A platform guard blows a whistle. The train lurches forward and Perry looks up. The boarding passengers are scrambling for seats. A tall youth, dressed in a shiny black tracksuit, plonks himself down on the seat across from Perry. There is a slight suggestion of aggression in that slide into the seat. The young man's thick-soled white sneakers don't knock against Perry's shoes, there is no actual physical touch, but there is the threat of it, of the desire to claim more space. The youth shoves a wireless bud in each ear, tilts his phone horizontally and fixates on the screen.

Perry switches off his own phone, returns it to his pocket. He looks out of the train window at the rushing vista. The dark is beginning to settle and now his reflection is more visible in the glass. Once again, his fingers reach for the knot of his tie. And again, he drops his hand. He has made his decision.

He had signed on to Grindr when he had first arrived back in Australia, had used it a few times for quick, anonymous sex. But not long after his return, the Covid pandemic had swept the world. Even after the passing of the immediate threat of the virus, he still found himself tentative and unsure of sex. He was alarmed to find that his confidence had diminished. There had been a particularly humiliating encounter when he failed completely to get an erection and the man he hooked up with leapt up from the bed and, while pulling back on his underwear and overalls, hissed scornfully, 'Well, you're a fucking waste of time, aren't you?' Perry's body shudders at the recollection.

The train glides into another station, the automatic doors groan as they are released, and people surge through the train. A young woman sits beside him. She crosses her legs away from him, deliberately shifting her body. She is attractive, except for a pinched, equine aspect to her face that suggests something splenetic in her character. She too has pulled out her phone and is speaking loudly, with a marked terseness, almost spitting the words, as if her teeth are clenching on every consonant. And Perry is almost relieved by the woman's hostility and the arrogance of the young man sitting opposite. They are a distraction from his apprehension about the evening ahead.

Once they were a little more comfortable with each other via texting, he'd asked Ivan why he had chosen that particular dating site, one whose clients were predominantly heterosexual. Ivan had replied, briefly and equably, that, as he had stated in his profile, he was looking for a relationship. Perry had read his response on a Thursday night, just before getting ready for bed, and when he had woken the next morning, as he was brewing the first coffee of the day, he saw that there was a further message from Ivan. This follow-up had begun with an apology: *Hey, mate, sorry, I should have asked why you were on this site and not on grindr or something like that? Can I ask that now?* Perry had read and reread those words, wondering how to reply. It was then that he'd sent Ivan his phone number with the message: *Ring me if you'd like to go out to dinner. You can ask me anything you like!* Ivan's use of the now unfashionable word 'mate' and that surprising hint of gentility in the apology had made Perry decide he'd like to meet him.

The train is now almost at a crawl, sliding into the terminus of Flinders Street Station. Parents take their children's hands, women sling bags over their shoulders. Perry tells himself not to rush, that there is plenty of time and he doesn't want to arrive all flushed and sweaty. The train lurches to a stop. People heave through the carriage to the doors. Perry breathes deeply, then stands up.

The city, this warm autumn night, is dazzling. Perry exits through the western gate onto Flinders Street. A homeless man has his arms outstretched, palms up, almost as if in prayer, his head bowed. Cars crawl past on either side of the street, their drivers navigating the constantly changing traffic signals and the groups of teenagers crossing against the red lights. A tram clangs furiously as three young women in the sparsest of dress dash across the tracks. One of them, wearing a skin-tight lime-green singlet, the thin straps biting into her burnished skin, turns around and gives the driver the finger. Her friends burst into laughter, then scoop her up in an embrace as they run to the other side of the street. A child is hopping furiously from foot to foot in front of a gelato stand, her mother gripping her tightly as if terrified her daughter will evade her grasp and rush to her father, who is ordering ice creams. Anodyne electronic music drones out of a bar. A short, crabby-faced old woman lurches past, screaming to no one in particular: 'Give me some fucking money, cunts!' Above one of the buildings across from the station a rectangular screen bursts into the neon sparkling colours of the rainbow, the word PRIDE emerging from the glitter in bold sans serif before being replaced by the logo of an insurance company now emblazoned across the rainbow flag. The old woman keeps shouting: 'Give me some fucking money! Now! Cunts!' Movement, thundering noise, a cacophony really, the river not visible, the buildings shoddy, the most humdrum and uninspiring of late twentieth-century architecture, their brick and concrete facades dulled into an ugly dark grey from accumulated decades of traffic exhaust and air pollution—here is a city at its most aesthetically unattractive. Yet as Perry merges with the crowd surging across Elizabeth

Street, he feels a delirious rush through his body. Will he and Ivan have sex tonight?

Caught up in the charge, his pace increases. The dusk is about to be enveloped by night; there is only the dimmest trace of light lingering in the purple sky. With no breeze to disperse it, the collected heat of the day lies across the city. Perry feels a trickle of sweat down his spine. He slows his steps.

Perry hadn't answered that first call from Ivan, not recognising the number. Ivan's firm baritone on the voicemail message had taken him by surprise. He hadn't expected such a firmly masculine voice, and he had forgotten the choppy roughness of an ocker accent. Ivan had called the evening of the day that Perry had sent him his phone number. That had impressed Perry—the man was decisive, and not a game-player. Perry called him straight back. They had both been polite, low-key. Very quickly the men established that they lived across town from each other, Ivan in a suburb called Bonbeach that was unknown to Perry. 'It's between Mordialloc and Frankston,' Ivan had explained, a hint of defensiveness in his tone now. And then, clearing his throat, the gruffness returning, he continued, 'I know Preston; I have family out that way. Should we meet there?'

Perry had been momentarily flustered by the need to make a decision. Ivan's silence on the other end had only increased his anxiety so he had blurted out, not really thinking it through: 'Why don't we meet in town?' Even as he had spoken, he had winced, realising that he had no idea where to eat in the city these days.

Thankfully, Ivan's response had been to ask, 'Do you like Italian food? I know this good place on Hardware Lane. It's not overpriced, good basic grub and you can hear yourself speak.'

'Great,' Perry had answered. 'That sounds perfect.'

Approaching the restaurant now, he wonders if it has been there for years, since before he left Melbourne. It is impossible to gauge; it shares the slightly kitsch aspect of so many Italian restaurants throughout the city and around the world. A tall waiter in black pants and a white shirt is standing by the door. Treacly Italo-pop is murmuring from a speaker attached to one of the posts holding up the olive-green awning. Identical posies of red and white carnations are placed in small glass vases on each table. Though the lighting inside is sombre, Perry recognises Ivan immediately. He is sitting at a small table on the other side of the window, swiping at his phone. Grateful that Ivan had not glanced up and spotted him, Perry takes a deep breath. The waiter smiles, ushers him inside.

As soon as he enters, Ivan swings around. The waiter escorts Perry to the table and then discreetly moves away. Ivan leaps to his feet, offering his hand to shake. Perry makes sure his grip is staunch, and that it doesn't last too long.

He's bought a new shirt, thinks Perry, as they take their seats. He realises he needs a drink. There is a slight drilling feeling at the back of his head and, though it has been a long time since he did drugs, it reminds him of the first effects of ecstasy, that strange limbo of anticipation and fear, before it really started to kick in. The music seems louder, there are frequent shouts and laughter from a large group in the middle of the restaurant, the sounds of cooking, of clanging, coming from the kitchen. And there is the solid man across from him, and the subtle citrus whiff of his cologne. It is all overwhelming.

Ivan takes his phone off the table, puts it in his trouser pocket. The civility of the gesture is admirable.

Perry is released. 'It's been a long time since I've been on a date,' he says, pocketing his own phone. 'Please ignore anything I say for at least the first ten minutes.'

Ivan's laugh is loud, delighted. 'I know, mate, I'm bloody terrified.'

They order wine and the conversation proceeds, stiffly at first. Perry comments on the appeal of the restaurant and Ivan explains that he had first visited for a business lunch. That opens the topic of work and Ivan becomes more animated, explaining that he owns a landscaping business, offering a short summary of his working life, from horticultural college and apprenticeship to his decision in his late twenties to risk working for himself. Perry listens attentively, finding himself charmed by the evident pride Ivan takes in the trajectory of his career. He employs three full-time staff, but it is clear that he still enjoys the work. It explains the optimistic masculinity of the man, the callused symmetry of his large hands and the curve of the muscles that strain against his tight-fitting pastel yellow shirt. It suits him, Perry notes, as it accentuates the gleam of his olive skin. He surreptitiously pats his tie, realising it had been a sound choice. Ivan clearly cares about his appearance: the new shirt, the polished black leather shoes, the aromatic cologne. His head is carefully shaved, with a hint of grey stubble at the temples. Perry finds himself wondering whether the man opposite is anxious about being bald or whether he is making allowances for age and nature. Ivan's shirt collar is unbuttoned, a flash of pale, smooth skin visible beneath. He wonders if that is natural or whether Ivan shaves his body hair.

The thought feels intrusive at this early part of the evening and snaps him back to attention. Perry starts talking about his own work as a translator for a media production company. He is gratified to see that it impresses Ivan, the singularity of his occupation. It also allows him to explain that he has only been back home for three years, that the last two decades have been spent in Europe. They ask each other questions about family and heritage. Ivan's is Serbian and Perry explains that his mother and father were both migrants, that his heritage is Greek. He speaks about his father's death, how the old man had fallen ill four years ago and precipitated Perry's return to Australia. Ivan nods, offers that his own father has also passed away. The natural gruffness of his tone deepens as he speaks of his father and Perry is struck by the gloom that for a moment seems to settle on him. They are both relieved when a waiter interrupts.

Once they've ordered, Ivan asks, 'So, what made you choose the site? Why are you not on Grindr or something like that?'

Perry is about to joke, 'How do you know I'm *not* on Grindr?' but stops himself. He'd have meant it in jest, but he intuits that the sense of sadness he perceived in Ivan might require a little gentleness. At that moment, the challenge of meeting a new person seems wearying, and he wonders if he will have the patience to last out the evening.

'I didn't mean to offend you.' Ivan's smile is embarrassed, and Perry catches a glimpse of the youth he once was. The sweetness of that image is captivating.

He shakes his head. 'No, no, I'm not offended. I'm just wondering how to answer your question honestly.'

Which is a lie. He hasn't been wondering that at all. Then he remembers something a therapist once taught him. David worked out of a cramped office above a tobacconist, and the room always smelt of cigarettes and the musky odour of old books. 'Périclès,' David would say, 'Sometimes by saying things out loud for the first time, we come to understand what we really want.'

Ivan's handsome, weathered face is open, waiting.

'I don't want to be lonely,' Perry says, feeling the chill of fear that always accompanies courage. 'I want to find someone to share my life with.'

Ivan's right thumb is obsessively scraping the edge of the table. Perry recognises the action; he is immediately reminded of Gerard.

'Ivan,' he says, smiling to assure the other man that he does not disapprove, 'would you like to go outside for a smoke?'

Ivan gives a gratified sigh, and his thumb stops. He shakes his head. 'Thanks, I wouldn't mind it, but it's not worth it. You can't smoke out the front—some bullshit City of Melbourne rule. Antony, the owner, lets us out the back for a smoke, but it's not a very inviting space out there with the garbage bins.'

He reaches for Perry's hand, offers the gentlest of taps before withdrawing. 'I want to hear about you. Why are you lonely?'

Perry thinks that if he were to fall in love—and it is too early for such impossible dreams, he knows that—its beginning would be marked by the grace and kindness of that simple gesture.

'Why am I lonely? 'Cause I'm a dickhead.' His voice changes for a moment, as if stripped of the polish of education and travel. He knows it is revealing, that that sharp pitch only returns in moments of shame or humiliation.

'Why are you a dickhead?'

'Because I spent twelve years of my life in love with a married man.' Perry rubs his forehead nervously as he takes a gulp of wine. 'Do you disapprove?'

Ivan gives the slightest response, a quick shrug. His face is unreadable, and Perry's confidence falters. He has said too much, and too soon. A heaviness falls with such alacrity that he physically slumps. He is too old to go through this ritual that seems more suited to the emotions of adolescence. Not for the first time—and he always thinks this heretical, would not dare utter it—he wonders if there isn't something stunted in the experience of being homosexual. He is on a *date*! What a ridiculous situation for a man of his age to be in.

'You haven't told me enough for me to decide whether I approve or disapprove.'

Ivan's words are precisely the jolt that Perry needs. Yes, he's fifty-three, and yes, he's on a date. Yet the man he is with is attractive, and clearly has innate perspicacity. Perry scans the restaurant. They are not the only middle-aged people here trying to negotiate the ever-shifting terrain of contemporary courtship.

'I guess I am judging myself.' That stark truth is a relief. 'I definitely regret spending all those years with someone who never told his wife about us, who had three children. I met his family a few times. It was awful; I felt so ashamed.' Perry's smile is weak, rueful. 'I guess that tells you something.'

'Did you want him to leave his family?'

Oh, God, where does he begin! There is no possible way he can explain, not at this moment, not to a near stranger—for though his instinct is to trust this man, the truth is undeniable: they do not know each other—how he has no straightforward answer to that question. It has tormented him for years, and it still plagues him, can still obliterate his peace.

'I never said that to him. I never gave him an ultimatum. Did I want him to do it? I don't know. I really don't fucking know.'

During the week he had told himself to be careful with expletives. He didn't want to appear crude. But the obscenity feels right, imbuing his words with anger, certainly, but also admitting a heartfelt candour.

'Was this in Greece?'

'In France. Gerard is French. Though we met in Thessaloniki. He's a professor at a university in Normandy, a classicist.' He hesitates. Does he need to explain that word? Should he have called Gerard a historian? He steals a glance; Ivan looks unperturbed.

'He was attending a series of lectures in Greece,' Perry continues. 'I was living in Athens, but I'd gone up for the same conference. I ended up interpreting for him and his colleagues.'

Their meals arrive and Perry starts tucking into the *scaloppine al limone* that has been placed before him. He can smell the tanginess of the lemon, the sweat of the garlic in the sauce. He knows he has only provided the most cursory sketch of his first encounter with Gerard. He doesn't know how to explain the astonishing heat and turmoil he experienced at that first meeting; the man's overt Gallic haughtiness; the Teutonic power of his height and colouring; the refinement of his immaculately tailored suit, the sheen of the clearly expensive material; the strong jaw; the crisp line of tawny beard. The other men and women around him, both the European delegates and the members of the Greek reception, had seemed shabby by comparison. As they shook hands, Perry noticed—all at once— that Gerard was wearing a wedding ring, and that his clear blue eyes were appraising him with evident regard.

Perry and Ivan eat in silence, one that is neither companionable nor awkward.

Perry is enjoying the food, and, more, he is enjoying watching the other man eat. Ivan slurps his ragu-coated pasta greedily. The suggestion of plumpness in Ivan's sturdy build suits his large frame.

The sommelier asks if they would like more wine.

'Neither of us is driving,' Ivan says, and turning to the sommelier he orders two more glasses. Then, immediately, he asks Perry: 'Or should we get another bottle?'

Perry hesitates. He is enjoying the slight narcotic fug from the wine. But it would be unwise to get drunk.

The sommelier smiles. 'If you're going to have another wine after this one, then it's cheaper to get the bottle.' She winks conspiratorially. 'You don't have to drink it all.'

And the suggestion of the bottle also indicates that the evening will not have an abrupt end. He nods at the young woman.

As soon as she has stepped away, Ivan asks, 'How long did you live in Athens?'

'Five years.'

'And then you moved to France. Did he ask you to?'

'He organised a position for me at a college in Rouen.' Perry's laugh is sharp, sardonic. 'To translate some Byzantine texts from Greek to French. It was very niche.'

The sommelier has returned with the new bottle. Perry admires how, with a warm smile, an assertive shaking of his head, Ivan indicates that there is no need for them to taste it.

'But I liked Rouen; it's a picturesque medieval city without being too Euro Disney. And it's convenient, an easy drive to Calais, to Belgium and to Holland. In an hour and a half you're in Paris.' He shrugs. 'And we're Australian—nothing seems too far away for us when we're in Europe.'

'I've never been.'

It's a shocking revelation and Perry can't hide his surprise. And something of disdain? For the first time, Ivan withdraws— not physically, but a coolness appears in his eyes. And just before his face had settled into that aloof severity, Perry had seen a flash of red-hot rage. Summarily controlled, smothered; yet it had been there.

I must seem like such a bloody snob, thinks Perry. And I bet he's got a temper.

'I'm sorry if I looked so surprised. I think I assumed that with your parents being Serbian you'd have been to Europe.'

Ivan's gaze doesn't shift; his eyes are still cold, unfathomable. Then one side of his mouth curls into a grin, and with an almost imperceptible shift, the slightest leaning in, the distance between them no longer seems unbridgeable.

'Though my father's Serbian, his village is now in Croatia. Neither of my folks ever went back. I don't really speak the language. Don't have any connection to the place.' His finger is gently tracing the rim of his glass. 'I have been to Asia.' There is pride in that final statement.

'Whereabouts?'

And Perry is sincerely curious. Since he got home he has become aware of how limited his travel has been: Australia and Europe and those few months in Japan; that week in New York City, where Gerard had disappointed him with his frustrating French parochialism, the timidity of his insularity.

'Thailand.'

'When did you go?'

Ivan coughs into his elbow, reaches for his water. 'When I turned fifty.' And this time he takes a sip of his wine. 'It was a birthday present. From my sister and my daughter.'

Clearly—for with this last word the man releases a deep sigh—it is a relief for Ivan to tell him this. He's been sitting on it all night, Perry thinks to himself, wanting to tell me he has a child.

'What's her name?'

'Katerina.'

'How old is she?'

'Thirty-six.'

'Jesus.'

And at this, Ivan bursts out laughing. 'I was only nineteen when she was born.'

'That's young.'

'That's way too young.'

Ivan's smile has vanished, along with the almost boyish pugnacity that Perry can't help but find appealing; it reminds him of the boys he revered in high school. The seriousness ages Ivan.

'It was a mistake getting married—my ex is a piece of work. But Katerina is worth it. She's absolutely fucking worth it.' No sign of embarrassment about his swearing: it is there to underline his love for his daughter. And with that, his lightness has returned.

'I need to tell you, Perry: I'm a grandfather.'

Perry knows the face to show: he consciously maintains his genial expression, forces the muscles at his neck not to stiffen. Perry has become expert at this mastery of his body. That first year after Gerard broke off their relationship was an absolute plunge into the misery of ruin; not only the collapse of his emotions and his will, those terrible, debilitating, emasculating—that is the *right* word—descents into weeping and sleeplessness and shame, but also the collapse of his very body itself. Perry had shed weight, had developed shingles, even suffered the humiliating return of his adolescent acne, with raw red boils across his neck and shoulders. And that horrible last autumn in Athens, getting sodden drunk night after night, taking those unconscionable risks in the basement sex cinemas off Omonia, almost willing himself to get sick, beaten, robbed. He wanted pure annihilation. Love sickness: that had been his name for it; the only name for it. He can still remember the taste of it with horror, the bile that seemed permanently to be rising to his throat, so he can never now forget what resentment and bitterness taste like. And returning to Australia, like a dog with its fucking tail between its legs, and devoting that next year to training his body to stop releasing that pain, from revealing that pain, demanding it not expose any sign of his mortification, so that he can sit opposite this man at this table tonight and nod cheerfully as he speaks of his granddaughter called Natasha, and can answer, 'What a lovely name,' in a tone that is warm and convincing, and so when he says, 'Excuse me, I'm just going to the toilet,' he can be sure that Ivan has not noticed his distress. Perry has mastered his grief.

He finds the toilet. He breathes in deeply.

It had been that word: grandfather. It had been Gerard's clinical announcement, over the scuffed metallic surface of a table in the café in Rue du Général-Leclerc, overlooking the sports park where a steady stream of fit youths in their gym wear walked past, their stupendous vitality mocking

Gerard's carefully rehearsed words: 'My dear Périclès, Marie is having a baby and Mathilde and I are to be grandparents. You and I must end. There is nothing else to do.' He had tried to counter the impenetrable barrier that Gerard had created between them—the older man had seemed almost furious, as if the conversation filled him with scorn—by offering up the only defence he had: 'Gerard, I love you.' The sound that Gerard had made, an almost comic rasping sound from the back of his throat, there was anguish in that suppressed moan. 'That doesn't matter now. I am to be a grandfather. To continue would be *incovenant*.' He hadn't immediately grasped the meaning of the word, had to look it up in English. Unseemly. By which he meant dirty.

Perry flushes and looks at his reflection in the small mirror blu-tacked at a precarious angle over the basin. It wasn't the contempt in Gerard's tone that had crushed him. No, it was Gerard's pride in announcing that he was going to be a grandfather. Perry smiles joylessly at his own image. This is progress: at least his face isn't flushed. The shame is lessening. He draws his face closer to the glass and whispers, '*Pédé, pousti*, poofter.' His breath clouds the mirror, and he finally feels released.

On his return he smiles at Ivan and asks, 'So, were you married for a long time? Is it only recently you've realised you're gay?'

Ivan laughs loudly. 'No way, mate—I think I've known since I was seven years old.'

'That's very specific. What happened when you were seven?'

'Tim Papadimitris happened. We were in the same class at Clayton North Primary. We used to spend every recess and lunchtime together holding hands. I loved him.'

It is expressed simply, the declaration pragmatic and forthright.

'So, you have a thing for us Greeks?'

A shorter, equally affable laugh. 'Yeah, I think I do.'

'What happened to Tim Papadimitris?'

'Grade four happened. At the start of that year he said we couldn't hold hands anymore. He said only poofters did that.'

Ivan's glass is nearly empty. Perry takes the wine out of the cooler, refills Ivan's glass and then his own.

'Thanks.' Ivan takes a sip. He suppresses a cough, that tell of a smoker. He quickly drinks some water. 'They say that we develop in cycles of seven years. I think there's some truth in that. I definitely noticed it with Kat. She changed suddenly from being this inquisitive tomboy to wanting to dress and act like other girls.'

There is a lull; both men have fallen quiet.

'Do you think it's true?' Ivan asks quietly.

'What is true?'

'That we develop in stages of seven years.'

Perry calculates. Like flashes, moments of being seven: playing hide-and-seek in Studley Park with his siblings and cousins, the dappled light falling on the ground; then fourteen: the fumbling, almost aggressive mutual masturbation in Colin Attwood's bedroom, Fleetwood Mac's *Tusk* spinning on the turntable; then twenty-one: the rush, the terror of navigating the buses from Istanbul to Trebizond. And twenty-eight: applying for his EU passport.

Ivan is waiting patiently. Perry realises he has been lost in memory.

'I think it might be true when we are very young,' he begins in a rush. 'I did first-year psychology at university . . .' Perry falters. He was about to mention Piaget's theories of childhood development but thinks how pretentious that could sound to the man sitting opposite. Or is it arrogant to think that Ivan wouldn't understand? 'I studied a man called Piaget,' he continues. 'And I was convinced by his notion that at around seven years of age there are phenomenal spurts of emotional and physical development in children.' He glances across the table. Ivan is looking at him intently. 'I think similar changes occur at around fourteen, in puberty.' Perry pauses. 'But I don't think it's the same for adults. I'm not sure if there was a big difference between being forty-two and forty-nine.'

Ivan nods, and at that moment the waiter arrives holding two small cards.

'Dessert, gentlemen?'

The question seems to unsettle Ivan. A grizzled, old-man's frown creases the edges of his mouth, reveals the depth of the furrows above his eyes. For a brief moment he is ugly.

'What do you think?' There is something almost beseeching in his tone.

'Let's have a look.'

Ivan's smile returns, is expansive.

The selection is standard. There is cheesecake, chocolate mousse and tiramisu. The cheeses are local. He glances across to Ivan and sees consternation once again gathering at his brow. It is odd, as if his straightforward confidence, which had been so immediately appealing—even before tonight; from when he first heard Ivan's voice on the phone—seems to have vanished.

He's a big man. Satisfyingly big, with those broad shoulders, the strength in his arms: that must be from the landscape gardening. But yes, certainly, there is a paunch, there is softening at the jowl.

'Do you want to share the tiramisu?'

Ivan gives Perry a grateful smile. And with it comes a welcoming revelation: Ivan likes Perry too.

Ivan beckons the waiter and orders.

'I was forty-two when my father passed away, so that was a big year,' he says. 'Definitely a big year. And it was only when I turned fifty—you know, five years ago—that I think I was settled in my grief.' His fingers have resumed their soft tapping on the table. And he swallows, as though he had been about to add something and had then thought better of it. Then he gives a good-natured shrug, with that almost impish grin of his. He would have been a very good-looking teenager, Perry muses, and in allowing himself that glimpse of fantasy, he is aroused. He wants to know what it would be like to kiss the man, to have those strong arms hold him.

'So maybe it is the rule of seven,' Ivan continues. 'Or maybe that's just another superstition, a way of us humans ordering and making sense of the world. Who knows?'

'How long were you married?'

Impossible to not make some of this sound like an interrogation. And impossible not to have to feign interest in some of it—Perry knows that he will soon be asking the age of the fucking grandchild.

'Nearly ten years. They were a nightmare. We were both nineteen and dumb and selfish and way too young to be parents.'

'Is that why you married? She got pregnant?'

Ivan nods firmly, sadly.

'But you knew you were gay?'

'Yes.'

There is an intrusion of noise. Something has smashed on the floor in the kitchen. There is a loud roar and rush of Italian. The disturbance is welcome. Perry feels he is floundering over the expectations of this assignation—oh, for God's sake, man, it's a date, call it a bloody date—and he doesn't know if he should probe further to show he's not self-involved and narcissistic . . . or is that being too inquisitive?

'I feel for the poor bastard.' Ivan's tone has dropped to a whisper. 'That chef is really telling them off.'

'You speak Italian?'

'Dana's Sicilian. My ex. I picked it up from her folks screaming at me.' He shakes his head. 'My ex. That sounds so stupid. It was all so long ago.' He reaches for his wineglass, cradles it without drinking. 'It was the mid-eighties and I was just out of trade school. I got terrified about AIDS; that was all you heard about back then. I thought I'd give being a straight guy a crack.' He is smiling again. 'Didn't last long.'

He clears his throat and drinks some wine.

'I was never in love with Dana, that's where I fucked up.'

He settles the glass back on the table, rolls his shoulders, and faces Perry, his gaze genial but direct. It makes Perry a little anxious, as if Ivan is letting him know that he is assessing him, taking notes.

'Were you in love with this man, this French fellow . . . ?'

'Gerard.'

'Gerard,' repeats Ivan, and the heaviness of the Australian accent, the stress on the first syllable, the abrupt cut to the second, the complete absence of melody, makes Perry want to laugh. How Gerard would hate it.

He answers honestly: 'Yes, I was.'

He wonders if he has been too candid, for Ivan's gaze has strayed. But it is because the waiter is bringing their dessert.

'And you are fine for wine?'

Ivan glances over. Perry shakes his head.

'We're good.'

The waiter pours the last of the bottle into their glasses. Perry looks at his glass; only a few mouthfuls of wine left. He suddenly feels weighed down by anticipation. He doesn't know how he wants the evening to end.

'I'm sorry.'

Perry is taken aback. 'What for?'

'This guy must have hurt you very much.'

It is too intimate an observation. Ivan's eyes are too generous, too fucking pitying.

Perry deflects, points to the tiramisu. 'It's enormous.'

'It'll be good, I promise you.'

They attack the dessert and Perry notices again that Ivan's appetite is impressive; he enjoys the gusto with which the other man eats. His own mouthfuls are much more modest. It is a good tiramisu, firm and creamy and not overly sweet nor drowned in coffee. There is a clump of cream above Ivan's lip. Perry brings his finger close, Ivan leans in so there is touch. It is quick—Perry softly wipes Ivan's mouth, then cleans his finger with the napkin. There is a spark; he is sure that the other man felt it too. Perry feels elated.

Ivan is looking lovingly at the last morsel of tiramisu. Perry pushes the dish across to him with a smile. Ivan scoops the morsel into his mouth, takes a large swallow of water, follows it with a sip of wine.

He pats his stomach, looks doleful. 'I love their desserts a bit too much.' He then says with startling candour, 'Getting hurt by love stinks, doesn't it? It really fucking stinks.'

He finishes his wine. 'Perry,' he says, 'would you like to go somewhere for another drink?'

'Yes.' Perry's answer is immediate.

As they leave the restaurant, Perry is disconcerted by the crowds in the alley and the loud autotuned pop music blaring out of the bar opposite. The streetlights are blinding, as are the green, white and red globes hanging from the restaurant's awning. The youth of the swirling bodies all around them—the women in their strapless tops and short skirts, the men in T-shirts and skinny jeans—is both dazzling and intimidating, along with the manic percussion of the music drumming insistently in his ears, the explosive glare of light. Perry realises he is a little drunk. And chilly—the luxuriant warmth of the day has disappeared with the full descent of night. He puts his jacket on. Ivan stands beside him, hands in his pockets, observing the action of the street.

Across from Ivan and Perry, Rani, a young woman, is talking on the phone to her sister. She is huddled in a doorway between a bar and the music shop next door, the shadowy alcove hiding her from clear view of the men. She is trying to support her sister, who is bemoaning the selfishness and laziness of her husband, who has once again left her alone at home with their three-year-old to go out with his cousins. But Rani is also impatient to get back to the bar where she has been flirting enjoyably with a guy, Dylan, who works with her friend Bianca. It has been a long time since Rani has experienced the frisson of attraction in real time, not had it mediated by the safe distance of a screen. She likes Dylan. Her sister is prattling on about her husband's egoism and Rani is listening, bored, ready to pounce into a gap in the monologue to say that she will come around first thing in the morning. She cursorily examines the two older men across the alley. They are both tall, the thinner dark one looking Lebanese or Greek. The other one is hard; even the flab of his belly appears solid. He seems Anglo, though there is something about the sharp angle of his cheeks and the prominent broad chin that suggest otherwise. They are both dressed simply but well. She is sure they are gay, though the big bald one has just glanced her way with an admiring look. But she feels sure there is nothing sleazy in his appraisal. She doesn't acknowledge his stare, just gazes impassively. 'Bhakti,' she finally interrupts, 'it's cold, I'm going back inside, I'll be round tomorrow. Love you.' She steps out of the doorway, slips her phone into her handbag from which she then removes a small compact mirror. She checks her teeth, her smile. Then, after an adroit fluffing of her long dark hair, she strides back inside.

Perry notices Ivan watching the young woman. 'She's very attractive,' he says.

Ivan nods then looks across at the bar. 'It seems a little full-on in there.'

'Yes,' says Perry, 'and a little too young.'

Ivan laughs in agreement. 'Should we walk up to the top end of Bourke Street? There's some quieter places around there.'

Perry wonders if there would be any place open at this hour—not quite midnight—that won't be full of sound and glare and people.

Then Ivan adds sheepishly, 'And I wouldn't mind finding a place with a beer garden or courtyard—somewhere I can have a smoke.'

Perry stops himself from saying that he's lived in Greece and France, where no one has to apologise for smoking. Instead, surprising himself, he offers: 'Would you like to come back to my place for a drink?' And almost immediately he starts apologising, anticipating the rejection. 'Of course, it might be a bit far . . .'

Ivan touches his arm. 'I'd like that.'

'And you can smoke at my place. There's a balcony.'

In the cab there occurred an incident, slight, almost *en passant*. Nevertheless, Perry had been upset by it. The driver was listening to a late-night current affairs show. They had been waiting at the lights to turn right into Blyth Street when Perry realised that Ivan was concentrating on the conversation on the radio. An academic was being interviewed, her tone robust, impassioned. She was clearly struggling to maintain objectivity as she spoke about a recent scandal in which a young television journalist had accused an older colleague of sexually assaulting her after an awards night party. Perry had only followed the story intermittently, though he had watched the young woman's painful press conference after she had gone public with the accusations and been affected by the wounded, glazed fear in her eyes. He had felt immense sympathy for her; she seemed so very young. His sister Cleo had been galvanised by the woman's courage, as had many of his friends. So it had been a shock to hear Ivan snort out loud during the interview. And then he had said in an undertone which Perry and the driver both heard: 'Maybe don't get so drunk you pass out and can't remember what happened.' The driver's eyes had flashed gleefully in the rear-view mirror as he nodded approvingly with a superior smile.

Perry had sat there, wanting to say something, to interject, yet fearful that it would precipitate an argument; and also, to be honest, knowing that very similar opinions had often crossed his mind. Not meanly, and certainly not dismissively. The woman's disbelieving, devastated face on the television had been sincere. Perry was convinced that she believed she'd been violated. The words had started forming in his mouth—'That may be, but it doesn't condone a man taking advantage of her' . . . Christ, they sounded so fucking pious, so fucking trite!—but the conversation had moved on, Ivan and the driver having bonded over their derision. He had looked down at his phone: the driver's name was Ehsan. As he did so, Ehsan asked Ivan where his family was from, and when Ivan replied, 'Serbia,' Ehsan had said, 'Then you are not an Australian. Australians are very bad drunks, the boys and the girls—it is terrible what I see.' Ivan had nodded affably and Perry had deliberately turned away from him, his forehead almost touching the window, as he looked out at the blunt ugly stretch of St Georges Road.

Then Ehsan had asked about family and Ivan, sounding assured—no, Perry decided, sounding *smug*—had answered, 'Mate, I'm a grandfather.' Perry hated it when taxi drivers asked such familiar questions. 'No,' he always wanted to shout, 'I'm not married, I don't have fucking children!' He'd wondered what would have happened—the temptation was immense—if he'd leant over and said, 'Yeah, he might be a grandfather, but he's coming back to my place to suck my cock!' It did not matter how polite Ehsan had been, how capable a driver, how clean his car; he'd give him a terrible rating. The car had stopped right outside his building's main entrance. Perry had given Ehsan a five-star rating and left him the minimum tip.

His mood was lifted by Ivan's enthusiastic response to the apartment. Purchased in an almost hallucinatory state when he had arrived back in Australia, his resilience shattered, overwhelmed by shame over Gerard's betrayal, that futile waste of years, he had relied on the counsel of his brother-in-law, Benjamin, when it had been time to buy the flat. All he had asked was that it be north of the river and close to public transport. That first year he had hardly even noticed the space; certainly, he did not regard it as home. Benjamin had been a saviour, not only finding the apartment but also securing him work for a law firm that was negotiating a contract between a mining company and the French government. Perry had enjoyed the banal minutiae of the work, poring over long documents of legalese, dry economic statistics and regulations that he translated back and forth into unadorned French or commonsense English. His efforts had impressed one of the consulate staff, and he'd been offered further work preparing for the annual French film festival. That had led to the job at the media company. Then had come Covid: the long lockdowns and, with that restriction of freedom, the first sense of the boons and shortcomings of the apartment.

As soon as he had stepped out of the cab, Ivan had turned to him and said, 'It's a great place.' And indeed, with the moonlight striking the solid red brick, the recently repainted frieze announcing the names of the original owners of the factory, Perry had been struck anew by the impressive elegance of the exterior. He was proud of his home. A bar across the street was bathed in soft yellow light, languid dance music was gently burbling from the outside speakers, and he could see a shadow-play outline of a group of people smoking on the bar's rooftop. It gave the neighbourhood a sense of motion, of activity.

They had climbed the stairs to the third level, and Perry found he was holding his breath as he opened the door, turned on the lights and led Ivan through. The interiors were functional, designed in that sterile contemporary mode, all matt white surfaces, with internal walls ridiculously thin compared to the monumental framework of the original factory. There had been two apartments up for sale when the building was still being renovated, with this top-level apartment being the much more expensive one. Benjamin and Cleo had been adamant that it would be worth the extra money, the strain of a larger mortgage. And they had been right: the vaulting ceiling, with the long skylight running along the northern gradient, gave the room an exaggerated sense of space which had been a blessing during lockdown.

'Would you like a whisky?'

'Yes.'

'Neat? I have single malt.'

'A splash of water, thanks.'

While Ivan had excused himself to use the bathroom, Perry scrolled through his music. He had no idea what music Ivan would like. He selected a compilation of old Stax soul and RnB. A sinewy bass, a lazy strolling drum pattern, the music suddenly picking up intensity and focus just as Carla Thomas's effortlessly powerful voice started in. Perry swayed his hips as he poured the drinks. When Ivan returned, Perry took him and the drinks out onto the balcony.

That was when he'd recalled the cab ride. And further remembered the promise he had made to himself since returning to Australia, a refrain that had become the closest he came to prayer: You will not live your life anymore in silences and evasions. You must never do that to yourself again.

He has steeled himself, so he says the words carefully, clearly. He has rehearsed them in his head: 'I was offended by what you said in the cab.'

Ivan is startled, clearly not knowing what Perry is referring to. They are sitting on the balcony, they have just clinked glasses, and Ivan hasn't yet lit his cigarette.

'What you said about the young woman who was raped.'

The click of the lighter, the flare of flame.

Ivan sucks on his cigarette. 'Right.' He leans forward in the chair, looking over the long flat roof of the apartment block across the street. Just visible are the tops of the skyscrapers of the distant city. 'I can't quite remember what I said, Perry, but I didn't mean to offend you. I apologise.'

Perry is relieved. All he needs is that simple apology.

Ivan flicks some ash onto the saucer Perry has provided. 'My daughter was raped when she was nineteen.' It is not only the horror of his words that shocks Perry; it is also the Herculean effort Ivan makes to contain his emotion. He sits absolutely still, legs apart, hand holding the cigarette frozen in the air. Its swirling smoke adds to the sense that there is a violent commotion taking place within him, though there is no indication of it on his face.

He takes a deep breath. 'She was heading home to her mum's place. It was bloody daylight, late afternoon. There's a park, she had walked through it a thousand times and it just happened that on this particular day there was this psycho, this useless, pathetic piece of shit. And he dragged her into the toilets, put a knife to her throat, and he raped her.'

And now Ivan's body is quivering as he brings the cigarette to his mouth and sucks it hard. It is Perry who is absolutely still.

Ivan exhales. 'My little girl,' he whispers.

Perry feels as if he shouldn't be hearing those words, or be witness to the despairing catch in Ivan's voice.

Ivan releases his breath. He shrugs weakly as he turns to look at Perry. The strain in his voice has disappeared. 'She is amazing, Kat, just fucking amazing. She thought he was going to kill her. She was sure of it, he . . . he . . .' He expels the words in a rush: 'He told her he was going to slit her throat if she said a word.'

Perry cannot speak. He taps the cigarette packet. 'May I?'

'You smoke?'

'Very rarely.'

Ivan lights the cigarette for him. The first lungful of the smoke is horrible; Perry can feel the noxious burn of it. But he perseveres. He's not smoking for the taste—he wants the calming balm of the nicotine. And to express some kind of solidarity with the man sitting across from him.

'She took that witness stand and told them all exactly what that low-life did to her.'

Ivan stabs the tail of his cigarette into the saucer. He takes a sip of his whisky. 'Kat was calm. Didn't flinch from telling the court exactly what happened. The vile things he did. I was so proud of her.'

Perry sees that Ivan is eyeing the packet lying on the table. 'Here,' he says, offering him his half-smoked cigarette. 'Finish it for me.'

'I think there's a difference, Perry, between what happened to my daughter and what happens when a girl drinks too much and the next day can't remember what happened. I'm not excusing the degenerate cunt—if he did have sex with that journo when she was too drunk to know what was going on he needs to cop his punishment. But it's not rape. What happened to her and what happened to Kat are not the same thing. Otherwise that word loses all meaning. I'm sorry I offended you by what I said. But I'm not sorry for what I believe.'

The silence isn't uncomfortable. They sit in that gentle stillness until their respective glasses are empty.

'Another one?'

Ivan hesitates for the barest moment. He nods.

Perry deliberately pours himself a half-shot. Ivan's revelation is enormous, terrifying in its emotional intimacy. On standing up, a wave of drunkenness had briefly dazed him. Had Ivan noticed that slight wobble? Perry is moved that Ivan chose to trust him with such a confidence yet fearful of accepting such trust. He is chastened by the man's forbearance.

He quickly turns on the tap, gulps down two glasses of water to straighten himself out.

He walks out onto the balcony with the whisky glasses. 'Are you cold?'

Ivan takes his glass, raises it. 'Cheers. I'm okay.'

'Sure? I can grab you a jacket.'

There is a chuckle, Ivan wipes the spray of alcohol from his chin. 'Sorry.' He laughs again. 'It's just the thought of me fitting into one of your jackets . . . I'm a big man.' He looks down at his paunch. 'Maybe too big,' he adds ruefully.

'Not at all,' says Perry. 'I think you're very handsome.'

It is astonishing how that admission has returned him to a preposterous adolescent state. Perry doesn't know where to look, how to sit, what to do with his hands. My God, is he blushing? He is grateful that the light out here on the balcony is so dim. He *is* blushing.

Ivan shifts in his chair; there is an ugly screech as the legs scrape across the concrete. He has moved closer to Perry, so close that Perry can smell the tobacco, the alcohol, the onion and garlic. He can feel the warmth of Ivan's breath.

'I think you're fucking beautiful.' Ivan falls back in the chair, as if exhausted by the confession.

Perry fights the urge to say something self-deprecating, to dodge the compliment. 'Thank you,' he says quietly.

Perry sips his whisky, savouring the burn and the bitterness. His unsteadiness has gone. 'I've been meaning to ask all night,' he says. 'Why did you sign up to the dating website?'

'Didn't I explain it in a text to you? I'm looking for someone.'

'I get it. But why *that* particular site?'

Ivan cocks an eyebrow. 'You mean why didn't I trust my luck on Grindr or Tinder?'

Perry nods.

'I'm lonely too,' Ivan states, then coughs. There's a very slight movement of his hand, as if he were about to grab at the cigarettes then thought better of it. 'And I hate those sex apps. All those fucking acronyms and codes. I have no bloody idea what any of them mean.' He shrugs his shoulder. 'But the truth is, yeah, I'm lonely.'

Ivan has sat up, has crossed his arms. He is looking out onto the street.

'Those sex apps end up making me feel lonelier.'

'Have you had a relationship with a man?'

As soon as he asks the question, Perry is embarrassed. It sounds so damn condescending. But Ivan hasn't taken offence. His gaze shifts back to Perry.

'Oh, yeah. A bit like you, I wasted fifteen years on someone who wasn't worth it. His name's Joseph. Joe. He's a right prick.' He clears his throat again. 'He started using the apps. I found out he had been cheating on me for years. And I had no fucking idea.' Ivan is looking down at his glass. His voice is shaky.

He broke your heart. Perry doesn't say it out loud, but he's sure of it. Ivan's not giving anything away, but Perry has a preternatural sense of the misery that Ivan has endured.

Too much, too fast, thinks Perry. Immediately followed by: It's the whisky. It is a heavy drink.

He excuses himself and visits the toilet. Washing his hands afterwards, he peers into the small mirror. His face is flushed and there is something caught between his two front teeth. He slides his fingernail between them, loosens the scrap, rinses out his mouth. He takes one last critical look, uses his damp hands to smooth back his hair. There's already a shadow of stubble darkening his chin, the telltale grey whiskers. Well, there's nothing he can do about that now.

Ivan is standing by the shelves, examining the book collection. He turns on hearing Perry come back into the room. The music has ended; there is only the dim roar of traffic from the junction and from Bell Street in the distance.

As Perry goes to his laptop to find some music, Ivan steps forward and the two men almost collide, only a deft side-step from Ivan avoids impact. Perry starts a rushed apology as Ivan raises his hand to Perry's collar and expertly tightens the knot of his tie, straightens it.

'Thank you.'

Ivan's eyes are shining, a mischievous gleam. 'You're welcome.' Then he kisses Perry.

It is thrilling; thank God it is thrilling. There is a firmness to the kiss, there is the taste of tobacco, of alcohol, of the rich food, all of it tempered by the scent of Ivan's cologne and the salty tang of his perspiration. Perry accepts the kiss, they briefly break contact, and then he returns it with equal fervour. When they next pull apart, they are both breathing deeply.

It is a particular form of dance, thinks Perry, as he guides Ivan to the sofa. As soon as they are seated, they are kissing again, Ivan now almost aggressive in his urgency. Perry wishes he could banish consciousness, that sense of floating above, watching himself. He is not unaroused, but there isn't the intoxicating swoon that came with the initial kiss. Ivan's fingers run through Perry's hair, his lips are on his neck. Ivan's other hand drops onto his crotch. Perry's cock is soft.

They are so close it is the first time that Perry notices the almost metallic grey hue of Ivan's eyes.

'Do you want me to stay?'

There is no reticence and no pleading in Ivan's question. Perry intuits immediately that it would be a mistake to answer with a question.

'Yes.'

Leading Ivan into the bedroom, Perry almost says the words out loud: We are no longer strangers. He turns on the bedside lamp, wanting a soft light. They are not strangers and so this is unlike any of the sexual encounters he has had since separating from Gerard: this night doesn't wear a cloak of anonymity, and so he is both more expectant and more tentative. Ivan too seems unsure, standing there in the doorway, looking around the bedroom, at the framed Polish poster of Pasolini's *The Decameron*, at the eerily austere seascape that Perry's friend Amelia had photographed when he and she had been holidaying in Crete many years ago, the blue of the Aegean so vibrant that its luminance hurts the eye, makes the colour of the sea seem as starkly white as the pebbles and sand of the beach. The fragile thread of spiderweb hanging between the light bulb and a cornice; the wardrobe door that Perry had not completely shut when he had been frantically looking for the right tie earlier in the evening; the battered copy of *Remembering Babylon* on the bedside table, next to the tall glass of water: the wariness, the anticipation means that every colour, every surface and every object is outlined in vivid relief, as if Perry is experiencing the wild ambush of a rushing drug high. And every sound amplified: their breathing so loud in the silence.

He walks quietly to the toilet, his bladder almost painfully bloated, his stomach all growls and rumbles. The sun has not long risen and the apartment is in half-shadow, in variegated streams of light. The sound of his pissing, two whistling farts and then the shudder and release of his bowels, all of it seeming improperly loud. He flushes, takes his aftershave out of the cabinet and sprays it around the small room. He makes a note to himself to buy a deodoriser for the bathroom, or at least a scented candle. This is what comes from being on your own for too long, Perry chides himself: you get lazy.

He treads carefully down the corridor to the bedroom, into the darkened room, grimacing at the smell: mustiness and sweat. Ivan is still sleeping; most of the doona now covers his bulky form, as if unconsciously he'd pulled it all over him when

Perry had risen from the bed. Perry stands silent, listening to the deep wheeze of Ivan's snores, inhaling that strong perfume, carnal and animal, the blatant odorous pungency of a man.

Perry had watched Ivan undress. First he unbuckled his belt then, with his head still lowered, took off his shirt, only looking at Perry when he let it fall onto the wooden floor; that coy grin, that flash of knowing. Perry had walked over to him and touched Ivan's chest, the strands of grey hair, then moved his hand lower to stroke the firm, round belly. He had felt Ivan's involuntary intake of breath. He grabbed Ivan, bringing him in closer. Perry felt a rush of exhilaration. He hadn't been with a man of Ivan's size since his youth. As Perry started to undress, Ivan demanded, 'Look at me.' He reached for Perry's tie, unknotted it, then undid the first, the second button of Perry's shirt. Perry started to unzip Ivan's trousers, making a motion to kneel. 'No,' Ivan hissed. 'Please keep looking at me.' His eyes were that metallic grey but there was an amber light just visible there now, a hint of warmth, and the two men were gazing at each other in unashamed curiosity, with something akin to wonder.

Perry was aware of all blemishes, all asymmetries, his too-large earlobes and uneven, discoloured teeth, the sagging jowls, but none of that mattered because Ivan was handsome, so very handsome, with an intense, undiluted severity, and, still looking into those eyes, he grabbed Ivan's cock, which was straining against the cotton of his Y-fronts. The cock was heavy and hard in his hand, and he tightened his grip on it, and as he did, Ivan moaned, still looking at him, and then Ivan was unbuckling Perry's belt, their gaze not once drifting, and reaching under the waistband of Perry's underpants. Perry shuddered at his touch, and there was a momentary intrusion of that silly juvenile fear: Would Ivan think his penis too small? But there was no easing of Ivan's fervour: in his kissing, in his thrilling stroking of Perry's cock. Perry was relieved, furiously eager.

Standing there, deliberating whether he should return to bed or make himself a coffee, Perry is aware that Ivan's snores have ceased. There is a short, harsh bout of coughing and Ivan's hand is scrambling for the water glass on the bedside table. He drinks it all in one large gulp, then coughs again. Ivan yawns, his arms reach out in an unhurried stretch. It is then he notices the shadow by the door.

'Did you sleep well?'

And as he asks the question, Perry realises he has answered it for himself. They have slept amazingly well, undisturbed, somehow finding an immediate satisfaction in their physicality together. Ivan's arms had been around him most of the night. Perry had fallen straight to sleep.

He comes and sits on the bed. The two men reach for each other, the kiss is awkward and tender at the same time.

'I can make a coffee. Or better yet, I can go downstairs and grab some from the café.'

'A latte, please, one sugar.'

Perry pulls on his running gear, the holey Nike sweat top, the faded navy trackpants. He feels like a kid, a young man. He bounds down the stairs.

Perry was the first to break their gaze. He dropped to his knees, an action lacking all grace as he gripped one of Ivan's arms to steady himself while he stripped off his own trousers and jocks. He was still in a state somewhere between consciousness and a drug fugue, one moment aware of the indignity of his ageing body, the next only cognisant of the perplexing mix of familiarity and strangeness as he took Ivan's cock in his mouth. Ivan's fingers kneading his hair. It was exhilarating, the taste and the odours, the hint of urine along the silken glans. And it was disconcerting, the intrusion of the unwelcome memory of Gerard's thinner, smaller penis, how the Frenchman had always escalated his gyrations into a manic jabbing at Perry's mouth and throat. Perry was no longer hard. He clambered awkwardly to his feet.

'Can we please just keep kissing?' he asked quietly.

They have their coffee sitting at the island bench. A patch of light streaming in from the window haloes Ivan, and Perry is aware of the silver sheen of uneven stubble on the man's scalp. And of his morning odour, acrid yet bracing. They sip their coffee in silence. Every sentence that comes to Perry's mouth, that he is about to ask or say, seems silly or predictable or banal. There is that unshifting control in Ivan's gaze; the cool scrutiny of it unnerving.

Impossible to say how long they were lost in their kissing. At first, desire was quashed by the intrusion of memory. Gerard could only convey submission in the act of the kiss, as if that intimacy freed him from his constant need to be respectable and masculine. He was a timid kisser, and Perry would take the lead, be both instigator and guide. So when Ivan's tongue first dug deep into his mouth, as his strong arms tightened their grip on him, as their lips and tongues mashed against each other, Perry found himself hesitant, resisting. Yet Ivan remained unafraid as his fingers explored Perry's body. Maintaining the intensity of the kiss, Ivan traced a gentle line down Perry's spine with his fingers. And then suddenly, their mouths unlocked, Ivan drew breath, and then his lips gently caressed Perry's neck, rising to his cheek, sucking and licking his ear; the wetness, the gentle tease of Ivan's breath, reignited Perry's arousal. Perry's lips brushed Ivan's stubble, his chin, his neck. He was startled by the coarseness of the skin, the unabashed salty taste of it. With an action quick and savage, Ivan seized Perry's chin and clashed their mouths together again. The roughness, the zeal, was intoxicating, and this time Perry did not hesitate, exhilarated by the brutality and longing in the kiss. All there was and all there needed to be was in that unquenchable expression of desire. Impossible to say how long they were lost in it. Perry's hand dropped to his own crotch. He was bone-hard.

The men finish their coffees, share a large almond croissant that Perry has brought back from the café downstairs. They ask each other innocuous and unthreatening questions of the order of: 'What are you doing today?' The nerve-racking silence returns as the two men look out of the large casement windows to the streetscape below. A jogger expertly dodges a couple wheeling a pram, her blonde ponytail skipping from shoulder to shoulder as she runs past them. Three girls, their arms linked, are striding with spirited intent to the lights, one of them wearing an oversized white T-shirt emblazoned with the words CHOOSE LIFE. It's a reminder for Perry of a long-ago youth.

Ivan is laughing. 'I haven't seen one of those for a long, long time.' He mock dances in his seat, begins to sing the chorus to 'Wake Me Up Before You Go-Go'. It's the sweetest of images, the incongruity of the bulky older man, his comical twisting on the stool while singing that old song unashamedly out of tune.

'Ivan,' Perry says, interrupting, 'I'd like to see you again.'

Ivan beams.

It had been the discovery of Ivan's skin that was enticing, that deepened Perry's longing. The rough, scarred and callused hands and fingers, the bristly scrape of his chin, the tautness of his biceps and shoulders and chest made a thrilling contrast with the remarkable softness of the man's belly. Ivan showed an equally avid curiosity, kissing and caressing Perry's arms and his neck, groaning softly as his face rubbed the thick down of Perry's chest and stomach and groin. Yet he always returned to the kiss, as if it were a resuscitating force. The power of it intensified, their tongues laced with each other's odours. They had taken turns sucking each other off; returning to the kiss, Perry smelt the sour-milk stink of his cock on Ivan's lips. That too was rejuvenating, the smells of another body, the coarse sting of Ivan's armpits, the saline bitterness that dampened his skin. Perry breathed in every aroma as their lovemaking settled into the kiss and the slow working of each other's cocks. Ivan drew away with a grin, sucking his own fingers. His hand lowered to Perry's arse, the wet thumb pushing hard into his sphincter, the jolt both pain and bliss. 'Perry,' Ivan whispered, 'sit on me; I want to lick out your arse.' The force of those pornographic words was shocking.

They decide to meet for lunch again the following Saturday, with studied restraint but obvious pleasure, punching the details into their phones. Perry insists this time that they should meet on Ivan's side of town. Ivan suggests a pub in Mordialloc. Perry nods at the suggestion, thinking to himself, I haven't been to Mordialloc since I was a kid. All he remembers of it is the long stretch of placid bay, the scores of Italian and Greek and Slavic and Turkish families on the beach.

'I'll have a quick shower,' Perry says, 'and then I'll drive you home.'

Ivan argues that it's too long a drive, that he has to get ready to visit his daughter and grandchild almost as soon as he gets home. Perry dismisses his objections with a shrug. 'I'll drop you off,' he says. 'I won't come in.'

Ivan agrees to the offer with grace. 'Alright, thanks,' he says. 'You can see my place next week.'

Ivan looks down at his empty coffee cup, then turns sharply to look out the window again, as if worried he may have revealed too much, been too daring in his expectations.

It is a dance, thinks Perry as he heads to the bathroom, a thought both bemusing and wearying, and we're both trying to remember the steps to it.

'*C'est dégueulasse*,' was how Gerard had once dismissed him. Perry had been massaging his naked back and had pulled down the older man's underwear and then daringly spread the firm small buttocks and flicked his tongue into the anal cleft, licking at the wispy grey strands of hairs there. The heady rank odour had aroused him, and he had pushed his tongue deeper. Gerard had recoiled, his whole body snapping upright. That's when he'd said those words. They had been so unexpected that it had taken a moment for Perry to decipher their meaning, to translate them into English and then back to French. *It's vile, it's disgusting.* Perry had stammered an apology, burning with shame.

Ivan realised his mistake immediately as Perry instinctively recoiled. The ravenous longing disappeared from his eyes. He said sheepishly, 'I'm going too fast, aren't I?'

Perry didn't answer. He felt a burst of panic. And then, not speaking it aloud, scolding himself—'Say something, dickhead!'—he reached up, his finger brushing Ivan's lips. That was words enough. Ivan smiled, took Perry's hand, and kissed it. 'Lie on top of me,' Perry urged. Ivan did, grinding his body against Perry's, and with that dizzying sensation of the man's heaviness and strength, and his pungent odours, the intrusive memories paled. Both men kept their eyes open as their bodies writhed and pushed into one another. Gerard retreated, and instead it was the generous and bolstering stranger Perry was looking at, the man with clear, unafraid eyes, and it was Ivan's penetrating stare that made him realise they had resumed their lovemaking, and their rutting against each other quickened. Ivan lifted himself off Perry, took both their cocks in his hands, spat, and the rubbing was near pain, but it wasn't pain, and as Perry's breathing shortened, intensified, Ivan pleaded, 'I want to see you come,' and Perry was thrusting his hips and Ivan was tugging only at Perry's cock, each pull faster, frantic, and Perry jerked his hips high, eyes shut tight, head slamming deep into the pillow as he roared his release. He fell back, shivering, panting, and watched as Ivan scooped up the cum from Perry's belly, slathering it across his thick cock, leaning down close to kiss Perry hard, almost violently, until with one final brutal motion he lifted and his body spasmed fiercely.

Chest heaving, Ivan slumped to his side. His eyes were gleeful as they looked at Perry. And it was that joy, that letting go that was also a return to naivety and wonder, that prompted him to crouch over Ivan and take the man's spent cock into his mouth, to suck and swallow the last sour trickle of him.

In the shower, lathering under his arms, Perry remembers that bitter taste and grimaces, biting his bottom lip in embarrassment. He had wanted to show Ivan that he trusted him, that within only a few hours of knowing each other, he had faith in Ivan's integrity. Now he sees how his action might have been misconstrued. He probably thinks you don't care about *your* health, he chides himself. He probably thinks you're a *con*. It is instinctive, this settling on the French word. In Perry's understanding, it is one that conveys both the sting of the abuse of *cunt* and the disgrace of *whore*.

There is a knock on the door and Ivan enters the bathroom. Perry watches from behind the steamy glass as Ivan pulls down his jocks. Perry opens the shower door.

It is such a long drive. They cross the river at Richmond and take Williams Road up to the Nepean Highway. On the stretch through Balaclava, as he sees the observant Orthodox Jews heading to the synagogue, Ivan says, 'Is it wrong that I find yeshiva boys so fucking hot?' Perry laughs out loud.

Ivan lives in a nondescript, late-sixties orange-brick apartment block. 'It's a ten-minute walk or so to the beach,' Ivan says
as he gets out of the car, as if ashamed of the dull ugliness of
the flats. There is that uncomfortable moment when they look
at each other and neither knows whether they should embrace.
Ivan does the right thing. He leans across the passenger seat,
kisses Perry on the lips.

'See you next Saturday.'

It takes another hour to return home, the traffic heavy as he
approaches town. Yet Perry is not infuriated, not exasperated.
He doesn't put on the radio, doesn't listen to music. He is
eliciting sensation: the deep rumble of Ivan's voice; the raw
brace of his odour on waking; his rough and gentle fingers
exploring Perry's body; the heft and force of Ivan's cock in
his mouth. He is awash with all of this and more, so that the
other man is almost a presence in the car.

It is only when the car is stuck behind a tram in High
Street, Thornbury, that Perry's reverie is broken on seeing a
kitsch row of tiny French flags flapping from an awning. And
he has a sudden, overwhelming craving for a freshly baked
brioche, pliant and buttery and just out of the oven, the way
Marie-Louise made them at his local boulangerie in Rouen.
He knows he'd have to cross the river to find anything as
good here. And that thought leads inevitably to a memory of
them in the same café, Gerard reading the paper, dressed in
a pale yellow short-sleeved shirt, navy pants and sandals, his
feet crossed, absent-mindedly taking a small piece of pastry

from time to time, never looking up from the newspaper, not looking across to Perry, who is content, sipping his coffee, eating his own brioche, admiring the elegance and gentlemanly refinement of his lover.

The tram rumbles forward, the cars start moving slowly. Perry switches the radio on; an old Talking Heads track is playing on Smooth FM. And the memory of Gerard is gone, replaced with the image of Ivan's awkward dancing as he jubilantly sang the old Wham song. Alone in the car, Perry starts to laugh.

2

'You know why, Dad.' Kat is clearly exasperated. 'She's still angry with you. She's angry with everyone.'

Ivan is rocking on his heels, testing the floorboards; there is a pronounced wobble there and a creak every time he pushes down. He squats and turns up a corner of the clammy acrylic carpet. There is heavy mould on the underlay. He raps his knuckles on the wood. The boards are solid—old hardwood.

He looks up at his daughter. 'It needs restumping. But the boards are good. I can do the sanding for you. They'll come up beautiful.'

He sees it in Kat's eyes, knows by the glum twist of her mouth that she's pissed off with him.

He rolls his shoulders, sighs. 'It's okay, *lutka*,' he says, and he's glad to see her smile at that familiar endearment. 'Perry doesn't have to come. He'll understand.'

The smile is gone. She even stamps her foot, and Ivan has to stop himself from laughing. Kat finds it impossible to hide her ire, a trait probably inherited from both parents. He still has delicious memories of her as a child, with her hands on her hips, face grimacing as she uses that same foot stomp to convey her fury.

'That's not the point, Dad. I want Perry to be there. Tash wants him to be there.'

Ivan nods, appreciative of his daughter's kindness. And her loyalty. Tashie's only met Perry once and he is certain she has little memory of him. Not yet five years old, she only cares about routine and security. Her innate curiosity is indeed a pleasure—Ivan is indefatigably proud of her—but as yet it is contained. He is sure that Kat has diligently explained to her that Perry is Deda's new boyfriend. He is equally confident that the information is irrelevant to Tashie. She has to get to know Perry, to meet him again and again, before he becomes real for her. He silently rolls that word—*boyfriend*—along his tongue, and winces. They are too old for such a word.

He shakes away that unwelcome thought. He needs to get on with looking through the house so he can figure out how much work is required before Kat can bid for it at auction.

Bloody Dana. Yet again he wishes he'd never met her. And then, immediately, as always, comes the indisputable realisation:

but then, with no Dana there would be no Katerina. And that is unthinkable. He shakes his head.

'Thank you—it means a lot to me that you want him there. But it's Tashie's birthday and she'll be devastated if her Nonna's missing.' He walks over to his daughter, who is still looking mutinous, her arms crossed tight, her body tense. He puts his arm around her shoulders. 'You, Tash, Perry and me will go for a birthday picnic another time.' He feels her relax into him. He kisses the top of her head, inhales the sweetness of her perfume.

He gently pushes her off him. 'Okay, now let's take a look at this house.'

He is confident he has not revealed it, the knot that has tightened inside him, the shadow that has enveloped him. He shudders at the ferocity of his anger.

He walks along the dark, narrow corridor, which reeks of the chemicals the real estate agent has used to disguise the stink of the mould and rot. He goes into a small room. There is a large double-sash window with light spilling through it. It looks out directly onto a zebra crossing on the street outside. The thought is automatic: that's good for Tashie. He tries opening the window but there is a bolt lock and no sign of a key. The wooden frames are freshly painted, the most basic and cheap of acrylic off-white. He runs his thumbnail along a groove that has bubbled along the surface. The paint peels off immediately and his nail scratches along the seam of the wood. It can't dig in far. He nods in satisfaction.

He gives Kat a thumbs-up. 'Good windows.'

An archway leads into the kitchen. It is tiny, but then so is the whole place. He takes the measure of the room. There is hardly space to fit a small table. One of the cupboards has a door missing, and the basin is scuffed and stained. He opens the door under the sink, and the hinges shudder and squeal as he peers at the pipework: cheap and shoddy casings, an ominous crack visible on the S-bend. He sniffs. It stinks of mice. The whole bloody kitchen will need to be replaced.

A small screen door opens to the narrow yard. Standing on the top step he understands why Kat has fallen in love with the place.

The sea isn't visible; it's a few hundred metres to the highway and there's the whole of Bayside Plaza to cross before you hit the beach. And there's the uninspiring red-brick wall of the back of the bicycle shop across the alley. But the house sits at the top of a shallow rise, and the breeze from the bay is bracing and fresh.

Kat comes up beside him and puts her head on his shoulder. 'I know it needs a lot of work, Dad, but I really like this place.' She jumps off the steps, throws her arms out wide. 'And I know it's small, but there's a yard for Tashie.'

Ivan is making swift calculations in his head. The property *is* small. At the moment there's enough room for Kat and Tash, but when his daughter gets together with someone in the future that will present a problem. And the kitchen and that foul bathroom, all of it will need to be redone before they move in. There's the restumping, but that's par for the course. The walls are solid, at least; when had Kat said it was built? The 1950s? They built them to last back then. And it's only a five- or ten-minute walk to the shops, to the station. Fifteen minutes and you're at the beach. It's rare to find homes so close to markets and malls in the suburbs, but the house is part of an old industrial estate, a subdivision of a much larger property, the auto shop next door. The real estate agent had explained to Kat that the previous owners had been two artists and that they had moved in illegally, that it had never been zoned for residential. Fortunately for the artist couple, and now maybe for Kat, a provision in one of the local by-laws transferred full ownership of the property if it could be shown that there had been continuous domestic use for seven years. The couple had been living in it for nine years when they applied for the exemption and now it is the only fully residential property on the block.

Ivan runs his thumb across his bottom lip, feels the rough scratch of his stubble. His hand instinctively goes to his head. He needs to shave it tonight. All of that recent history boded well for the house. It revealed that the shop owners in the block weren't arseholes; none of them had reported the couple to the council. And it meant that inevitably the area would be rezoned at some stage, that apartments would be going up all around. Great resale value.

Watching him, Katerina stays silent.

'How much are they asking for it?'

She knows he knows. She also knows that this is a necessary part of his decision-making. 'Around six hundred thousand.'

She shrugs. 'But you know real estate agents, they always underquote.'

The only competition will be developers. But the size is a risk for them. The owners of the warehouse next door or of the bike shop behind would have them over a barrel when it came to negotiations. The other side of the house runs along the street, so there is no potential for expanding on that side. Families want to move into Frankston, but the place would be too small for them. And luckily the yuppies still look down their noses at the suburb—too far from the city. Kat had rolled her eyes when he used that word, and only the other week, Perry had laughed too. 'Yuppies?' he'd exclaimed in feigned shock. 'Who the fuck uses that word anymore!' Ivan is adamant: he is going to keep on using it. He hates calling them hipsters; that was just yuppies wanting to self-aggrandise. Young urban professionals. That's what the cunts are. That's what he's going to call them.

'Offer them seven hundred.'

'You don't think we should wait for auction?'

'We might have to.' He drops his voice to a low whisper. Never know who's listening. 'I think you should be prepared to go up to seven hundred and fifty—maybe seven-sixty. But let's see what they say after the first offer.'

Katerina rushes to her father, embraces him with so much enthusiasm he is both embarrassed and delighted.

'Seven hundred and sixty thousand for Frangas?' she replies. 'Can you believe it. It's just not right.'

'No,' Ivan responds, the word resounding so emphatically that Katerina pulls out of their embrace, looks quizzically at her father.

'You okay?'

'Yes.' A growl to that syllable as well. He strides the short distance to the back fence and squats next to an untended seedbed, a few spindly and meagre twigs the only evidence of the plants that used to flower there. Ivan pulls out a handful of weeds, and then scrapes and digs into the earth, examining the soil.

It's not right. The words are swirling in his head, and as his fingers rub the clumps of sand, he repeats them—*it's not right, it's just not right*—till they become a mantra. Ivan grew up in Clayton, hardly salubrious itself, and not blessed with a beach to escape to. Yet for most of his life, Frankston had been mocked by many of his peers and neighbours. Dole bludgers and welfare mums. Drunks and junkies. And the old joke: What does someone from Frankston call their father? Answer: Uncle Fred. The snobbery against the suburb summed up by its nickname: the ocker slang for a condom. And now it costs seven hundred and sixty thousand dollars to buy a dilapidated hovel there. Ivan's never bought into the scorn. He loves the beach and the surrounding hills. His fingers push into the hard sand which crumbles into vapour over the neglected garden bed. His own flat, that little shitbox down the road in Bonbeach—would he have been able to afford it at today's prices? The city's getting too big. And everyone's getting greedier.

He's mashing into the dirt now.

'Dad, please stop.' Kat is crouched down next to him, her hand on his.

Ivan looks down at the knots of green leaves and scrub that he has piled into a small stack beside him.

Katerina shoves the pile of weeds and twigs onto the garden bed. 'I might not get this house, Dad. We don't have to do the gardening for them.'

They lock up the house and return the keys to the agent.

Ivan checks his phone. 'I've got an hour before I need to get back to work. Want some lunch?'

Kat is looking up at the pearly winter sun. She zips up her jacket collar. 'Let's have it on the beach.'

'Good idea.'

Kat never wearies him. He gets fearful, he gets agitated—she's his daughter and he'll never not feel that kernel of anxious concern that was embedded within him from the first, when, after all the anguish and violence of her birth, she had emerged bloodied and wet, looking like an alien from some sensational horror film, encased in a caul of plasma and tissue. Then she had started to cry and Dana had offered her to him to hold—and in recalling it, Ivan still shivers, from the gratitude—and in holding her, that outraged squashed little monkey face of hers, he was awed by the everyday miracle of birth and did in that moment thank God for the gift of his daughter. With the immediacy of that love, he also felt the burden of parenthood take hold, that fierce concern for his daughter that has never diminished. It has been a part of him for so long now: in his terror for her, in his frustration with her, in his undiluted love for her. Yet Kat never wearies him. There isn't a moment, a glimmer of it, when he imagines a life without her in it.

A ridiculous squabble takes place at the kebab shop, with each of them insisting on paying for the other. As he tries to get the bemused young man at the counter to accept his money, Kat smacks Ivan's hand away and offers up her card instead. They jostle and argue for a few seconds, until Ivan realises his actions and stubbornness remind him of his mother, and of how often he had been embarrassed by her. She was always too loud, too belligerent, too strange. With that recollection, he withdraws his hand, allows his daughter to pay.

They sit on the cold stone wall. The sky is overcast, and the shallow waters are the colour of wet slate. Only further out, halfway to the horizon, where the soft pulsing glow of the sun penetrates a thinner sheet of cloud, does the sea sparkle, become a deep green.

Kat is eating faster than he is. She devours the last of her falafel roll, wipes her mouth, carefully wraps the soggy paper in the napkin and carries it over to the rubbish bin. Ivan is chewing slowly, only half-done with his chicken kebab. He swallows, sips from his water bottle.

'Was it a busy morning?'

'Yeah.' Kat stifles a yawn, gently rubs at her belly. 'It's good to eat. I organised an early class to make up for coming out to inspect the house. And I didn't have much for breakfast. Stupid of me; I was anxious.'

'I hope you get the place.' He takes another bite.

Kat shudders. 'Don't, Dad, don't jinx it.' She taps her head gently with her knuckles. 'Touch wood.'

He grins at this; yet his own hand is on his chest, his fingers slipping under his jacket to find the solid shape of his crucifix.

Onion and slivers of meat drip from his kebab and he kicks them away, watches a trio of squalling gulls snap at them. He takes a last bite and, before he can collect the rubbish, Kat takes it and drops it into a bin.

She stands over him. 'You got time for a walk?'

He takes out his phone. There is a missed call from Perry. 'Twenty minutes.'

Ivan is impressed by the work that has been done on the foreshore. His family had rarely visited Frankston when he was a child; his father preferred the closer beach at Mordialloc. On long drives for a daytrip or to go camping, they always bypassed the suburb for Dromana or Rosebud or Rye, the beaches further along the peninsula. It seemed almost like a homing instinct, that so many migrant families chose those same beaches for their holidays. Without it ever being stated as such, it was assumed that Frankston belonged to the Aussies. As a teenager, and when he began his training in horticulture, he'd often ended up in one of the big Frankston pubs on the weekends. He remembered lots of wasted young men, fights, driving home drunk along back roads to evade the cops. There had been stretches between the beach and Clayton that were like bush, or open farmland. Now, of course, it was all new estates and shopping centres. And Frankston had changed. It didn't seem so isolated from the city now. It was far—forty fucking kilometres—yet suburbia had stretched all along the swing of Port Phillip Bay. Dromana, Rosebud and Rye were now an extension of suburban Melbourne.

He breathes in the chilly sea air, the briny niff tickling his nose. 'I like what they've done to Frangas.'

Kat slipped her arm into his. 'Dad,' she said, and he could hear the seriousness in her tone, 'I want Perry to come to Tashie's birthday.'

Ivan swallowed, turned to his daughter. 'You owe me nothing. That money was always yours, always Natasha's.'

She groans. 'You and Mum are exactly the same.'

He's confused; feels a stir of exasperation. He means it: him helping Kat buy a house places no obligation on her. She's selling her crappy one-bedroom flat in Dandenong. There was always going to be a deposit. The extra Ivan will put in is money that is pledged to her, to his granddaughter. She owes him no gratitude; nevertheless he's pissed off.

Money. He knows how money poisons everything. He must not let it come between him and Kat.

'As I said, you wanting Perry there makes me so happy.' He squeezes her knee. 'Let's give it some time. He'll be there next year. Your mother will come around.'

She draws away from him, clearly furious. 'Both you and Mum think you know what's best for me. Sometimes you do, sometimes you don't. I don't want Perry there as a favour to you. I want him there for us. For Tashie, for you. For *me*.'

Her vehemence underscores that final word. 'That should be enough for you; that should be enough for Mum.'

You don't know Perry, you've met him a handful of times—why do you want him there? Do *I* want him there? Of course he voices none of this. He recognises the tremble in her voice, the proximity of tears. He remains silent.

'Perry isn't Joseph, Dad.'

There, the name is said, the word released, and still, even after all this time, its very mention splits him open, as brutally as fire on flesh. That terrifying vertigo, so severe the pain, so fucking ugly the memories. Ivan knows his own strengths, the imperturbability he has affected since childhood and which he has, for the most part, mastered; that is where he hides his weaknesses. He is sitting rigid in his stillness. He doesn't look at Katerina; he doesn't dare. Eyes are a breach between the physical self and the soul; in their candour, they mock his futile attempts at control. He fixes his gaze on the sombre sky and the murky water, on the lines of the waves, concentrating on the layers of grey. In doing that, he gives silent thanks to Paul, the counsellor he had been ordered to see. Back then the very utterance of that name—*Joseph*—would unleash such a riot of hatred and self-loathing and humiliation that the only way through seemed to be to kill or to kill himself—the only anti-dote for the pain was the wrecking of mind and soul through the annihilation of blind rage. He had initially thought Paul was too young, too foolish—what would he know about life? What experience would he have of torment? But Paul had taught him to look out into the world at that point of terror and find five shades of a single colour around him. He does this now. Grey, the layers of grey. There is the eggshell haze that glows just above the line of the horizon. There are the funereal patches far out at sea where the water is deepest. The almost-black wooden posts of the pier, slimy and studded with sea moss. His eyes scan the beach, find the ash-coloured jumper of a woman walking her spaniel. The steely slabs of cloud up above. Five. He lets himself exhale.

He has been silent for too long. He has to answer his daughter. 'I know Perry isn't Joe. But we've been seeing each other for barely a year. It makes sense why Dana doesn't trust it yet.'

Wrong thing to say. He senses the eruption even before her outburst. The furious pull away from him. 'I just don't fucking get it!'

Two women are strolling past. The taller one, whippet-thin, her grey hair blowing around her, turns on hearing Katerina's raised voice, glares at Ivan.

'What don't you get?'

His emotionless reply only maddens her more. 'Joe stole from *you*, Dad, this has nothing to do with Mum.' Her tone softens. 'Why does she need to constantly be a victim?'

Ivan has no answer to that. He has known Dana since they were in high school together. She has always been angry: furious at the strictures placed on her by a fearful Sicilian migrant family; pissed off with the blunt prejudices of their teachers, which curtailed her opportunities and her vision; enraged that the young man she had fallen in love with and had thought of as her escape from family and stunted suburban expectations had turned out to be a poofter. She had reasons to be angry. Yet once upon a time, she had also been fearless, vital. Now there is only the bitter residue of the anger. Ivan often wonders if there is a chemical response to martyrdom that gives women a rush equivalent to the frightening elation a man feels when challenged to violence—an urgency that is cellular and seemingly spontaneous in its detonation.

He puts his arm around Kat, kisses her on the top of the head, whistling softly into her hair. He's been doing it since she was an infant. He feels her relax into his arms. And he suddenly understands. With Perry there, precisely because he is still a partial outsider, Dana will be required to show some restraint. Ivan knows that his daughter's wish to have his partner there is genuine. He has no doubt about that. But Perry's presence will also be a buttress. Natasha's dad will be there; Dana has never forgiven Eddie for being feckless, incapable of accepting the responsibilities of fatherhood. Truth be told, Ivan hasn't forgiven him either. But he knows there's no point getting angry with weak men like Eddie—they just walk away. Kat needs Perry to be there. It will ensure that it remains Tashie's day.

Ivan finds the immensity of his respect for his daughter impossible to measure; he might as well try to calculate the terrifying perpetuity of the universe. She has repeatedly said that it would kill her to be a victim. And he believes her, believed her back then, during that awful and senseless trial, with that lump of human excrement calmly sitting there—that manifestation of pure evil—when she had responded to every question and slight and insinuation fired at her by the defence lawyer with courageous resolve. Ivan had wanted to kill before—had certainly wanted to kill Joe. Yet never had he so longed to physically destroy another being as he had done while enduring his daughter's testimony. Of course it hadn't shocked him. This was the modern world; the defence lawyer had attempted to paint the rapist as the victim, trying to ameliorate the outrages he had enacted on Kat by blaming poverty and homelessness and addiction. As if they excused anything. And weren't they the same excuses that had the cunt out on bail in the first place? Even though he had only recently broken his girlfriend's face? Ivan had dreamt, night after night, of the violence he would inflict on that piece of filth. And also on his lawyer: the thrill of the fantasy in which he slammed her face repeatedly into the brick wall of the courthouse. He had wanted to destroy the whole world.

With the same supreme effort of resilience that enabled Katerina to sit only metres away from where that evil shit was smirking, blaming anyone but himself, she had refused to allow their legalistic platitudes and pathetic excuses to obscure the enormity of what he had done to her. The final morning of the trial, she had found her father smoking in the alley behind the courthouse. He had started to speak, wanting to express his pride in her, but had collapsed into mortifying sobs. She had taken his cigarette and had two quick puffs—she *never* smoked—and handed it back. She kissed him and said, 'Dad, it would kill me to be a victim.' Impossible to measure such courage.

'Joe stole from all of us,' he says quietly, his lips still brushing her hair. 'Perry will come to Tashie's birthday.'

He drops Katerina off at work at the gym in Dandenong. Then, instead of driving straight up Springvale Road, he turns back towards the beach. It isn't until he swings the car into Bay Street that he realises what he is doing. He parks the car, gets out and lights a cigarette. He leans on the bonnet and looks across at their old house.

His old house. Ivan sucks hard on the cigarette. He'd bought it, renovated it, landscaped the small front yard, all native plants, hardy shrubs and grasses, defiantly tolerant of the searing summer heat and the harshest of winter chills; plants capable of withstanding the bruising blast of sea air that rushed across the road from Parkdale Beach. The new owners aren't gardeners. He is distressed to see that they have removed the striking kangaroo paw he'd planted to the right of the front gate. The house had been dilapidated, an eyesore really, when he'd bought it, with rotting window frames and the brick-veneer facade loosened and cracking, the damage burrowing deep into the substratum. And the house had stunk: of mildew and damp, and of generations of accumulated grease and oil that seemed to weep from the kitchen walls. The walls were filthy, as was the rangehood, the stove: all of it had to go. Yet Ivan had seen the potential as soon as the real estate agent had opened the door. There was, of course, the prox-imity to the beach; but also the layout of the property meant a second storey could be built without blocking a neighbour's view. The front yard was just lawn and he had immediately started imagining the plants he could fill it with. The first two things he'd envisaged: the kangaroo paw, the comfort of their small, scarlet flowers against the harsh coastal landscape; and a second storey, so that he could wake up to that astonishing view of the bay spread out before him. He had dreamt of such fortune since he was a child, when his parents would take him and his sister, Sonja, to that very beach, and he would float on the water, squinting in the munificent glare of the sun, and imagine what it must feel like to grow up so close to the bay, to have the sea as your front yard. Ivan drags deep on his cigarette. He had worked so hard on the house, forgoing holidays, spending every Sunday for a year stripping it, doing as much of the labour as he could. It had been his obsession and it had made him happy.

He remembers that first morning after Joe had slept over. Ivan had woken to find himself alone in the bed. With his arm shielding his face from the glare, he saw Joe standing by the window, the blinds open, rays of sun shining through the interstices. He will never be able to forget how joyful Joe had looked. 'My God, Ivan,' he'd said. 'This is beautiful.' Ivan had felt so proud of the home he'd created. It was in that moment that he had also realised that he loved Joe.

Ivan takes one last pull on his cigarette and puts it out under his boot. He is still terrified by how much he wants to destroy Joe. There is no other word that can do justice to his hate. He wants to annihilate him, extinguish his life, abolish his shade.

He wants him never to have existed. He takes a final look at the house that has been taken away from him.

Back in the car he shakes his head at the entirety of his humiliation. He has mentioned Joe to Perry, but only in the most imprecise terms. I was in love with someone for fifteen years. He left me for a younger guy he found on Grindr. I had to sell my house. I'm glad that prick is out of my life. He was toxic. No words about how the pain of Joe's desertion had pushed him dangerously towards madness. Ivan had spoken freely of his daughter's pain on that first night he and Perry had spent together, but about his own suffering, he has remained silent.

You have not suffered the way she did, he berates himself, with a strict and adamant purpose. He will not allow himself the indulgence of misery and martyrdom favoured by the rest of his piss-weak generation.

By the time he gets to Mrs Zangalis's house, his only thought is for the work that needs to be done.

Leon and Vicki have been working hard. A foretaste of the approaching winter is in the air, in the cutting nip of the wind and the drizzle that seeps into the cuticles of leaves, into the damp earth. Yet Leon is stripped to a T-shirt and Vicki has unbuckled the straps of her work overalls. As Ivan walks in through the small gate that opens up to the backyard, the others take the opportunity to lay down their tools: Vicki her trowel and Leon his hammer and nail belt. 'Hey, boss,' Vicki calls out, pulling an already sodden cloth from her pocket, wiping her face and neck. Leon is standing in what remains of the old vegetable garden, his boots sunk into the soil. Ivan can't hide his grin. He is always struck by the comic contrast between the two of them. Vicki is short, stout and full-bosomed whereas Leon is tall, all sharp angles and severe lines, the high flat brow, the deep furrows of the lines that cut into the side of his lips, over his eyes. Though his parents were Greek, there is an austere Slavic paleness to his colouring; his receding hair, closely cropped tufts at the side of his scalp, is grizzled, silver. Vicki's skin, flushed now, is a creamy gloss, and her face is a constitution of curves and dimples, her Pacific heritage clear from the black, spongy curls of her hair, the expressive jut of her features: the wide nose, the thick full lips. Vicki and Leon are the best of friends.

'Good job—now time for coffee.'

Ivan swings around. Anna Zangalis has stepped out onto the verandah. Ivan has to curb his instinct to rush up and help her to a chair. She is alarmingly thin. Her neighbour, Irena, had recommended Ivan to Anna; and Irena has spoken to him of Anna having cancer, whispered it in the hushed, reverential tone that older people still use to ward off the evil of the word. Irena had no further details and Ivan hasn't asked Anna himself. He admires her stoic acceptance of fate, her fragile shrug, her bemused smile when they talked occasionally about age and illness—his parents' passing, her husband's long sickness and death—and how she points a finger up to the ceiling or to the sky and says, 'We are toys for God.' No lamentation, no whining in her voice, just that cool acceptance. He adores Anna Zangalis.

'Thanks, Mrs Z,' Vicki gives a thumbs-up. 'You're a legend.'

'Greek coffee?' asks the old woman.

'Of course! Not bloody Aussie.' Vicki mimes disgust.

Anna laughs, a surprise to hear that deep sound coming from that tiny frame.

The old woman insists that they all come inside to drink their coffees, that it is too cold to sit outside. They take off their boots. Ivan walks into the kitchen, realises from the sputtering sound coming from the ducts that Anna has only just switched on the central heating. She must have been freezing. He recognises that stubborn peasant frugality—both of his parents had it. Anna resembles them in this way, but in her kindness and her bold sense of humour, she is nothing like them.

There has been little need for Ivan to drop in to Anna's place. Leon and Vicki don't need his supervision—they are diligent and hardworking, and both from homes and backgrounds that make them intuitively respectful of an old migrant woman like Anna Zangalis. The truth is that Anna gives him joy, her uncomplaining humour is a tonic and it tempers his cynicism. Ivan is far from a romantic. He knows that Anna's generation, his parents' generation, can be spiteful and small-minded, that they can be intolerant. Yet they have courage, and they have humility. Joe's shadow can't penetrate the warmth of her kitchen.

He has just sipped the last of the thick coffee—he doesn't particularly enjoy Greek coffee, but he drinks it out of respect for Anna—and is about to make his farewells when there is a knock on the laundry door. And almost immediately the door opens with a rush of cold wind, and a man walks into the kitchen, Anna's youngest son. Anna gets up and rushes to kiss him. Arthur leans down, offers his mother his cheek, but his eyes are fixed on the coffee drinkers. Vicki is already standing. Leon quickly downs the last of his coffee. 'We should get back to work,' he says.

They thank Anna and go outside to put on their boots.

Arthur is glaring at Ivan.

Ivan nods at him, asks dryly, 'How are you?'

The man doesn't answer. Instead, he turns to his mother. 'Make me a coffee.' And with that he storms off to the toilet. Ivan could knock his fucking block off. He feels revulsion for him: there is no civility or humility in Arthur. Ivan detests him. And he also detests how attractive he finds him.

He gets to his feet. 'Thank you—for the coffee,' he says to Anna, using his clumsy schoolyard Greek.

She smiles, her eyes still solicitous, but they are wandering, looking over his shoulder in anticipation of her son. Ivan has grown up with Greeks, went to school with them, has worked with them, has been mates with them—he's now seeing a Greek, for God's sake—and is resigned to the adoration she bestows on her son. His protective affection for Anna in part arises from how she reminds him of his own mother, of what they share as migrants, and also what they had in common before that. He remembers Anna saying she was from northern Greece; her village and his mother's village were probably closer

than Melbourne is to Ballarat. Yet he can never get used to the
infatuation that Greek mothers feel for their sons. That depth
of maternal reverence unsettles him. Ivan has had more contact
with Anna's daughter, Melissa. She is the one who takes her
mother to the doctor and to the hospital and does all the shopping for Anna, but not once has he seen that expression of
worship in Anna's eyes when she looks at her daughter. That
is reserved only for the son. Ivan hears the toilet flush, and
goes outside to start putting on his shoes.

Angeliki, Perry's composed and taciturn mother, is less
effusive than Anna. Yet she too betrays that devotion when it
comes to her son. Not Perry; towards Perry and Cleo, Angeliki
is coolly loving. It is Tass, the oldest, the number-one son,
whom she pampers. Tass is a charmer, and an egoist.

He walks over to where the others are working. The old
vegetable garden, that fertile wonder, is almost gone. In a week
or so the job should be done and the whole of the yard will be
lawn. Anna has kept the lemon trees and the herb garden. Her
eyes had filled with tears early on in the job, when Ivan had
asked about the fig. She said something in Greek, before adding
in her hesitant English, 'I like figs very much, they remind me
of home.' But she shook her head. 'Too much work; it is not an
easy tree.' The tears had started to fall and she abruptly turned
away from him. 'Cut it,' she'd ordered flatly. 'Take it away.'

'Okay,' he says to Leon and Vicki, 'I'll be off.'

Still squatting in the dirt, Leon tilts his head to a pile of
bluestones. 'Does Anna want to keep those?'

Anna was meant to get back to Ivan about them. Her initial response had been to ask if he could dispose of them for her. It was evidence of the esteem in which they all held the old woman that the three of them had remonstrated with her, explaining how sought-after the old rocks were. 'If you don't want them,' Ivan explained to her, 'then we can sell them for you.' She had answered that she would consult her children.

'I'll go and ask her.'

There is a sudden shout, an obscenity screamed out with the ugliness of a crow's caw. And then, like a spray of artillery fire, the same obscenity screamed again and again, rapid and insistent: 'Fuck! Fuck! Fuck! Fuck! Fuck! Fuck! Fuck! Fuck, Mum, you're a fucking idiot!'

To insult the gentle old woman like that . . . Ivan could break Arthur's neck. The muscles have tightened in Leon's face, usually so impassive, accentuating his leanness. He too is furious. As for Vicki, her abhorrence is clear. 'That guy is a cunt,' she mutters.

Ivan is caught in indecision, a state he cannot abide. Clearly this is not the time to ask about the bluestone. He can only imagine the old woman's humiliation if he were to disturb them now. But Arthur's shrieking tantrum is frightening. He makes up his mind. He won't leave yet.

An argument is raging in Greek. They can't hear Anna, can only imagine she is attempting conciliation. Only the expletives are in English.

It is Vicki who, turning to Leon, asks, 'What are they saying?'

Ivan frowns. He also wants to know, but he thinks the question indecent. He dislikes gossip, finds it a weakness in women and is repelled when men indulge in it.

Leon answers quietly, 'It's about money. The prick is complaining about the money she's wasting on the garden.' Vicki snarls in contempt.

Anna would be mortified if she knew they were speaking about her and her family in this way. She was being shamed enough.

'I'll clear some more rubble,' Ivan growls, stripping off his jacket. He gestures for Leon to throw him the extra pair of work gloves lying on the top of the compost bin. Vicki and Leon have caught the reprimand in Ivan's voice. Vicki drops to her haunches and resumes work on the garden bed. Leon slams his foot down hard onto the step of the shovel, digging for the remains of the tree roots. Ivan squats, grimacing as he strains to pull the roots from their tight hold in the soil. He knows his labours are superfluous, but he isn't going to leave. He doesn't trust Arthur.

There is a crack, the sound of breaking glass. Arthur screams further insults. Then they hear a loud thud, something slamming against wall or floor. Ivan springs to his feet. Leon and Vicki are frozen.

The back door flings open and Arthur is there, screeching, his face red and contorted. 'Why the fuck aren't you working?' he screams. 'What the fuck are we paying you for?'

Ivan clenches his right hand into a fist, wills himself not to get into a fight. Not to scream, in equal outrage: 'You haven't paid a cent, it's all your mother's money, you useless cunt!' He tightens his fist.

Anna is a shadow at the screen door. She is imploring, begging, in Greek.

Ivan swings around, says quietly, 'Ignore him, get back to work.'

Vicki obeys immediately. For a moment, Leon doesn't move: the lines on his face cut deep, and his mouth tightens as he stares at the quivering man standing on the deck. Then, turning away from Arthur, Leon jams his shovel into the earth.

Ivan's phone vibrates, that irritating juddering against his thigh. A text from Dana, her antagonism clear in capitalised letters: *WHAT THE FUCK DID YOU SAY TO MY DAUGHTER!!!* He shoves the phone back into his pocket.

There is another shout from the house, clearer now; the back laundry door is still open. But this time it isn't angry; instead it is frightened. And with that, the three of them drop their tools. Ivan runs towards the house, alarmed by the fear they have all heard in Arthur's cry. Through the fine lace curtains on the kitchen window, he sees Anna's shadowed outline, and then he sees her drop. One moment she is standing and then there is the sickening thump of her body, the sharp bang of her head on the floor. Ivan hears his own blood rushing through his body, sees his hand pull open the screen door as Leon and Vicki run up behind him, hears Arthur's wails. The man is kneeling before his mother's prostrate body, rocking back and forth, his words a dumb chant: 'Mama, are you alright? Mama, are you alright?' Looking down at Arthur, Ivan doesn't see an overweight and ungainly middle-aged man; he sees a racked child.

He kneels beside him, says quietly, 'Don't move her.'

Ivan presses his fingers to Anna's throat. He swallows; cold charges through him. And then he feels it, the slightest flicker of a pulse. 'Call an ambulance.'

Arthur scrambles to his feet, starts dialling. Ivan carefully shifts Anna's head to one side and equally cautiously opens her jaw, checks that her tongue hasn't rolled back in her mouth. There is the faintest of wheezes. She looks terribly old and yet the frailness of her body bent into itself reminds him of a just-born kitten or puppy. The memory punches into his consciousness: the sight of his father in hospital, the same contradictory vulnerability; the awfulness of a casing that was the dying man's body and those incredulous, trusting eyes. He shoves the memory aside. Not now.

'Will she be okay?'

Ivan appreciates that Vicki is anxious, but he doesn't want her anxiety to escalate Arthur's state. Without turning to look at them—for he knows both Vicki and Leon are standing behind him, as if the adrenaline still coursing through his veins is amplifying everything in him that is most animal, most instinctive—he says, 'Can you two wait outside for the ambulance?' They accede straightaway. He senses their relief, and that of the man beside him.

'They'll be here soon.'

He's not sure that Arthur has heard him. He's now sitting cross-legged, his eyes not moving from his mother's face. The contrast between that position and the man's grey, thinning hair, the silver spray of stubble across his plump cheeks and chin, is incongruous. Ivan, who is still gently holding Anna's tiny, bony wrist, sees Arthur raise his hand and then immediately drop it.

'Go ahead,' Ivan encourages him. 'You can touch her.'

With that permission, Arthur clambers to his knees, bends over and lightly kisses his mother's brow. Anna doesn't stir. Ivan sits impassively, holding the woman's wrist. Where the fuck is the ambulance? His own phone has buzzed twice while they have been sitting there. But he doesn't want to make any movement that might alarm the other man. There is something shockingly childish about Arthur; his current subdued meekness as disconcerting as his wild aggression had been in the moments before his mother collapsed. There is even something reminiscent of the school locker room in the stale smells of the man, the pong of his sweat, the sharp ammonic stink of his dirty trackpants. His lips are moving, there is a subtle rocking: the man is praying.

Ivan turns back to the old woman, and fusing with his own prayer is an apology. Anna is a canny woman—he is sure that there is nothing about men and their appetites that would shock her. How ridiculous they are. Here were he and Arthur, both praying, pleading for Anna to be returned to consciousness, and even now, in that life-or-death moment, Ivan still can't help it: that indelibly primal part of his brain—no, not his brain, the instinct is buried deeper, is truly mysterious, as if it belongs to that other ancient element, the soul—is carnally assessing the distraught man opposite him. Arthur is overweight, his face is asymmetrical, his clothes are stained; nevertheless, those rich aromas are intoxicating. His arms are fat but also muscly and strong, and Ivan has noticed the outline of Arthur's penis under the stretch of the cheap polyester of his trackpants. He feels his own cock bud.

Arthur finishes his silent prayer with three quick rotations of the Orthodox cross. Ivan follows him. The siren is growing louder. Ivan allows himself to—briefly, firmly—clutch Arthur's shoulder.

'It's going to be okay, Arthur. They're here.'

Ivan is relieved to step aside, to allow the young paramedics to assess Anna, to prepare her for the stretcher. Arthur answers their questions, says nothing about his argument with his mother. Ivan remains silent.

Once Anna is laid on the stretcher, one of the paramedics turns to Ivan. 'I'm afraid only one of you can come with us.'

Ivan points to Arthur. 'He's Anna's son.'

There is a quick locking-up, then Ivan, Leon and Vicki call out their condolences and best wishes as Anna is hoisted into the back of the ambulance.

Arthur turns to Ivan. 'Thank you,' he begins with a stutter, and then adds more firmly, 'You were so calm. I'm so glad you were there, mate.' And then, impulsively, with an ardent warmth, he is hugging Ivan, holding him tight. Without looking back, he steps inside the cavity of the ambulance, drops the flat seat and sits beside the prone body of his mother. The paramedics slam the door shut.

Ivan crosses himself one last time. He turns to Leon and Vicki. 'Could you two please clean up. Then take the rest of the day off.'

As he's about to turn the key to his ute, his phone starts vibrating. Dana's name flashes across the screen, and he declines it. He has now missed three calls from her. He puts his phone on speaker, rests it on the dashboard, and listens to the messages.

The abuse is vile. At first it's almost funny, the demented logic and the incoherent fury: the words *cazzo* and faggot intermingled with the accusations of him being a sexist and a misogynist and a toxic male. It makes him chuckle, and that feels good; it relieves the tension at the back of his neck, at the saddle of his right shoulder. But as Dana's invective continues, his laughter is stilled. Dana's derisive scorn is undiluted, and in the closeness of the cabin of his car, it takes on an intensity, as though she is there with him. She is now accusing him of putting Katerina between them—'As you always have, you useless Slav *cazzo!*'—and of undermining her—"Cause you hate women, you cunt!'—and he listens in stony silence. She's drunk, he tells himself. And then, her voice dropping to a dangerously measured tone, she sounds placatory. 'Don't do it again, Ivan,' she urges. 'Don't let another man make a fool of you.'

He lunges at the phone, bangs his finger on the speaker icon, stops her infernal, cruel tirade. The messages continue; her voice is tinny on the phone's internal speaker, as if coming through water.

Ivan lays his head on the cool glass of the driver's window. He looks out on the quiet street. A little further up, where the road bends, there is an old man shuffling slowly, wrapped in a large black coat.

He can't expunge Dana from his life because that would exile him from Katerina.

If she's drunk, she'll keep ringing. He knows he needs to call her. Yet he hesitates. Though the day is cold and the glass is icy against his brow because he hasn't started the car, there is also something tranquil in this moment. But then, as if a demon has entered the car, the stillness is sundered and her final words slam into his head: Don't let another man make a fool of you.

He looks at his phone, willing Perry to ring or surprise him with a text. If he made contact now, that would be proof, would it not—evidence of love?

'Jesus, fuckwit!' he reprimands himself out loud. He finds morally contemptuous the kind of religious observations that insist on supplication before God. He has superstitions that he regards as necessary: crossing himself at intimations of danger, and mouthing the name of the Virgin Mary when he suspects malice or insincerity in others. Those rituals are tied to the traditions of his Orthodox Christian faith that illuminates the darkness lying between birth and death. But to barter with God, to demand proof of His existence? No, for him, that is weakness.

He quickly punches the following text, sends it to Perry: *I miss you, I want to kiss you so hard.* And he winds down the window, not minding the cold, embracing it, inhaling deeply.

The thought of kissing Perry, the fervour of their kissing, is arousing. His hand falls to his crotch, feels the satisfying hardness there. He closes his eyes, imagines his finger tracing Perry's lips. Then, unbidden, he sees Arthur's fleshy face, recalls his acrid stink.

He opens his eyes, takes his hand away. He's not guilty that his fantasy includes both men. If there is shame, it mostly comes from the thought that Anna is in hospital. And he knows he can't put off doing what he has to do. He owes it to Kat.

Ivan calls Dana.

She answers on the first ring. 'Finally. What took you so long?'

Yet her fury is muted, and the words are slurred. He suspects that after leaving him the spiteful blast of that last voicemail, she's taken some kind of pill.

'It's been busy with work. This is the first chance I've had to call you.' He's not going to mention Anna.

'Bullshit.' Some spunk is returning to her tone. 'Absolute fucking bullshit, Ivan. You're just too much of a pussy to speak to me 'cause you know I'm fucking right.'

And now he explodes. 'Dana, what the fuck is your problem?' He looks up, furious with himself for losing his temper.

Her voice becomes light, almost musical now, with just a slight narcotic drag on some of the syllables. He's sure she's gloating because he lost control—that she got to him. 'You, prick, you are my problem. Why do you want to bring him to Tashie's birthday?'

'His name is Perry.'

'I don't care what his fucking name is.'

'Katerina invited him.'

''Cause you made her invite him.'

'I did no such thing.'

'I don't want him there.'

'Then tell Kat.'

'You'd like that, wouldn't you? So she'll blame me? You'd love that.'

He's drained. 'Dana,' he sighs into the mouthpiece, 'he's a nice guy, he really is.'

He's spoken his thought, and his hope; he's spoken it out loud. He winces, prepares for another lashing. Dana is silent. He hears the click of her lighter, the intake of her first drag on the cigarette. He leans over, releases the catch to the glove box and takes out his packet. He winds the window down completely and lights his cigarette.

'You haven't given up?'

'Nope. I've cut down.'

'Me too.' She giggles, an offering of armistice. 'Does he want you to quit?'

'He lived in France for years and he's Greek. He's not uptight about those things.'

'Not like Joe?'

He stiffens. Even the lull of the nicotine can't dull that wrench. And it is in his bloody heart. The romantics and the dreamers are right: inside his chest, deep within, the mention of that name causes a tearing right there. He presses his finger hard against his pecs, as if searching for the ache, as if making it hurt more would negate the sting of that name.

'No, he's not like Joe at all. He's a much better man.'

'That wouldn't be hard.'

He laughs, and so does Dana.

'Kat told me that you're putting in seventy thousand towards her getting a new place. That's real good of you.'

'Not a problem.'

He hears her inhale, sharply and suddenly. 'I can't afford anything, Iva.'

'I know that, Dana. Don't worry.'

He can, and she cannot. His business survived, even thrived during the worst of the pandemic. With travel made impossible, everyone decided to landscape their homes. Whereas Dana lost her job in the first lockdown and started working shifts at the local supermarket. And then her hips needed work and there was that long wait to get on the disability pension. He pities her. There is no equivocation there; he genuinely believes she is unlucky. He waits for her to speak. He knows any expression of consolation would be a terrible mistake. She is ashamed that he pities her.

'If he didn't take our money, Iva . . .' she moans. 'If that cunt hadn't stolen our money.'

He feels his goodwill beginning to dissipate, as if draining from his body. And he is alert again. The drag in her voice has returned; he can hear the competing battle of the alcohol and whatever sedative she has taken for dominion over her body.

She could fly into a rage at any moment, descend into self-pity. He doesn't know which of the two he hates more.

'Why'd you let him do it to us?' she whines. 'How could you let it happen?'

No, he's sure: he hates the self-pity more.

Joseph did it to *me*. He betrayed *me*. He destroyed *me*.

'Dana, I've got to go.'

'Fuck you. You're always having to go—you have no fucking balls.' She's a fighter, she is wrestling against the drugs. 'That's why Joseph took you for a ride all those years, stole everything from you, fucked around, made you a fucking *cazzo*, a fucking cuckold.' And she's laughing now. 'You've never had any balls.' And then her voice, remarkably, is steel. Sober. 'I've learnt not to trust faggots. You're not bringing that Greek prick to my granddaughter's birthday.'

He ends the call. He ends it to save himself from unleashing his wrath. Ivan sits absolutely still. He is praying. Oh God, destroy her, let her never have existed.

But there is Kat, there is Natasha, there is the will and order of fate.

'Lord,' he whispers aloud, 'forgive me.'

He takes a last drag of the cigarette and flicks the butt out the window. He starts the ignition. He's trembling, the words going around and around in his head, a demonic swarm: You've never had any balls.

Marrying Dana because it was easier than telling the world, his family, that he was a homosexual. For years, when they were together, ignoring Joe's secretive calls, his relentless texting and scrolling, because it was easier than confronting him. And it is so much easier not to tell Perry about Tashie's party. There's a rancid sourness in his mouth: the contempt he feels for himself. Even Katerina knows he has no balls. As he releases the clutch, a new text comes up on the phone.

Perry: *Kiss sounds good. Real good. Can't wait to see you x*

Ivan ignores it.

Kat had put the radio onto a Classic Hits FM station, and just as he turns left into Canterbury Road he hears the threatening riff introducing Split Enz's 'I Got You'. He turns up the volume, glad that the traffic is heavy, that he doesn't have to concentrate on the road. The song always makes him think of Dana. She had so much energy, was always up for a dance. He owes her. He knows that.

'*I don't know why sometimes I get frightened.*'

He's singing, screaming the lyrics. A middle-aged woman in the car beside him turns, grins, gives him a thumbs-up.

And Dana was smart, she should have gone and studied. But she fell pregnant in her final year of high school and never went back. He was still in his trade school overalls when she'd come around to tell him. 'Are you keeping it?' he'd asked. She had said yes. He hadn't hesitated. 'Then let's get married.'

He'd been so shit-scared. Not of having a child. They were so young they didn't know what it meant. It was all those images of young men dying, the poofter disease. Back then marriage had seemed a lifeline.

He turns the volume low. The song hurts.

The first two years had been tough, but they were united. Ivan completed his apprenticeship, and after a year at home with Katerina, Dana found a job working in admin. They were working towards buying a house, saving all their money for the deposit. On the eve of Kat's fifth birthday, Ivan decided to make a go of working for himself and had registered a business in both their names. This was going to be their future. This was going to make their lives. And there had been Katerina, watching her grow into an infant, become an inquisitive child: that had been thrilling.

It was in the tenth year of their marriage that Ivan came home drunk on a Saturday night and left his wallet open on the kitchen bench. Dana had found it there the next morning. A business card was sitting on the wallet with the words *Call me, spunk* scrawled across the back in blue biro. It was signed *Patrick.*

Ivan still shrinks in mortification at the memory. His gutlessness. He was drunk, but he knows he left his wallet out on purpose.

'I don't know why sometimes I get frightened.'

He so fucking owes her.

In the subsequent maelstrom of rage, of terror and sadness, of relief and recrimination, there had been moments of clarity, when the honesty between them had moved them both. They had never talked so openly before. And never would again. Dana came to understand the weight of her husband's shame and Ivan to comprehend the enormity of his wife's humiliation. They negotiated alimony and custody with calm forbearance.

Dana remained his business partner. He owed her that. Ivan *still* believes he owes her that.

Joseph Tuala had started working for Ivan in the early years of the millennium. Ivan was in his late thirties and Joe was just entering his twenties.

Ivan had not expected to fall in love with Joe. The dalliances that had preceded their relationship seemed embarrassingly insignificant by comparison. Until then, Ivan had been cocky, arrogant, in his sexual liaisons, assuming always that he would be the one adored. That had been true with Dana, and it was true with the boys he had fucked at high school and trade school, the men who'd sucked him off in parks and toilets and change rooms. Some of those encounters had involved affection. And he did feel genuine responsibility to Dana. But with Joe coming into his life, he experienced the transfiguration of love: Joe meant more to him than he did to himself.

A car behind honks impatiently. The light has gone green. Ivan presses hard on the accelerator. Be fucking honest, get some balls. He is burning. But he admits it. Joe meant more to him than Katerina.

He had been high on Joe, drunk on Joe. From the moment the boy had come in for the job. From the moment he had first smiled at Ivan. He was still feeling the rush of that love over a decade later, long after that drunken night when they'd all been out together at that pub in Mitcham and Joe had come up next to him at the urinal, winked, and said, looking down at Ivan, 'You got an awesome cock, boss,' and Ivan, still pissing, had leant across and kissed him. He had been lost in that kiss for over a decade. The intensity of it had never waned. Joe just had to look at him with those blazing black eyes in that broad handsome face, and Ivan would fall onto the boy and wrap himself around him, and in doing so it seemed to Ivan that the boy would not let go of him, would never release him. Locked in that mutual obsession, Ivan felt his own strength and luxuriated in it, believing that he was succour and haven for Joe. Even though he had bought the house by the beach before Joe started working for him, Ivan thought it was fated that it would be their home, their eternity. How could he ever have thought that he and Dana had a future together? Joe was his destiny and his purpose. Until that night when Joe had said, his voice coldly dismissive, 'I hate it here, Ivan. I want adventures and I want to have some fun. Being with you is making me old before my time.' Uncomprehending, Ivan had answered, 'But I love you.' That was enough for him. And then Joe had uttered the words that could never be erased, that would lash at him till the day he died: 'Jesus, don't you get it? I'm fucking bored. I've met a guy, Brett, and I want to be with him. Sorry, Ivan, but it's over. I'm not in love with you.' Stated as simply as that, as though remarking on the weather, or talking about a TV show. How Ivan hated him for that. How he wanted to punish that indifference. And then, further devastation, uttered again in that calm and dispassionate tone, 'And you'll have to sell this house or buy me out. It's half mine. By law, I get half of everything.'

'I don't know why sometimes I get frightened.'

In that moment, realising that the cruelty was premeditated, Ivan knew that Joe had been making plans to leave him for a long time.

It still has the stunning clarity of a silent nightmare. He is looking down at Joe, the boy screaming, bucking, as Ivan's fist rises and falls, smashing again and again into Joe's face. Joe's resistance quietens, there is a spray of scarlet exploding from Joe's burst lip, and it is only with that final punch— was it the third? the fourth? the fifth? He honestly cannot remember—that sound returns and he hears the crunch of Joe's jaw breaking. He will never forget the shocking sound of that impact. He could hear the gurgling in Joe's throat, his struggle to draw breath. Ivan still asks forgiveness and offers thanks that he was not drunk that night. He knows that if he had been, Joe would be dead.

Ivan had called the ambulance.

Dana cannot get over her outrage that Ivan had to sell his house, sell their business, and give the lion's share to Joe. She considers him a fool, thinks the young man took advantage of him. But only Ivan knows the enormity of his offence. So Joe's leaving made him poor. What did that matter? He started working for others again, worked hard and long and eventually registered a new business. He'd done alright, enough to put down the deposit on that one-bedroom flat in Bonbeach, and enough to take care of his family. He doesn't even bear a grudge against Joe for taking his money. His violence had been unconscionable, unforgivable.

Even now, when kissing and making love to Perry, his eyes are shut tight as his hands try to claim a younger body, a smoother body, Joe's almost hairless cinnamon skin. He's still addicted: he wants to taste Joe when he kisses the older man. Will he be forever addicted? It is not Joe wound tight around him. Ivan is now the one who cannot let go. The wrenching apart had to come from violence.

'It's half mine. By law, I get half of everything.'

'I don't know why sometimes I get frightened.'

There are times he wishes he could tell Dana about that night, about what he did. Maybe she would finally forgive him. But he won't. He can't. Because to confess would be to give her the power to tell Kat of the monstrous violence her father is capable of, and he cannot do that to her or himself. Better that Dana thinks him a gullible cuckold poof than Katerina learns the truth about him.

Ivan shudders, his body trembling. The memory is excoriating. But worse, he knows he has to tell Perry what he did to Joseph. Perry needs to know the truth if they are to have a future together.

The traffic clogs as he approaches Elwood. His back is sore, his shoulder won't stop tingling. He hasn't boxed for a few weeks; he's let that slip. He needs to get back to the gym. With that thought, his right hand on the steering wheel reflexively transfigures to a fist, it clenches and unclenches. That simple motion delivers him from agitation.

———

The house is a California bungalow, the renovations only recently completed, with the facade and porch returned to their original splendour. The restoration has been expensive, with the piers and balustrades rebuilt with pressed bricks, and original casement windows fitted. The rear of the building, however, has been gutted, and a two-storey extension built. From the glimpses Ivan has had of the open-plan kitchen and dining area, the decor is rigorously contemporary. One wall is dominated by a huge painting, a bewildering swirl of colours in thick daubs of paint. Over the last month, as Ivan has come to assist Stu with the landscaping work, he has often stopped to look across the garden at the painting. If the sun is out, the seemingly random strokes and colours fuse. The varied dashes of blue—some the cyan colour of open sky, others a livid purple darkness—rise out of the mashed turbulence of the surrounding colours, and the painting reveals itself to be a vision of the sea, viewed from above, as if painted by a god. Ivan still doesn't know if it is ugly or one of the most beautiful things he has ever seen.

He has never been inside the house. Simon and Clarissa seem like decent people; they are always polite, and their expectations are neither outlandish nor unrealistic. Ivan appreciates the matter-of-factness with which Clarissa has negotiated prices and payments. There is the slightest hint of accent in her poised, clear English; he guesses that she was born and raised in Hong Kong, for in her straightforward manner with finances there is something of the unashamed bluntness he associates with the Cantonese. Her husband is more aloof, undoubtedly vain, with a constant formal smile that shows off perfect white teeth. Ivan doubts Simon's sincerity. He knows it is prejudice. The man is handsome, with fair hair, unblemished skin and a slim body. But he's too pretty. And the confidence of the couple is astonishing. Though they have only one child who is not yet twelve months old, they have built the extension to accommodate an extra two bedrooms for the further children they are planning. Clarissa had let that slip when she was taking Ivan and Stu around the garden, explaining what she wanted. She had pointed out where she wanted a path built, one that led to a shady liquidambar. 'We're thinking it would be lovely to build some stairs into the tree and have a treehouse built up there for the children.' Ivan had asked how many children she had, and she had replied, 'We are going to have three.' As if life was preordained according to their desires.

Stu is busy filling in the grout for the quartz pavers. He's stripped to his singlet; the waistband is drenched with sweat. As he crouches, the top of his shorts stretches down, releasing the bottom of the singlet. Ivan spots the trail of tawny fuzz disappearing down Stu's lower back. Through the window, he can see Clarissa walking around the dining area, speaking into a headset. She acknowledges Ivan with a curt nod, returns to her conversation.

He thinks of Anna, wants to know if she is alright, if she is being looked after at the hospital. He knows he has her daughter's number somewhere, but that it would be an indecent intrusion to call her.

'Stu,' he calls out, 'tuck in your fucking singlet, mate, we don't need to see your arse crack.'

Stu, without bothering to turn around, gives him the finger. 'What's up with you, you Slav fuck?' he asks lazily, scraping at the wet render. 'Don't you like my sweet ginge bum?' He swings around, still crouching, a big grin on his face. 'Aye, that's right, you like 'em darker, don't you?'

Ivan chuckles. He likes Stu, enjoys the ease of the banter between them, and prizes the man's loyalty. In the collapse of his first business, in the fog of separation from Joe, Ivan had learnt that being betrayed is a drowning. He had been left alone, thrashing and going under. Stu had saved him. He'd said, 'Till you get on your feet again, I'm gonna help you out. That's a promise, Ivan.' The man had kept his vow, working alongside Ivan when he wasn't on another job, while Ivan faithfully kept a log of the money he owed him. Ivan had not drowned. After two years, when Ivan handed the money back to Stu in rolls of cash, Stu's blue eyes had narrowed and he had growled in his Glaswegian brogue, 'No need for this, mate.' Ivan had answered, 'Yes, there is. Please, take it.' Stu had tugged at that luxuriant beard of his, its thick orange coils now peppered with grey, and had finally assented. His loyalty had reminded Ivan that virtue existed, and that was how Ivan had been saved. He genuinely loves Stu, and as that love has not been sullied by desire, it is the deepest friendship he has.

Ivan lands a soft kick on Stu's backside, teasing him. 'Your dirty arsehole is dark enough, mate!'

They both burst into laughter.

For close to an hour, laying the pavers and turning and mixing the grout, they work in silence next to each other. At one point, Clarissa slides open the glass door to say a quick hello, and then shuts it again. Soon after, Ivan rises from his crouch, and massages his lower back. That damn insistent pain. He goes to the ute, mops his brow, and guzzles from his water bottle till it is empty. He checks out the windows, peers into the rear-view mirror, then, sure that there is no one around, he unzips and places the tip of his penis to the bottle's opening. He nearly fills the bottle. When done he places it on the passenger seat. To toss it in the back is to risk forgetting it. He has learnt from that mistake.

His phone vibrates just before four o'clock. It's Dana again and he ignores it. He groans, forces his body to a stand. The last of the pavers have been set and now they have to wait for them to dry. He knows there is no forecast of rain, yet he scans the skies nervously. The grey is parched, washed out. There is no hint of rain.

'We're done for the day, mate.'

Stu attempts an abrupt leap to his feet, almost stumbles, and Ivan lays a steadying hand on the man's shoulder. Stu's skin blushes pink in the patches of his neck and chest not hidden by his beard, and his cheeks are flushed. But the top half of his face remains an almost alabaster pale, a whiteness so translucent that the fine webs of veins at the side of his temples are blue.

'We're getting to be old cunts.' Stu yawns and looks around the garden, his hands on his hips. 'Nearly done, boss.'

'You think we can get it finished by Friday?'

Stu scratches his beard again. 'Maybe.' He falls quiet and Ivan doesn't speak. He knows Stu, knows that his considerations are slow and thorough.

'How much else you got on?'

It is Ivan's turn to deliberate. 'I can do a half-day tomorrow, in the arvo. I've got that job in Beaumaris in the morning and that's just down the road. And Thursday's fine.' He wipes his wet brow with his shirtsleeve. 'Friday's hard: Vicki's got the day off and it's something to do with her kid, so I don't want to take it from her. But that means I'll need to help Leon.'

And then that sinking in his stomach. Anna might still be in hospital—they might not be able to work in Blackburn. There might be no job. Anna might be dead.

The churning in his belly vanishes abruptly. It's as if he has to force the two fingers and the thumb on his right hand to join. But once done, he taps them against his brow, his chest, his right shoulder and then his left.

'Friday.' Ivan spits out the word like a decision. He walks carefully around the edge of the pavement work, steps onto the welcome mat and taps on the glass sliding door. There is no answer, and he peers into the house. He can't see Clarissa. He taps harder. The dining room is muted in the shadows of late afternoon, and the colours of the enormous painting have lost all their vividness. It looks like a mess, Ivan thinks: it is ugly. He slides open the door, calls out.

Ridiculous, at his age, that he experiences a moment of guilt, as if he is a boy back at school, defying a teacher. The shame really is his reaction to the Reardons' affluence and rudeness—so wealthy but they won't offer their toilet for poor Stu to piss in after he's been there all day. While Anna Zangalis, who has worked in factories all her life, who hoarded and saved her money to bestow it on her children, offers her homemade shortbread, Turkish delight, her coffee and tea, water and apple juice, and always, if it is a Friday night, a short neat whisky before they head home.

'Anyone there?' He shouts it, loud and coarse, deliberately rough. When he had slid open the door he'd heard a tease of piano music, like the dash of soft rain. It stops at the sound of his shout. His eyes roam the dim space, all planes of charcoal and slate and grey, with occasional glints where the pallid wintery sun lights up the flecks of blue quartz in the polished granite benchtop. Expensive. Everything about this house is expensive.

Clarissa steps forward, as if conjured from the shadows. 'Is everything alright?' There is a crispness to her voice, and her eyes are both anxious and annoyed.

'I just wanted to say we're done for the day—we've got to wait for the grout to dry now.' He looks over his shoulder, gestures out the back. 'We're nearly finished. Stu and I reckon we'll be finished Friday arvo.'

And looking out at the prospect of that deep plot, the simplicity of the newly paved courtyard, the symmetry of the two paths Stu has made, one leading to the imposing liquidambar, the other curving around the bluestone enclosure of the small vegetable patch, he is proud. Of course, there is a nakedness to the vegetation and flora, the sparseness and the fragility of the new seedlings and flowers, the still-emerging plants and bushes. Yet he can envisage what the garden will look like by summer, see where there will be shade and serenity, where there will be a blaze of colour.

Clarissa has come up to the door, also looking out. It's rare for them to be so physically close to each other. He can smell the discreet florals of her perfume.

'Marvellous.'

It is astonishing, some alchemy of schooling and privilege that he will never be able to understand, how much suggestion someone of her class can load into just one word. She is pleased, certainly. But also glad to be dismissing him and looking forward to having the house and garden back, just for her, her husband and her child.

He steps back. 'Well, Stu'll be here in the morning. I'll see you later tomorrow.'

Her smile is courteous. 'Thank you, Ivan, it's splendid work. Please invoice us early next week and we'll pay immediately.' She raises her voice, only slightly. 'See you tomorrow, Stuart.' With that, she slides the door closed.

They pack up and walk to their vehicles.

'You okay?' asks Stu.

'Yeah, why?'

Stu throws the tools into the back of the van, then rests against the open door. He pulls a pouch of tobacco from the pocket of his work vest, starts rolling a cigarette.

Ivan taps his own pockets. His fags are in the ute. 'Can you roll me one?'

Stu nods, his fingers agile. He expertly pushes a filter into the rolled cigarette, hands it to Ivan. 'You seemed out of sorts back there.'

'Yeah, I probably didn't show her enough deference.'

Stu gives a deep-chested laugh as he lights Ivan's cigarette. Ivan can't help laughing in return.

Stu sucks on his smoke, shrugs his shoulders, pointing the lit cigarette towards the Reardons' house. 'She's alright. He's a bit of a knob.'

Ivan wants to tell him about Anna—there's a rush of words forming in his head, awaiting release. But Stu hasn't worked on the Blackburn job and has never met Anna Zangalis.

'I'm a bit tired,' he says instead. 'Didn't mean to sound pissed off.'

They smoke in silence, neither needing to fill in the space with unnecessary words. When done, they stamp on the butt-ends, give one another a quick, solid embrace. Stu's odour is harsh, defiant, that compound of sweat and tobacco and earth, the masculine scents simultaneously sour and stirring.

He's nearly home when his phone starts ringing in its console.

He answers. The voice he hears is remote and stripped of any resonance, distorted by the ute's shoddy speakers.

'Is this Ivan Pavlovic?' She gives the last consonant a guttural emphasis.

'Yes, speaking.'

'Ivan, this is Melissa Sotiropoulos.'

He doesn't recognise the name or the voice. There are muffled background sounds coming through the speakers, as though an old radio is being tuned: a robotic announcement over a PA system; muted voices in the background; and was that a cry of distress?

'We've met briefly. I'm Anna Zangalis's daughter.'

'Of course. How's your mum?'

He hears it in her pause, the clutch of her breath. 'My mother passed away an hour ago.'

'I'm so sorry.' Instinctively, he lifts his hand to his mouth, to cover it as he gulps and holds back the threatened sob. The last thing she needs is to bear witness to the grief of a stranger. He recalls in that instant returning to work the weekend after his mother's funeral, when he was still a contractor. The woman whose front yard he was landscaping, matronly and plump-chested, had wanted to hug him as soon as he came in the gate, tears rolling from her eyes, copious, enormous teardrops. He had hated her in that moment, wanted to scream at her, *This is not your fucking loss!*

'I'm really sorry,' he says again, and that ugly memory is gone. 'Anna was a wonderful woman.'

Was? Already, so quickly, *was.*

'Thank you.' Melissa's voice is abrupt, but not unfriendly. He understands the mundane tasks and caretaking one must do immediately after a parent's death, the antechamber of grief. 'We were very fortunate to have her as a mother.'

The anguished voice he had heard in the background before is now wailing, distinct even through the speakers.

'For God's sake, Arthur, keep it together!' Melissa's voice explodes.

Ivan pictures Arthur's bloated eyes, snot running from his nose, phlegm on the sides of his mouth, dribbling down his chin, his large body shuddering from the crying. He's prepared to hear obscenities, primed for Arthur's inchoate rage. Instead, he just hears the relentless sobbing.

'Melissa, we don't need to discuss things at the moment,' Ivan quickly offers. 'You can call me next week.'

'Thank you.' Her voice has returned to that original emotionless pitch. 'Of course, we still have to work things out with the house. I just wanted to make sure that you and your colleagues didn't turn up tomorrow.'

'No worries. I'll wait till I hear from you.'

'Thank you.'

'Please pass on my condolences to your brother.'

There is no reply. She has ended the call.

The light is shutting down, the wind is brisk and the world is dark by the time Ivan gets home. He unlocks his door, flicks on the lights. They seem too bright, invading all the available space, leaving no shadows.

Ivan turns on the heater and the standing lamp, turns off the main light. He draws the curtains, orders Thai takeaway, strips off his work clothes and slips into a windcheater, old trackpants and thick woollen socks. He takes out his phone, puts his laptop on the bench that divides the small kitchenette from the living room, and turns it on. He wants images and sounds and the soporific drone of technology to fill in the silence, to remove him from the world.

There is a message from Katerina, thanking him, a selfie of her and Tashie waving at the camera, a bank of symbols—plump full hearts, hands brought together in gratitude, red lipstick kisses—and a rushed promise to ring him tomorrow. Ivan touches his lips, kisses the image of his smiling child and granddaughter. He won't ring Kat now; she and Tashie will be having dinner, there are the long preparations for bed. And Perry is out; he has texted that he is having dinner with friends. There is no one else he wants to talk to.

Mechanically, resenting the feeling of expectation as he does so, he fires up his laptop. As he waits for the browser to activate, he realises what he will search for and what he will do. There comes the sickening self-awareness, the polluting sense of his own baseness. Then he puts all such thoughts aside. He logs on to the porn site, already feeling for his cock. He clicks on to the place where his favourite videos are collected.

He knows what he is looking for and he wonders—a rise of bile at his throat, so distasteful that he pulls his hand back—did he know how this evening would end while the old Greek woman lay dying on her kitchen floor? When his senses had been full of Arthur's smell; the shudder of his belly as he cried, and the curve and fullness of the bulge under the cheap fabric. Grimly, purposefully, resisting the allure of other temptations—the pixelated images of drunk youths somewhere in the Caucasus taking turns to orally and anally fuck a fat transvestite; the too-pale, too-thin Eastern European boys dutifully, almost conscientiously sucking on each other's outsized penises; a huge silver-haired and silver-bearded man in a suit forcing a young man to his knees—he searches. His fingers stop their relentless scrolling. He's found it.

It's amateur. There is no set-up—the camera filming the encounter does not move—and no cutting: the time bar at the bottom of the video reads from zero to nine minutes and thirty-seven seconds. Surprisingly, the colours are sharp; there isn't the washed-out tone of most home videos. It begins suddenly, with a middle-aged man sitting on a couch, talking. He is overweight, in a big black T-shirt and shiny black trackpants. His arm muscles are huge. It is an American accent, the drawl lazy, though the sound quality is terrible and his words are hard to hear. From the snatches of conversation that Ivan can make out, it seems the man is discussing a basketball game. The feeble whine of a song drifts from a speaker in the background.

By this point, Ivan would usually have forwarded the video, rushed to where the sex is starting. Tonight, though, he is determined to watch it unfold in real time, not to speed to its conclusion. And so, for the first time, he recognises the song, though not the singer or the title. He's sure he's heard it, the stuttering vocals, the juddering electronic pulse of the music. Maybe Kat has played it in her car? Maybe he's heard it on the radio while working alongside Leon and Vicki? A second figure comes into frame and Ivan's attention snaps back to the images.

The man on the sofa looks like Arthur. His heritage could be Italian or Spanish, could be Greek. His dawdling tone, the way he seems to forget himself in the middle of a sentence, suggests he is stoned, but there is a pleasing twinkle to his eyes. Even though he is seated at a distance from the camera, whenever he glances directly at the lens, his eyes shine.

The second man is much younger, thin, with ginger wisps on his sharp chin. He is wearing plain black Levi's and a white T-shirt, generic male attire. There is something studied, almost rehearsed about the way he sits next to the older man, coquettishly placing his long, slender hand across the man's crotch. His hair is dyed an unnatural blond, and that too seems a calculated attempt to convey effeminacy. Arthur—for the older man is Arthur now, this is who Ivan needs him to be—has fallen silent. The boy whispers something to him, the words inaudible, and Arthur nods. He leans over the arm of the sofa, and as he does so his T-shirt rises, revealing his hairy belly. Ivan spits on his fingers, gently pushes back his foreskin from his cockhead. He releases a low growl of pleasure, resisting the urge to fast-forward.

Arthur pulls a screen pad off the floor. The youth, now squeezing at Arthur's cock and balls, leans in so he too can see the screen. The irritating pop song has finished and now there are the hysterical euphoric shouts of advertising. The boy says—and Ivan's never sure if these are his exact words, most times he skips over this part—'You like her?' Arthur's answer is clear. 'Fuck yeah! Look at her tits!' It's at this point that the boy, almost violently, pulls at the waist of Arthur's pants and grasps the older man's cock. It is erect, not exceptionally long, not especially thick.

The youth starts sucking him. Ivan starts gyrating slowly in his chair, his buttocks moving back and forth. He's wrapped his hand around his own dick, massaging it.

And then the visuals seem interminable. The unwavering gaze, the young man mechanically sucking on the older man's cock. Ivan's erection is waning. He closes his eyes, imagines himself kneeling in front of Arthur, pulling down the man's pants, sees Arthur's hairy belly, a coarse, dense pelt of pubic hair, black fur across the man's balls. He inhales, trying to recall the scent, the rankness of the man. He takes Arthur's cock in his mouth, he is sucking him.

But it's not working. All he sees is Anna's face.

Ivan stares blankly at his laptop screen. He clicks the window. The two men disappear. There is a faint electrical throbbing in the room, the menace of silence. Desperately, he scans the images of the saved videos. None will do. He needs to get off. He needs to forget the old woman's face. He enters another site, views the columns of videos recommended for him. Sees an image of a young man, possibly Tamil, his body slender and hairless. Ivan starts the video, watches the youth masturbate. Ivan starts tugging at his still-soft cock. The boy is handsome but it's taking too long. Ivan just wants it finished. He quickly types three words into the search box: *Latino. Dad. Son.* He glances at the result, clicks on a thumbnail of a young man in a shower, on his knees. The video plays, also one unchanging shot, three other naked men are in the shower cubicle, all Ivan can see are their hirsute torsos and large cocks. The youth, who is handsome with his body shaved, has a furious glare in his eyes, sucking first on one cock then the next and then the other before returning to the first. The glare in the boy's eyes is rage. Yet he doesn't stop sucking, takes two cocks in his mouth. Ivan's cock is not exactly hard but his tugging of it is so fast, so brutal, that the friction does what he needs it to do. The boy has his eyes squeezed tight as the first slash of cum strikes his face. His mouth is closed tight in an unnatural grimace. Finally, thankfully, it happens: Ivan ejaculates. A few gobs of semen fall across the keyboard. The rest trickles over his fingers. Ivan closes the browser. His screensaver is a recent photograph of Katerina and Tashie. Burning with shame, he slams the laptop closed.

The burr of electricity, the indistinct throb as if a motor is running, that sound is everywhere. The soft light from the lamp, the constant thrumming, it all feels ominous. Yet Ivan can't summon the energy to stand up, to go to the bathroom and clean himself. The semen is drying on his fingers, the stench of it overpowering. Revolted, he wipes his hands across his shirt. And with an audible groan, hating himself, he lifts the computer lid, launches the search engine, and types.

Joe's Instagram page. A new photograph. Joe is beaming at the camera, Brett has his arm around him, is the one taking the selfie. In the background is the azure splendour of the Pacific Ocean. Joe is wearing a tight yellow singlet; his skin is a dark gleam, his chest shaved. Brett wears a light pink linen shirt, and his profile is sharp and distinct. Both men look happy.

Stu has said that one day Ivan will come across a photo of Joe and it won't hurt: 'I promise you, Ivan, one day it won't hurt.'

But today it hurts. The pain is wretched, so acute that Ivan is shaking. His guts are squeezed, and his throat is dry. He exits the browser and again there is the wrench of that image of Kat and Tashie. He shuts down and the screen is black. He looks at his ghostly reflection. The speckles of white in his stubble, the uneven spread of bristles across his scalp. He is looking at an old man.

The disgust finally gets him moving.

Without turning on the light in the narrow bathroom, he grabs the electric razor, shaves his head. Once done, he strips, walks into the shower, washes himself, scrubbing at his hands, at the clots of semen matted into the hair on his belly. He turns the hot-water tap off, and the water is tepid and then it is freezing. His jaw clenching, he stands under the freezing torrent till his teeth are chattering, till his testicles seem to have been sucked up into his guts. He suffers the pain till it is all that there is in the world, till the memory of the photograph of Joe and Brett fades, becomes indistinct, finally vanishes. Till all he is capable of conceiving is the stabbing pain of the cold water. He turns off the tap.

After drying himself, after throwing his clothes into the washing basket, he puts on a pair of boxers and his favourite sleeping top, an old U2 tour T-shirt. There are small holes under both arms, and the white cotton is now discoloured.

He stands in the middle of his flat, feeling the incessant thrum of light, of wires and current and machines, as if his apartment is a body and he is deep inside it, the sound of the electricity coursing through capillaries and veins and arteries behind the walls, across the floor and ceiling.

The emptiness of it. He had wanted to stay close to the water, but the flat is ugly, cheaply constructed. There are no paintings, no posters, no photographs on the wall. There is the TV, the black vinyl couch, the matching armchair, a coffee table he bought at a sale at IKEA. In November it will be five years since he moved in and it still looks desolate, like the most basic of motel rooms.

Perry has only stayed over a couple of nights. He was polite the first time, but Ivan sensed his lover's unease at the bare emptiness of the apartment. That first time, that first morning, they had walked to the beach and it was then that Perry had turned to him and said, 'I can see why you like living here. I'd come down here every day if I could.' Walking back, they had stopped for a coffee, and while they waited for it on the street, Perry had gone next door to the op shop. He returned with an outrageous thick-bowled ashtray, the heavy curved glass a day-glo pink. He had shown it to Ivan, and both men had laughed: at the ugliness of it, at the comforting familiarity—it turned out that both their parents had exactly the same ashtray.

The moonlight falling through the venetian blinds finds the ashtray, sitting on one end of the coffee table. The colours swirl: crimson and pink and lavender.

Ivan breathes heavily. It's late. Perry is out with friends. He shouldn't call.

A cold serpentine chill across his back: the humming of the house, the sense of it being corporeal and organic; the coursing of blood.

He rings and Perry answers immediately.

The stifled drone of laughter and music and chatter in the background.

'Hi! Where are you?' Perry's voice, warm and delighted.

'Home.'

'You okay?'

No, he is not okay. He is lonely, he is wretchedly lonely.

'Ivan?' There is rising concern in Perry's voice now, a sharpness. 'What's the matter?'

'Anna Zangalis died.'

Has he talked about her? Would Perry remember if he had?

'Jesus.' The noise from the bar recedes. 'Hold on a moment,' Perry says. 'I'm heading outside.'

The relentless vibration has gone. Ivan is aware of the world outside the four walls of the room: the roaring of a speeding truck on the highway, the muffled sound of a TV next door.

'What happened?'

'I don't know exactly. We were working at her place this afternoon and she must have had a stroke or a heart attack. I'm not sure.'

Perry's breathing on the other line.

'Her son was there,' Ivan continues. And suddenly his words are out in a rush, and he describes running to the house, the distraught son keening over the body, Ivan trying to keep her warm and still till the ambulance arrived. He finishes telling

Perry about Anna and he is conscious of the heaviness of his breathing. He doesn't cry, and though in part it is because he doesn't believe he has the right to that grief—for after all, Anna was neither friend nor family—it is also because Anna's was not a wasted life. There was evidence of disappointment there, and traces of deep sorrow. Yet he had not glimpsed even the smallest fraction of bitterness.

'Ivan'—Perry's tone is firm—'I'm coming over.'

He looks at the empty walls of the living room. 'Stay, have fun with Claudia and Spiro. I'm okay.'

'They'll understand. I'll finish my drink and order an Uber.'

The drone, faint yet marked, has resumed. Ivan knows what he wants. 'Can I come over there instead?'

'Of course.'

'I've got the key. You stay out with your friends. I'm exhausted. I'll go straight to bed.'

'Are you sure you don't want me to come home now?'

'I'm sure.'

'I'm sorry, mate. I know you liked her a lot. You've been enjoying working on that place. I wish I'd met her; she seemed kindness itself.'

The sob begins as a tickle at the throat. Ivan gulps it down. 'I'll see you later.' He is about to end the call when he hears Perry's voice, loud, insistent.

'I love you.'

It has not been said before. Ivan is tempted to pretend that he hasn't heard, to continue the motion of sweeping his fingers across the phone's screen. To make Perry disappear. He raises

the phone back to his ear. And indeed, Perry has gone. He
has ended the call.

The boldness of it fells him. He is dazed too by the confidence with which Perry said those words, and how that
conviction is heightened by him not needing Ivan to repeat
them. Ivan knows that he has to prove himself equal to that
courage, tell him about the depths of his debasement. He
knows he has to make that confession—and that it will be
made in the future. Such hard truth needs time to be declared
and to be heard. He knows too that there are indignities and
mortifications that Perry has not yet revealed about his own
abandonment by Gerard.

His fingers tap the phone. He writes the words. *I love you too.*

He doesn't press send. There is that photograph, Joe's happiness with Brett. He owes it to Perry that his words are not
deceitful, must not be insincere.

She seemed kindness herself. Had Ivan said that about Anna?
Or was it that Perry had listened when he'd been jabbering on
about work? It was not an expression that Ivan had ever used.
There was something old-fashioned, bookish about it. Perry
had been listening to him as he chatted about Anna.

He taps the phone, he sends the words.

On the drive across town he flicks between radio stations until
he finds a yearning, plaintive song. He sometimes likes to find
a station broadcasting in another language. He guesses the song
is in Arabic. He doesn't change the station even when the

song ends. He listens to the voices of the two men who are now arguing earnestly; occasionally he recognises an English word, the name of the prime minister or a Melbourne suburb. He deliberately keeps the volume low, yet at a level where the chat and the music don't disappear into insensible murmur. As he descends Punt Road to the river, the sparkling aurora of the city to the left, the more muted spread of flickering lights across the great plain of the northern suburbs ahead, another song begins, the rhythm propulsive. As soon as he is over the bridge, a male voice, deep and rapturous, blares from the ute's speakers. He turns up the volume. He even sings along, making up the words.

Though it is a waning moon, it sheds enough light so that Perry's apartment is not in darkness when he enters. The curtains and blinds are open, the shafts of illumination forming silvery waves across the large living space. Ivan doesn't bother to switch on the light. He walks up to the large casement windows and looks down on the streetscape below. There are the pulsing neon lights from the Punjabi grocery across the street, and shadows are visible behind the darkened windows of the pizza restaurant. Ivan checks his phone. It is nine thirty-seven. He is distracted by a green square on the screen, a text from Dana. *I'm tired. You win.*

He stares at her message for a long time, perturbed by the finality of the words, puzzled by their meaning. Is she signalling her acceptance of Perry attending Natasha's birthday? Or is it nothing more than a sarcastic backhand indicating that she can't be bothered waiting for him to reply tonight, that the battle will continue tomorrow? He too is tired. He feels no victory.

He types quickly, the text replete with typos; he wants to communicate to her that they cannot continue to battle each other with this ferocious resentment, that he can't keep apologising, that he is weary of the battles. *Joe destroyed me.* Can she not understand?

He looks at the spray of words. Perhaps it might lead to conversation and not necessarily into argument. Yet their history together is too long and complicated for such a simple resolution. He deletes every character. Instead, he types, *Let's talk tomorrow, have a good night.* He hesitates. He types one last letter, an *x*. He sends the message.

On the rooftop of the wine bar on the opposite corner, there is a huddle of smokers under one of the tall standing heaters. The rays from the radiator are an unnatural orange. The red-glass candleholder shines a murky pink. Though the smokers look cold, the craving assails him.

Yet there is something he must do. The weak candlelight has been a reminder.

There are no candles in Perry's kitchen drawers but then he remembers the thick lemongrass-scented candle that sits on the basin shelf in the bathroom. It must have been a gift; the crepe wrapping paper hasn't yet been removed. He tears off the paper and the tart citrus odours fill the narrow room. Ivan unlocks the sliding door to the balcony.

There is not much wind, but where it does make contact the cold is bitter. Ivan dashes back into the flat, grabs an old hoodie that he's left in the bedroom. Back on the balcony, he can smell the sweet stench of marijuana floating from one of the balconies along the row. He lights a cigarette, and that reek is replaced by the smell of tobacco.

He stares at the unlit candle. His intention is to say his prayers and farewells to Anna. Ivan knows that, in the tradition of Anna's and her family's faith, he would be welcome at the funeral, possibly even the wake after, regardless of the brevity of their acquaintance. It would be easy to find out the date and the time of the church service. But he doesn't want to disappear into the anonymity of the silent, respectful congregation. He wants his leave-taking from Anna to be personal, and even though he is not convinced there is an afterlife, is even indifferent to its possibility, nevertheless he would like to mark her passing and their parting explicitly, vocally, as if in the enunciation the emotions can transcend and violate the adamant impasse between life and death.

He wonders if a candle will stay alight in the breeze. Yes, the wind is mild, but it could easily gather strength and extinguish the flame. Enough ancestral superstition remains in Ivan that he would be disturbed by such an auspice.

He draws heavily on the cigarette, pissed off with himself. He is not scared of irrational omens. Alone with his thoughts, preparing that singular ritual for Anna, he realises that he knows very little about her. He has only known her a few months—there is a long life that he can never fully comprehend: a life of suffering, of joy. He is still a stranger; better to merge into the anonymous throng of mourners and pay his respects traditionally.

Anna's laugh comes to him, clear and strong. They had been in her kitchen, himself and Leon and Vicki, and the television had been on in the lounge room with the sound turned down. Someone had glanced over, some politician had been embroiled in a sex scandal, one of those incidents that seem to swoop the media along with the force of a king tide before breaking and retreating. It had only been a few weeks before, but Ivan can't remember the names or even the faces of those involved. But he does recall Anna's joyous laughter. How she had placed an arm around Vicki, squeezed her affectionately, and said, still chuckling, 'You lucky, darling, being *lesbia*.' She had used the Greek word. And then, with a wink, she had swung her hand downwards. 'Men and their *poutsa*, they love it, more than their wives and more than their children.' Pleased at how the three of them had burst out laughing, she had looked heavenwards and added, her expression now serious, 'God forgives. Only He understands us.'

That laugh was solid. It was a guide. He knows it is impossible in the judgement of Eternity that he has suffered more than Anna. Yet there it was, her sparkling, buoying laugh.

The gas takes at the first flick of his lighter. For a moment, the wind rushes against the flame, so it seems to bend, then it trembles, gathers momentum and strength, shoots upright. In his parents' tongue he says his farewells to Anna.

———

From a flat across the road, a middle-aged woman is looking down at Ivan on the balcony. She is washing up, preparing for bed. Her name is Rudi. At least, that is the English name she uses—her birth name is in fact Rutna. She works as a nurse in the largest public hospital in the northern suburbs and the shift she has just finished has been long. She is bone-tired. She stayed at work almost two hours longer than she needed to, and in the strange ways of coincidence and synchronicity, she was moved for reasons that she finds inexplicable by the death of an elderly Lebanese woman. Rudi had been caring for her for the past week, the ministrations by now only palliative as the cancer had conquered and begun devouring her body. The old woman's family had kept a constant vigil at the bedside. She was loved. In the few moments when Rudi and the dying patient were intimate—as Rudi carefully cleaned her when she soiled herself, administered the opiates to quell her agonies, plumped up her pillow while her exhausted daughter snored lightly in the armchair next to the bed—the old woman always made sure to thank her. 'Thank you, darling.' They were the only English words she'd ever heard the woman use. It had been days since she had last spoken. Her dying had taken all the morning and stretched into the evening. It is often so: the desperate yearning for life was always humbling. Every so often Rudi would go into the room: to wet the cracked, darkening lips of the dying woman; to squeeze some drops of water from the sponge onto her tongue, always apologising to the exhausted family gathered around her bed. In the middle of the afternoon, after she'd rubbed the moist cotton wad across her lips, the old woman had muttered, her voice a watery splutter, 'Thank you, darling.' Rudi had insisted on staying until the death. Her colleagues understood, and they had quietly changed shifts around her. Only when the sun had completely set did the old woman finally let go. Rudi heard the relieved sobbing of the family.

She had defrosted some curry from the previous week, eaten it in front of the television, hardly paying attention to what was on. It was while she was washing up, looking down from her fifth-floor apartment, through the narrow aluminium-framed window, that she had spotted the thickset man lighting a candle and then crossing himself in the Christian manner. Rudi had quickly sponged off the last of the dishes, washed her hands thoroughly, and murmured prayers for her own family. And for the old woman. It had been a savage, rending death—for that was death—yet she was loved. Her room was never empty.

Ivan blows out the candle, allowing some time for the spark to be completely extinguished, and places it back on the basin in the bathroom. He brushes his teeth, strips naked, and gets into Perry's bed. The bedroom is cold, and he curls up for warmth. Soon his body relaxes under the flannelette sheets, the thickness of the doona. His breathing steadies. He closes his eyes and falls into sleep.

He stirs when he senses Perry's body sliding in beside him, as he inhales the fug of the whisky on Perry's breath when he kisses Ivan's neck and the crisp mint of toothpaste. It is the briefest of glimmerings; it does not take him out of his slumber. He feels his lover's arms enfold him, and again is lost in the consolation of sleep.

3

He's been home nearly five years, but Perry is still unsettled by how antiseptic Australian gymnasiums are compared to those in France. He thinks fondly of the dark, poky gym he used to go to in Rouen. It was in Rue Lafayette, on the third level of a late nineteenth-century armoury which now housed a halal grocery store below, alongside a hairdressing salon called Kings of Africa and a travel agent that organised cheap flights and tours across the Mediterranean. Running across one side of the old factory was the gym. *His* gym. There were a couple of rowing machines, three treadmills and a row of boxing bags. The old brickwork was exposed, parts of it crumbling after decades of water damage. A bank of radiators stretched along the far wall, with the dial apparently stuck on the highest level so the place was hot in all seasons—intolerably so in summer, when the sun seared through three long skylights, light flooding the building. A few of the men who were friendly with the gym's owner, Pierre, would demand of him, sweat pouring off them, 'Fuck, friend, can't you do something about the heating?' And Pierre, whose broad face had been smashed into twisted dough by the punches he'd taken as a professional boxer in his youth, would curse in turn and mutter, 'Go fuck yourselves, you're all soft. It's a gym—you're meant to fucking sweat!' Perry had never exchanged a word with the owner, just nodded if they happened to pass each other. Pierre usually kept to himself, in his tiny office lit by a cloudy window. He'd smoke at his desk, the tobacco odour drifting through into the workout area. No one dared to tell him not to smoke.

How it reeked. There was the menthol stench of Pierre's cigarettes, the dank undertone of the waterlogged bricks, and the stinging fetor that leaked from the toilets and the cramped communal shower in the men's dressing room. The urinal was a long aluminium trough and there were two confined toilet cubicles, one without a door. When Perry whinged about the state of the toilets, his gym buddy Imane would say, 'Périclès, please, there's only room for *two* of us in the women's change room. We have to wash tit to tit or ass to ass. Consider yourself blessed!'

But the keynote was the stink of sweat, the odours augmented by the unrelenting heat. The reek of shit, of alcohol and tobacco and chemicals being released from perspiring flesh. After his hour was up, Perry always felt drenched in the stench. He never bothered to use the showers at the gym—he could never trust that the hot water would be working, or that it wouldn't slow to a trickle just as he had lathered up with soap. He'd cycle back home and shower there. It was the only way he could be sure of ridding himself of the tenacity of those smells.

He loved that gym.

Perry slows the treadmill and wipes the back of his neck with his towel. He can see row upon row of gleaming machines, all of them in use. He can't hear the air conditioner but he is aware of the air around him being carefully sucked up into the unseen ducts and filters above them. The far windows look out to the soaring towers of Southbank, but the natural light is obliterated by the glare of the fluorescent lights above. There is a broad-shouldered young man galloping on the machine next to him, a young woman in a tank top releasing hoarse breaths of an almost metronomic consistency as she sprints on the machine to his right. He can't catch a whiff of either of them.

Perry steps off the now-stationary machine, grabs his toiletries and heads down the corridor to the men's change rooms.

All day he has been burdened by a gnawing sense of dislocation, a growing irritation. The starkness of the white walls, the frisky beat of the electronic music skittering out of the speakers, the humourless list of regulations and instructions fixed to the change-room doors, all of these things—the mild, smug officiousness of it all—are heightening the sense of resentment building deep within him. There is a heaviness in his belly, a sourness in his throat and tongue. Standing at the urinal, he deliberately aims wide so a stream of piss splashes on the rubbery foam tiles. It is a childish act but it brings a smile to his face.

A young man has finished drying himself. There is an unabashed sense of ease in his nudity. The deliberate unkemptness of his beard and hair, the solid blocks of Hebrew letters tattooed down his left arm, make Perry think that he is a student. His pubis is shaved, and his penis is long and thick. Only a metre or so away, a slightly older man is undressing. He too is attractive. He unknots his tie, puts it carefully on a hook and begins to unbutton his shirt. His black hair is almost a thatch over the dark sheen of his skin. Perry hasn't seen them exchange one glance. Yet he is convinced they are enjoying a covert and intimate dance.

As he steps out onto Little Bourke Street his phone pings. It's Ivan. The message flashes: *I'll be there at 6.30 x.* Perry has an hour and a half to himself.

The train rumbles into Parliament Station, he readjusts his face mask and gently jostles for a position against the waist rail, so he has an interrupted view. He pushes his earbuds into his ears. He wavers before switching on his phone, thinking about the hour or so he will have to himself in his apartment. Ivan's size—not only the physical mass of him, but also the intensity of his self-containment—can dominate a space. Perry doesn't resent Ivan's masculine authority, doesn't feel oppressed by it, nor diminished. But without doubt, he is losing sole possession of his home: slowly but inevitably over the last year and a half, it has become a joint ownership. He is looking forward to some time alone. He also knows that he is pleased that Ivan now shares in his home. Thinking back to the diffident play between the two men in the gym, he sighs in relief.

He activates his phone and selects a podcast. It is a history of the Byzantine Empire. Before meeting Ivan, Perry had listened obsessively to political broadcasts and analysis of current affairs. He'd listen to features on books and film, and there were a couple of queer podcasts he followed and a few true crime narratives. And, of course, he still listened to the news from France. On their first holiday together, a long-weekend drive to the old goldfield towns of central Victoria, he had put on one of the news programs. Ivan had taken the device, paused the podcast. 'Do you mind if we listen to something else?' Perry had nodded, assuming Ivan would choose music. Instead, Ivan had connected his own player to the Bluetooth, a fanfare had boomed from the speakers, and a lazy Midwestern American drawl started talking about ancient Rome. That whole weekend they had listened to episode after episode, and soon he had become engrossed in the complicated history of the Roman Republic. Even the twanging accent became attractive. It was only after they'd arrived home that Ivan told him he'd already listened to those early episodes but played them again so he could introduce the series to Perry. He'd admitted how for years now he had turned away from the news, grimly convinced that none of it was trustworthy, that every network and media service was compromised by venality and ideology. They had argued; oh, how they had argued! Perry had defended the notion of truth, the veracity of evidence, the power of objectivity, even though it was impossible to achieve. The striving towards it was what mattered. He insisted, and to some extent still believed, that there were journalists dedicated to accuracy and truth. But he also understood Ivan's wariness. There *was* respite in history. The belligerence and intolerance of the contemporary age was of no consequence to the past. And there was no shouting. The history of Rome had led him to the history of Byzantium. He was thankful to Ivan; he was now far less agitated on the commute to and from work.

He wishes he could get out of this dinner. The thought intrudes and he finds he is no longer listening to the words of the podcast. He's ashamed by his own petulance. He hasn't sat down with Cora and Yasmine for years now, which is ridiculous given that they live so close, a mere half-hour walk from each other. When he'd bumped into Yasmine at the market they'd had a genuinely warm and enthusiastic conversation. It had been so good to catch up. She'd reminded him how long it had been since they'd all been in the same room. That had been for Cora's forty-fifth birthday, and Perry had surprised them all by coming back to Australia for the celebration.

'It's ridiculous we haven't seen each other for so long,' Yasmine said. 'You're one of our dearest friends.'

He had begun to stutter an apology.

'Don't,' she interrupted. 'The pandemic made us lose touch with so many people and life gets in the way. I understand.' She clutched his arm. 'It's so good to see you.'

As they walked to the delicatessen she said, 'I really thought you'd go back to France. How come you're staying here?'

That question still flummoxed him. Did she even know about Gerard? He had told Cora, revealed it to her in a drunken conversation when she and Yasmine and the children had been visiting him in France. In a crowded bar off the main square in Rouen, with groups of students all around them, she had listened patiently and with kindness. Yet she had said, 'You must know, it doesn't have a future.' He had been humiliated, and from then had deflected her questions when they caught up on Skype. Cora had always been rigorously scrupulous about not betraying his confidences, even to her lovers. 'You know,' he answered Yasmine shyly, 'Mum's getting on.' And then, blushing, he added, 'And I've met someone. His name is Ivan.' They were easy snippets. They satisfied most people.

Yasmine smiled, slipped her arm through his. 'That's wonderful news. We *have* to meet him. You are both coming over to dinner.'

She texted him the next morning: *Cora is SO excited. We can't wait to meet your partner.* Yasmine had clearly forgotten his name.

I'll check with Ivan, he replied. *Will get back to you ASAP x.*

It was telling that he had yet to introduce Cora to Ivan, indicative of the cooling of their friendship. After all, it was coming up to two years now since his and Ivan's first meeting.

Inwardly, he groans. It had been a *date*—why couldn't he call it that?

Perry can't concentrate on the podcast. He switches off his phone, pulls the buds from his ears. He looks out the window. The sun is still high in the sky, throwing golden light across the rooftops. He considers autumn to be Melbourne's true summer, when the heat is consistent and not overwhelming.

His gaze shifts across the crowded carriage, settling on a stout woman standing in the middle of the aisle, in a neatly pleated skirt and an ironed high-collared shirt. She is looking out the window. Those seated, those standing next to her, all are staring at their mobile phones. She is clearly daydreaming. Suddenly she turns and their eyes meet. Just as swiftly, she turns away, deftly searching her bag while holding on to the hanging strap. Taking out her phone, she stares fixedly at its screen. He is sure he knows her, is racking his memory to make the connection. He is equally certain that the woman has recognised him. And then it comes. Not her name, but who she is. They'd been in a tutorial together in his first year at university. Cora will remember her name.

He looks back at the woman, thinks: My God, she's aged.

He silently reprimands himself. So have you.

It was a joy to run into Yasmine; he's looking forward to seeing her again. It is being with Cora that is making him anxious. As soon as that thought settles, he is relieved, as if the acknowledgement itself is also a release. He turns his face towards the window, rests his forehead on it, enjoying the judder of the glass against his temple. He is calm.

It explains the puzzling unease he has felt all day: the yearning for France, for Europe. Everything had made him peevish. Ivan's snoring, which had woken him during the night and poisoned his sleep. Having to rush through breakfast to make his train on time so as not to endure the tedium of waiting fifteen minutes for the next one, as if Melbourne were a provincial town and not a metropolis. The long queue for coffee at the café had pissed him off, as had his colleagues' inane chatter about the start of the football season, some stupid reality show, a trivial outrage erupting on social media. How could they be animated by such nonsense? And then the hour in that sterile, plastic gym. God! He hated this country!

And really, he now knows, all of it was about his anxiety at seeing Cora.

The train is decelerating, heading into Thornbury station. On impulse, Perry gets up, deciding to get off at an earlier stop. He needs a longer walk. He wants to delay his moment of arrival.

Cora isn't his oldest friend. He still sees Stella, whom he has known since high school. And he's in regular email contact with Kelvin, whom he worked with at Kmart during the final years of school, and with whom he had his first tentative forays into clumsy sex. Cora, however, had been his first friend at university, and that friendship had marked the leap he had taken from suburban Strathmore to the inner city: from home to share houses; from his staunch familial loyalty to the Australian Labor Party to his immersion in the plethora of sects and offshoots of radical sexual politics. From the furtiveness of the closet to coming out. From marijuana to amphetamines. From Bruce Springsteen to New Order. A whirlwind, a recalibration, a surrender and a euphoria. A remaking. Through those first two years, he and Cora had held each other's hands as they leapt into that revolution.

He walks straight down the long avenue under the trainline, oblivious to the riders speeding past in the bicycle lane. He is assailed by a memory. He is reclining on the frayed orange couch in the lounge room at Palmerston Street, in the three-bedroom worker's cottage that Cora shares with Anastasia and Maree. He is in a white shirt, the thin black tie he'd pinched from his father when he left home, and the pointy rockabilly black suede shoes that he'd spent all of his eighteenth-birthday money to buy. Cora is curled up next to him. She is wearing a lime green beret with a red star sewn on it. Her hair is dyed red, and her fringe hangs over her left eye. She is wearing dark navy stockings and a tartan wool skirt, a look so defini-tive and local that years hence, in Athens or Paris or Istanbul or Prague, he will see young women dressed similarly and ask them, 'Are you from Melbourne?' He and Cora are both smoking cigarettes, the ashtray is full, and he's refilling her empty glass from a cask of cheap red. Perry can even remember the conversation they are having. They have both recently read Jessica Anderson's *Tirra Lirra by the River* and both think it is marvellous.

A train roars along above and he's snapped back to the present. The days are shortening and the sun is hanging low, already disappearing. He realises that he has imbued the memory with nostalgia. There is a sepia filter across the images. They had both loved the Anderson novel. And they probably had been engaged in an earnest conversation about socialist feminism and gay liberation. As Perry turns into the alley that runs behind his apartment building, he grins to himself. Safely tucked away as undergraduates in the little college on the edge of the university, they had no idea that, across the waters, their communist utopia was about to implode.

It has been a long time since they laughed together. That isn't only a matter of distance, of him being away for so long. They'd spoken on the phone and via Skype while he was in Europe, but a terseness had entered their dialogues. They didn't enjoy the same books anymore, they disagreed about what was happening in the world. He was not interested in the insularity of Australian politics or her obsession with what was going on in the USA. She probably thought he was turning into an elitist European wanker. It had always been a relief to finish those conversations.

He hasn't forgiven her. Those cruel and true words. *You must know, it doesn't have a future.*

As soon as he gets home, he plants his phone on the speaker, scrolls through his music till he finds The Jam. He remembers nicking his dad's tie, sure that it made him look a little like Paul Weller on the cover of *In the City*. He hears the screeching chords, the countdown, and the first track kicks in. Its abrasiveness is exciting, but before long it becomes grating. He stops the track, scrolls the playlists absent-mindedly. He looks at the time. He has forty minutes to get ready.

In the bedroom, he is wavering between a deep red linen shirt that he worries is a little too tight for him or a more conservative mustard cotton one when he hears the unlatching of the front door over the slowly building euphoria of the final movement of 'A Love Supreme'. There is a swift, reflexive press of his tongue against his cheek—he hears the click—and he thinks that he would have liked to hear the music play out in its entirety, to claim some more of that in-between time for himself.

Ivan walks into the room, and that trifling annoyance is forgotten.

Ivan is clean-shaven, wearing the dark blue shirt that Perry's mother had bought him for Christmas. The honeyed scent of his cologne, his bulk, the sheer force of his presence, makes Perry grin. They both fall into each other to kiss.

Perry runs his nose along Ivan's neck to his chin. He inhales and releases his breath.

'You smell nice.'

Ivan's grey eyes are glinting. His palm strokes the down on Perry's belly; his fingers deftly unbutton Perry's jeans and slide into the pouch of his underwear.

Ivan chuckles. 'Your cock's cold.'

'I'm just out of the shower.'

'The hot water fucking up again?'

With that sudden intrusion of the quotidian the men pull away from each other. Ivan pecks at his lover's cheek, sits on the edge of the bed, careful to not crease the ironed lines of his shirt and trousers. Perry sees this with a rush of gratitude for the effort Ivan is making. He will wear the mustard shirt, he decides. The more subtle colour will complement the elegant navy hue of Ivan's shirt.

'What's this?'

'John Coltrane. Do you like it?'

Ivan leans forward, his eyes ahead, as if he can see right through the wall to the source of the music. 'I'm not sure. I think I'd need to sit down and really listen to it.' He shrugs. 'I don't *not* like it. I'm just not sure.' He smiles. 'Sometimes you play jazz and it just sounds like a headache. This doesn't.'

Perry is about to speak, to be encouraging, to confirm that Ivan is indeed right to withhold judgement, to do the work justice by giving it concentration and time; and to further explain how Coltrane, as composer and musician, fully aware of his sins and sinning, is also giving thanks for grace and redemption. He is about to say these words: 'It is Sunday morning music. It is asking forgiveness for the mistakes of Saturday night; it is being indebted to a compassionate God.' They are French words, not English. Gerard had first introduced the record to him in that way, in the music shop on Rue des Arsins, the surly shop assistant playing it for them on the turntable.

He has been thinking of Europe all day, in the sourness and confusion of his mood, comparing and judging Australia. Yet he has not thought once about Gerard during all of that musing. Not until now.

Tucking his shirt into his black jeans, Perry smiles and kisses the top of Ivan's head. It tastes of the cologne, and though freshly shaven, there is a faint roughness. 'You look very handsome.'

They decide to take the tram to Cora and Yasmine's house. They pick up two bottles of wine at the boutique bottle shop downstairs; the tables outside its adjacent bar are already filling up with people. The tram is just ramming through the junction as they leave the shop. They quickly scan up and down High Street, then Ivan risks a dart across the road in front of a slowly approaching car, holding tight to the bottles. Perry waits for the tram to stop before crossing cautiously.

Ridiculous really, he thinks, as he takes a seat across from Ivan, that I should be fuming. But he is.

Ivan flops into his seat; his face is flushed from the run. He grins, his smile open. Perry's anger evaporates, leaving the intriguing thought that there is so much more to know about the man across from him. Prudence is one of Ivan's traits. It is how he navigates the world, watchful and careful. And yet there are times when he seems deliberately daring, even careless—the reckless dash across the road just now or sudden bursts of raw speed on the highway for no apparent reason, as well as his readiness to indulge any of Perry's sexual whims and his refusal to set limits to their exploration; exhilarating but often unsettling too.

His knee brushes against Ivan's. 'You shouldn't run like that across the junction. It's dangerous.'

He sees the flare of annoyance at being reprimanded, the mulishness in Ivan's eyes. And then the conciliatory grin returns.

'You're right.' Ivan slaps both thighs. 'These old-man reflexes aren't as good as they used to be.'

'They're not that old.' Perry smiles. He turns to the window, looks down at the world.

They are not deliberately visible as a couple. They don't hold hands. Of course they will show affection at a restaurant, kiss on meeting in public. It has been unspoken, the consensus that their physicality is largely sequestered to the intimacy of the private realm. Is it because of age, or a legacy of generations of secrecy? Of course it is both, thinks Perry. He turns back to Ivan, who is content to be sitting looking straight ahead, not immersed in his phone. The elemental solidity of him is strikingly endearing, and he is indubitably handsome. A flush of pride floods Perry's body, a warmth delicious and gratifying. His knee grazes Ivan's again.

Cora and Yasmine's house is down a lane that runs parallel to the railway tracks. A group of adolescents, three girls and two boys, are laughing loudly, walking towards them on the narrow, cobbled street. The five of them are in short sleeves, and one of the girls has her yellow cotton shirt tied in a knot under her breasts. One of the young men is in an oversized LA Lakers singlet, the purple stark against the paleness of his skin.

A flush of freckles marks each of his bare shoulders. There is a moment when the group of youngsters seems to be on top of them, and Perry experiences the urgency of needing to make way for them. He notices an almost imperceptible exchange between Ivan and one of the youths, a heavyset young man with a strong clear gaze. Without a word he steps down from the pavement onto the road and the other four follow, swinging out of the way. 'Cheers, guys,' Ivan says as they pass. 'Have a good night.'

There is a cackling behind them, and for a moment Perry wonders if they are being mocked, laughed at. Yet Ivan is striding along, unfazed. The ardour, the swell of pride returns.

Ivan stops at a low picket fence, the wood recently painted a matt pale lavender. Number forty-two.

'This their place?'

Perry nods. Ivan pushes open the gate and there comes the sound of loud barking from inside the house. As they step up onto the front verandah, the sound becomes a growl.

Perry can't remember the exact breed of the dog, only that it is cantankerous and large. 'Their dog doesn't like men,' he whispers.

Ivan looks up from examining the front garden, the straggly rosebushes and the gnarled branches of a pomegranate tree in the far corner. 'Did someone mistreat it?'

Almost before the words are out, the front door opens. Cora is bending over the growling dog, whose body is taut, straining. Cora is holding tight to its leather collar.

'Rosie,' she warns, a growl in her voice as well, 'behave!'

The dog doesn't relax; her nostrils quiver, and she bares her sharp teeth.

'Just walk around us,' Cora says. 'She'll be fine once you're in the house.'

Perry walks sideways past them and slides inside. Ivan is behind him. They are in a narrow anteroom containing only a coat stand burdened with thick winter jackets, beanies and umbrellas. Cora shuts the door behind them and the dog finally goes quiet.

She ushers them along a dark corridor and then they are in a spacious open living area, with high ceilings and an alcove fireplace along the long far wall. The fire is lit, the flames blazing. Yasmine is in the kitchen area, and she beams as they walk in. Rosie, her stubby tail now wagging, bounds up to her, then rushes back to a large, frayed rug in front of the fire. With a quick shake of her body, the dog circles and settles.

Cora extends her hand to Ivan. 'Sorry—Rosie doesn't like men.'

Perry checks his impulse to quip, 'Of course not, she's been trained by lesbians.' Instead, he observes the cool interaction between Ivan and Cora. As they shake hands, there is an uncomfortable moment where it seems both are wanting to lean into each other for a kiss on the cheek, but both think better of doing so. Thankfully, Yasmine's greeting is effusive. She hugs Perry, embraces him solidly, kisses both his cheeks. She shakes Ivan's hand on being introduced, immediately offers him a kiss on the right cheek, the left, then another on the right.

'Three kisses for Serbs?' she asks. 'That's right, isn't it?'

Ivan nods and grins then holds up the bag containing the bottles. 'Should I put these in the fridge?'

'Yes,' answers Yasmine, leading him into the kitchen. 'We've opened a lovely vermentino from McLaren Vale. Are you happy to start with that?'

'Does the Pope shit in the woods?'

Yasmine's laugh is bright, unforced. Perry lets out a grateful sigh. Cora is next to him, puts her arm around him. He lays his head on her shoulder. When he left for Europe, Cora's hair had been brunette. Now her hair is silver and white. It occurs to him that she was probably dying it for years.

Cora shifts, shuffles. Perry pulls away. Yasmine has poured the wine and Ivan comes over with a glass in each hand, gives them to Cora and Perry, then returns to the kitchen for his own. Cora indicates the dining table. Only then does Perry notice that it is set for six.

'Are the kids joining us?'

Yasmine sits down next to him, clinking his glass with hers. 'No,' she answers. 'Nathan's going out tonight.'

'He's just getting ready,' Cora adds, pulling out the chair next to her for Ivan. 'He'll be out in a minute to say hello.'

'And Hannah?'

He notices the flick of Cora's eyes, the nervous glance at Yasmine. Equally swiftly she turns back to Perry.

'Hannah's living with her father at the moment.' Cora's tone is deliberately offhand.

Perry deliberately says nothing. Cora knows he has never liked Victor, the children's father. Yasmine hadn't mentioned that Hannah wasn't living with them when they'd spoken about the children at the market. Cora sits stiffly in her chair. In the awkwardness neither she nor Perry can look at one another. The silence is beginning to thicken in the spaces between them. Leaning forward—and so clotted has the hush been that the gentle motion is almost startling—Yasmine says breezily, 'Well, you two are lucky that you don't have to deal with teenagers. You can be the good uncles.'

Perry's jaw is straining, wanting Ivan to speak. He has to stop himself from speaking for him.

'I'm a father,' Ivan says brusquely. He clears his throat. 'Katerina's now in her late thirties, so we're way past the teenage stage.' He winks at Yasmine. 'Actually, I'm a grandfather too. Natasha's the best kid in the world.'

'That's wonderful.' Yasmine raises her glass. She smiles over at Cora. 'I guess that's the next stage of life for all of us.'

Ivan smiles across at Perry, and Perry gives a thin smile in return. But there's a knot forming deep in his belly.

'So, who else is coming then?' he asks.

'Evelyn and Jed.'

The names mean nothing to him.

'You know Evelyn,' Cora says. 'I used to work with her at the DV centre in Footscray.'

He doesn't know what she's referring to. DV? All he can think of is the shorthand his colleague Renée would use from time to time when he'd cross himself and mutter resignedly.

Yasmine is tapping her shoulder. 'Long curly red hair. Tall. Drop-dead gorgeous, always dressed as if she's in a 1960s black-and-white movie.'

He remembers. A very beautiful woman. And of course, DV didn't mean *si Dieu le veut*; it was an acronym for domestic violence.

'Hey, Perry, how you doing?'

The voice is low, booming, and one he doesn't recognise. He swings around in his chair. A giant of a young man is smiling at him.

'My God!' Perry knows him. 'Nathan, you're all grown up!' He rushes to hug him.

Nathan laughs and returns the embrace. Perry is more than a foot shorter, and in the embrace he smells the heavy musk of boy and the oversweet cologne he has doused himself with. He pulls away, keeping one arm across the boy's wide shoulders.

'Come and meet Ivan.'

Ivan has already stood up, and they shake hands, then Nathan instinctively grabs the older man and pulls him in for a kiss on each cheek.

'It's really good to meet you.'

Ivan, momentarily surprised by the effusiveness of the greeting, smiles and kisses Nathan in return.

Perry is overjoyed. There is, of course, his happiness at seeing Nathan again. He has the fondest memories of the boy who had travelled to Europe with his mothers and his sister at age four-teen. Even then, he was indelibly handsome and already over six feet tall. He had become friendly with a group of boys who shot baskets every evening at the end of Perry's cul-de-sac in Rouen. His zest for motion and his friendliness had charmed all Perry's neighbours: Marie-Louise at the boulangerie, who would always give Nathan a pastry in the morning; Monsieur and Madame Chaïbi at the *petit magasin* underneath his apartment building, the old gentleman kissing his fingers and muttering, '*Quel homme*'; and even the recondite Madame Bayard, who rarely ventured out of her basement apartment but who made the effort to knock on the door on the family's last day in Rouen, to wish Cora and Yasmine and Hannah a 'pleasant journey', her small lined face blushing deeply at her use of the English words, before she turned to Nathan and gave him two quick, shy pecks on his cheeks, saying, '*V'avec Dieu.*' Perry had always adored the boy; there was an easy bond between them. That attachment had stayed strong, despite how far apart they lived and the time that had passed. The love he feels for Nathan is sincere and unencumbered, and he delights in Ivan's evident admiration for the lad.

The adults resume their seats.

'You want to stay for one drink?' Yasmine has brought a platter to the table, a mound of steaming golden cheese pies.

Nathan takes out his phone, glances at it, and shakes his head. 'Nah, I've got to go.' He grins. 'But I'll take some *fatayer* to eat on the way.'

Perry starts to rise, but the youth shakes his head. 'Don't get up.' He comes over and hugs Perry from behind, kissing the top of his head.

He proceeds around the table, kissing Ivan and his parents in turn.

'Where are you going?' asks Cora.

'We're starting off at the Peacock for a few drinks and then heading off to a new club in Sydney Road, the Coburg end. Tosca's DJ-ing. Should be good.'

'Don't get too smashed.'

Nathan cringes, and Perry has a flash of the young boy he'd escorted around the streets of Europe. Then Nathan winks at him, and the boy is replaced by a man. 'Do you want to come along, Perry, be my spirit guide?'

Cora spins in her chair, slaps him lightly. 'Go on—off you go!'

Laughing, and after a quick roistering with Rosie, Nathan lopes to the door, calling out a final goodbye.

It is as if Perry and Cora have wordlessly agreed to an experiment in which they are both silent and ignoring each other but are attentive to Ivan and Yasmine. Perry sees how Cora's eyes move from her partner to his, and he is aware that he is also engaged in the same curious yet detached activity. Yasmine, who is more naturally ebullient than Ivan, is asking him questions: about Katerina and Natasha, about his work. Ivan responds openly yet economically, prompting Yasmine to probe further. She's ageing well, Perry decides. Her focus is so relentlessly on Ivan that he can allow himself a thorough scrutiny. She is still dyeing her hair. She is heavier, with a puffiness to her cheeks, and he discerns how she has deftly placed the blue silk scarf around her neck to conceal her soft jawline. Her large chestnut-coloured eyes are striking. She was handsome as a young woman; now she is beautiful.

Cora's body is twisted in her chair as she examines Ivan. There is something merciless in her detachment, as if she were an ancient deity bemusedly considering mortals. He is relieved when the dog springs from her bed and begins a fevered barking. Her claws scrape on the polished floorboards as she runs to the front door.

'Jed and Evelyn are here,' Cora says, rising and placing her napkin on the table.

The endless introductions. Evelyn is indeed the attractive woman of Perry's memory. She is splendidly attired in a tailored pantsuit, black tapered trousers and a matching tux jacket, which she removes on entering the room. Over a white shirt she wears a dark mauve fine-wool vest. Her make-up is expertly applied. Her stylish grey hair has been recently cut and emphasises a leonine aspect to her face. He remembers: she always did intimidate him. Wickedly, gratefully, he notices an unfortunate tiny droop to the left side of her mouth. Her polite smile at being introduced is spoilt somewhat by the effort she has to make to overcome this small flaw. She is clearly aware of it, and the effort to hide it clearly frustrates her. It makes a grimace of the smile.

Her partner, Jed, is also well dressed, in a salmon-coloured shirt and neatly ironed dark linen trousers. He greets Ivan and Perry effusively. It is impossible to pinpoint his age; fifty, sixty? There is a dry, tight stretch to the skin on his face, a splay of fine wrinkles spreading from each corner of his smile. Yet his hair is lustrously black, with only a small sprinkling of grey in his short sideburns. His body is tall, slender, and it will not surprise Perry when, later in the evening, Jed will mention that he is an avid swimmer, that most mornings find him at the pool. Only the presence of a small paunch at his middle betrays the entropy of ageing.

They sit down to eat. There are the cheese pies for entrée, and creamy baba ghanoush, topped with crumbled feta. Yasmine has also prepared toum and hummus. She admits, however, that the tart, delectable taramasalata was bought from their favourite delicatessen stall at the market. Yasmine brings over a platter of warmed flatbreads and sets them in the middle of the table.

Cora is filling the wineglasses. 'I just did some chopping and cutting,' she says. She points to her partner. 'I think you all know that Yasmine is the true cook in this marriage.'

Jed claps his hands in delight, pounces for a piece of bread, and munches on it. 'Yas, these are fantastic.'

Yasmine bows her head modestly, yet is obviously pleased.

They raise their glasses in salute to her, then they all attack the food.

The conversation is genial, curious, and does not stray into any controversial or difficult terrain during the first course. Nevertheless, Perry finds he cannot settle that sense of unease. He is too aware of Ivan, who answers the questions asked of him with courtesy and calmness. Yet he conspicuously refrains from contributing to the discussion. Jed is an academic, a professor at the School of Biological Sciences at Monash University.

Perry is conscious of the assumption of a shared language and system of beliefs among the five at the table who have university degrees. At one point, just as Yasmine rises to take the plates away, Evelyn asks Ivan, 'Where did you study?'

Perry freezes. He has never quite understood that metaphor before: that the sudden snap of chill that infiltrates his very blood isn't the consequence of fear but of humiliation.

'I did trade school at a horticultural college. I started my apprenticeship when I was sixteen.' Ivan takes a piece of flatbread, piles hummus onto it. 'I hated high school—couldn't wait to leave.'

Perry lays his napkin on the table and excuses himself.

He sits on the toilet, trousers still on. The icy assault he felt has completely vanished, and there is a dryness in his throat. He needs some moments of calm. The small cubicle suddenly seems intolerably hot. Yet he sits staring at the off-white door straight in front of him. There are fingermarks staining the wood just under the steel handle. He grabs a knot of toilet paper from the roll, scrunches it up, spits into it and starts wiping off the stains. When satisfied that the wood is clean, he opens the toilet lid, throws the paper in and flushes.

He washes his hands in the bathroom, rinses out his mouth. He can smell the strong perfume of gardenias. He turns around, trying to locate the source of the sweetness, and finds a small bundle of perfumed sticks in a glass on the edge of the bath. Satisfied, he dries his hands, walks back to the dinner.

A large red tagine base sits steaming in the middle of the table. In it are pieces of chicken and yellow chickpeas immersed

---

in a thick red sauce. There is a big bowl of salad, one of chicory and chunks of feta, and a smaller bowl of couscous sprinkled with coriander. The odours are enticing.

Before sitting down, Perry walks up behind Ivan, squeezes his shoulders.

Ivan is the first to raise his glass at the table. 'Yasmine,' he says, '*shukrun, el-akel beshah-he.*'

She laughs in delight. '*Sahten, ahla wsahla. Btihki arabi?*'

Ivan shakes his head, laughing as well. '*La! La! Shway bas.*'

The food is wonderful. The chicken is succulent and the sauce is tangy and fiery. The vegetables are beautifully cooked. Perry eats with ravenous pleasure. The exchange between Ivan and Yasmine has surprised him. He had no idea that Ivan knew any Arabic.

It is Cora who asks, 'Where did you learn Lebanese Arabic?'

'My first boss was a Leb. Lovely guy. Musa. He was tough on us, but I learnt so much. And his mother was a terrific cook.' He grins at Yasmine. 'But you're better.' His eyes dart upwards, he touches his brow with two fingers. 'Bless your hands.'

Cora immediately turns to Evelyn. 'Thank you for the wine; it's superb.'

Perry cringes inwardly: neither Cora nor Yasmine had said anything about the wine he and Ivan had brought.

They settle into a rhythm, the metre of it supplied by the appreciative sound of good food being eaten, of fine wine being sipped. Evelyn and Jed have indeed brought an exquisite wine: an Italian grape that Perry has had before in France and in Italy, but it has never tasted as sharp and full as this vintage does. They are on to their third bottle now and the music of the night becomes a blend of light exchanges between Jed and Ivan and Yasmine, gleeful reminiscences, a shared and unforced communion in being the children of migrants, a conversation punctuated by humour and an inevitable melancholy: each of them has lost a parent, and Yasmine and Ivan have lost both. Countering this joyful exchange is the more solemn dialogue between Cora and Evelyn: about their work, about the intransigence and conservatism of Australian institutions, about the unrelenting, crushing enmity of unrepentant racists and misogynists.

Perry has become mere audience. He had to restrain himself from rolling his eyes moments before, when Evelyn had blithely claimed, 'Australia is such a racist shithole.' He cannot abide this tendency of middle-class Australians to endlessly deride their own country. He finds it jejune, ignorant of the world. But Christ, he scolds himself, that's the habit of the bourgeoisie the world over—he is being unfair. Cosmopolitan Europeans are just as annoying in their shallow, condescending generalisations.

Evelyn mentions a scandal currently engulfing one of the football codes, in which a player has abused another with a homophobic slur. Her fury has silenced the others. Yasmine is nodding in sad agreement.

Cora slides back in her chair, folds her arms. 'It never fucking changes, does it?'

As he half-listens to the impassioned denouncements, he wonders why Cora invited Evelyn and Jed. Of course, it could have been Yasmine who insisted on a third couple. Yet he doubts it. Evelyn is clearly closer to Cora. Mischievously he wonders if it is to satisfy some odd politically correct symmetry: one lesbian couple, one heterosexual and one pair of poofters. He enjoys the delicious irreverence of that thought, even if only in his own head. He dares not utter it out loud—it would be considered worse than the footballer's insult. He has discovered that Ivan hates the word. When he had used it some time ago, early in their relationship—'Shut up, you big pooftah!'—he had been shocked at the loathing that flashed in Ivan's grey eyes.

He snaps his attention back to the conversation. They are still condemning the footballer. And the game itself. He feels sorry for the young man. Perry doesn't follow sport, though he's getting used to Ivan watching it over the weekends. He recalls the poor man at one of the press conferences, looking genuinely contrite, his shame all too evident.

Ivan hasn't said a word, has remained silent throughout their criticism of the footballer. The background music has stopped.

Perry gets to his feet, points to the stereo. 'Can I choose something?'

Cora and Yasmine still have racks of CDs and there is also a turntable on a small table next to the stereo, a stash of vinyl records lined up under it. Perry gives them a cursory glance. Bands and singers he doesn't recognise except for the occasional surprise: the lurid, perverse cartoons of Robert Crumb on Big Brother and the Holding Company's *Cheap Thrills*; the floating naked baby in the serene blue universe of Nirvana's *Nevermind*; the grieving monkey etched in white on The Pixies' *Doolittle*; and the seducing, confident smile of a prelapsarian Michael

Jackson on the cover of *Off the Wall*. He's sure this must be Nathan's collection.

It is when he turns his attention to the CDs that he stumbles across it, almost overlooking the calligraphy of the title on the spine. It is the cool emerald colour that reminds him, and he pulls it out. It is only as he inserts the silver disc into the slot and then presses play that the vague stirring of sensations coalesces into firm memory. He is at the wheel of Gerard's 2009 Citroën, his lover beside him. Gerard has his arms crossed and his eyes closed, yet he is not asleep. And there it is, ahead of them, the road that leads towards the alpine terror, the ascendant splendour of eastern France. The disc clicks into place, there is a whirring that now sounds archaic, and then there are the first mourning drones of the synthesiser and the answering ecclesiastic ringing of the organ and all those notes— clear, precise, epic—and it could be this clarity that jolts the memory into place. The sound mirrors the majesty of the snow- clad peaks. He is back in France, approaching the ascent from Grenoble, enjoying the freedom of the two of them being alone together for the eternity of a week. Gerard's wife is visiting her sister in Montreal and his children are away, and Gerard is showing Perry the world he first knew as a child. And he can hear Gerard beside him, arms crossed and eyes closed, not asleep but humming softly to this music. Perry is glad that he is crouching by the stereo, his back to the clamour of the dinner table. He needs that moment to compose himself.

It hurts still. That week alone with Gerard was the happiest time of his life.

Jed says, 'Jeez, I haven't heard this song for a long time.'

He can turn around; the sorrow has gone.

Returning to the table, he stops, rests his hand on Cora's shoulder. 'I seem to remember you had this on vinyl when you were living in Canning Street?'

Her hand finds his. 'Maybe I did . . . or maybe it was Cleo's?'

Sitting down at the table, he looks across to Ivan. 'Do you like this album?'

'I know the song. Don't think I know the album.'

'It's fucking terrific.' Jed's response makes Perry elated.

'My favourite is the title track,' Jed continues, his chin upturned, alert to the music. 'It's the next track. I'm going to turn it up.'

'Clearly you made a good choice,' Yasmine says. 'You've made Jed happy.'

'One of my friends in France loved this album; she played it all the time.'

He is pleased to have altered the pronoun. He understands the involuntary shudder that Ivan has to suppress when he mentions Gerard. He experiences it when Ivan speaks about Joe. They are learning to protect one another.

Jed has turned up the music and returned to the table. 'While You See A Chance' is fading.

'I think it sounds dated.'

Jed's vehement shaking of his head is a rebuke to Evelyn. 'Well, you're wrong.'

She laughs dryly, turning to Cora. 'That's right.' She rolls her eyes. 'Only men can know about music.'

Everything about her is sour, thinks Perry. The warmth of the fellowship he felt towards Cora only minutes before has evaporated on seeing her smug smile of agreement at Evelyn's jeer.

'Do you want me to choose another CD?'

Evelyn has felt it as a rebuke; he can tell by the way her eyes swing towards him.

Yasmine has started collecting the plates. 'No, Perry,' she says. 'Let it play. I haven't heard it in an age.' But Jed is already turning down the volume on the stereo.

Ivan is on his feet. 'Let me help.'

While Yasmine and Ivan load the dishwasher no one at the table speaks. The dog's snores are an eruption in the uneasy quiet.

Yasmine too loudly declares that they should have a break before dessert, and Cora asks if anyone wants more to drink. The three men all nod, and so does Yasmine. Evelyn shakes her head. Cora opens one of the bottles he and Ivan brought. Perry notices she doesn't refill her own glass. Jed has asked whether everyone is watching a new series on Netflix. He and Ivan haven't watched it. Cora dismisses it as lightweight. Yasmine disagrees. The conversation stalls once more.

Into that breach, Ivan asks, 'Who's Hannah and Nathan's dad?'

He has asked Cora the question, was looking across at her. Her silence is excruciating.

'His name is Victor,' Yasmine blurts out, too quickly. 'He's their biological father. He's gay, his husband is Cameron. So, they have two fathers as well.'

Perry recollects Victor's sallow features, that censorious ferret-like face. Perry knows he is being unkind. It is true, he and Victor had never got along from the time they were both students. He can't remember ever seeing the man laugh. Victor had been ferociously in the vanguard of ecological activism, his hand-knitted jumpers festooned with feminist and anti-racist badges and slogans—he'd always made Perry feel frivolous.

'Does he live close by?'

And now Perry is pissed off at Ivan. It is clear from her manner that Cora is annoyed. The feeling of long-term friendship surges, returns to him. He wishes it were just the two of them, out to dinner on their own. It must be so painful that Hannah has chosen to live with her father. He is troubled by how little he and Cora have seen of one another, how little he knows of her life.

'They live in Yarraville.' Yasmine shrugs. 'Not close but not too far.'

'How old is Hannah?'

Perry interjects. 'I've told you—she's seventeen.'

He can tell that Ivan is startled by his cranky response. He's being unfair; he probably hasn't mentioned it at all.

'She's doing the VCE,' Yasmine says quickly. 'Cameron's a teacher. He's a good tutor for Han; he's very patient with her.'

'He indulges her.' Cora's hand reaches for the bottle. She pours herself a wine. Evelyn gives a slight nod of her head. Cora fills her glass as well.

'That's not true, Cora,' Yasmine says. 'He doesn't indulge her.'

'That final year is always hard.' Ivan's tone is calm. 'Kat hated it. And she was unbearable.'

His bid for conciliation is successful.

'That's exactly the right word.' Evelyn is smiling now. 'Our son Matt gave us hell during his final year. I felt like I was tiptoeing around him the whole time.'

'And that was during lockdown.' Jed, remembering, rolling eyes and shaking his head. 'God, I hated that year.'

And with those words, a collective shudder unifies them. They are Melburnians, and during the years of the pandemic they lived in the most locked-down city in the world.

'Yeah,' says Ivan. 'It was like living in quicksand.'

Evelyn claps her hands. 'That describes it. That's exactly right.'

'Remember,' says Yasmine, 'just getting up every morning and waiting for them to announce the case numbers. Feeling elated if they were zero and then your stomach sinking if there was a community case.'

The reliving of a shared experience banishes the previous tension. Perry finds himself nodding along. He says nothing. The unease of difference has returned; yet alongside it the warm pleasure, deep in his gut, which he associates with his feelings of being an outsider. The pandemic emails from friends in Rouen and Athens, in Glasgow and Thessaloniki, the texts from Neha in Mumbai. There was fear there too, confusion and anger. But also acceptance of illness and death. Resignation, not constant whingeing. He remembers writing back to Céline:

Touts les australiens sont comme des enfants. By which he meant: I am not like them.

'What was that?'

He has spoken the words out loud.

'Nothing,' he answers Cora. 'I was just recalling those times.'

'I had to give up on the news for a while,' Jed says. 'I was so sick of that word, Covid.'

Evelyn is shaking her head. 'I couldn't. I was obsessed.' She sighs. 'Thank God we had a government in this state who cared. Pity we had those conservative fuckwits in Canberra then. God, they really fucked it up.'

Perry steals a glance at Ivan, whose face is giving nothing away.

Jed laughs. 'No one ever went broke underestimating the intelligence of the Australian voter. Blame the dickheads who voted for them.'

'Don't worry,' Cora snaps grimly. 'I still do.'

He notices that Ivan's hand has dropped below the table. Patting his pockets, searching for his cigarettes.

The awkward silence resumes. And as if by instinct, some prescient sense of the interloper, everyone is glancing at Ivan.

Yasmine—and Perry realises that she is the one working hard to make the night a success, not only in the care and attention she paid to the dinner but in maintaining conviviality at the table, wanting the six of them all to get along—asks, 'Did you also become obsessed with the news, Ivan?'

Ivan is looking straight at him. Perry cannot read what is being demanded of him.

'I'd given up on the news long before that,' Ivan answers finally. 'It doesn't make me happy.'

'Is that what news should be, something that makes us happy?'

Perry stiffens at the antagonism in Cora's tone.

Ivan doesn't respond immediately. Perry is impressed by his lover's resolve. He is thinking the question through.

'No,' Ivan says. His finger is scratching at the side of his neck. 'I guess maybe the real reason is that I don't . . .' He hesitates. 'I don't trust journalists.'

'You don't trust journalists, or you don't trust the publishers?'

'I don't know what you mean.'

'I think what Cora is asking,' says Yasmine, her tone measured, 'is whether you don't have faith in the people who own the media. Is that what you mean when you say you don't trust journalists?'

It seems an age, it seems that time has slowed to a quiet pace, before Ivan responds.

'Both?'

It is definitely a question.

Jed leans forward. 'Where do you get your news, Ivan?'

'I used to read *The Herald-Sun.*'

Evelyn laughs out loud. 'Well, of course, that's the Murdoch press; I wouldn't trust them either.'

'And I'd read *The Age* online.' Ivan is persevering, answering Jed's question. 'I'd watch the ABC, SBS sometimes. The Channel Seven news if I was home on time.'

'And you don't trust any of those sources?'

'No.'

'How about the radio?'

Ivan swings around to face Yasmine. 'I don't like talkback.'

'So, you get your news from what . . . Facebook, YouTube?'

It's the patronising sneer in Cora's voice. At this moment, Perry detests her.

'I said'—and for the first time there is a commensurate mettle in Ivan's voice—'I don't trust any journalists.'

'I do.' Perry catches it, Evelyn's wink at Cora. 'I trust *The Guardian*, I trust the ABC, I trust *The Saturday Paper* and I trust *The New York Times*.' And now Evelyn is leaning on the table, looking directly at Ivan. 'You see, Ivan, I don't read or watch the news to be happy. I do it so I can be informed.'

Perry is suddenly weary. He's going to ask Ivan outside for a smoke—anything to leave this sanctimonious interrogation.

'Why would I read *The New York Times*?' Ivan's question is innocent; there is no guile or slyness in it.

And that is why Evelyn is taken aback. 'As I just said,' she begins, her mouth tightening, 'to be informed. I read *The New York Times* to know what the world does to black people, to women, to LGBTQ+ people. I read it to find out how we are destroying the environment. I read it to know where injustices are occurring in my world.'

'And what knowledge of the world does *The New York Times* give you?' Perry breaks in. He can hear the aggression in his voice. The bellicosity is exhilarating. 'I'm not going to hear anything about Australia in *The New York Times*, am I?'

Evelyn is about to answer but he cuts her off.

'The only thing you'll learn from that paper is how hard it is to be a whining Ivy League student these days. And maybe what movies you should be watching or books you should be reading if you want to feel like a smug cunt from Williamsburg.'

He sees it, the blow landed by the obscenity. Everyone at the table has recoiled from it. Even Ivan, who won't look at him. And Perry's defiance bleeds from him. I'm doing it for you, he wants to say. He feels like a child who has disobeyed a parent. It just feeds his rage, that toxin of resentment. He can't stand any of them. He should never have come back.

'Perry, I'm sorry, I don't know what you mean.'

Ivan must have sensed his withdrawal. The moment is too raw and too intimate. The tenderness in Ivan's voice only makes him feel more chastened.

'I think that Perry's referring to how'—Jed is struggling for words—'he is suggesting that the purview of the *Times* is now . . . elitist.' Jed turns to him. 'Is that what you mean, Perry?'

Evelyn snorts. 'Right. For the first time in history women and people of colour are editing newspapers such as the *Times*, they're finally on the ABC, and of course they're now considered elitist. Clearly those institutions were paragons of democracy and inclusion before.' Her exasperation is scathing. 'That's such a typically privileged tone-deaf attitude.' She raises her glass in mock salute to Perry. 'What a surprise, gay men can be sexist too.'

And he knows that in the nights to come, when he is awoken by the sharp reminiscence of humiliation—the pain a jabbing at his side, in his chest, slamming into his head—he will come up with a thousand cutting responses to her derision. But now, sitting here, his cheeks aflame, he feels weightless, useless, as if a hand has reached deep down inside him and turned him inside out.

'Of course gay men are sexist.'

'Thank you, Ivan.' Evelyn raises her glass.

'You know, when I was a young poofter, I felt different.' And now Perry looks up. At how Ivan has stressed *that* word. And breath comes back to him. He intuits it. The others don't know. He's being defended.

'I thought back then that being gay naturally made me connect with women. You know: we both knew men could be cruel and that they could hurt us.' Ivan is looking straight at Evelyn, his gaze unwavering; not unfriendly, not warm. 'And then, 'cause I was a dumb-fuck kid trying to impress those types of men, wanting to belong, I pretended to be straight and I got my girlfriend pregnant and I found out women had their own ways of being cruel, of hurting you.'

There is a slight tremor in Ivan's voice. Perry can see the strain the confession is causing him. Not that the others have a clue how well he knows what cruel men can do. Perry has said nothing to Cora, or to any of his friends: he knows it is Katerina's story to tell and to use it would be to sunder Ivan's faith in him. Perry realises he has accepted this truth as a precondition of their relationship's future. All of these thoughts are whirring around his head as Ivan speaks, so when Cora makes to interject, to parry Ivan's argument, Perry almost barks out the words: 'Let him finish.'

'I have a daughter. I've tried to teach her to stay away from violent men and from angry men. To never trust a man who despises and disrespects women.'

His voice is close to breaking. Only Perry can hear it.

'I haven't always succeeded.' Ivan swallows, then sucks in air. 'But if I had a son, I'd teach him to walk away from angry women, from women who complain and undermine and who can't bear to see anyone happy. You all have sons; you don't want them to end up with bitter women.' Ivan's smile is sad. 'Bitter people are cruel.'

It is Evelyn who responds. She is furious. 'It is not the same thing. Men make women cruel.'

Ivan gets to his feet. 'That's bullshit. There are cruel men and there are cruel women.' He takes his cigarettes from his pocket. 'Can I smoke outside?'

Yasmine nods.

Perry rises. 'I'll have one too.'

It's a messy backyard. Perry looks at gardens through Ivan's eyes now. He notices that the vegetable plot lies nearly abandoned, fallow, the soil has reverted to clay. The flowerbeds need weeding. He is surprised. He has a clear memory from just before he left for Europe, going around to make his farewells: Yasmine, in dirty old jeans, hoeing and digging in the dirt.

He remembers how proud she was of that garden. But that was a long time ago now, before the children came into the women's lives.

Ivan lights Perry's cigarette for him.

They both turn their backs on the shabby garden, turn to look into the house. Evelyn is gesticulating wildly, and Cora has an arm around her. Jed has his back turned to them. Yasmine is taking a cake out of the fridge. She is closest to them, and as she places the dessert on the bench she looks up, spies them observing her. She winks. The generosity of it shocks Perry. He'd assumed all three women would be furious with Ivan. With him.

Jed is calling out something, coming towards them. Freed from his slouch on his chair, he stands tall and lean, his stride long and elegant, almost feline.

He slides open the door, steps onto the narrow deck and shuts the door behind him. 'Mind if I have a smoke as well?'

Without saying anything, Ivan hands Jed the packet.

'Been a long time.'

'Yeah?' Ivan doesn't sound convinced.

Perry hardly puts his cigarette to his lips. His intention was one of solidarity, to gauge Ivan's emotions after the bruising argument. If it was bruising—Ivan seems unperturbed. He smokes languidly. Unlike Jed. Jed sucks hard on the cigarette. He may not have smoked for a long time but Perry can tell that Jed is still an addict.

'I thought it was a good point what you said inside about how girls . . . women . . . can be cruel. I think about that with

Matty. We kind of know what to say to girls these days. How they don't have to put up with male aggression and misogyny. But it's hard to know how to speak about it with boys.'

There is something dog-like in the way Jed speaks directly to Ivan, as if seeking approval and confirmation. Perry is bemused. The reversal has taken him unawares, from the faint condescension with which Jed addressed Ivan at the beginning of the dinner to this near deference. Even the triptych they form underscores this transformation. Ivan stands with his feet apart, directly under the naked globe, the sheen of his skin and the weave of his shirt vivid under the illumination. Perry and Jed are in the shadows, the red glow of their cigarettes the only colour.

'I think it must be hard raising any child at the moment.' Perry feels he has to say something to fill the long silence after Jed's comment.

Jed looks around for a possible ashtray. 'You don't have kids, do you?'

The question is proffered innocently. Jed is smiling as he asks it. Nevertheless, Perry feels the inevitable sting.

'No.'

Then Jed's next words chasten Perry. 'Sometimes I think that makes you the better judge. You can be objective. I really don't like that I can't be objective about Matty. I keep thinking, am I fucking it up? How do I know if I am fucking it up?'

It's a rare, exceedingly rare gift: a parent inviting him into fellowship. In that moment Perry's feelings towards Jed move from neutral to affectionate. He jumps off the porch, examines the shallow, unkempt flowerbed at the side of the short steps. There is a glint of metal. He picks up the crushed beer can, shakes off the dirt, offers it to Jed as an ashtray.

'Thanks.' Jed squashes the end of his cigarette into the can. He steps off the deck, looks around, finds a tap on the other side of the garden. He turns it on, washes his mouth, his face. He walks back up the stairs, drying himself with a white handkerchief he pulls from his pocket.

'Evelyn hates the smell of ciggies,' he says by way of explanation. Before sliding open the door, he turns to Ivan. 'The argument isn't over. Evelyn's not finished with you yet.'

As soon as Jed is inside, Perry steps over to Ivan, kisses him softly on the cheek. 'You okay?'

Ivan smiles, kisses him back, on the lips. It's just a touch, but there is hunger in it. 'I'm good. Looking forward to dessert.' He pats his belly. 'Yasmine told me it's cheesecake.'

Perry thinks to himself: I'll have to do a double session at the gym tomorrow.

'The boys have had their smoko break. Good.' Evelyn rubs her hands. She smiles mirthlessly at Ivan. 'We're not done yet.'

A subtle rearrangement has taken place while they were outside. And yes, Evelyn's playful use of the word 'boys' has alerted Perry to how the party has indeed split into two since the men went outside and the women remained indoors, replicating generations of segregation. The wineglasses and the napkins have been rearranged, and Evelyn is seated next to Ivan. Perry can't overcome his distrust of Evelyn's erudition, his sense that she will entrap Ivan with rhetoric as much as with reason.

As soon as the men step inside, however, Cora pulls him aside. 'Come and help me with the dessert.'

It is a lemon cheesecake, with a bowl of berry compote, the fruit swimming in blood-red juice. Cora deftly cuts the cake into slices and Perry uses a spatula to transfer them to the plates. The sugared waft of the cream, the tartness of the citrus; his mouth is already watering.

His focus remains on the voices at the table. Has he heard right? Has Ivan just asked, 'What does patriarchy mean?'

'Do you think the slices are too small?'

He returns his attention to the task. 'No, they're fine. We can always have seconds. It looks delicious.'

He realises that he is not sure if he could define patriarchy. 'I like Ivan.'

It is a relief; and a release. He thought she'd been diffident, removed, all evening. He'd assumed she was sitting in judgement. Cora had never been reckless in her opinions.

'Good. I wasn't sure you'd—' he searches for the word, lands on it '—approve.'

'Jesus.' Cora looks surprised. 'That makes us sound like we're horrible snobs or something. Why wouldn't we approve?'

Her green eyes have him pinned. Words fly into his consciousness, words like self-righteous, academic, dour. He feels that sensation of always being on guard, of language being a weapon.

From the table, he hears Evelyn snort, and then her defiant retort: 'Biology has nothing to do with it, Ivan.'

Quieter, but equally adamant, Ivan's reply: 'Nah, I can't agree. It's all about biology.' And then a tempering in his tone, his confusion clear to them all: 'How can you say biology has nothing to do with it?'

'I like that he's prepared to argue.'

He will concentrate on Cora, this moment together, apart from the others. She's one of his best friends. He needs to see more of her. He needs to not be so wary of her.

'And,' Cora continues, 'I like that he's looking after you. Making sure we're not being unkind to you.'

He kisses her on the lips. She bursts into pleased laughter.

'Is there cream?'

'Cream and ice cream,' she replies.

He finds the cream, and then opens the freezer door. As he is taking out the tub of vanilla ice cream he notices a clear plastic container filled with what looks like frozen tofu in a congealed sauce. Hannah's name is written in black ink on the lid.

He puts the tubs on the bench. 'What happened with Hannah?' he whispers.

He's right to whisper. Cora's eyes immediately flick to the table, where Yasmine is sitting, listening to the to-and-fro between Evelyn and Ivan.

'Not now,' she murmurs.

He is alarmed. Those cool eyes are welling with tears.

She puts a hand to his cheek. 'She thinks I'm a hypocrite.' She brushes away her tears. 'Let's talk later.'

At the table, a further shuffle has occurred. Evelyn is still next to Ivan, but she has shifted in her seat, away from him, and is leaning across the table in an ardent exchange with her husband. Yasmine has come to sit on Ivan's other side. As Perry walks over and puts plates in front of Jed and Evelyn, both conversations drop away. He is aware that Ivan, having satisfied his craving with the smoke, and done his duty by defending Perry, is probably tired of the argument. Perry certainly is. In snatches he heard from the kitchen, he had caught Ivan answering Evelyn's questions with polite, meaningless phrases: 'I think I get what you mean there,' or, 'That's possible.' Yet they offered no real concessions. Perry has already learnt how annoying such defences can be when arguing with Ivan. The only defence against them is by direct attack, and that is not a possibility available to Evelyn. It would have broken the rules of polite dinner parties. Evelyn is making her feelings known by turning away from him.

Perry brings another heaped plate of dessert and places it before Ivan. He kisses the top of his lover's head and the scrape of stubble on his lips carries a frisson of the erotic, a drop in his belly, a charge in his cock.

As soon as he and Cora have sat down, Ivan takes a large mouthful of dessert. His pleasure is unmistakable.

He smacks three fingers against his lips, blows Yasmine a kiss. 'Mate, you are an amazing cook.' He brings his hands together in thanks. '*Shukran!*'

Perry usually finds cheesecake either too sweet, or too heavy. Neither is a problem with Yasmine's creation. The aromatic bite of the citrus balances the sugar, and the filling is surprisingly light and delicate. Everyone voices their appreciation with the first bite. Calm is restored. Apart from the barest conversation—Jed being teased for adding cream to the ice cream and Evelyn asking Yasmine whether she had used frozen or fresh berries for the sauce—the six of them are too busy enjoying the food to speak.

The first to start is the first to finish. Ivan clinks his spoon on the plate. 'Beautiful!'

Yasmine points to the island bench in the kitchen. 'There's more. Have another piece.'

Ivan playfully clutches at his belly. 'I wish. But I can't.' He winks at her. 'Anyway, you should save it. You and Cora can have some for brekkie tomorrow.'

Yasmine laughs, shakes her head. 'No way. You're all taking a piece home tonight. If we leave it, Nathan will eat the whole thing when he gets home.' She pats Ivan's knee. 'You and Perry can have brekkie cheesecake tomorrow.'

It's satisfying for Perry to see the sympathy already established between Ivan and Yasmine. Part of the day's long yoke, that disturbing sense of not belonging, that unease, is loosened by the promise of this emerging friendship. She asks Ivan's advice on the garden, sheepishly admitting to having let that part of the house go. Perry is content to sit back and listen to his lover and Yasmine talk. He must not forget to ask Cora and Yasmine over for dinner next month.

'Do you miss Paris?'

Jed's abrupt question shifts his focus. Perry notices that Cora and Evelyn are now sitting together, shoulder to shoulder. Evelyn has her feet up on the chair, Cora's smile is wide and relaxed. The tension that has been evident for most of the evening has gone.

'I've never lived in Paris,' Perry answers. 'I lived in Rouen.'

'That's right, I think Cora said. She stayed with you, yeah?'

There's a nervousness to Jed, an almost frantic eagerness, and Perry wonders if the man is ever comfortable in silence. A distant yet distinct premonition, a warning to be wary of this attractive, seemingly placid man sitting across from him. Jed is addressing the questions to Perry, but his eyes keep darting across the table to where Evelyn and Cora are sitting.

That's when he guesses it, when the machinations of the evening fall into place. Cora's untroubled manner as she listens to Evelyn, the flirtation between them. Yasmine is explaining to Ivan that she has had no luck over the years in combating the leaf curl on the peach tree. Ivan says he'll come around and have a look. Perry hears the tenderness in Ivan's offer, but also discerns the strain in Yasmine's voice.

'Yasmine and Cora stayed with me in Rouen,' he replies to Jed. 'Hannah and Nathan were there too. We had the loveliest time.'

And with the uttering of that memory, the tenor of the table shifts again. The wariness returns to Cora's face and Evelyn's feet drop to the floor.

Yasmine reaches across, holds his hand. 'It was a joy spending that time together.'

'Where's Rouen? I don't think I've heard of it.'

Perry recognises then the accuracy of his foreboding. Instinctively his hand moves to his chest, three entwined fingers press hard there, where a crucifix might sit, or the evil eye. Jed has enunciated the name of the city perfectly. Perry now senses what has been submerged under Jed's gentility all night: fury.

'It's in the north of France,' Cora answers.

She has moved away from Evelyn, has her elbows on the table. The memories are a cord that binds Cora and Perry and Yasmine together. 'I loved the light in Normandy. It was so beautiful: a soft light, yet so bright.'

'That's right, that's right.' Nothing forced in Yasmine's delight. 'Bright but not overwhelming.'

She turns to Ivan. 'Has Perry ever shown you photographs of Normandy? That magic light? Every photo we took seemed to come out right.'

'Yeah, but why Rouen?' Jed interrupts. 'What took you there?'

'Yes, Perry.' Evelyn is looking straight at him. 'I always wanted to know, why Rouen? It seems such an odd choice.'

She knows. Cora will never confirm it, but Perry can tell, by the callousness of Evelyn's tone, that she knows exactly why he was living in Rouen.

He knows he should simply say, *For work.* They couldn't probe further. He certainly can't confess to Evelyn and Jed, could not bear the humiliation of saying: *For love, I ended up in Rouen for love.* He's not afraid of letting the spectre of Gerard invade the room. He's just so fucking tired of it.

Ivan comes to his rescue. 'I've never been,' he says loudly. 'It would be great to go one day.'

'Never been to France?' asks Yasmine.

'Never been to Europe.'

Ivan has saved him. The others are incredulous. Perry smiles to himself, a secretly wicked grin. Ivan has understood them only too well.

'You've travelled other places, though, right?' Jed asks the question with arrogant certainty it can only be answered in the affirmative.

'I've been to Thailand,' says Ivan, embarrassed under the scrutiny. 'I liked it.'

'Nowhere else?'

Ivan shakes his head. 'Couldn't afford it. There was Kat to look after, running the business.' He smiles across at Perry. 'I'll get to travel now, I'm sure.'

'Where in Thailand did you go?' Evelyn asks.

'Bangkok and Phuket.'

Perry sees the glance between Cora and Evelyn. Is it a sneer they are sharing?

'I loved Phuket the first time I went there. It was so beautiful.' Jed shrugs. 'But I think tourism's spoilt it.'

'I think it's still beautiful.'

Is that the quietest Ivan has ever sounded?

'Of course,' Jed agrees quickly. 'It's a wonderful country. And Bangkok is one of the world's great cities. So bloody alive. It takes us a while to readjust whenever we've come home from there. Melbourne seems to be in slow motion in comparison.'

'Yes,' Evelyn agrees. 'Bangkok is a thrilling city. Well, it is if you avoid the Australians.'

'That's easy enough to do.' Jed turns to Ivan. 'Last time we went we stayed in the old town. It was beautiful. And blessedly quiet.'

'I'll remember that for next time,' Ivan says cheerfully. 'I definitely didn't stay in a quiet spot. I stayed in a shitty hotel off the Khao San Road—one step up from a backpackers, really. But it was cheap. There was this tiny window between five thirty and six in the morning when it was quiet. The rest of the time it was *doof-doof-doof-doof.*' He shakes his head, gleeful. 'It was mad. But I loved it.'

Yasmine is smiling at him. 'Amazing how we could all do the backpacking thing when we were in our twenties.' She grimaces in mock distaste. 'I couldn't bear to do it now.'

Perry looks down at his lap. Ashamed. He feels as if he's uttering a deplorable, selfish prayer to Ivan: Don't tell them you were there for your fiftieth. Please don't tell them.

He looks up. Ivan is staring straight at him, unsmiling.

'I couldn't bear it even then.'

They all turn to Evelyn.

'I was never a good backpacker. Everyone stoned and drunk and off their heads all the time. I found it so annoying.' The smile she gives Ivan is cold. 'I get it, we were young, and we hardly had any money, so we all stayed in those places. But Khao San Road—I could never bear it. Any more than I could bear Kuta or Seminyak—or De Wallen in Amsterdam, for that matter. There's so much more to see in the world.'

She's trying to control that squint, that tremor at the edge of her smile.

Perry steals a look at his partner. There's an almost mulish aspect to Ivan's face. He's trying to comprehend Evelyn, those abrupt shifts between politeness and goading, amity and hostility. It took Perry years to work it out, being dumbfounded when he first encountered such rituals of competition and contempt at university. Only slowly did it dawn on him how that superiority and antagonism were formed from childhood in moneyed households and within elite private schools. He had felt like an alien, those first few years at uni. He is sure that is how Ivan is feeling now.

'I think I know what you mean,' Ivan says. 'Yeah, all the drunks and dickheads are annoying. 'Course they are. But my daughter had a great time in Seminyak just after the pandemic, when she went to Bali with some friends. There were lots of Aussies there; she ended up being part of a big group of young girls just wanting to party and have fun. She said to me it felt really safe, knowing that those Aussie girls there had her back.'

There is a pause. Perry takes his wine, has a long sip, trying to think of how to change the conversation. Away from travel, away from gender politics. Evelyn is silent, observing the man sitting next to her. Perry feels a rush of anxiety. Is she going to pounce on Ivan for the heresy of defending Seminyak and drunk Aussies?

She surprises him.

'That's a good point, Ivan,' she says. 'It's true, I did feel more at ease having Australian women around me when I was a young traveller. Safety in numbers, I suppose.'

Perry exhales so loudly that everyone turns to look at him. 'Sorry,' he says, reaching for his glass. 'I suddenly felt hot.'

Ivan throws him a look of concern.

Perry mouths the words, 'I'm okay.'

'I think Ivan might be the most ethical one among us,' Jed says suddenly. 'Unlike the rest of us he hasn't contributed to fucking up the planet with indulgent air travel.'

'Oh, Jesus, we're not starting on that again!' Evelyn has crossed her arms. She is glaring at her husband.

'What?' Jed replies belligerently, crossing his arms as well. 'It's true. Air travel requires fossil fuels; it contributes greatly to carbon emissions. I'm not making that up, Evelyn. It's a fact. It's *science*.' He says the last word like he is grinding it into her face.

'Jed's right,' Yasmine says. 'We do all take travelling for granted. We're guilty. We all vote Greens, and we all get outraged at how little the government is doing about climate change, yet we won't give up travel.'

He can see the effort Evelyn is making not to glower at Yasmine. He takes another sip of his wine and reaches for the bottle.

'I'm not disputing the facts, as Jed likes to put it.' And now she does scowl at her husband. 'I'm not disputing the science. I just hate the moralising part of it all. Yes, we could all do more. But the real culprits are the multinational mining companies and the big carbon emitters. That's where the focus should be.'

Cora is shaking her head. 'Sorry, Evelyn, I can't agree. Yes, the big polluters are most culpable, but we are all responsible for what's happening to the environment.' She lightly brushes her fingers against Evelyn's wrist. 'People in nations like Australia or America or in Europe, we use an obscene amount of energy compared to the rest of the world.'

Yasmine stands up. 'I'm going to put some music on.'

Perry has caught the agitation in her voice. He drinks more wine. He knows he is drinking too much, that he should refill his water glass. He's conscious of Ivan, sitting silent. He tries to catch his eye, but Ivan is listening intently to Cora. Perry half-turns in his chair, watches Yasmine searching through the CDs.

He can't concentrate on the conversation. He *has* drunk too much, and it is a discussion that he finds exhausting, a circle without end, where cause and effect are entangled and where the enormity of what is at stake makes any solution seem either pitifully inadequate or a utopian impossibility. Yasmine has chosen. Jed and Evelyn are arguing. He focuses on the music.

It is an ethereal piece, simultaneously acoustic and electric, with the sparse bass notes a simulacrum for a gently strummed guitar. The vocals begin, an uneasy soprano trilling. The words are in English but he can't make them out. He's sure he has never heard the song before. The singer's intonations owe a debt to soul music but he's sure she is white.

They're talking about bushfires and floods. Surely soon they will have to mention the plague. He stifles a giggle, feeling blasphemous: so, when are the locusts coming? He's not immune to the gravity of the shifting weather cycles, of the severity of their effects. Nevertheless, that gnawing irritation that has been with him all day—it is still sitting deep in his belly—has been rekindled by Jed's dour pessimism, by the apocalypse he is outlining so animatedly. At this very moment, with an evangelical fervour, he is insisting to Ivan that Frankston and all the bayside suburbs will be underwater in a matter of decades. Perry can't help it; he thinks it a uniquely Australian solipsism. He was in Frankston just the other weekend; he had taken off his shoes and socks, taken Natasha's hand and walked her to the water's edge, had delighted in her fearlessness, how she had unselfconsciously stripped off, walked into the gentle lapping water. It had been crystalline, no rubbish in it at all. And with that recollection a mashing of memories, of taking the ferry to the Elephanta Caves in Mumbai Harbour, sitting next to a loquacious old American couple, and staring out to the filthy black waters of the Arabian Sea. Sewage and plastic and shit—literal shit: human faeces—bobbing by as the craft cruised to its destination. The waters there had stunk. And the fishermen on their catamarans and small boats. Which in turn reminds him of the sampans gliding on the putrid grey waters of the Yangtze, of how the great mouth of that enormous river seemed to be vomiting out refuse and waste. That was where real disaster and tragedy was occurring. Not in fucking Frankston!

That shrill singer is still trilling. There is a persistent throbbing at his temple.

Yasmine has returned to the table. 'Ivan,' she blurts out suddenly, interrupting Evelyn, 'what do you think?'

Perry snaps to attention.

She smiles. 'I mean, you must be aware of what is happening with the climate in the work you do as a gardener. You probably have a much better idea than any of us here at this table about what is really going on.'

Everyone has turned to him.

'I guess so.' There is a long pause. Perry marvels at how they are all waiting for his answer. Gravitas. That's the word: his lover has gravitas.

'The seasons are definitely changing. I miss that about Melbourne. Everyone jokes about us having four seasons in one day but I'm not sure that's true anymore.' Ivan is opening and closing his hands. 'The soil is changing as well. I was talking about it with my mate Stu the other day—I work with him.' Perry watches Ivan's hands, that motion of clenching and releasing. He's there, he thinks to himself, working the soil.

Ivan drops his hands to his sides. 'I'm no scientist,' he offers unapologetically to Yasmine. 'I don't know enough.' He hesitates again with a slight frown. Digging again, thinks Perry, trying to find the words. 'I do think that climate change is real. You're right, I see it in my work. But there's a lot of opinion out there, not a lot of facts.'

'You have to look for them,' Jed says quietly.

Ivan nods again. 'I guess that's true.' He beams, and Perry knows, even before he says anything, that he's going to delight in being mischievous. Grinning, Ivan says, 'Sorry to disappoint you, Yasmine—I don't vote Greens.'

'You don't like the Greens?'

Ivan turns to Jed. 'Nah, I think they're—' He stops himself.

'Sanctimonious?' Perry suggests.

There's a flicker of anger there, in the rigid set of Ivan's jaw. Perry is wounded. I was only trying to help, he wants to insist. And now he feels a prickle of resentment.

Ivan clears his throat; tries again. 'I think they're up themselves. And they don't know the first thing about small business.'

'That's not their priority.'

'Alright, I get that.' Ivan nods at Jed's point. 'But it is a priority for me. There's a lot of red tape that we have to put up with in my work, and the Green councils are the worst. They don't seem to be interested in getting people like me on side.'

'So, you only vote out of self-interest?'

It's clear that this stumps Ivan. There isn't belligerence in his frown, though Perry can understand how looking at him they might think that he resents Jed's question. It is as if together they are approaching a lightness. He is coming to really know Ivan. His lover is taking the question seriously.

'I don't think you've done too badly, have you, Ivan?'

'What do you mean?'

Perry catches Ivan's surprise, how his body swings around, facing Cora and trying to make sense of the taunt in her voice.

'Tradies have done very well out of this economy.' Cora turns to the others. 'We've all had renovations done or needed tradespeople to come in. None of it comes cheap, does it?'

Perry draws a breath, wondering if Ivan will explode. He sees his lover reach for his wineglass. Then, changing his mind, Ivan grabs his water and drinks. He sets down the glass and faces Cora.

'I think tradies work hard. They deserve the money they make.'

'I'm with you, Ivan.' Perry is sure that Yasmine is purposefully not looking at her wife. 'I hate this assumption that working-class people don't deserve to be paid well. That's such a fucking entitled opinion.'

'You can still work hard and not be a manual labourer. Lots of women—'

'You don't have to tell me,' Yasmine interrupts Evelyn. 'Cleaners, nurses, childcare workers; I know how hard women have to work. My mother was a cleaner and a factory worker.'

Cora's thumb is scratching at the inside of her palm. Perry watches the obsessive repetition of the action.

'Your father was a Collins Street surgeon. And your mother a principal at PLC? Have I got that right?'

Evelyn nods coolly at Yasmine's question.

'I'm sure each of them worked hard and that their work was mentally draining. But my father's body was broken by all those years as a bricklayer.'

The tension remains, but its focus has shifted. Neither Yasmine nor Cora can look at one another. Perry feels a wave of nausea. Is it the alcohol, or the constant sniping? Does everything have to be about politics? He'll ask about the music, about who is singing. At the moment, his stomach rumbling, his head woozy, he can't stand the singer or her songs.

He's about to ask Yasmine when Ivan turns to Jed.

'I don't always vote out of self-interest.'

Perry sits back in his chair. Ivan must also have been formulating words. There is a measure to his tone. 'Sometimes I vote for those who I think are going to make the best leaders, even if I don't necessarily agree with their politics.' He leans into the table. 'But aren't you all voting out of self-interest, when you all vote Green? You all work for the public service, or non-profits.' He glances at Perry. 'Or, you know, media or arts organisations. You're voting for the people who are protecting your jobs and lifestyles, aren't you all?'

Ivan breathes heavily, and this time does take some wine. He looks across at Perry, and winks. Perry wants to knock the fucking glass out of his hand. *Aren't you all* . . . He thinks Perry is the same as the rest of them, that he belongs to another class and another world to his. The humiliation stings. He forces himself to smile back at Ivan.

'I've been voting Greens for a long time,' Evelyn says quietly. 'And not because of self-interest. I care about the planet. I care about my child's future.'

'That's not fair, Evie,' Jed says, shaking his head. 'Ivan cares about all that—of course he cares about his daughter's future.' He sends a conciliatory smile around the table. 'We all do, right? We don't want our children to inherit a broken planet.

We want them to have more opportunities than we did, we want them to be safe.'

Perry's not one of them. It's Ivan who belongs to *them*.

'You know, discussions about climate change bore the shit out of me,' Perry says, swooping on his glass, holding it at an angle, deliberately flicking his wrist, adding a dash of effete ennui to his voice. Which he's sure Ivan hates. 'We always end up going round and round in fucking circles, wondering who is most to blame. The reality is that there are too many people in this world.' He flourishes his glass dramatically, and wine splashes onto his shirt. 'What is it, eight billion people and counting? This planet can't support that. You want to do something about climate change? Stop having children.' And he swings around to Jed. 'And Jed, your children *are* safe. They're the safest of any generation in history.'

Ivan won't look at him.

'Perry.' He turns to Yasmine, hears the conciliation in her voice. 'You have a point: compared to so many people in the world, we're doing fine. But it's still an unequal world. And it's still not a safe world for girls. Hannah can't walk down the street at night the same way Nathan does. We can do better. We need to do better. That's all we're saying.'

The joyous righteous anger seeps from him. And now he wishes he hadn't said a word. But he still feels distaste for their sentimentality. Just concede, he tells himself. Just let it go.

'You're right,' he says with a sigh. 'I'm being unfair.' But that fucking word is still revolving in his head. Safe. How he detests that word. 'You can't have a perfectly safe world,' he pronounces bluntly. 'That's impossible. I think we do girls like Hannah a disservice if we pretend otherwise.'

'Maybe you think that because you've always felt safe. Maybe you don't really know what it is to be unsafe.'

He swings around to face Jed. 'Bullshit.'

'When have you ever felt unsafe?' Jed insists.

'Perry knows what it is to feel unsafe.' Cora is leaning on the table, her chin in her hand. 'He was a young gay man in the eighties—he definitely knows what it is to be unsafe.'

He's drunk, he knows it. He also knows that he must remember this, this surge of gratitude. The friendship between him and Cora is solid—they mustn't abandon it.

'I'm sure it wasn't easy for you,' Jed is saying, though with little conviction. 'But I think you're being blasé in your argument. Sure, we can't have total safety, but we can raise our sons not to be misogynists. We can try to make the world safer for our daughters.'

He glances over at Ivan as he speaks. Perry is gutted by the conspiratorial self-satisfaction of that exchange.

'Yeah,' he slurs, deliberately exaggerating his inebriation, 'that's right. I don't have a son. Or a daughter. Maybe that's why I don't get it. Maybe that's why I think the little shits should just toughen the fuck up.' He pushes his seat out and stands up. 'Excuse me, I need to piss.'

In the sanctuary of the bathroom, Perry gives vent to his rage. Safe: how he has come to hate that word! As if the world can ever be free of risk and danger. And the sanctimony in

Cora's voice as she delivered her tirade: as if her grievances were commensurate with the pain in the world. She, who can marry the woman she loves, raise children independently, who has completed two university degrees and who has blithely escaped the strictures of tradition. As if his own heart doesn't thump when faced with a dark alley and an approaching loud group. He should never have come back. Their childishness floors him. He hates it here—precisely because it is safe.

The sounds of his urine thundering into the bowl and of his turds splattering in the water return him to his body. There's an awful hint of sulphur in the pong of it. He has drunk too much.

Stuck on one of the panels on the back of the door are four photographs, the colours dulled from age. A surly teenage Hannah poking her tongue out at the camera. A young Cora wearing a wide-brimmed cowboy hat and a defiantly bare-headed Yasmine in a red singlet, her face and bare shoulders tanned a magnificent honey, the backdrop an exquisitely ramshackle colonial-era town square, the large diagonal planes of the Cuban flag adorning the far wall. An old woman staring at the camera with an echo of Hannah's diffidence, a large gold crucifix shining out of the black of her dress. Hannah's *teta*, maybe? In the mountains of Lebanon? And there he is, on the esplanade at Cabourg, in an unbuttoned white shirt, those silly mid-century-style cream bathers that he had thought were so refined, one arm embracing Hannah, who is smiling this time, and another arm around the waist of the adolescent

Nathan, who is already a full foot taller than Perry, his shirt also unbuttoned, a dense sweep of black curls below his navel. He remembers that daytrip, how surprisingly cold the water of La Manche had been, how Nathan had been oblivious to the icy jolt, had swum out far into the distance, to the alarm of some of the French tourists. Had Cora taken the photograph?

He shakes his cock, wipes himself, looking in the mirror as he washes his hands, seeing the grey of his thinning hair, of his stubble, and his anger dissipates. His cheeks burn as he recalls Nathan's breathtaking beauty, and how dazzled he was by the length and power of Nathan's legs, their astonishing hairiness. That night, in the cheap hotel they had stayed in, that shook with the gusts blowing in from the Atlantic, he had lulled himself towards sleep with thoughts of kissing those legs, that belly, kissing and taking Nathan. The pleasure of it when he had finally come. He slaps cold water over his burning face.

Maybe the world is right. Men cannot be trusted. He's mortified by the recollection of that fantasy—not that he had done anything to Nathan; not that he ever would. He loves the boy—loves the young man—with a protective and absolute love.

Perry knows what he must do.

He bursts into the room. The others abruptly go quiet. The shame flares again, the heat at the very roots of his hair. He stutters, gets it out: 'I'm sorry.' He is speaking directly to Cora. 'I am a dick. I drank too much.'

The sympathy is unexpected. Cora waves away his apology, and Evelyn says, almost kindly, 'We all drank too much.'

He sits next to Ivan, who immediately puts his arm around Perry, bringing him close. He sinks into his lover.

There are still twinges of unease. Perry still feels like an intruder; there is something forced about the bonhomie around him; it feels too easy, too deliberate. He wishes he could close his eyes, rest his head on Ivan's shoulder.

Yasmine whispers, 'Perry?'

He opens his eyes. Is there drool on his chin? He had fallen asleep.

He sips at a lemon and ginger tea, listening to the conversation. The talk now is carefully uncontroversial. Evelyn mentions the holiday she and Jed are planning in Japan, and Yasmine talks about how she and Cora are going to take a fortnight to go down to their property at Marlo and work on the house. Ivan is excited to hear about the beach house, saying how much he loves the coast of East Gippsland. Perry is enjoying the comfortable chitchat when there is a sudden dawning: there is no mention of the children. He doesn't even care if that change of direction in the conversation has had anything to do with his outburst. His tea has gone cold. He yawns.

Ivan looks at his phone. 'Time to go?'

Evelyn and Jed are also making a move.

There are thank yous, embraces, pieces of cheesecake wrapped in baking paper, effusive gratitude for the food, the company, as Perry apologises once again. Jed offers them a lift and there is a tentative look between Ivan and himself. He is pleased when Ivan says, 'Thank you, but I think we could do with a bit of a walk.' Then the final kisses, the chilling blast of night when they are outside, the send-off from the gate by Cora and Yasmine. The two women are standing together, but Perry wonders if he can detect a melancholy distance there, intruding between them. A wave to Evelyn and Jed as they get into their car. Then, sweet relief: the evening is over.

The men walk in silence. Perry hears the chugging of the tram, wonders if it is northbound. He hears Ivan chuckle, and looks at him.

Ivan's grin is cheeky. 'They're an intense lot.'

'You didn't like them?'

Some of the good cheer leaves Ivan's face. 'I didn't say that,' he answers.

The silence resumes. They are approaching the imposing neo-classical bulk of the town hall.

And then Ivan stops suddenly. Perry feels a sudden wrench, as if the fear is squeezing his heart: *he's going to break up with me.*

Ivan's grey eyes are serious, though not devoid of warmth. 'Perry, you don't have to be a father to Kat. I don't expect you to be a parent. She doesn't want that either, eh. She's an adult.'

Ivan's words are incomprehensible to him, so focused is he on the fright that overtook him when he thought Ivan was leaving him and also overwhelmed by humiliation at that abject expression: *he's going to break up with me*—the damned adolescent sound of it. It would be impossible for someone his age to speak it out loud. It is simply laughable.

Ivan is waiting patiently. There is a clicking sound, a quick flash of light. A couple across the street are walking to their car.

Perry's awareness of his own egotism, his own selfishness, banishes all other thoughts. Ivan's words return, their meaning clear.

The sound of laughter, the words muffled. Two women are getting into the car.

Perry pulls Ivan in close, enjoys the assertion of belonging. 'I love Kat and I love Natasha. I love them because I love you.'

And Ivan surrenders. Perry feels the weight of that submission, and it is enormous, yet it also brings an incredible lightness to him. He tightens his embrace, and Ivan whispers into his neck, his breath warm: 'I love you too.'

Stated, accepted, consecrated. The men pull apart.

'Should we walk?'

Perry thinks of the rich meal they have just consumed, the abundant alcohol.

'All the way?'

Ivan chuckles. 'Let's see how we go.'

For the first kilometre or so of the walk, descending the gradual slope of Ruckers Hill, avoiding the high street and following the railway line along the back streets and alleys, Perry listens to Ivan chatter away. Once or twice now he has seen the heaviness when Ivan has drunk too much, the scowl that takes over his face, as if an enraged sculptor has manipulated it into a mask of hostility: that Ivan he certainly doesn't want to be around—that heaviness is exhausting. But, thankfully, it is rare. He does, however, adore the tipsy Ivan, when he is playful and cheerful. As he is now, remarking on the pompous earnestness of the conversation at the table, the snide competition between the couples. Perry is taken by his lover's acumen, the way Ivan—who doesn't know the jargon, who has no experience of such codes—has recognised the self-consciousness of much of the evening's political and moral posturing. He is listening intently, but he is also focused on the sombre bluestone of the cobbled lane they are walking down, the clanging of the boom gates announcing a train's arrival, the autumnal colours of the restored Victorian and Edwardian houses, the slightly repellent sweetness of a thick lavender bush sprawling over a low picket fence. And he is marvelling at the startling ease with which they have declared their love for one another, the clear truth of the pronouncement. He had loved Gerard, passionately and completely, so much so that Gerard's swift, cruel termination of their relationship had almost driven him mad. He sees that now. Yet even in its most intense, serene, moments there was never future in that love. With Ivan there is a future—such a future. Of course, he still dreams individual dreams. Was he not doing that earlier in the day? Fantasising about returning to Europe, alone? But they were fantasies, encouraged and fed by petty resentments and anxieties, such as his wariness of Cora, of the tedious constancy of work. Ivan is part of his calculations now, part of how he imagines the world to come. And he suspects that the kind of disloyal fantasising he had indulged in is part of the imaginary life even of those couples who have survived and loved for more than fifty years.

'I never wanted children,' he suddenly blurts out. 'Never.' Ivan slows his pace and Perry continues breathlessly, letting the words fall out. 'I adore my niece and nephew. Cerise and Ilias are great kids.' He stops, recollects. 'They're great young people. And I love my friends' children. I love Nathan, and Hannah. My cousin Yana's kids in Athens. You've got to meet her; she's wonderful. I think I'm a good uncle, and I like the role.' His voice rises. 'That's what I want to be for Kat, for Tash. I want to be a good uncle.' He pauses, adds, 'A good great-uncle.'

Ivan bumps into him gently, grabs his chin, rubbing his finger along the harshness of Perry's grey stubble.

'I wasn't pissed off tonight because I was the only non-parent in the room. I didn't mean to give that impression.' Perry takes a deep breath, and in that pause there is the assembling of his thoughts. 'I haven't said anything to you about it, but I think I've been anxious about that dinner all week. I was away from here for a long time, Ivan. And then I came back home, I was older, and nothing seemed familiar. I felt strange with all my old friends.' Excitedly, in a flash, he lands on the correct metaphor. 'It was like they were speaking another language that I had only just begun to learn. I was bloody scared every time I opened my mouth.' This time he moves sideways, his shoulder grazing Ivan's. 'I think I just want to be with you.'

It is a full minute or so before Ivan speaks, though his arm comes up to caress Perry's back. Perry has become attuned to the time Ivan takes to weigh his thoughts and his words. A car glides past, the young male driver searching the house numbers. There is the bright flare of an automated house light. A young woman in a lusciously flamboyant red coat walks confidently to the car, takes a seat in the back. As she does there is a reveal of the jacket's lining, a bold faux-leopard print.

'Are you saying you don't like your friends?' Ivan asks finally.

Is that what he is saying? Perry pauses, thinking through the emotions of the evening.

'We all met at university. It was exciting.' He hesitates, takes a quick look at Ivan. The man's impassive face betrays no emotion. 'Really exciting. I came out; we were experimenting all the time. With ideas, with drugs, with sex. And then AIDS came along, and we found our cause. It was so fucking thrilling.'

Bernard's face flashes, lodges as an assault into memory. Handsome and tall, the serene aplomb of the astonishingly beautiful. Then the physical desecration of illness; and then death.

'And heartbreaking and frightening as well,' he corrects himself. 'But that was a long time ago. I'm not the same man and I think my friends want me to be the same man.'

'But do you like them?' Ivan asks again.

He feels a scurry of annoyance, a lick of impatience: is that really what is at issue? He bites back on his irritation and as he does a low heavy cloud slides from under the half-moon and the dark street they are walking down is bathed in a pale light.

'I think I'm more concerned that they might not like *me* anymore.'

They have crossed a roundabout and are approaching a railway station, the ramp leading to it buttressed by a stout concrete wall.

Ivan points to it. 'Let's have a rest.'

There is the steady low roll of traffic from High Street, and from St Georges Road across the railway line.

Ivan cocks his head, peers down the street. 'I worked on a garden here. A long time ago. A lovely lady: Gladys.' He turns, grins at Perry. 'That's a name you don't hear much anymore. She was real old-school Aussie, born and bred in Thornbury. She was sweet.' He chuckles to himself. 'And tough. Bartered the price right down. My boss wasn't too happy about it, but he was no match for Gladys.' Ivan bangs his fist on his thigh. 'Gladys Hutchinson. I haven't forgotten her.'

'Should we go and have a look? Maybe she's still there.'

Ivan shakes his head. 'It was a long, long time ago, Perikli. She'd be long dead.'

Perry is thinking of how much he likes it when Ivan attempts his name in Greek. The intonation isn't quite right; too brusque. But there isn't the nasally twang that most Australians bring to its pronunciation.

'Your mates have changed as well. Maybe Cora is also worried that you've grown apart. That happens.'

'I just hate how we're all expected to think the same way. I spent the whole evening worried that I was going to say something they all disagreed with.'

'Well, they're an opinionated lot. They care about politics; that's not a bad thing.' Ivan turns to him with a gentle frown. 'You stood your ground. What are you worried about?'

'That they all think I've turned into a right-wing cunt.'

Ivan laughs out loud. 'Mate! That's ridiculous, you're a Labor voter!'

Perry wonders if there is any way to make Ivan understand the binding hold of the past, and that of once-shared ideologies.

Ivan's hand reaches for his. Perry feels the roughness in the caress, the calluses of Ivan's palm, the newly acquired scratches and blisters. He reminds himself that when he and Cora were undergraduates, snorting speed and reading French feminist psychoanalysis, Ivan was already a father to a toddler, and that he had been hard at work for years.

Perry is suddenly buoyant: the inexplicable fear that has shadowed him all day and night—has it gone? He glances down the street, quickly kisses Ivan on the lips. 'Yeah, I noticed that you didn't mention you're a swinging voter.'

''Course not! I can read a room. I wanted to make a good impression.'

'You did. They all liked you.'

Ivan shuffles closer, leans into Perry. 'Don't be hard on Cora. I liked it when she defended you during that bullshit argument.'

'Which one?'

'All that stuff about safety. What was the word you used?' Ivan scratches his chin. Perry waits patiently. 'Disservice,' Ivan announces, and now there is steel in his voice. 'You're right.

You can't make the world one hundred per cent safe. I know that. Kat knows that. I bet Hannah knows that too.'

Guilt swoops on Perry. Of course. Kat. He's mortified that he hadn't paid attention to what Ivan must have been experiencing during that conversation. I must try harder, Perry tells himself with furious injunction. I must try harder with Kat and Tash.

'What?' Lost in his thoughts, he hasn't heard what Ivan has said.

'I said, you know what danger is.' Ivan hesitates then asks, 'Cora knows about you getting bashed?'

The memory is always like a shard of glass slicing into his throat, but thankfully now it revisits him only in the rarest of nightmares. The four young thugs in the toilet block in Royal Park; the shock, greater than the pain, of how he had dropped to the piss-stained concrete floor after the first punch; how ashamed he'd been of his impotence. They had taken turns kicking him and he had curled himself into a ball, pleading with them to stop, recognising the inevitability of submission. When he had staggered home it had been Cora who'd answered the door and who had washed him and cleaned him up and taken him to the police, that old cunt of a sergeant who kept asking with a sneer, 'Yeah, mate, but did you touch 'em? What did you do to piss them off?' He thought they would arrest her when she started yelling at the bastard cop, calling him every foul word she could think of until Perry had begged her to stop. And with the thought of her ferocity and love, the sting of that memory is gone.

'Yes, she knows. She was there. She was amazing.' He puts a hand on Ivan's knee. 'I'm going to try harder. She's a good friend.'

Ivan is quiet, staring straight ahead. And then his body shudders, and he lets out a despairing moan. His body rocks with his crying. Perry puts his arm across his lover's back and waits for the sobbing to diminish. The weightlessness that settled on Perry a few minutes ago remains. No longer ecstatic: distilled now into purposeful care. Whatever it is, he is determined to share the burden.

Ivan snorts and wipes his eyes, then wipes the back of his hand across his nose and mouth, collecting the gobs of phlegm and snot. He sniffs, stares at his hands.

'I'm doing a wash tomorrow,' Perry says quietly.

Ivan nods and wipes his hands on the legs of his trousers. He is staring straight ahead. Perry waits patiently.

Ivan releases a long, shuddering breath. He turns to look Perry in the eyes. 'I sent Joe to hospital. I beat him up real bad.' His eyes are gleaming, still wet from the tears. But the crying has ceased.

'I know.'

And Perry realises that he had known. Not about the actual incident, but he has read it in Ivan's reserve, in the choke and terror of his buried shame.

'What do you mean you know?' Ivan is shaking his head. 'You have no idea, Perry. I nearly killed him, I hurt him so bad. What I did to him was evil.'

'Was it just the one time?'

The words fervent: 'That was the only time I hit him.'

Perry thinks back to that awful night when he was being kicked and spat on. Called those shameful names. He recalls the mortification of his surrender to their violence, and wonders that now he can barely remember any of it. It meant nothing. They were strangers.

Yet Gerard's words, his rejection, the disgrace he felt because of their love: that still cut him up—would it never go away?

The thrum from the traffic on High Street, the gentle whistle of the night's breeze.

'There's no excuse for what I did.'

'I know.' Perry says it because he has to. Not now, but at some future time, when the betrayals they have experienced no longer hurt, maybe then he'll have the courage to say more. But tonight he's learning from his lover. He lets the quiet sit between them. He tightens his grip on Ivan.

'I will never hurt you like that, Perry. I promise you.'

'I know.'

In the serene silence, he sits next to Ivan as the other man smokes.

'I liked Yasmine; liked her a lot.'

Ivan stubs the butt against the wall.

There is a long pause. And when Ivan speaks again, Perry realises they have been having similar thoughts.

'Is Cora sleeping with Evelyn?'

Perry shrugs and sighs. 'I don't know. We've drifted apart. I don't know.' He throws out his hands, the gesture deliberately exaggerated. 'I don't even know if Cora and Yasmine are monogamous.'

As soon as the word has been said, Perry regrets it. He wonders if it will force a conversation that has not yet been had around how he and Ivan are to negotiate the boundaries of their own relationship. He isn't ready.

'Does it matter? Yasmine's clearly not happy.'

He raises his head. Ivan is looking at him.

'No,' Perry says. 'But maybe nothing is happening. I'm not going to assume anything.'

'Come on, mate.' Ivan's tone is definite. 'They were making it pretty fucking obvious.'

The surety in his voice, the judgement. It compounds the tingling of fear deep within Perry. He does love this man, he does want to be with him. Yet he wonders if he can forsake those exquisite, illicit thrills, those photos and clips on his phone of cocks and faces; and only a few days ago, the lean muscular frame of the older man drying himself on the other side of the bench in the gym locker room, the silver buzz cut, the thick halo of bristly pubes around his cock. They were both getting hard, until there was the shocking bang of the door slamming open, the loud yells of the teenage boys strutting in. The two men immediately wrapped their towels around their waists and doggedly ignored each other.

Ivan is standing, looking down at him. 'Still up for a walk?'

Perry doesn't move. He can't be scared of revealing himself to Ivan. The promise he has made. No more silences, no more evasions.

'Poor Yasmine,' he says, still not getting up. 'And poor Jed.'

Ivan snorts. 'He's a bit of a coward.'

Now he sounds flippant.

'So, it's okay for a straight woman to cheat on a guy, is it?'

Ivan looks startled, and then exasperated. 'Of course not. That's not what I meant.' His sternness is replaced by a wan smile. 'I just don't think he's honest. He kept saying all the right things at the dinner table, and then he comes outside when we're smoking and is all blokey and shit.' Ivan starts mimicking Jed, deliberately makes his voice go up an octave, exaggerates the man's full, elongated vowels. '*I thought it a good point you made about how girls can be cruel.*' Ivan's voice shifts to a growl. 'I didn't trust him.'

Perry gets to his feet. 'I think you're being too hard.'

Ivan's hand reaches for him abruptly, grabs his arm. There's nothing savage in the gesture. Perry turns back, ashamed. It seems childish, that urge to walk off, to walk away.

'Perry, what's going on?'

And he says it: 'I think we should move in together.'

Ivan's smile is joyful. 'You know I want that as well.'

They have fallen into a stride, side by side.

'I need to be close to Kat, though—especially now that she and Tash have just got the new place.'

'I know,' Perry answers quietly. 'I get it.' He draws a deep breath. 'I think we should get a new place together. Somewhere close to where you are now; close to Katerina.'

There is only the hushed tread of their walking. Then the rumble of a tram in the distance.

'That's a big move. It's the other side of the city.'

The sudden clanging of the boom gates. This time Perry grabs Ivan's arm, turns into a street leading away from the railway line.

'I'm ready for it.' He draws Ivan closer. 'It makes more sense to move to the south side. I want to do it for Katerina and Tash as well.' He is bashful, daring himself to express it. And he does: 'They're part of my life too now.'

Perry doesn't add, though he nearly does: and moving away from here, it will be a new start for me. It's not that he doubts Ivan's ability to understand; it is simply that the hope is still too precious to be articulated carelessly. The fullness of that desire is as yet unvoiced, unthought, even to himself. All he knows is that he longs for that promise of relaunching. Returning to Australia was not enough. He needs to make a home.

Just before they turn into High Street, Ivan seizes Perry's hand, brings it to his lips. 'I'm ready too.'

A group of young women, laughing, haughty and beautiful, are streaming out of a bar, rolling and lighting cigarettes. The electronica blares and then is abruptly silenced as the door closes behind them. Ivan drops Perry's hand, strides forward, and deftly weaves past the women. The carefully curated outfits, the mash-up of eras and styles, the wild dyes in their hair and their brutally chic cuts all indicate that the young women are students, undoubtedly cosmopolitan. There would have been no disquiet if the men had continued to hold hands. In fact, the opposite. But Ivan doesn't know these codes. These neighbourhoods are not part of his world. And it's hard to shake off the hold of one's generation. Ivan will always prefer discretion. It is his age as well as his history.

As it is mine, Perry suddenly understands. He passes the women, reaches Ivan, and once again they fall in step. Their bodies do not touch, yet they are so close as they cross the road to Perry's apartment that their hands brush together from time to time.

Chloe, one of the women they have just passed, has had too much to drink. She is not insensibly drunk, yet as she puffs on the cigarette her girlfriend has rolled her, as the smoke drags and tears down her throat, she has to will herself not to give in to nausea. Don't you dare be sick, she warns herself. That'd be *so* embarrassing.

Her lover, Erina, puts an arm around Chloe's waist. 'We're going home.'

And the next morning, having experienced a night of fitful sleep, her head pounding and her stomach roiling, Chloe will make herself a coffee and sit on the narrow balcony of her girlfriend's flat to drink it while looking down on the street below. Her head still thumping, she will muse on the street's silence. There are only old women, all dressed in black, shuffling to the Orthodox church on the corner, or to the large Catholic church at the summit of the hill. An old man, not as elderly as the matrons she has been watching, will come out of the building across the street. For some reason, he seems familiar. He is bald, strong-shouldered and thick-bellied. She will ponder: do I know him? Then that question will be forgotten. Instead, she will look wistfully, and a little resentfully, across at the apartment block from which he has just emerged. She thinks they have done such a brilliant job, converting that old factory, the structure so solid and the facade so elegant, with those enormous light-filled windows. She can't see the balconies from where she is—they are only visible from the side street— but she has noticed them when she walks up to High Street from the train station, admired their size. Not like Erina's flat, which is not only small but made of grey concrete, already battered by the rain and weather, the walls stained and blotchy. How she envies that old man; how she envies his generation. Erina can barely scrape together the rent to pay for this ugly shitbox. The rooms are tiny—too small for a couple. It's unfair. Until she's finished uni, until she gets a proper job, she'll have to live at home. She watches the man stride past the old women and turn into the street that leads to the Orthodox church. Surely, he can't be going to church? He doesn't look *that* old. Chloe belches, and then farts, all of the night's toxins rising. She rushes to the toilet. She will never have cause to recall that stranger again.

As Perry yawns and stretches awake, he realises that Ivan is not beside him. There is a momentary confusion. And then he remembers: Ivan is at church.

Not yet ready to rise, Perry rolls over, inhaling Ivan's sweat on the sheets. But he can't stay in bed; he has to piss. And then he grimaces, remembering. He drank too much last night. He embarrassed himself. With a groan, he rolls off the bed.

He fires up the coffee machine, glances at his phone. A message from Cora. *Lovely to see you. Yasmine and I think Ivan's HOT! Coffee this week? xx*

He starts composing a reply. There's too much to say. He hearts her text. He'll call her in the afternoon.

His laptop is open, sitting on the coffee table. And he remembers then, the final whisky he and Ivan had together on coming home, the excitement of looking at houses and apartments.

Over a breakfast of toast and coffee, he scrolls distractedly through the open pages. He looks at maps, at photographs of streets, of images of parkland and beaches. His is a vast city, he muses; so much of it is unknown. He is hungry to discover it.

4

Ivan is standing with his feet apart, hands clasped behind his back. His jaw is clenched, his body rigid, his spine straight. He is on the patio of a penthouse in an eight-storey building that towers over its immediate neighbours. He is looking over the river and the expansive parks—their lawns still impossibly green, watered continuously through the height of a punishing Melbourne summer—and straight down to the water. The late summer sun has only now started to set, and in that sparkling luminescence the waters of the bay are not their usual slate-grey; they are emerald. The soft hues of the early evening are enchanting. But Ivan looks upon it without really seeing it. He is examining his conscience.

He has been lying to Perry, and he knows that this night will be both the culmination and the annulling of that lie. The surety of that conviction does not shame him. He is pondering this precise point: how the origins of this present betrayal of a man he now loves began before they had ever met. Three times he has been tempted to speak of it; he has clear memories of each of those moments. The first was on their first date, at that Italian restaurant in town, when he had drunk too much too early and almost blurted it out. But how to explain it without it sounding sordid? An equal timidity had overcome him the second time, that weekend away at the Grampians, Ivan's birthday present from Perry. There had been the daily hiking to see the world from the magnificence of those outcrops soaring over the surrounding plains. There was the sprawling apartment, those wonderful meals at the hotel in Dunkeld. On the final evening, walking back from the restaurant, the sky crystal on ebony, coruscating with stars, he had found himself falling into a punitive despair: that in the wickedness of his treachery he was as culpable as Joe. Yet again he could not find words, and when Perry asked what was wrong he'd used the excuse of overindulgence to explain his distress. The last time had been on that unseasonably icy November day, when they'd started house-hunting together. After dinner that Saturday night, Perry had said, 'If we are going to live together, we need to make a decision about monogamy.' He had heard the tremor in his lover's voice, knew how fearful he would have been to initiate that conversation. A wave of affection had overtaken him, and he had replied, 'Yes, please.' He had come closest then to revealing everything. Yet, again, fear had stopped him. But he and Perry coming to a solicitous, shared agreement had been wondrous. Perry having loved Gerard, and he having loved Joe—there was no romance left for them in the valorisation of absolute monogamy. Nevertheless, they both had agreed that love in itself was no safeguard against dissipation occasioned by heedless promiscuity. They would be each other's only love—those were Perry's words—and if each of them had to stray, that hunger was to be satisfied anonymously. 'We can't know their names. They have to be complete strangers.' These had been Ivan's words.

The concentration of memory and sensation shatters and disappears. The evening light is so clear that Ivan can see the silhouette of a cargo ship gliding on the placid waters of the distant horizon. He abruptly turns from the peaceful vista, reaches for his cigarette packet. Troy isn't a stranger. There is a loyalty he owes to him. That is what he can never explain to Perry, for the nature of such fidelity is elusive even to himself. He must live with this one lie, and he must swear to be humbled by it. He whispers, half in his parents' tongue and half in English, declares to his Lord: 'If I betray Perry again after this night, strike me down.' A snap of fear, and then it is gone. He lights a cigarette.

As the smoke fills and settles in his lungs, he walks around the L-shaped balcony, the wide expanse of the south-facing patio narrowing to a balcony on its western flank. There's a parapet of thick, opaque glass, but he is tall enough to rest his arm on it as he smokes, to look down across the railway lines of Jolimont to the jutting skyscrapers and fluorescent blocks of light in downtown Melbourne. The vista strikes him as unreal, a quick sketch of a city as might be drawn by a precociously talented child. In the soft falling light of the evening, everything else has been erased. The air is thicker here, and Ivan feels a wetness at his armpits. He runs his thumb along his upper lip to wipe the drops of sweat. He walks back to the patio, where the southern breeze comes off the sea and cools his skin.

He's already finished his first Coopers. He drops his cigarette butt into the empty bottle.

It is 7.18 by his phone. There is a text message from Kat asking if he and Perry are still coming around for Sunday lunch. There is a missed call from Perry and a follow-up text: *Hope you're enjoying your quiet time. The boys send xx.* It is momentarily unsettling. Perry is out for dinner with his friends Spiro and Kai. They might be in Collingwood; they might even have decided to come into town. They might be a stone's throw from where Ivan is now. He types *xxx* into his phone. He then answers Kat. A thumbs-up emoji. *CU Sunday.* A red love heart emoji.

He pockets his phone, retreats into the apartment, to the bathroom. It is ridiculously spacious, as big as the bedroom of his flat. The shower stall runs the length of one wall, with a large square mirror over the cabinet. A rectangular mirror runs the length of the opposite wall. He'd laughed when he first walked in there. Apart from being ridiculously rich, the owners must also be ridiculously vain.

He leans over the basin, gives his teeth a quick scrub, making sure not to drop any toothpaste on his shirt. He rinses his mouth. He steps back, undertakes a fearless scrutiny. He has put on weight. It is inevitable: the comfort of being with someone he loves. But he's been working hard, and he's been scrupulous about going to the gym. He's big, but built. He smacks his belly, winces at the wobble beneath his shirt. He punches harder at his chest, taut as a drum. He nods at his reflection with satisfaction. His head, shaved today, is gleaming. He takes his crucifix from under his shirt and kisses it.

The buzzer is a shock—it sounds like an alarm and lasts for seconds. He doesn't have to check his phone. He knows it will be seven thirty. That's Troy, meticulously punctual.

He buzzes him in.

He wonders at his excitement, at the quickening of his heartbeat. Then he reminds himself that something momentous is happening, and with this thought his body relaxes into a familiar stance. He faces the door, hands clenched behind his back.

Waiting for Troy's knock, he is unexpectedly assailed by his father's stern commands: to walk in step whenever they were together; to keep his back straight; and, most vehemently, *Don't slouch!* Invariably followed by the insult in his father's broken English: *Fucking Aussies, lazy bastards, always slouching!*

Joe had asked him, early on, 'You been in the army, bro?'

He had swelled with pride. Funny that all those seams of memory are coming to the surface now. Ivan cocks his head, amused. They are untainted by the underlying terror of angering his father, or the scalding humiliation that used to come with remembering anything about Joe.

He faces the door, his hands clenched behind his back. He knows to be prepared. They were important lessons.

Nevertheless, at the first loud rap on the door, it is a relief to drop his arms to his sides and open it.

'How are you doing, old man?'

Ivan grins at the youth's cheekiness. Troy unhooks his backpack from his shoulders, tosses it on the floor, and strips off his black Puma hoodie, the white shirt underneath rising at the waist and revealing the flush of hair at his belly. From what Troy has told him, Ivan knows that his paternal grandparents were from the Punjab and that his mother is Anglo and Yorta Yorta. The strong slender frame, the well-proportioned face. The dark bronze sheen of his skin, the abrupt contrast of his sharp blue eyes. Ivan draws in his breath; as always, he is awed by the young man's beauty.

'I've got the money,' he says, and the boy nods.

From the outset, he and Troy have been scrupulous in observing the rules that define their relationship. Ivan reaches for his wallet and hands $1700 to Troy. While the young man counts out the notes, Ivan heads to the fridge.

'Want a beer?'

'Yeah, sweet.'

Troy pockets the money. 'Thanks for the extra two hundred.'

That thank you has also become part of their ritual.

Troy is taking in the breadth of the apartment, the immense view out to the bay. He whistles in appreciation.

Ivan offers him a beer and they clink bottles.

'Is this your new place?'

'I wish!'

The boy has a deep, husky laugh, a rasp that carries through to his speaking voice. Ivan loves the sound of Troy's voice.

The man, he corrects himself. In the four years that Ivan has been his client, Troy has become a man.

Lured by the gentle warmth of the night, by the magnitude of the view, they walk out onto the patio, sip their beer while leaning on the balustrade. The final streaks and wisps of daylight flare orange and red near the horizon; up above them, the sky is night. Yet the lingering of the summer sun is such that they can see the whole of the long curve of the bay.

Troy stretches out his arm and points. 'That's your place there, right?'

Ivan shifts closer to him, murmurs, 'Further south,' and then they kiss. And that kiss unsettles all his planning. It is why he has paid for the whole night: to avoid that sense of rushing, the constant demand of time. They would go slowly through the arc of the greeting and payment, to the settling drink, to the acts he has fantasised about for days, weeks or months. Most of his requests are standard, but a few fill him with such abject shame that he can't face the boy as he asks for them. They bring to the surface of his consciousness an ancient terror that maybe his lust is truly evil, the sin of his desire exposed in his rush to expunge its traces once sated. This is not a night to end quickly with Troy's hurried showering and departure, with having to squeeze it all in to that beckoning and threatening hour. Not tonight. Time would not have dominion tonight. But the kiss is hard, consuming, and Troy's tongue and mouth so expert that Ivan cannot contain his excitement. He and Perry are ageing men, and the comfort of their kissing is in its tenderness. But now he is renewed, inflamed by Troy's life force, that zeal which no one Ivan's age can possess: that conviction of immortality. There is a harsh chemical hint on the youth's skin, even on his breath; he is on some drug. The thought arises, passes immediately, and Ivan is pressing hard into Troy, he is kissing him so vehemently—almost grinding his teeth against the boy's lips—that Troy pulls away. Ivan's breath is hoarse; Troy's chin is wet with spit.

Ivan's hand is on Troy's shoulder, a soundless decree. He pushes Troy into the living room, and then exerts further pressure on his shoulder as Troy sinks to the floor. Troy's face rubs against the crotch of Ivan's jeans, his lips grazing the zipper.

'Fuck my throat.' Troy commands it in an urgent whisper, knows the power of the coarse, pornographic words.

Ivan looks down at him, at the alluring glory of a face so handsome and young, those imploring cobalt eyes, as if he is not just performing, as if he is indeed ravenous for the older man. It's an undermining thought, and Ivan rejects it: those contortions of guilt and conscience can wait. In this splendid moment, he truly wants to believe he can possess this boy.

'Open your mouth wide, faggot!'

As he sprays out that last word, hisses the abuse, his cock stretches, surging against the fabric of his trousers so strongly that it hurts. He's scared to unzip, thinks he might come if he touches himself. He grabs Troy's hair, pulls his head back.

'Wider,' he demands.

The boy obeys.

Ivan hawks it into his hand, then brings it to Troy's mouth. The youth sucks greedily on Ivan's fingers.

'Can I suck you?'

Ivan shakes his head. He knows he will break. Just the touch of Troy's lips on his cock and he will break.

Troy reaches up; one hand clamps against Ivan's crotch.

Ivan moans, then slaps Troy's hand away.

This is not the way he wants the night to go. An image of Perry smiling flashes into his brain; he feels a contortion deep inside him, his heart twisting at the depravity of his betrayal. And Troy's beauty, the sharpness of those cheekbones, the glint of those cold eyes.

'I want to suck you!' Troy's tone is insistent.

'Get up.'

The boy accedes.

'Turn around.'

Troy does so, and Ivan shoves him against a wall with unexpected force. Ivan is behind Troy now, pushing himself against the youth. He kisses his neck. The sourness of the sweat, that unpleasant taste of chemicals. He gnaws at that skin.

'Hey, careful.' Troy's tone is direct, and it is a warning. He is only feigning submission. Ivan accepts the reprimand. He steps back. 'Drop your fucking pants.'

The dance resumes. Troy lowers his trackpants and arches his back. Ivan looks down. And moans.

And now there is no controlling his desire. Ivan brings his hands to those solid buttocks, the fine hairs, the puckered opening, the pink flesh contrasting against the darkness of hair and skin. Ivan sucks on his forefinger and pushes it hard into the man. He knows that Troy will have washed and douched; even so, as he shoves his finger in further, as he feels the silky softness of the bowel, there arises a faint whiff of shit. Ivan unzips, spits again into his hand, and massages the shaft of his own cock. He pulls down on his foreskin and rubs the tender head along the crack of the youth's hairy arse.

He's close, and Troy knows it as well. He tightens and releases Ivan's finger, and then turns and drops to a squat in front of Ivan. His lips bite on the foreskin and then he takes the length of Ivan's cock down his throat. Ivan pushes forward, and as his pace quickens there is an ugly choking sound, but Troy persists and there is the tiniest of groans and now Ivan is spasming, and he is thrusting so fast and so hard that the back of Troy's head is banging against the wall. Looking down at the same lustrous dark skin, Ivan doesn't see Troy, he sees Joe and he shoves harder and further. And then Ivan shouts: 'Don't you spill a drop, you fucking faggot cunt!' He jerks, a series of shudders, each subsequent surge abating till all that's left is a weak quiver. His cock slips out of the youth's mouth.

Troy leaps to his feet. He spits the clag of semen into his palm, wipes his mouth with his other hand.

He winks at Ivan. 'Can I have a shower, mate?'

Mortified, not able to look at him, Ivan points to the bathroom. Alone, he takes out his handkerchief, turns on the faucet over the kitchen sink. He waits till the water is warm, and then he scrubs his cock clean. Stumbling, his jeans still around his ankles, as if he is in some ancient slapstick film, he searches the kitchen drawers, finds a napkin, and dries himself.

He goes out to the patio, reclines on a sunlounge and lights up a cigarette.

Troy comes out, his hair combed back so it looks silken in the fading light. He reaches for the pack, takes the other lounge. The men sit in companionable silence.

'Are you hungry?'

Troy nods.

'What do you feel like?'

'Don't care.'

'Thai?'

'Sure.'

Ivan stubs out the cigarette, gets to his feet. 'I'll order some wine as well. Do you want another beer in the meantime?'

'Yeah, why not?'

There is a sheaf of takeaway menus in one of the drawers, and a fridge magnet advertising a local boutique bottle shop. Ivan orders the meal, texts instructions to the delivery driver to pick up the wine.

The men clink their beer bottles. There is a lone shimmering glow over the horizon.

'So, how long are you staying here?'

'Just tonight.'

Troy glances over at Ivan. 'You didn't want to meet at your flat?'

Ivan steels his nerves. He has prepared a speech, a declaration of sorts, and hopes for it to be an acknowledgement of gratitude, and possibly even of tentative friendship. Now, with the memory of the fervid sex in the kitchen and Troy's obedient surrender during it, a matter of professionalism not desire, the sentiments seem not only compromised but obscene. He recalls looking down at the handsome face, the boy calmly lapping the spit from his fingers, and he winces.

'I hate my flat.'

The words, the ferocity with which he has expressed them, surprise even him. He feels a blush suffuse his face. He takes a sip of the beer, and the cooling bitterness evens his temper.

'It's small and it's cramped and it didn't seem right for tonight.'

It's sudden and intimate, the way Troy reaches out to him, lays a hand on Ivan's knee, squeezes it. 'Are you okay?'

The older man nods. 'Yeah, I'm good.'

Ivan looks up at the night, as if seeking guidance there. It doesn't matter how foolish it might sound. He believes he owes Troy this explanation.

'I want tonight to be a thank you. A thank you for you being real good to me, Troy.' The words fall in a rush, yet he neither stammers nor falters. 'I was a bit of a mess a few years ago; I didn't think I was worth shit, and those times we were together made me feel like maybe I'm okay, that I'm not a complete cunt. And I don't mean the sex. Though, don't get me wrong, I love having sex with you. You're a beautiful man, Troy; I look at you and I can't believe how beautiful you are. Just holding me was enough, sometimes. You made me feel less lonely. I was so lonely.'

His voice shakes on that last word. He says firmly to himself: Don't you fucking cry! He understands now that he is not making a declaration; it is a confession.

He turns, forces himself to look at Troy.

The youth gives him a half-smile, the warmth there sincere. Ivan sighs in relief.

Troy sets his beer bottle on the ground, gets up and kneels before Ivan. There is nothing obsequious in the pose. His clear eyes are alive, electric—so much so that Ivan has to turn away. Troy grasps Ivan's chin, forces Ivan to look at him.

'You're alright, Ivan. I enjoy being with you.'

Ivan mutters something unintelligible.

'What?'

He repeats himself, almost in anger. 'Even after some of the things I ask you to do?'

Troy bursts out laughing, so that Ivan sees the impossible whiteness of his teeth. He's had them done. Then he swipes away that trivial thought.

Troy gives him a quick, firm kiss on the lips. He gets to his feet. 'We all have our fantasies, mate. And fantasy isn't reality.' He reaches down for his beer. 'You're not a cunt, Ivan. Trust me: you are so not a cunt.' He is about to sit. Then his eyes narrow. 'Is this a goodbye?'

Ivan answers immediately: 'Yes.'

As Troy lowers himself onto the sunlounge, there is a sudden thudding reverberation; a beam of stark yellow light sweeps the night. The sound gains strength, momentum, the relentless whirring of the helicopter is almost above them. Then, with an abrupt glide, it sweeps up and over the apartment block, disappears. There is the receding whine of a siren from the streets below. Then silence and the gentle hum of traffic.

'Does that mean you're not lonely anymore?'

The directness of the question takes Ivan by surprise. He ponders it for a moment, tries to comprehend exactly what loneliness is. The detachment that has been part of him for so very long, since boyhood, hearing his parents bicker. The petty cruelties of school, willing himself not to take sides. How he was there physically in his marriage—his body functioning as husband and then father, and always diligently executing the role of a worker—yet also not there. That was his greatest cruelty to Dana. He does understand why she's hated him for so long. Then the long years with Joe, that tiny seed of suspicion, not trusting that such a beautiful man could love him. The doubt was always there; the discovery of Joe's betrayal was its confirmation. That was the real betrayal, knowing he was alone all those years. He thinks about waking up a few weeks ago; the door to Perry's bedroom was closed, but he could hear music playing faintly. When he walked into the living room, there was Perry, his eyes closed, swaying in one spot, listening to a honeyed voice that was, for Ivan, both new and strangely familiar. Then Perry whirled around, eyes open, seeing Ivan and chuckling in embarrassment, though the pleasure was still there in his eyes. He admitted shyly, 'I love Dusty Springfield.' That moment had been the opposite of detachment; it had been its annihilation.

'I'm not lonely when I'm with my daughter and my grand-daughter,' he answers Troy. 'I'm not lonely when I'm with Perry.'

'Perry?'

'I've fallen in love.'

'Congratulations.'

Is there sarcasm in Troy's tone?

The youth has raised his beer, and Ivan does the same, saluting the night scape.

'What's he like?'

'Gentle and kind.'

'Good-looking?'

'Very.'

'How old?'

'A couple of years younger than me. Fifty-five.'

'How long have you been seeing each other?'

'It will be three years this March.'

Troy turns to him and Ivan sees that there is affection in his smile. He's not making fun of him.

'Do you want to get married?'

Ivan feels his top lip curling, knows how obvious he has made his distaste at the question.

Troy laughs out loud. 'What's wrong with asking that?' Then he adds cheekily, 'You're such a dad.'

'Maybe I am.' And Ivan's annoyance vanishes immediately. 'I don't know, I can't get my head around calling another man "my husband".' He shakes his head. 'It isn't for me.'

'I'd like to get married.'

He's about to ask the question—'To a man?'—and then he bites back the words, confused. He was being honest when he thanked Troy for alleviating his loneliness, assuaging that gnawing pain, the unhealable wound caused by Joe's desertion. He will miss Troy's head resting on his chest after sex, smelling the odours of salt and cum, his fingers tracing patterns on Troy's chest. And them talking, Troy revealing, bit by bit, something of himself. Though there would always be a wall, built by the exigencies of commerce: how much of what he has been told is what Troy thought he wanted to hear?

What are they? Something not quite friends?

He has been silent too long. 'Married? To a man, you mean?'

'Yeah, you dickhead. To a man.'

There is something in Troy's mocking that makes Ivan shift uncomfortably in his chair. The teasing tone is reminiscent of the exasperation Katerina often expresses over his awkward- ness and inadequacy about the digital world. As Troy just did, she will roll her eyes or shake her head in frustration. It feels unnerving to draw a connection between his daughter and the prostitute sitting beside him, so casually drinking a beer. He thinks of the money he has paid Troy, money that could have gone towards Kat's mortgage, or to the deposit he and Perry are saving for a new home. The sleaziness of what he is doing suddenly overwhelms him. *You know nothing about* this boy, he reminds himself with fury. How many times have you . . . ? He has to pause on the ugliness of the thought. He asks himself: How many times have you rented him? Eight times? Yes, it has been eight times—nine times including this final encounter. His mind, attuned to the calculations of his work and his business, immediately snaps to a count. Eight times $350, which is what Troy has charged for an hour over the last four years: $2800. Add to that the $100 tip he has dutifully added from their first transaction: $3600. And the $1700 he has paid him for tonight: $5300. He has been a fool. So much money for sex he could have arranged to have for free with some pick-up on Grindr or at a toilet after work. And for all that money, he has known the boy for only eight hours. One day's work. He knows nothing about him.

He glances over at Troy, who seems oblivious to his turmoil. Ivan has observed subtle changes in him over four years. Troy still wears clothes of simple utility; but unlike the first time they met, when his cheap short-sleeved shirt had been thread-bare, a rip visible at the pits, the hoodie he wears now is expensive, and his black trackpants are no longer cheap knock-offs but a designer brand. His hair is better styled. Yet his cheerfulness, his openness, the letting down of his guard that became apparent from their first few minutes together: that has not left him.

'Are you seeing someone?'

He has been quiet for so long that Troy is initially confused by the question. The young man's face breaks out into that attractive, frank grin. 'You're hard to follow sometimes, Ivan. You really like your silences, don't you?'

'My daughter says that.' He gives a wry chuckle. 'Perry says it too. I guess everyone I know says that about me.'

'I like it. You think before you speak. The world's too full of bullshitters that do the opposite.'

Ivan clocks it, the turn—like a drop in temperature.

'I was seeing someone,' Troy continues, both men stretched out, not looking at each other, 'for ten months. I thought we were going somewhere but he was a timewaster.' Troy sculls the remainder of his beer. 'He was a fucking liar.' And now he does raise his head and look at Ivan. 'Why are so many faggots liars? Is it in our fucking DNA?'

A prejudice stirs, so deeply embedded within him that he thinks it must be innate. And maybe prehistoric, traceable to that primal evolution of bodies: the fear of violence and the terror of exposure, that thin tissue of instinct and biology that connects so many women to homosexuals. Good Lord, he understands it. As always, with such contemplation of the awfulness of what men can do, he thinks of his daughter; the shudder, involuntary, is noticed by Troy, who looks up, concerned. Ivan doesn't condemn the fear of violence. It is gossip and slander, the guerrilla tactics of undermining and sabotage, of making envy a virtue and a weapon that he detests. Bitchiness. He hates it in women. He hates it in gay men.

'You're young,' he says to Troy. 'You have no idea what it was like living your life scared of everyone finding out you were a poofter.'

Troy scrunches his face, the reaction so extreme that for a passing moment he looks ugly. 'I hate that word.'

'Faggot, then. The word doesn't matter. You grow up being scared that people are going to bash you or insult you or chuck you out because of who you are—'course you're gonna be a bit of a liar.'

'You're not.'

The thought—fast, cruel—arises immediately: You don't really know me.

And as if the notion has miraculously been shared, Troy then continues, 'I mean, as much as I know you from our time together. But you seem a straight-up kind of dude. You're my mum's generation, right?'

Ivan nods. He remembers the lad has told him his mother's age. She is five years younger than he is.

'You probably experienced heaps of homophobic shit. Damon didn't. His fucken Mum is at a drag show every Friday night. So why the fuck is *he* a liar?'

'Is Damon's dad around?'

'Kind of. He knows him. I think he lives in New South Wales somewhere. Nah, I guess he wasn't round much.' He pushes the sunlounge back, leaps to his feet. 'Is there more beer?'

'Yep.'

As Troy gets up, Ivan notices that there is a wet patch, small and perfectly spherical, on the dark fabric of his trackpants, the outline of his cockhead clearly visible. Ivan wants to reach for it. Reach for his cock, raise Troy's shirt with his other hand, rub his hand across the boy's firm, hairy belly. The eternal battle between wickedness and charity plays out in his head, and even deeper: in his soul. Why not reach out and touch him? You paid for him.

The ugliness of the thought shames him. 'Can you get me one too?'

When Troy returns, he brings the lounger closer to the older man. He sits on the side of the long seat, facing the reclining Ivan.

'Cheers.' He takes a swill of beer. 'Why did you ask about Damo's dad?'

Ivan tries to think back to what it was that prompted the question. It's the third beer, and it is filling him up, both physically in the swelling of his belly, and also in the mellowing from the alcohol. His thoughts are wandering.

Troy's face is unsmiling.

'Maybe your mate Damon thinks his father doesn't respect him for being gay.'

'He probably doesn't respect him for being a liar.' The statement is delivered with unflinching finality.

Ivan remains silent. His curiosity is roused, as is his concern. Troy is hurt; really hurt. Ivan doesn't ask any more questions. He doesn't think that men can be coaxed into revelation, and even though that might not be true, that Troy's generation of men may indeed be less circumspect about intimacy, it is an aspect of himself that has been so constant for so long that Ivan believes it unalterable.

The boy's breaths are steady, drawn out. Ivan sits up and turns to his side, so that the men are now looking at each other. The boy isn't going to reveal anything.

Ivan kisses the pad of his thumb, raises it, and gently rubs it across Troy's lips. 'Well, he sounds like a dickhead, mate.' Ivan lowers his hand. 'You're a good lad, Troy. Don't waste your time with liars.'

The abrupt urgency of what follows unnerves Ivan. Troy's hand reaches for Ivan's crotch. Then Troy cups his hand so tight that there is a jolt of pain. The boy doesn't release his grasp, though the grip lessens. Now his palm is also gently massaging. This assumption of authority is an abrogation of the rules fixed from the evening of their first encounter, when Ivan had made it clear in a series of texts that he would be the one taking charge, directing their activities. Those initial communications had been tentative, evasive—out of the fear of incrimination or arrest, of public shaming—but even early on he had made that part clear. Troy had never initiated the sex before.

The youth is unzipping him, his hand digging in, squeezing him.

There is the screech of the doorbell. Ivan pulls away and rushes to zip himself up like a frightened schoolboy. His fingers feel like rubber, useless, and he gives up. He dashes to answer the door, Troy's laugh booming behind him.

'Delivery?' a bored voice asks through the speaker.

He buzzes them through. Finally getting his jeans zipped.

Leaving the trays of food on the kitchen benchtop, Ivan goes through the unfamiliar drawers, finding a folded tablecloth which he lays over the small circular dining table. He opens cupboards, finds four of everything: plates, bowls, wineglasses.

For all its practical modern amenities, its astounding views over to the bay from the patio and over the rooftops of the city from its bedroom, the apartment is sterile, from its bland white walls hung with mass-produced black-and-white framed photographs of Paris and New York and the Greek islands to the functional generic Scandinavian furnishings. He wonders if there has been a divorce, a separation that has also torn the soul out of the place. A droll eye roll: it was so much more likely to be a rich person's tax dodge. He tips the steaming food into bowls, pad Thai and beef salad, green chicken curry and chilli prawns. He opens the wine, fills the glasses.

Troy has been leaning against the wall with crossed arms, his face neutral, deadpan. Ivan's first thought on looking up, knowing he has been watched, is: Does he think I am a ridiculous old fool? There is something embarrassing about the effort he has gone to, all this preparation and expense, to culminate in a cheap takeaway dinner. He blushes. The heat he feels is not just from the awkwardness; the boy is ravishing.

Ivan holds up a glass. 'To you, Troy.'

Troy smirks and lifts his glass. 'And to you.'

His own appetite is huge, he is scoffing the food, but he notices that Troy only picks at it. Ivan orders himself to slow down and is reminded that Perry always shows the same restraint his mother urged: *Slow down, you eat too fast, it's not good for you.*

The food is delicious. He scoops out more chicken and sauce, piles it over a mound of rice. The spices are hot; there is the tart and sweet tang of lime. He swallows mouthful after mouthful.

Troy is watching him.

Ivan sets down his fork. 'You're not hungry? You don't like it?'

The youth shakes his head. 'It's good food.'

'Then eat.'

Troy's grin is as charming and unguarded as one of Natasha's smiles.

For the first time Ivan fully acknowledges what the evening augurs. He will never see this beautiful man again. His appetite is gone and he pushes his plate away.

Troy's fingers close over a prawn tail, and he brings it to his mouth, crunches the whole of it, wipes his hand over lips and chin.

'I don't want to eat too much because I want you to fuck me. Hard.'

Amazed by the audacity of the request, that further upending of rules, Ivan takes a long moment to allow the implications of Troy's words to sink in. So full is the pause that Ivan can even formulate the question to himself: What does his not eating have to do with my fucking him? Then, a dawning that is also a humiliation. He doesn't want to shit himself. He both deplores and envies the boy's pragmatism. He's too old. His repugnance feels integral to him. He looks down at his wineglass.

'Eat up. I'm not gonna fuck you.' He can't help it, and he can't hope for a younger generation's nonchalance with the mechanics of sex. He's reminded of the earliest schoolyard taunts. Dirty filthy poo-jabber. Would Troy even know that term? Ivan has known heterosexual union and comprehends that the body's fluids and emissions are strange and uncontrollable in every encounter. Yet, deep inside of him, he carries the sense of homosexual union as being unnatural, against a pleasing order. He does not experience this in kissing his lover, in sucking the cock of a man he desires. Even inhaling the perfume, the musky reek of an arsehole does not repel him: his tongue reaching deep into a man's cunt is one of his greatest pleasures. But no matter the depth of the pleasure he has felt while fucking another man, when he looks down and sees the stain of shit on his cock, the foulness seeping from his partner's anus, he is appalled. At those moments a precise understanding overwhelms him: this is unholy, this is unnatural.

And so, he says it: 'Eat up, I'm not gonna fuck you.'

Troy's eyes flash. Ivan wonders: Is he furious?

The youth spits out the words. 'Okay, boss. You're paying.' He brings a heaped spoon of chicken to his mouth, gobbles it so fast that the oily sauce drips down his chin, splatters across his T-shirt. Indifferently, he wipes at his front. He swallows some more food, then burps. 'It's fucken good, innit?'

Ivan's first impulse is to grab the boy as if he were a dog, by the scruff of his fucking neck, slam his head against the wall, pull down his pants and fuck him. Hard, without tenderness, let the cunt shit himself as Ivan bores into him. The desire is so sudden, its vehemence so thrilling, that he knows it has made him hard. He knows it would be possible. He *is* the boss, *he* is paying, only *his* word holds power: he can do whatever he wants to Troy. Ivan looks straight into the youth, who cannot hold the older man's fierce and unforgiving stare. It is this meek surrender that reminds him of both Katarina and Natasha, of how a child, after a long tantrum, after weeping and screaming with a fury that seems unending and a stubborn resistance that appears unflagging, will suddenly hunch her shoulders and submit. He is glad to feel sudden compassion. He smiles at Troy. 'I'm sorry.'

Troy glances up, and now he is beaming. 'S'right,' he says.

They finish their dinner, quickly now, in the peace of Ivan's apology. Ivan is the one now grazing as Troy demolishes the remaining curries, spooning up the last vestiges of the food. Ivan finds something appealing, something sensual and heated, in such an unashamed appetite.

He pours another round of wine.

'I'm getting drunk.'

'Is it a problem? Do you have an early start tomorrow?'

Troy shrugs, pats his expanded belly. 'I probably need to be at the gym all day tomorrow.'

Ivan points to the fridge. 'I got us dessert too.'

Troy brings back his head, releases a tremendous bellow of laughter.

Ivan is delighted by its unrestrained joy. He raises his glass once more. 'You are fucking beautiful, mate.'

It's not that Troy's laughter ceases abruptly, nor that its waning is conspicuous. Yet Ivan is conscious of an emerging solemnity in that moment.

The boy says, serious now, 'You spoil me.' And as he does so, his hand reaches across the table and squeezes Ivan's.

Ivan is truly awed. Are they friends? he asks himself.

He sips the wine, the satisfying oaky fullness of it, and it indeed gives him courage. 'I wish we could be friends, Troy.'

'Can't we?' There is a pleading in his question that accentuates Troy's youth.

Ivan shakes his head.

''Cause I'm a whore?'

Ivan is appalled. At the meanness of the self-description, and at himself for not considering the misapprehension his words could cause. 'What? No.' He shakes his head emphatically. 'No. Perry and I love each other. And we've made a promise that from now on we will love *only* each other.'

Troy's eyes do not waver; they stare right at him.

'We're old men, mate, and we've both been around the block a few times now. Monogamy is hard.'

And this time it is Troy who is insistent: 'Monogamy is impossible.'

'Maybe it is for men. But you're young, you do lose that . . .' He stops, tries to think of what it is that is lost with age. He searches, stumbles on the precise answer. 'You lose that drive, it lessens. That does happen.' He takes a sip of his wine; there is a gnawing for a cigarette. 'I couldn't promise full monogamy, though I will try.' And at this he smiles wanly at the youth. 'Though I guess I'm not really trying tonight.'

They both chuckle dryly.

'We made a vow. If we do get that bloody itch, it will have to be satisfied with strangers, people we don't know.' He clears his throat, and he knows he is blushing, his cheeks are on fire again. 'You know, anonymous sex.' Having confessed, he allows himself a long exhale. 'That's why you and I can't be friends.'

'We don't have to have sex.'

He appreciates that gentle hope. Ivan takes a long look at Troy. The depth of those intense blue eyes, the gleam in them. The lean symmetry of the face. The large hands, with those fine, long fingers. The black down on those powerful arms.

'I'm not strong enough, Troy. I wouldn't be able to keep my hands off you.'

Troy leaps up, agile. 'I need a smoke.' He looks down at Ivan, his expression sneering. 'So, if we bump into each other in the street, if you're with this Perry, we don't know each other?'

'No, son. I would never lie about knowing you.'

Troy grips his glass so firmly that the wine swirls and splashes. 'Don't ever call me that. I'm not your fucking son.'

Ivan sits in silence, trying to make sense of the rage, appreciating its righteousness. The glass sliding doors have been flung open and tobacco smoke wafts through the apartment. He goes out onto the patio. He grabs a cigarette, goes and stands beside Troy at the balustrade. 'Can I have a light?'

The night has cooled, and Ivan shivers. His skin prickles. It seems like Troy will ignore his request, but then he takes his lighter from his back pocket, lights the older man's cigarette.

Ivan hesitates; then he lifts his hand, places it warily on Troy's shoulder. 'Are you warm enough?'

The convulsion is so furious, the heaving of the boy's body so unexpected, that for a terrible moment Ivan can't move. The thought that races through his mind is numbing: Is he going to throw himself off the balcony? Then, thankfully, there is swift comprehension. Ivan lunges at the youth, grabbing him around his middle and dragging him away from the balustrade. Troy's body has quietened to a few shudders, but Ivan doesn't relinquish his tight hold. And he is right not to. There is one more violent pitching, the neck and spine at such abrupt perpendicular angles that Ivan wonders how a bone doesn't snap. Then there is a quiver and the body slackens, a dead weight in Ivan's arms. He slowly lowers himself into a kneel, cursing his aching hips, and gently lays the boy on the cold stone. He settles Troy's head onto his lap and wipes the spittle and foam from the young man's lips. Troy's eyes are wide open, the pupils rolled back; the blank whiteness makes Ivan nauseated. He suppresses a retch. Then there is a tiny flicker, the rapid back and forth of the boy's left wrist. Troy blinks, looks up. He has returned to their world. Ivan will not relinquish his grip.

Troy's left hand is still flicking, an insistent tattoo at his jeans.

Ivan searches the pocket, finds a tiny plastic case made to hold earphones. One arm still holding onto Troy, he clicks open the container. There are two white pills.

Troy grunts.

'What was that, mate?'

A gurgling, a desperate urging.

'Give it to me!' The voice sounds as if it is coming through deep waters.

Ivan puts the tablet to Troy's mouth. The boy starts grinding it with his teeth, and then swallows.

The sound of a siren from somewhere in the city. Ivan can hear his own heavy breathing, the shallow struggles of Troy's breath. The siren fades, disappears.

Troy turns his head. His smile is rueful, abashed. 'Sorry, Ivan. I think I shat myself.'

And pissed himself. Within moments Troy has come back, his strength returned, his speech no longer strained and slurred. Ivan finds stunning that sudden shift from epileptic oblivion to sober reality; there is something superhuman in the speed of that recovery. He carefully guides the boy into the bathroom to shower, strips him, placing the stained pants and jocks onto a towel, painstakingly ensuring he stays clean. He is thankful to have noticed a small washing machine and dryer in a narrow cupboard in the kitchen, and even more grateful that the shower had two types of head. He keeps hold of Troy, propping him against the tiles, and uses the hand-held nozzle to wash away the shit that has run down the back of the young man's thighs, then gently manoeuvres him into a corner as he increases the water pressure to flush the putrid mess down the drain. Troy has watched him throughout, not saying a word. Ivan lowers the pressure and leaves the boy to shower himself. He gingerly picks up the trackpants, removes the earbud case and a wallet from the front pockets, a comb from the back pocket. He throws the soiled clothing into the machine with the towel. It is only when he has turned the dial to wash and heard the rumble of the machine, the gush of water through the pipes, that Ivan shudders. That terrifying moment he thought Troy was going to leap into nothingness.

Needing a smoke, he goes outside and finds two cigarettes on the concrete, burnt to their butts, the length of each now a long noodle of grey ash. He fetches a dustpan from the kitchen and goes back outside to sweep up the mess. He takes a pot from the kitchen, fills it with water, and douses the cement until every trace of ash is gone. Now he can breathe properly.

'Thank you.'

Troy is standing shivering in the doorway, his arms wrapped tightly around his body, naked except for the thin white towel tucked around his waist. Ivan rises, pressing the fingers of his right hand hard on his gently throbbing neck—a reflex conditioned from years of manual labour. His only thought is that the boy will catch a cold.

He ushers Troy through the large living area, into the narrow corridor that leads to the main bedroom. He switches on the light.

'Get into bed. It's chilly out.'

Troy nods obediently. He releases the knot of the towel and, now fully naked, falls onto the bed. The bedclothes are all a pristine white, so it seems that Troy is floating on a cloud. The young man doesn't bother to cover himself. He sprawls across the sheets, his hands behind his head, his left leg stretched out, his right bent at the knee. The whiteness of the bed covers accentuates the dark hue of Troy's skin, the thatches of raven-black hair in each exposed armpit and on his chest, across his taut belly, the shocking lushness of the hair crowning his cock and his balls, the coils still wet from the shower.

His voice gruffer than he means it to be—for again he is enraptured by the young man's splendour as well as taken aback by Troy's insouciance—Ivan orders: 'Turn on the light.'

Troy leans over, searches for the button to the bed-lamp, and as he finds it and clicks on it, Ivan switches off the main lights, throwing most of the room into darkness. Troy's face is half in shadow. He beckons Ivan over.

'Come lie with me,' he says, moving to one side. Ivan lies next to him, carefully dangling his feet over the edge of the mattress so as not to dirty the bedclothes with his shoes.

'Hold me.' Troy's voice is insistent.

Ivan slides his arm under Troy's head, and as soon as he has done so, the other man turns, curls into him. Ivan shivers.

Troy's breath is on his neck. 'Tell me about this guy.'

'What guy?'

'This guy you're in love with.'

'His name is Perry,' Ivan says. 'It's Pericles, but he calls himself Perry.'

'I like the name Pericles. It's better than Perry.'

'I like it too. Pericles was a Greek god.'

There's a rustle beside Ivan as Troy shakes his head. 'Nah, Pericles wasn't a god. He was like the . . .' He searches for the word. 'Like the leader of ancient Athens. He was a mortal.'

Ivan chuckles. 'You know your history.'

'I like history. Always have. When I was a kid, my dad used to read to me from a book about ancient Greece. He said Greece was one of the few places in the world that could compare to India when it came to history and to culture.' Troy sniffs, and a bitterness creeps into his voice. 'He was a snob when it came to culture. Thought all Aussies were barbarians.'

Ivan can hear the mocking insults of his own father: *Uncultured thugs. Australians are dogs.*

'All migrants think that,' he responds quietly.

'He wasn't a migrant.'

A child of migrants, in the in-between, like me. Ivan doesn't speak these thoughts. He doesn't think Troy will understand and he isn't sure he can explain them.

Troy has curled deeper into Ivan, putting his arm around him.

'Mum wanted to call me Ganesh.' The giggle is warm against Ivan's chest. 'Dad wouldn't have it, insisted on Troy, 'cause of his love of ancient history. Saved me from spending my life being called Gav, I guess. Or Elephant Boy. The old cunt was good for something.'

Ivan is shocked at the casual force of Troy's bile. The boy has spoken about his mother before, and he knows that Troy loves her. This is the first time he has referred so openly to his father.

He asks casually, 'So Troy's your real name?'

It is a mistake. The boy rolls away from Ivan to the other edge of the bed.

'Yes,' he answers, something in the tone conveying distance even more acutely than the physical separation. 'Troy is my real name.'

Ivan, shamed, turns on his side, looks at Troy's naked back. The maple-hued skin is unblemished. There is a small dot, a dark freckle, just below the sharp jutting of a shoulder blade. Apart from that the skin is smooth, hairless, until the base of the spine where a few tufts of black hair begin, thickening as they spread across the boy's arse, culminating in the dense bush in the cleft between the buttocks. Ivan determinedly holds his breath, his cock straining against the fabric of his jeans. He is aroused by Troy's hirsuteness, his forthright masculinity. Equally, he is stirred by the flawless skin. An image stirs for him. Perry's skin is paler, the hair more sparse. Spots mark Perry's shoulders, and there are unbecoming patches of hair sprouting from both shoulders, at the base of his spine. Unflattering they may be, but Ivan finds them beautiful. They indicate age and experience. Troy is so young.

He doesn't reach out, doesn't touch the boy. Instead, he whispers, 'I'm sorry.'

He exhales. The only sound is their breathing. The large window of the bedroom is locked. Ivan sniffs, suddenly aware that he is hot, that he has been sweating. His shirt is damp. He stifles a groan as he rolls off the bed; to make the sound of an old man would be too humiliating. He releases the latch, slides back the large pane of glass. The muted rumble of the city invades the room.

Troy is sitting up, smiling now, his arms folded across his bent knees, his cock flopping between his legs. That nonchalance: Ivan would find it impossible.

'Apology accepted.'

Ivan nods, turns back to the vista of the nocturnal city, the geometric patterns of towers, the tiny squares of neon light shining out of thousands of apartments and offices. The breeze is soft, caressing.

'And thanks for being so good back then about my fitting. You didn't seem scared at all.'

That isn't true.

'My mate Stu is epileptic,' is all he says. He returns to the bed and sits down. 'I've been there when he's had a seizure.'

'That explains it. You didn't panic.' Troy rests his head on his folded arms. 'It happened once before when I was with a client. I came to and I was alone in the motel room. He must have been terrified. Just left me there.' Troy raises his head. 'What a prick.'

Ivan turns to face him. 'How's the deposit on your mum's house going?'

Troy's grin is mischievous. 'You sure I wasn't lying about that?'

Ivan grunts in contrition. Though the truth is that he has always doubted it. He has doubted the truth of Troy's name, doubted the stories the youth has told him.

'I've saved up a good amount. She and I have started looking.'

'Where?'

'Werribee. Laverton. She likes Point Cook, but the prices there are bloody crazy. She needs to be near a train station. And not far from Geelong. Her sister lives there.'

'And you?'

'I might move in with her when we get a place. Not for too long.' Troy laughs aloud at the thought. 'She can't stop fussing, treats me like I'm thirteen.' Troy stretches back, leans against the bedhead. 'She wants me to get married. To a nice tradie. She says I need the security.'

He yawns, raises his arms straight, puts them behind his head and slides further down the bed. 'But I love her. And I won't need to worry about rent and shit for a couple of years before I can afford my own place.' He looks across at Ivan. 'That's the plan, anyway.'

In the ensuing silence, Troy leans over, drags the white sheet across his lower body.

'Are you cold? You want me to close the window?'

'Nah. All good. I like the breeze.'

Ivan has been sitting askew, not quite lying down. The soreness in his neck now twinges. He undoes the laces to his shoes, takes them off, carefully stuffing his socks deep into each shoe. A fresh memory is rekindled.

'Why are you laughing?'

With a contented sigh, Ivan flops down on the bed. 'The other night, I was at Perry's place and getting undressed and he was looking at me. I was doing what I did just now, taking off my bloody socks, rolling them into a ball and stuffing them in my shoe. And he said—'

Troy interrupts immediately: 'What the fuck are you doing?'

'Yeah, exactly.'

'I get why you're doing it tonight. I'm assuming you didn't bring a change of socks for the morning?'

Ivan turns, his smile radiant. 'No. I did. I did bring a change of socks. And jocks. I'm always prepared.'

'So why put the socks in your shoes? Why not chuck them in the corner, or put them in a bag?'

'I have always done it like that. Since I was a small boy. We'd only change our socks three or so times a week, not every day. My father was very strict about it.' Ivan deepens his voice, deliberately exaggerates his father's brooding accent. '*I learn this in army. Fucking Australia. No army. So weak men.*'

Ivan pats his bloated belly. Unbuckles his belt. 'I ate too much.'

'Does that mean I don't get to fuck you?'

Ivan flicks his hand across Troy's shoulder, lightly smacking him. 'Ha! You're a cheeky fucker.'

'How often do you change your socks these days?'

'Every day.'

'Thank fuck!'

'It was a different time, Troy. We didn't have a washing machine when I was little. Mum had to wash everything in this tub and then there was this wringer thing.' Ivan stretches his hands out as far as he can. 'It seemed enormous to me at the time but that was 'cause I was so small. And Mum would be sweating in the middle of summer, putting the clothes through this bloody contraption.' Ivan sits up in the bed, mimicking those actions. 'Raising two kids and working full-time at a factory. Thank fuck for washing machines.'

Troy is shaking his head in disbelief. 'How old *are* you?'

Ivan lies back down. 'Anyway, Perry, God bless him, asks me about it the other night. "Why do you roll your socks up, Ivan? Just put them in the laundry basket." And I explain like I did to you just now, how my dad taught me to do it from . . . from before I can remember. And Perry says, "Okay then, if you've been doing it for that long then keep on doing it. I can live with that."'

Ivan recalls the sweetness of the moment, of Perry leaning down, lifting his chin, kissing him softly on the lips.

'I like him.'

'What?' Troy's interjection erases the recollection.

'I get a sense of Perry from what you said just now. I think I like him.'

Ivan turns on his side. He concentrates on the slope of Troy's firm shoulders and arms, the lustre of his skin against the stark white of the sheets. The boy doesn't age. And he's about to say this to Troy, when suddenly he is struck by the sight of three fine lines at the corner of Troy's mouth. They further remind him that there is a hardening to the man, and not just physically. There is an aloofness in the eyes that he is sure wasn't there before.

Ivan hesitates. He has announced that this is their final time together. It had seemed decent, the appropriate thing to do when he planned the evening, had scouted the internet for the right apartment, the correct setting for this farewell. In announcing it, it all seems pompous. They are not lovers, and they are not friends. He should just keep his mouth shut.

Ivan dares it, goes by instinct, what he has learnt from being a father. 'Have you given more thought to what you're going to do after this?'

'After what?'

Ivan doesn't answer. He is confident that Troy understands the question.

With a sigh, the young man slides further under the sheet, turning so they are now facing each other.

'The money is good, mate. Real good.'

Ivan remains silent.

'You think I should give it up?'

The shrill rise of a siren. Ivan waits for the sound to fade before answering.

'You're still young, Troy. And you're gorgeous. I'm not surprised it's easy to make good money. But at some point, you're going to have to think of an alternative. You can't do this forever.'

That glint has returned to Troy's eyes. 'I know this guy, Lachlan, he's forty-seven. He's been doing sex work since he was nineteen. He's got a good life. Real nice place he owns in Elwood, a new car.' Troy crosses his arms. 'I'm clean, I'm not a druggie, I know what I'm doing. Mum and I looked at a place in Hoppers Crossing the other day, near the station. New place, solid, three bedrooms, two bathrooms. Mum loved it. I can put down twenty per cent of the asking price.' Troy unfolds his arms, raises his right hand, slaps it hard on the mattress. 'Twenty per cent. There! On the table. Now. I'm making money, I'm doing alright.'

How old is he? Ivan tries to recall when Troy had told him that he had turned twenty-three. Two years ago? Ivan was divorced and a father already by that age. And he remembers that in your twenties being forty-seven seems an impossible amount of time away. But somehow, the years rush past so fast it still astonishes him.

Ivan reaches out, touches the young man; his finger traces the line of Troy's bottom lip. 'Is this where you want to be at forty-seven?'

Troy's mouth twitches towards a smile. Ivan thinks the lad is about to kiss his wandering finger. But then Troy snarls, his blue eyes unyielding: 'You're not my fucking father.'

Ivan takes his hand away and turns onto his back. There is a ripple along one side of the ceiling where the paint has puckered, the air bubbles resembling a line of beads. There is a crack a centimetre or so deep in the corner left of the window. It needs to be seen to, Ivan thinks to himself; it's visible even in this dim lamplight. The construction is shoddy—the developers must have cut corners. It isn't that he is oblivious to Troy's rebuke or dismissive of that steely anger. He's been put in his place, and it is fair. He'd assumed an intimacy that wasn't there. The night had been a mistake. There was no need for a goodbye—they didn't mean anything to each other.

His neck throbs. He's not looking at the boy, because to look at him is to be reminded of how much he wants to kiss him hard on the mouth, to take in the reek of his sweat, to rub his face in the hair on Troy's chest, to suck his cock, to lick his balls, to put his tongue deep into his arse, to taste him.

He's right, he tells himself silently. I'm not his father. I'm here because I want to fuck him. I'm not fooling anyone.

'No.'

He turns at the boy's word.

Troy is still on his side, looking at Ivan. 'I don't want to be here at forty-seven. I don't want to be here at thirty.' This time his smile is sheepish, awkward. 'I've applied to do my real estate certificate. I reckon I'd be good at it.' He glances over at Ivan. 'I think I will be, anyway,' he adds uncertainly. He quickly averts his eyes.

And there, unexpectedly, that curious regret, occurring so rarely now, but more often when he was younger. It has been the longest time since he's experienced the sensation, yet here it is now. So intensely does it swell and fill his chest, his lungs, that he can't help it: he slides closer to Troy, lifts him so that the young man is lying in the crook formed by his embrace of him: the regret—not poisonous, for it has no essence of bitterness—is more of a wonderment: what would it be like if he were also a father to a son?

Ivan is overwhelmed. And grateful. 'Troy,' he whispers, so close to Troy that he speaks the words into the man's still-damp hair, 'I think that's a great idea.'

'I've liked going round with Mum, looking at houses, working out what's needed to fix them up right. Working out what makes a good location, a good position. I love doing that.'

Ivan is imagining Troy clean-shaven, in an elegant, conservative suit, white shirt and a black tie. 'I can see you doing that.'

There is a pause.

'Yeah,' Troy says decisively. 'I can see myself doing it too.' He swings to his side, away from Ivan. 'Hold me tighter.'

Ivan grabs him, folds his arms under and around him, embraces him. He smells the trace of soap on him. Ivan closes his eyes, kisses Troy's skin: one gentle kiss on his arm and one on his shoulder, then one final kiss on his neck. Almost as if he is offering a prayer, beseeching protection for himself and this young man. The number three as a talisman. The Trinity. He repeats his prayers, the kisses on the skin. And a memory blares, so radiant that Troy and the bedroom disappear and he is with Joe, early in their love. They had driven to Echuca one oppressively hot summer's day. They had parked near one of the muddy beaches along the river, had stripped naked and jumped into the icy brown water. They'd been swimming. They had swum and played and splashed each other, and there had been a moment when Ivan had dived down into the impenetrable water and had come back up, opening his eyes, to find Joe wide-eyed, frightened, frozen in terror. Ivan had followed the line of his gaze to see two tiger snakes swimming rapidly downriver, only a metre or so from where Ivan was treading water. One snake following the other. There had been an instant of cold panic as the snakes disappeared from view, and then his own fear had vanished. He had been struck by the magnificence of the gleaming, banded skin, their shimmering grace. And then he'd realised that Joe was still unmoving, terrified. He'd swum to his lover, held him, whispered to him to close his eyes and then had led him to the embankment, pushing him onto the bank to safety. It must have only been a few minutes, but in his memory it was an age, in which he had dried Joe with his own T-shirt, had sat him on the grass and held on to him. The tightest embrace he had ever given him.

He realises why the memory has returned with such intensity. He had kissed Joe three times then as well.

Ivan holds Troy, concentrating on the release of his own breath and on the way his lungs fill with each inhalation. His lips are still on Troy's skin, yet he concentrates on bringing Perry to mind, making Perry's shade and shape fill the room. Of the becoming twist at the edge of Perry's smile. The delicate slant of his eyes. The soft plumpness of his balls. The toughness. The power in his kiss.

He wakes. It is cold and dark. He is alone in the bed.

It's not complete darkness. The city's lights are like a wash of stars across the window. Ivan raises his head, rolls over to his side, gets up. A line of light shines under the closed door. He pushes it open.

Troy is sprawled along the sofa, naked. One hand is tugging at his erect cock, something about his unrushed motion seeming almost distracted. It is an intuition: he's bored, thinks Ivan; and then marvels at the energy of youth, to stay hard even in languor, even in disdain. Ivan stays by the doorway, looking on. Troy is wearing an earbud and the hand that holds his phone is extended out, the light from the screen illuminating his torso and groin as the young man moves the phone slowly across his body. Ivan coughs loudly.

Troy turns his head, still holding the phone. He indicates for Ivan to be quiet. There is not a hint of shame in the young man's grin.

There is the unbroken hum from the air conditioner. Feeling foolish in his T-shirt and underwear, Ivan keeps watching. Now Troy's tugging is faster, frantic. Then, with an abrupt expletive—'Fuck!'—he switches off the phone's beam.

'You can turn on the light,' he says lazily.

Ivan does and both men blink in the glare.

Troy places his phone on the coffee table. 'I'm going to upload that video.'

Ivan is confused, scratches his chin. 'Upload it to what?'

'I've got an Only Fans site,' Troy says with a shrug. 'I'm shit at refreshing it. Thought while you were sleeping I could make a video of me having a wank.' Distractedly his fingers touch his phone again. He glances at a message, pushes the phone away.

'I need a piss.'

Ivan rushes to the toilet and the relief is exhilarating.

He washes his face, rinses out his mouth.

When he returns to the lounge room, Troy is manically scrolling on his phone, still erect.

'Put on some fucking clothes!'

Why is he so angry? He is threatened by the unconcern of the young. That too-easy comfort with his body and with his desires.

Troy hasn't glanced up from the phone. 'I can't,' he says icily. 'They're in the dryer.'

Ivan stops himself from blurting out: *Then go and fucking get them and put them on!* It's not the boy's fault that he is old.

He sits down on the sofa next to Troy, who lunges for his hand and brings it to his cock. Troy giggles. 'Your hand is freezing.' He puts down his phone and reaches under the elastic of Ivan's jocks, begins to softly massage Ivan's balls and cock. He shifts closer to the older man, his lips against Ivan's ear, his tongue darting, licking the lobe. 'I love your cock, mate,' he whispers. 'I want you to fuck me.'

There is that metallic reek again on Troy's breath. And there is a fixed urgency in his unblinking eyes. He's taken more of that drug, Ivan realises. His energy is ferocious.

The boy whispers again, 'Will you fuck me?'

Ivan's cock stays flaccid. Troy pushes himself off the couch and gets onto the floor. On all fours, he arches his back. 'Fuck me!'

The moment will recur in the most unexpected moments. Ivan will recall his body stirring, the charge of lust flooding through him as he looks at Troy, following the line of his slender back, the fine hair at the base of his spine. When the memory is revived—whether in dreams or in fantasy—he will be startled by its brute power. He will be grateful every time that he has experienced the abandonment to pleasure, that he has submitted to desire. That image of Troy's nakedness will recede and merge and become one with him being sixteen, in the bedroom of that party in Strathmore, where he and Craig Harris and Jimmy O'Donnell and Tony Di Stanza are snorting speed, and then he and Jimmy are kissing and they know that the other boys are watching them and that makes them kiss more ardently. It is the first time he has felt the tongue of another boy in his mouth, and the fact that Craig and Tony are watching them only makes the exhilaration purer, more intense, and the drug is in every cell of his blood and every pore of skin and every fibre of hair on his body and soon he doesn't know whether it is Jimmy or Craig or Tony he is kissing; he is kissing them all. And the memory of the four boys kissing will bleed into the first time he experienced the warm melt of ecstasy, the Smashing Pumpkins' track 'Mayonaise' on the stereo, and Stu and his girlfriend Adriana sitting with him on the floor, one on either side, Stu stroking his hair and Adriana holding his hand, and her saying, 'Just ride the rush, Ivan,' and him feeling that first frightening wave ebbing to be replaced by the exquisite calmness of the high. That remembrance will glide, become entangled with the sensation of fucking a stranger for the first time, of the man he had sex with at midnight on the beach in Seaford, the two men jerking each other off, the man's moans rising to shrill shallow screams as Ivan pumps his cock, as the man climaxes, as Ivan himself climaxes, shuddering and laughing at the man's savage gulping yells, whispering to him, 'You okay, mate? Not so loud,' and the man's eyes looking straight into his and Ivan realising only then, for they had not said a word to each other, that the man was deaf. This night, too, will blur into the united memory. It will be making love to Joe. It will be making love to Perry. It will be every cock he has sucked and every mouth he has kissed. And he will be grateful to his God that he has known each and every one of these thrills.

And every time, in bringing his mind back to this precise moment, in the apartment at the very edge of the city, the naked boy in front of him, the desire to fuck him, to submit once more to intoxication, he will also recall his acquiescence to age. He looks down at his own body and notices that liver spots are now freckling the tops of his hands. He is aware of the fustiness of his scent, that blend of sleep and sweat. He recognises that, if he wanted to, he could muster the will that would lead his body to enact the frenzies of sex. Yet his neck is tight, there is that dull pain in his shoulder, and he is tired. It is only seconds that pass between Troy's command and Ivan's decision, and so impossible in such a brief slice of time for him to comprehend how his past and his future touched in this resolution. All he knows is that there is no humiliation in what he is experiencing; it is galvanising. He does not regret his life and he feels the peace of attaining a mellowness which makes it easier to resist the commands of the body. With that aware-ness, only dimly conscious of how fortunate he has been, his fingers press against his crucifix.

None of this can make any kind of sense to the boy. When he is ready to express it, it will be to Perry, who is of an age and an experience to understand it and possibly to have shared it.

He gently slaps Troy's buttock. 'I'm real sleepy, mate. We're not going to do that tonight.'

Troy drops back on the sofa. His hands drop across his crotch, as if suddenly aware of his nudity. One foot keeps tapping ceaselessly against the wooden floor. 'I don't think I can sleep.' Troy grabs his phone, checks the time. 'It's only gone midnight.' He turns to Ivan, his smile self-conscious. 'Do you want me to go?'

They are not lovers, and they are not friends.

'I think you're too wired for sleep.'

'Probably.' And with that, Troy leaps to his feet. 'I should get my clothes.'

Ivan is stacking the used plates and cutlery in the dishwasher when he hears his name being called. Troy is standing in front of the bathroom mirror, his mouth stretched wide, examining his teeth.

He smiles at Ivan in the mirror. 'Can you get my backpack?'

Ivan returns with it and leans against the bathroom door, watching as Troy gets ready. The young man unzips the backpack and pulls out a small toiletries bag. He quickly flosses, spits into the sink, and then wets the corner of a small cloth, wipes his face with it, and then the back of his ears and his neck. Troy sniffs at his shirt's pits, wrinkles his nose, and then lowers the T-shirt's sleeves to wipe at the moist hairs there. Finally, he squeezes some gel into his palm, rubs it vigorously over his hair, and then takes a comb and diligently brushes it in firm long sweeps.

He catches Ivan's eye in the mirror. 'You have to comb it following the natural groove of your hairline. Then you can style it however you want it. Too many people brush against the natural flow of their hair line and that's a disaster.' He winks at Ivan. 'Not that you have to worry about any of that.'

That's right. He remembers that Troy had told him that his mother is a hairdresser. Was that their second or their third time together?

Troy throws the damp washcloth into the basin. He steps back from the mirror and scrutinises the reflection.

'You look very handsome.'

Troy, clearly pleased, kisses Ivan briefly on the lips as he squeezes past him. The older man follows him into the living room, where Troy puts the toiletries bag back into his rucksack. He scrolls through his phone, from time to time using the thumbs and fingers of both hands to message, with a dexterity that seems astonishing to Ivan. Then Troy slides his finger into the card slot on the sleeve of the phone protector. He pulls out a small plastic baggie that holds three capsules, opens it, and sticks one of the tablets in his mouth. He motions for water. Ivan fills a glass at the sink, brings it over.

'Take one.' Troy wipes his mouth. 'It's good MDMA. It'll make you horny.' He is holding his phone to his side. 'I'm happy to stay. You've paid for it.'

And for a moment he is tempted. The perfection, the youthful, arrogant beauty of Troy's face, the slim and powerful body. The illicit rush from a pill that will flout the boundaries of night. He shakes his head. And he catches the intake of breath from Troy. They are both relieved.

'Right,' says Troy, returning to scrolling through his screen. 'I'll order an Uber.' He taps at his phone, then turns it to Ivan. 'What do you reckon? This one?'

The phone's screen is filled with a photograph of a large penis, the glans peeking under the foreskin startlingly pink against the dark ebony sheen of the shaft. What is visible of the pubis has been shaved.

Troy flicks the screen. 'Or this one?'

A smiling young man, the hair on his scraggly beard near orange, a light fuzz on his chest and his belly darkening to an almost ochre hue in the thatch above his cock and around his balls.

'Or maybe this one?'

He must be even older than Ivan. The photograph is heavily pixelated, and the old man's face is cut off just above the nose, so that his eyes are not visible. His skin is ruddy around the jowls, but also the naked chest, the flabby teats, the hard round belly sprinkled with silver. The photograph is shot from below, so that it accentuates both that enormous stomach but also the oversized scrotum bulging out of rugby shorts.

Not him, he wants to answer, *not the old bastard, definitely not him.*

Troy's smile is impassive, waiting for Ivan's answer.

And Ivan, understanding that it is the spark of jealousy that is causing his violent objection, a roaring spite that has settled in his chest, marvels at the possibilities available to a young man like Troy, that he can so blithely flick through his phone and find someone to fulfil myriad fantasies. The world in your pocket.

He's aware of Troy's odours, and not just the chemicals. The strong fragrance of his sweat is like clay soil after rain, dizzying in its intensity. That petrichor smell which is quarantined from the digital world. Emotion floods him; relief that he doesn't live in that world.

'I like the red-haired guy,' Ivan answers wryly. 'I'm always going to trust a face.'

'Uber's five minutes away.'

The final goodbye is rushed, haphazard, their embrace clumsy. Troy seemed resistant initially, then relaxed into the older man's arms.

'Thank you,' Ivan whispers.

And then, with a small wave, Troy is gone.

The weight of the silence overwhelms him, and a heaviness bears down on Ivan.

The three men that Troy is choosing between to fuck that night. Eugénio is a young man from São Paulo who has been living in Australia for the past five years. He had only been in the country a year when the Covid pandemic began, and though he was frustrated and sometimes enraged by Australians' obsession with safety, their ridiculous puritan fear, he had been grateful to escape the scourge of the virus in his home country. Australia made him feel as if he were floating, that life here was lying on a still, clear body of water, whereas in Brazil it was a constant struggle against tempestuous and savage swells, and it felt impossible to touch the ground. He desperately misses the excitement of his birthplace. Australian men, whatever their colour, their heritage, they all seem cold to him.

The red-haired man, Shannon, is a student in his final year at La Trobe University. He is originally from the country, the far east of the state, and though university and city life have been bracing, he has never quite lost the earnest fair-mindedness with which he was raised. He is puzzled by cruelty; his heart has twice been broken because he trusted men who felt no remorse about lying to him. His guilelessness, however, is also sometimes a form of defiant strength. He shows his face on the hook-up apps as a matter of principle.

The old man is Angelo, an immigrant from Italy. He arrived in Melbourne as a fifteen-year-old, and there is still the faint burr of Abruzzo in his accent, whether he's speaking English or Italian. He was married for twenty-five years and has three children. Only the middle child, his daughter Carmela, still speaks to him. His wife divorced him when a scandal emerged: he had been having sex with an apprentice, a youth called Adrian, at the auto shop his family owned. His son and his youngest child, another daughter, still refuse to acknowledge him, even though it has been decades since the divorce. For Angelo, life is lonely.

Troy, of course, has already made his choice. He presses his face against the window. The traffic is light, and the Uber is gliding along the southern banks of the Yarra. The seamless propulsive motion revitalises the drugs whipping through his body. He can feel it beginning deep in his belly. He exhales and now the balm seeps through his body. His nipples harden, his skin flushes, and he closes his eyes, cooling his brow against the pane. And then, with a jolt, he sits upright. The driver glances at him in the rear-view mirror, then quickly looks away. In that sudden jolt, he realises that the work is over: he doesn't have to be Troy anymore. He can be himself; he can be Aaron. That feeling is always an unshackling. Not that Ivan isn't a good client. It's a pity he's not going to see him anymore. Then again, who knows? Aaron thinks, smiling to himself. Old queens fall in and out of love all the time—he's seen enough of that. Though he's alright, is Ivan; he's a good man. But Aaron is clear-headed enough to know that his fantasies of older men are purely sexual, that the reality of such a relationship would be drab and constricting. He chuckles to himself again. Poor Ivan, wanting a special night, paying for him till morning and then passing out asleep before midnight. He is conscious of the bulk of his wallet. He checks his phone, locates a Westpac branch close to his destination, and quickly adds the address to his ride. He'll stop, bank the money, then head off to the hook-up. He's too high; he doesn't want to worry about carrying all that cash on him.

The driver half-turns, asks curtly, 'We making a stop?'

Aaron nods and sinks back into his seat. He is thinking of the sex he is going to have, of the drugs peaking in his body, of the beauty of the night and how full of adventure it feels. It is impossible, preposterous, to think of sleep.

Ivan stands looking at the door that Troy shut behind him for two, nearly three minutes. He is conscious of his breath, of the electrically charged humming of the urban night. At first, he is not cognisant of thoughts; there is only the awareness of sounds, those external and internal: the blood that moves through his veins, the air that fills and empties from his lungs. Then he moves, walks out to the patio. He lights a cigarette.

The night is darker now. He glances at his phone. It is only just past midnight. He'd like to call Perry, see if he is home. He'd like to go over, crawl into bed beside him, wrap his lover in his arms. But he cannot do that. He is conscious not only of Troy's scents on his body but something mystical, a sensual emanation of their encounter. It is, of course, absurd, nonsensical, but he fears that Perry will sense his infidelity on his very skin, through his breath, from his kiss.

The apartment has been paid for. Should he stay the night?

Ivan sucks hard on the cigarette. He shouldn't have one at this late hour. Yet he needs the meditative lulling that the addiction brings him. He is flooded with that warm sensation of relief. His body feels relaxed, unburdened. He has said farewell to Troy. He has been needing to do that for months now.

A dissenting voice in his head: You still have his number; you can call him anytime.

He shakes his head. He will never call Troy again. He is certain of it. The boy saved him, allowed him to experience joy when he had believed himself exiled from happiness. Joe's betrayal had annihilated him. Ivan smiles as he remembers that first nervous call, the tremor in his voice. Troy's touch had been tender, and he had been so grateful.

Yet there is something demeaning about paying for sex. He can't know if it is only old prejudices or if it is intrinsic to the transaction. He will never be able to abandon the fear that Troy could never respect him. Even the moments tonight in which the young man stepped outside the boundaries set by their transaction, when Troy's desire for him, for Ivan's strength and humanity, had seemed genuine and unforced, the kernel of doubt remained. He is grateful to the young man. He will never see him again.

Ivan is tired but he doesn't go to bed yet. The mechanical purring sounds of the city continue. At the furthest end of the pitch-black of the bay, there is a gliding light, the beacon from a cargo ship. His right hand grips the handrail and there is a sharp twinge at his tricep. He massages his arm, wondering where the pain has come from. Then he recalls Troy's spasming body, how he took the boy in his arms, how that had felt as if he were taking the seizure into his own body. And then there had been that abrupt cessation of motion as the youth's body lay supine. In that moment he had felt joy, and a benign power in his satisfying sense of capability. The recollection brings forth further memories, of how Kat as a young girl would fall asleep in his lap, trusting him. He had adored those moments, those sublime gifts of parenthood. If only he had met Troy in another scenario; if the young man had been his apprentice, perhaps. How he would have liked to teach him the pleasures of his work, explaining how to read the marks and colours and shadings of leaves, the hues and grains, the textures of earth and soil. It would have been an immense pleasure.

It is one o'clock now, and he works steadily, scrubbing down the kitchen sink, cleaning the toilet and the bathroom basin, stripping the bed and folding the sheets and pillowcases into a neat pile on the mattress. He collects the cigarette butts in a piece of paper, twists it closed and puts it in his coat pocket to dispose of at home. He finishes by removing the lint from the dryer. It's taken less than half an hour. He has laboured swiftly, methodically, and he wipes the beads of sweat from his upper lip. He checks that he has his bag, has packed away all his toiletries, that he has his keys, his phone. He shuts the door.

He drives home with the window open. There is a refreshingly cool breeze, and Coltrane's 'A Love Supreme' is playing. He can finally hear the generosity and warmth in the music. The temptation to drive to Perry's place is so strong it is almost an ache. But he won't give in to it. He is conscious of his deceit, his sin. Tomorrow is Sunday and he'll wake early, drive to the Orthodox church in Carrum Downs, light a candle for his daughter and his granddaughter and for the man he loves. He will say his prayers and make his atonement. He will also light a candle for Troy. Then he can head straight to Perry's flat, walk through the door, embrace his lover and kiss him. There is the breeze coming through the open window and the thought of that kiss. All he longs for is that kiss.

5

Léna wakes to the ringing of the bells. Their apartment is six floors up, on the top level of an apartment block in the Ampelokipoi neighbourhood. The church of Agios Vasilios is across the street, and its whitewashed dome dominates the view from their balcony. She has no issue with the hourly peal; it is part of the music of the city. Nevertheless, she always detects a militancy in the clanging of the Orthodox bells. This must be her imagination; the church bells of the Catholic churches in Rouen would have been made of the same material. But here in Athens the bellicose ringing suggests a ferocious and unappeasable god.

She counts the chimes. Seven o'clock.

One lone beam of the morning sun finds a crack in the thick curtains. It illuminates a section of the bare wooden floor, Vera's boots that she kicked off last night when going to bed. Léna watches the dust motes slowly surf in the channel of the illumination. Vera is folded into her, snoring softly. She smells of night. It is the last week of September, and the weather is blessedly clement, though the air still holds the warm caress of the end of an Athenian summer. During the night one of them has thrown off the light blanket and they have slept the night under the cover of a single sheet. Carefully she brings her lips to the top of Vera's head. They were late getting home, and it is Saturday morning, and she wants her lover to sleep in. She gently extricates herself from the embrace. Vera stirs, mutters inaudibly, turns over, and remains asleep.

Léna finds her skirt, her singlet and her phone. She quietly closes the bedroom door and goes to the kitchen to flick the switch on the water boiler. She grabs a fig from the bowl, eats it whole as she looks at her messages. *À dix heures? À café Ολγα, Υυρή. Á bientot, Périclès.* She smiles at the mixture of alphabets. She pulls on her skirt, types in reply: *Oui. À dix heures.* She pulls the top of the skirt around so it sits comfortably. She hesitates. Then adds an *x* to her message.

She does like Périclès. But she finds his formality annoying. She deletes the *x*. And sends.

There's some leftover coffee in the percolator. She pours it into the *briki* and heats it up on the stovetop.

She sips at it, sitting on the balcony. The morning sun is gentle. There is a clear view up the rising hill, the jumble of squat grey and white concrete buildings extending as far as her eyes can see. Directly in view is the church dome, with the stark symmetrical iron cross at its peak, the metal mottled and striped by the elements. Athens' din, the honking of horns, the steady rumble of traffic, makes her feel alive. She loves this city, has loved it from the time her parents first brought her here on a visit when she was young, just before her first term at the *lycée*. She has never understood why so many of her friends say it is ugly. The labyrinth of narrow lanes and streets, the unending patchwork of cement apartment blocks; certainly there isn't the medieval or early modernist beauty of the cities of her homeland. Yet it never ceases to thrill her, when walking to the market or heading downtown, that she can turn her head and suddenly at the bottom of an alley there is a glimpse of the ancient marble Acropolis.

'You couldn't sleep?'

'Did I wake you?'

Vera asks her question in English, Léna answers in Greek. They have been a couple for nearly five years and it has become part of their shared communion, this slipping in and out, shifting between languages. Vera's French is barely adequate, and from their first date together they found it more comfortable to speak in English. Over the years, Léna's Greek has improved, and sometimes she wishes that Vera would speak to her solely in that language. Yet she is forgiving. She understands that her lover is proud to have mastered a second language.

'Do you want me to put a coffee on?'

'No, I want you to come to bed.'

This time Léna has spoken in English, and Vera replies in Greek.

Léna takes a last gulp of her coffee, puts the cup on the ground. She takes Vera's hand, is led back through the galley kitchen into their bedroom.

The two women lie side by side on the bed.

Vera is stroking Léna's face. 'You are so beautiful,' she says in French. The urgent words, the hoarseness of the Athenian accent, sends a shiver through Léna. In Greek, with equal fervour, she says, 'Kiss me.'

Léna loves Vera's taste. She savours the burnt yet sweet tang of garlic and lemon from last night's meal on her lover's lips and tongue, then the saltiness of Vera's skin. Her hand reaches under the elastic of Vera's cotton knickers, rubbing the rough sweep of hair. Vera escapes from the kiss, releases a low moan.

Léna demands again, 'Kiss me!' And then in English she adds, 'With your eyes open.'

Vera stares at Léna with wide, steadfast eyes. Her hand reaches up, grabs Léna, they fall back into a passionate kiss, their tongues entwining. Still locked in the euphoria of the kiss, Léna splays the warm folds of her lover, her thumb stroking upwards along the smooth inner lips, sensing the ridges and bumps. Her hand comes to rest over the knob of Vera's clitoris. She presses firmly and now her finger, her thumb, her palm, are wet. Léna pulls away, looking down on Vera, and then brings the moist fingers of her right hand to her own mouth, brushes the thumb against her lips, sucks on her finger, tasting Vera. The intoxication is a wave that rolls through her body. They resume the kiss. She can still taste the musky bitterness. Then she slides her lips down Vera's body as she pushes Vera's legs apart and slowly settles to lap and suck there. The wave of fecund odours is in her mouth and in her nostrils and in her lungs. She inhales, filling her senses with the rich perfumes. She is drunk on them. Her fingers, her tongue, push further and deeper.

She realises that Vera is silent. She looks up. Vera's head is off the pillow, her eyes are closed, she is kneading her own breasts, two fingers squeezing at one of her nipples.

Vera's eyes flash open, and she looks at Léna. In English, she commands, 'Don't stop!'

Léna resumes her eager lovemaking. However she has also returned to the world: there is the insistent pulse of noise from down in the street, a slow rumbling and an annoying beeping as a truck is reversing. There is a subtle thumping against the apartment's walls. Antigone from the apartment next door must have pressed for the lift. But her attention goes back to her lover. She knows Vera's body as well as her own. Her tongue and thumb continue their dance, one seamless wave of sucking and rubbing. Vera suddenly raises her knees; her hand has slipped down, is gently pushing against Léna's head. Vera is preparing for climax.

Léna drops a hand between her own legs. Her sucking and drinking from her lover does not abate. She begins roughly kneading her own clitoris.

She needs fantasy. She is still inebriated from Vera's musky odours. But Léna's eyes are closed. She is a teen, not yet fourteen, and she is making her way down to the beach at Nafplio. Her mother is preparing lunch at the limewashed stone villa they have rented on the steep rise overlooking the cove, and she has asked Léna to go and fetch her father. There is no Anton and there is no Marie; she has banished them from her imaginings. She sees as if she is a camera, as if her perception has become film. The cottage is almost blindingly white in the fierce rays of the Peloponnesian sun, so that the glare is a dagger to the eyes. She is walking steadily down the narrow path that meanders to the sea, dry yellow grass forming a low wall on either side created by the constant herding of goats and sheep. Her tongue and her mouth work on her lover, diligently arousing Vera to climax. Yet is imagination contorting reality? The fluids in her mouth taste and smell of brine. Her sucking—no, her devouring—of Vera is so forceful that the sucking has become biting. Vera flinches, raises her head. Léna is ready to apologise.

'No, don't stop.' The hoarse order is in Greek, and Vera's hand is at the back of her head, guiding her return.

Léna closes her eyes, and she returns to the film in her head. Her pace accelerates as she descends, the crash of the waves drowning out all other noise. As she reaches the base of the hill, she can just glimpse her father sitting on his towel, looking out to the water. His neck and shoulders have started to peel from sunburn. It is then she stops, and instinct tells her to drop to a crouch behind an oleander bush. It is the unnatural trembling of her father's shoulders that halts her. And that he is not alone on the beach.

Léna's finger reaches deeper into Vera. She controls herself, does not allow the exertions to be violent. She kisses her lover's fleshy thigh. She declares her adoration in French.

Between the shrubs, she sees that a young man is lying on his back a few metres from her father. His face is indistinct but she knows from his black hair, from the dark honey hue of his skin, that he is Greek. Dark hair abounds on his torso and limbs; there is an impossible denseness to that fur on his crotch. She finds the sight neither appalling nor arousing. The man is slowly masturbating. Léna comprehends that her father is not looking out to the sea. He is staring at the young man. And he too is masturbating. That comprehension is not alarming. She intuited that from his shuddering shoulders, and that is why she hid herself.

As her fingers massage further and deeper into Vera, Léna takes her other hand down to her own cunt, rubbing it forcefully up and down so that her fingers slide back and forth over her clitoris. The sensation is near ache, an exquisite tenderness.

Her father and the young man do not touch. She is sure that the Greek youth wants her father to go over; his hand is beckoning. But her father stays where he is, his jerking intensifying, becoming more frantic. Then his body slumps in release. Only then does he get to his feet. And Léna is sure—and it is the only part of the recollection that makes her angry with her father—that he avoids the youth's gaze as he walks purposefully into the waves. To clean himself. To make himself pure.

She can't remember anything else about the young man. He must have scrambled back into his bathers, walked away in his fury. All that is firm in her memory is the image of her father in the water, scouring his belly with his hands, as if wanting to rip away the flesh there.

But she is making love to Vera. She must not forget that. She grasps at the fantasy.

She never dares give shape or definition to her father's face. He is known to her only by the peeling skin on the burnt shoulders, by the balding circle on the crown of his fair hair, by the length and thinness of his legs as he rises from the towel and walks over to the young man. She imagines the shadow that is her father dropping to his knees before the stranger, and she witnesses them both lean into one another for their kiss.

Léna brings herself up Vera's body till her face is pressing against one of her lover's breasts, her tongue teasingly glancing the tip of the engorged nipple. Her fingers are massaging Vera's soaking mound, expert and fast, pushing repeatedly as her hand slides back and forth. She sucks Vera's breast, wishing she could put all of it into her mouth, and Vera is moaning, calling in Greek: 'Like that, that's right, like that.' Léna draws harder on the nipple and the abandonment to savagery arouses her: she experiences an electrifying sensation of lightness, as if there is no bone or cartilage in her body. Lost in that giddiness, her free hand squeezing her own clit, her mouth pulling on Vera's hard nipple, as her father and the young man are ferociously kissing. Léna feels her lover buckle, spasm, Vera's thighs clamp shut tight, her calls are now whispers, hushed—'Don't stop, my love, don't stop'—and Léna maintains the motion of her hand and fingers, but slower now. Vera convulses again. Léna rubs herself hard, fast, there is the delicious pricking as she strokes herself. But the film is over. The world floods back in.

She wipes her mouth with the sheet, moves up to embrace her lover. She feels Vera's hand cup her breast then slide down her belly towards her crotch. Gently Léna takes the hand and brings it to her lips.

'I love sex with you,' she says in English. And then in Greek, 'But I mustn't be late.' She kisses Vera, and springs out of bed.

After her shower, Léna shrewdly surveys her wardrobe. The weather has tempered, but the sky is without cloud and the apartment is already warm. She puts on a sleeveless black dress and scrutinises herself in the long mirror resting against the bedroom wall. The cut of the skirt is full and looks good on her, falling to a length neither provocative nor conservative. Should she wear *des collants*? She doesn't want to feel hot or restricted. The dress is absolutely right for the occasion. She decides a little discomfort is worth it. She grabs the sheerest, finest stockings from the drawer.

She examines herself again in the mirror and is satisfied. She likes how the fine paleness of the stockings gives an alabaster sheen to her legs. She will wear the low-heeled pumps with pointed toes. They will be perfect.

She is about to call her mother when Vera emerges from her shower, naked, drying her hair with the towel. Léna knows that her partner is not completely at ease with her own body. Now entering their forties, the weight is harder to shed, and in her darkest moods Vera rants against the invincibility of genetics. 'My mother, all my aunts are fat!' she decries. And she resents that she has flat feet, that it limits the shoes she can wear, the freedom to roam barefoot through the forests surrounding her ancestral village, across beaches and shores. Yet alone, by which Léna means when they are together and united in their apartment, such anxieties and distresses are abandoned. Vera is—and there is no other word for it, and it is absolutely right that the word is redolent with those Sapphic connotations— Amazonian. A spark ignites a rush of desire through Léna's body. The dense black bush of Vera's pubes, those long sturdy arms, and the magnificence of those heavy breasts and belly: her lover is magnificent.

Vera has disappeared into the bedroom. Léna dials and her mother answers immediately.

'Madeleine? How are you? Is everything fine?'

'Yes, Maman. It is a glorious morning in Athens.'

'Well, yes. This is always the best time of year there.'

The conversation continues cordially. Léna can hear the snip of the shears as her mother speaks, and the occasional squeal and call of birds. It must be fine weather in Normandy this early morning.

A clutch of homesickness assaults her. She can almost feel the crisp air of her home and see the icy dew spread across her mother's lawn. She goes to make another coffee, holding the phone between her shoulder and ear. Out on the balcony, the haze of blue sky, the stark brightness of the light are dazzling. She walks to the shade at the furthest end.

Her mother laughs. 'That infernal noise, all those horns and traffic,' she complains, but with an indulgent affection in her tone. 'That makes me feel like I am there with you.'

'You should come. We'd love you to come.'

'Not this year.'

'Are you sure?'

There is a pause. Has her mother sensed her relief?

'I am sure,' her mother answers with finality. 'You know how much your father and I loved our travels. But now I find myself content to be here in the garden, to visit my friends who live nearby. I am not missing the world at all.'

There is the sound of the coffee starting to percolate. And her mother's concerned tone, her voice raised, asking: 'Madeleine?'

She has drifted off. She knows where her thoughts have been, or at least what has caused her inattention. It is her mother's mention of her father. She knows why she rang, why she had to hear her mother's voice. It is to deflect her guilt at allowing herself the indulgence of fantasy during this morning's sex—and also because of what the day will contain.

'Pardon, Maman,' she says, returning inside. Léna turns off the espresso machine. 'The offer is there. Whenever you want to come, Vera and I will be very happy to see you.'

Her mother's laugh in reply is teasing. 'You are kinder than your brother. He frets all the time, has almost forbidden me from air travel.' The warmth slips from her mother's tone. 'He's right. I am an old crone now.'

Léna is not fooled by her jocularity. She knows her mother. She knows how she detests getting old.

'Anton worries about everything,' she says dryly. 'He always has.'

'True, true. Those children are so pampered. I have to force myself to adore them when all I want to be is a strict and mean grandmother.'

It is naughty—wicked, really—how much they both enjoy making fun of Anton and his family. Then guilt resurges. Her brother is stolid, narrow-minded, yet he is kind. It is a cold cruelty in their family that she was her father's favourite, and that her sister, Marie, is their mother's favourite. Léna shifts the conversation to work. Having had a classical linguist for a husband and an archaeologist for a daughter, her mother has over time imbibed a passion for ancient history. Léna tells her about the new exhibits coming to the museum.

Vera emerges from the bedroom, dressed in jeans and a floral peasant blouse, a dramatic pattern of red petals on white linen cloth. Léna watches her grab the cups, pour the coffee. She mouths, 'Sorry.'

'What are you apologising for?'

Inadvertently, she has whispered the English word. 'I was talking to Vera.'

'My darling,' her mother says, 'will you make a prayer today for me? When you are at Sounion? Please pray for your father's soul.'

First there is the relief that her mother has said the words, acknowledged that today Léna will be scattering her father's ashes off the point at Sounion, into the Aegean Sea that he loved. Then there comes the tempest of shame. Léna forces herself to be steel. She must not betray the churn of her own emotions.

And as if she knows it, as if indeed there is an insight that all mothers share, she says quickly, 'Kisses to you and to Vera, we'll speak soon.' Her mother's adieus are always abrupt.

'Maman gives you her love.'

Léna has taken a cushion from the sofa, places it on the plastic terrace chair before sitting alongside Vera, who is sprawled out on a matching chair, rolling a cigarette. Even with the comfort of the cushion Léna is not quite relaxed, perching rigidly on the edge of her seat. She looks down nervously at the almost invisible seam of her stockings.

'You look very beautiful.' Vera has spoken in French.

The heat has soared over the last hour. The stockings might be a mistake. She gets up, finds the attractive straw boater she bought in Les Halles years ago. It was an inspired, inexpensive buy. The colour has hardly faded, it has kept its shape. She gives a quick glance at her reflection in the tall glass cabinet by the fridge, returns to the terrace. And only then does Vera's compliment resonate.

She presses her hand lightly on Vera's shoulder and sits down beside her. 'I'm sorry, my love, I'm distracted this morning.' She has spoken in Greek; however, she uses the French word *distrait*.

Vera blows out a long plume of smoke, then grins. 'Of course. You've taken on an enormous responsibility.'

For a moment Léna is disconcerted, unsure if she has understood the word. Then translating it—ah, yes, she means *responsabilité*—she is struck by how, as often with the Greek, the word implies an active purpose rather than a mere emotion or condition. *Ευθύνη*. She is undertaking a charge, a mission. An obligation.

'Maman asked me to offer a prayer on her behalf when we scatter the ashes.'

Instinctively, Vera touches the Orthodox cross that always hangs on the thin gold chain around her neck. 'She isn't reconsidering, is she?'

Léna shakes her head. They had laid their father to rest two years ago. The ceremony, so concise, as if to strip the religious formalities to their most rudimentary, was the way her mother wanted to farewell her husband.

Is she wrong to have wrenched him from eternal peace in that cemetery on the slopes beneath Bihorel, those woodlands and pathways so close to home, which he so loved to stroll? Léna wishes she could feel the comfort of grace epitomised by the cross around Vera's neck. An ancient superstition still haunts her, and though she knows they have debated it again and again, she once more gives voice to her fear.

'Am I doing the right thing?'

Vera cocks an eyebrow in confusion. Then, realising, understanding her turmoil, she grabs Léna's hand. 'Yes. Your father was a man who lived and loved in conflict, between two worlds. Two worlds of equal standing for him. It makes perfect sense that part of him rests in France and part of him rests in the Greece he loved.'

Léna sweeps Vera into a passionate embrace. Fuck the seam of the stocking. Fuck keeping her dress uncreased. She kisses

Vera so fervently that her hat falls off onto the ledge of the balcony, almost sailing down to the street below. Vera saves it.

The sonorous clanging of the church bells pierces the day.

Eight o'clock. Is it possible that only an hour has passed? She releases herself from Vera's embrace but finds she can't let go of her hand. In fact, she grips it tighter. Today she feels that she is on the border of time and floating above the world. As if she is in the in-between. As if she needs an anchor.

'I'm going to go down and get us some bread, do some shopping at the market. Do you need anything?'

Léna shakes her head, and Vera kisses her lightly on the lips.

'I'll see you tonight. It will be evening before you return from Sounion.'

Léna is still clutching Vera's hand.

With tender care, Vera separates from her. 'My Léna,' she whispers, a hint of hushed prayer in the words. 'Your mother understands that this isn't a matter of choosing between herself and your father. She has granted permission. You have her blessing.'

Léna remains sitting there after Vera leaves. The street sounds bleed in, as does the impatient cooing of the pigeons perched on the edge of the awning. Vera's parting words remind her of the astonishing perspicacity of her lover. Such acuity is preternatural, as if a lover can comprehend as much from the language of their partner's body as from the words they speak.

But there are things that Vera cannot know, that she cannot intuit. Léna has never told her about that day on the beach, when she had seen her father's longing for the young man.

The fantasy that she constructs out of that long-ago day, in which she imagines her father and the stranger making love, is scandalous, certainly, and she does not dare to share it with Vera. But all fantasy is forgivable. Less excusable is the delight she experienced on that day, spying on the desire between the two men. She had started to walk back up the rise and then turned halfway and retraced her steps, this time making sure that her tread was heavier and louder. She had started humming the words to a song that had been popular both at home and in Greece that summer, Roxette's 'It Must Have Been Love'. Her father had finished his swim and was drying himself. He had smiled at her singing. And the way she hummed that song had been truly joyous. She has rarely felt as happy as she was that day. That is the shame she carries. She understood the desire between the two men immediately, with a force in her gut, in the very pit of her. She knew too that her condoning it was a betrayal of her mother. But that didn't matter. Her father was as she was. Even though she never spoke to him about that day, it was a secret they shared. She was not alone in her desires.

The sun has moved and she is no longer in the shade. She feels it burning her bare shoulders. Léna goes inside.

She lays her hat on the kitchen bench. She can trace Vera's scents in the apartment, a mild perfume of tobacco, the brininess of her skin. Her eyes wander once again to the clock on the microwave. She has to be patient. She walks over to her desk.

Vera's personality and her work dominate the second bedroom; the sketchbooks and folios containing her illustrations lie across the workbench and in neat piles on the floor. They had tried to share the space for a while, but it proved impossible. The clashing audio from their respective Zoom meetings, and the inevitable frustration of another's presence while one was locked in the minutiae of work, was also distracting. Léna had announced that she was going to work from the living room.

Vera's brother, Konstantinos, had built her a long flat desk that ran the length of a wall. He had painted the wood white and fixed the bench on black brackets. The simplicity of the colours and the design were exactly to Léna's taste. The morning sun coming through the large picture window on the southern wall bathes the room with warmth and light.

She sits at the desk and opens her notepad. She is translating Marguerite Duras's *The Lover* into Greek as a way of honing and developing her facility with the language. It was a project she had started when she first moved to Athens. In that first year she had found a French translation of Yiannis Ritsos's poetry at a flea market in Psiri, and it was reading his words, wondering how they would sound in their original Greek, that made her decided to translate them for herself. She had bought a Greek edition of the poems. Back then, she would translate one poem at a time and then dutifully compare her translation with the original. The exercise improved her vocabulary, and gave her a great love for the allegorical force of her adopted language. She had then translated Georges Simenon's *Feux rouges* into Greek as a gift for Vera, whose favourite Greek film was also called *Red Lights*. Afterwards, she had completed a translation of Andrée Chedid's poems. And now she had started on Duras's *L'Amant*.

She had studied Duras at the *lycée*, and back then she had been dismissive of the writer's exacting austerity. However, working on the translation has given her a greater appreciation of the novel. She is proud of her increasing ability in Greek. Vera had a Greek edition of the novel, and the translator's work in it is careful, elegant even, but Léna thinks that she should have allowed herself greater freedom to utilise the power of the neuter gender in the Greek tongue. The Duras, after all, is constructed out of the conceit of evasion and non-identification.

Yet today she stares at the words on the page and is unmoved.

Un jour, j'étais âgée déjà, dans le hall d'un lieu public, un homme est venu vers moi. Il s'est fait connaître et il m'a dit «Je vous connais depuis toujours.»

Léna bites the tip of her pencil and swivels in her chair. The panorama through the picture window is ostensibly ugly, the endless patchwork of concrete squares and boxes, with the blue haze of Mount Vyronas hovering above the rooftops. But she finds the view compelling, has always found the geography of Attica elating, the mad crush of so many millions of people into the natural boundaries of mountains and sea. 'You exoticise Athens,' her colleague Yianni complains, and he is probably correct. She does not apologise for it. That it sits on the cusp, on the borders of west and east, is for her fundamental to her love of the city.

She checks her phone. Eight thirty-three. She should make a leisurely walk downtown. Yet she stays seated. She closes the work journal, then looks at the shelf where she keeps her father's diaries.

She finds the notebook with the black vellum cover and opens it. Her father's letter falls onto her desk.

The paper has begun to brown, and as she unfolds the letter, she realises that the creases have begun clawing into the page, fading the ink at the folds; in time, whole words might be illegible.

It doesn't matter. Léna reads from the page, yet she knows what sentence will follow. She knows this letter by heart.

My dear Périclès,
I love you. I have not said these words out loud to you before,
and I know that has hurt you. I have hurt you. Please know,
however, that my silence has come close to destroying me.
I know that all cowards will claim this. Yet I am asking you
to please forgive me.

The words *pardonne-moi* were underlined with such force, the pen had torn into the paper.

You often chide me for my making so much of the difference
between our ages. 'What is fifteen years?' you demand. My
character is quarrelsome, I do know that. The English word—
cranky—is I think an apt description of me. I am obstinate
and irritable. I haven't forgotten your forty-fifth birthday,
when you accused me of treating you with contempt.
You were turning forty-five and I was sixty years old. The
honest truth is that I was jealous of you that evening.
Fifteen years is a generation. I don't think you under-
stand how difficult it has been for me to accept the condition

of my homosexuality. I never wanted it, I have always been
terrified of it being revealed to the world. It may be that if I
were fifteen years younger it might have been different. In my
early years the homosexual had been the awful and degenerate
stereotype of popular contempt. Le pédé.

Impossible to translate the word into Greek. Or English
for that matter. When she'd first read her father's letter out
to Vera, translating as she went, she had stumbled on it. The
Greek insults were not as lacerating, and the English word
'faggot' didn't convey the malignant hatred of the French
term. The pause was only seconds, her brain had been whirring, all she had wanted was for Vera to understand the letter,
by which Vera might understand her father, and so, amid
the imperfection of the rendition, she had chosen to make the
word literal: 'The pederast,' she had read to Vera.

You have spoken to me of shame, Périclès. I am in no
doubt that you know that emotion only too well. You have
eloquently described your childhood and your family. They
are loving, which is a gift. Nevertheless, as migrants from the
Mediterranean world it was inevitably a hardship for you to
be a homosexual son and for them to be a homosexual son's
parents. You know that for me, Greece and the Aegean has
meant freedom. Isn't that the recurring joke between classicists?
That those fascinated by power choose Rome and those desiring
liberation look towards Greece? That you were a Hellene is
what first drew me towards you. However, I know that I am

288

always a stranger in that world, no matter how refined my language skills, and that what is permissible for the outsider is not so for the Greek.

Anyway, is France so very different? Discretion is permitted; it is revelation within the public sphere that is abhorred. France too has its migrants. The children and grandchildren of the Maghreb and West Africa cannot assume the lightness of homosexual love that the indigene French assume. You have taught me that, to see that.

So, ashamed of myself, I was determined from very young to marry, to raise children and to be a father. I have been successful. My other sexual life has been secret. Thus, being obliged to submit to the rule of shame, I decided long ago that the most dangerous thing I could do was to say 'I love you' to another man. To do so, I believed, was to damn myself forever. God and honour—which, for me, are indivisible—may forgive the carnal sins of the body. To give myself completely to another man can never be excused.

Then we met. By then I thought myself safely ensconced in the haven of a provincial bourgeois life. I began our intimacy convincing myself that the infatuation was temporary, that I was overwhelmed by your good looks, the understated confidence of your virility. I thought you beautiful, Périclès. I still do. I did struggle over whether I should see you again after that first evening together in Athens. So, it was not really a matter of convincing myself that our liaison was to be brief, unimportant: I had to lie to myself. I have been dissembling all the while, pretending that our time together is outside my life.

To this day I burn in scalding shame over calling you a 'foot-note', after that terrible argument in the summer gardens in Lyon. You had just told me of your affair with Hakim. That day I burnt with the torment of jealousy. And yet, and yet . . .

I did not say these words: I love you. I have loved you for so long now, Périclès. You are the essence of my life, the centre. I love you and I am prepared to risk everything for it. I am grieving over how this will hurt Mathilde. I fear that the coldness of our sexual relations has been a misery for her for a long time. Yet she has been stoic and kind as a spouse and a mother. She is a friend, and I love her with a boundless love. I regret that I haven't been able to give her the fullness of an intimate life. I do hope, I pray to the benevolent Lord, that she has found such love with someone. Even in this hope for her am I being selfish? Do I wish it true only so my guilt may be somewhat alleviated?

I am terrified of the reactions of my children. The thought of my son believing me less than a man is unbearable. I am grateful for my Léna. She understands me. Such a bond is incomprehensible to science and the moderns. It is instinctive, primeval. With few words exchanged between us, I am assured of her loyalty and love.

I am prepared. I am yours. I love you.
Gerard

Léna stifles a sob. She is about to return the letter to its place between the pages of the journal. Something makes her turn around and look over her shoulder. She had felt a presence, a premonition. Vera had been adamant when Léna had first read it to her: 'The letter was never sent, Léna *mou*. Whatever his reason for not doing so, you have to respect your father's decision. He never sent it.'

Vera's disapproval had been the spectre she'd sensed the moment before.

Léna snatches her handbag, unzips a pocket and slips the letter inside. She lowers the window blinds, checks that the water heater is turned off, then leaves the apartment, deadlocking the door behind her. Still uneasy, as if a spirit hovers behind her, she takes the stairs instead of the lift. Buzzing herself through the main doors, she is struck by the blast of hot, dry air, and then settles into a relaxed, unhurried walk.

She crosses the ugly asphalt channel of Alexandras Avenue, and then keeps to the shaded side of the narrow streets of Neapoli. The area has always fascinated her; she is charmed by the glimpses of the decrepit old-world Europe that lies beneath the utilitarian brutality of the modern city, the ochre, olive and chartreuse paint peeling from the lintel of an old door or the fine wrought ironwork of the small Juliet balconies.

This morning, however, she is not taking anything in. It is impossible to forget the letter she has slipped into her bag. Léna takes a breath, concentrating on letting it out gradually as she slows the pace of her walking. She wonders how she will let Vera know that she decided to give Périclès the letter.

She had always meant to, from the moment she had discovered it in her father's journal. The memory of that occasion, only two days after his unexpected death, after the terrifying violence of his stroke, also intensifies her guilt. Though Léna doesn't share the faith of her parents, she has enough veneration for the sacred and the inexplicable to even now offer a silent prayer of thanks that she had been visiting her family when her father died. The day after his passing, when they had all been in that otherworldly fugue, arranging the funeral and calling relatives and friends, she had offered to go to the private office that her father had kept for years in Rue de la République, the small rooms on the first floor of an austerely ugly 1960s terrace. Her brother had not asked to accompany her. He had been curt in his insistence on staying with their mother and Marie. 'You go,' he urged, then took her hand. 'Thank you,' he had offered quietly.

The office shelves were lined with books, neatly arranged in order of subject and then further filed alphabetically. Her father had been retired for a few years, so there was only one cabinet of documents and papers from the university. There had been the musky heaviness of male scent, the strong woody bite of his cigars. She had pulled out the drawers of his desk, had searched, and found only a few documents, some stationery, a few old pens. She had turned on the computer but realised that she had no idea what her father's password might be. She had stared at the screen, at the blinking, teasing cursor. She had thought of destroying the machine. But then she'd searched the desk drawers again and found a small and tattered spiral notebook shoved to the back of the bottom drawer. In the inside back cover her father had scrawled a series of digits and letters. She recognised the numerals of her parents' savings account. He had listed the birthdays of his children and grandchildren. And there, in red pen, was the word *platon*, the philosopher's name in lowercase, followed by three digits, 416. She had swallowed a sob, one that had arisen fast and unexpectedly. Her father had so loved the ancient world. Plato had set his *Symposium* in the year 416 BC, when Agathon had won the poetry prize. And Léna had heard her father's deep, cautious voice, whispering in that ancient tongue. Then those phantoms had fallen away and there were only the squawks of the gulls from the quay, the roar of a motorbike in the street below. She had quickly typed the password, and the screen had erupted into colour and light. There was the photograph of Poseidon's temple framed against the brilliant blue of the Aegean.

She had searched methodically for compromising files. She found a folder titled 'Photos et video', and within that folder there were countless photographs of family and friends and travel. Scrolling through them would have been wearying, and Léna had marvelled that even someone as sceptical as her father when it came to the computerised image had neverthe-less left behind an extensive digital history. She had searched further and finally came upon a folder marked simply 'X'. She had clicked and the first image that had flared up on the screen was a youth, naked, his hand thrown limply over his head, his pubis and his armpits shaved, his penis enormous. Photos of men fucking, video files. She had allowed herself only a quick glance at a few of the files. Some of the models were young, undoubtedly, but she had felt an enormous relief that nothing she had seen had been vilely illicit or illegal. She deleted the folder.

She had found no diary entries, no confessions. She resolved to return with a USB, transfer everything to it, and then erase the computer's hard drive.

Léna had opened the window, stood on the tiny narrow balcony. There had been the reek of brine from the river, and she had glimpsed the masts of the fishing boats down at the quay. It was then she had noticed the suitcase. It was old, battered, tucked underneath the daybed that ran along one wall of the office. She had knelt and pulled it out. The case itself was heavy, and she had marvelled that once people had travelled with such cumbersome luggage. There was a combination lock, the metal scratched and rusted. She had walked to her father's desk, fetched the heavy bronze paperweight in the shape of a horse's head, then knelt and hammered at the lock. Initially it would not give. She had swung the weight high, smashed it down across the face of the metal. There had been a splintering as the lock disintegrated into shards. The case was open.

The journals had been inside it, old exercise books that had once been used in schools: blue-lined pages and celadon-green covers. She had sat cross-legged on the floor, opened one of the journals at random, had started reading her father's life.

She hears her name being called and snaps back to the present. Aphrodite, the owner of a tiny café on Ippokratous Street, is sitting on the doorstep smoking a cigarette. They chat for a few minutes, and Aphrodite offers her a coffee.

Léna glances at her phone. She shakes her head. 'Vera and I will come by tomorrow.'

'It's Sunday tomorrow.' Aphrodite squints, and laughs. 'Tomorrow you make your own coffee.' She stands, takes a final puff and, with expert aim, throws the butt into the bin near the doorway.

Léna weaves past a small street market, vegetables and fruit laid out on narrow trestle tables. Cabs are parked illegally on the south side of the street and four taxi drivers have formed a circle under the shade of an awning, smoking while working their worry beads across fingers and knuckles. The youngest, with angular features, has styled his shiny coal-black hair into a pompadour. There is something defiantly old-fashioned in the way his white polyester short-sleeved shirt is unbuttoned to his chest. The cheap denim of his jeans has faded to a washed-out pale blue and is tight at the crotch. He has seen Léna looking at him and his returning stare is unsmiling, penetrating. She enjoys his admiration but is unsettled by the aggression in his eyes. She holds her head high, walks with assurance, asserting her strength, her dignity.

Léna crosses Panepistimiou Street, enters the office from the small lane at the side of the building. She is employed by the Archaeological Museum, but the staff are mostly housed in nondescript office buildings nearer Syntagma Square. She buzzes herself in and the lone security guard looks up from his phone, mumbles curtly, 'Good morning,' and immediately returns to scrolling.

She unlocks her office, goes to her desk, pulls open the long bottom drawer. Her father's ashes are in a square cedar box, the lid embossed with elegant block letters in the Futurist font. Her father had kept his cigars in it for decades; it is one of the mementoes she took for herself from his office.

Léna brings the cigar box to her lips, kisses the wood, and whispers to her father's ghost in their native language, 'I hope this will give you rest and peace, Papa.'

Carefully sliding the box into her shoulder bag, she grins to herself at the way she had reverently kissed the case as though it were an icon—clearly this Orthodox country is rubbing off on her.

Léna takes the stairs back down, farewelling the preoccupied guard. Her bag feels surprisingly light.

An image, memory replayed with the authority of an unspooling film: her mother, with the delicate china cup, its surface decorated with Flemish floral motifs, scooping ashes out of the ceramic funeral urn; turning to her, asking coldly, pointedly: 'Will that do? Do you want more?'

Léna stops in the middle of the narrow street. A young woman almost runs into her, hisses rudely, 'Excuse me, madam, this is a thoroughfare, not a resting place.'

Léna calls after her, 'Go fuck yourself, little girl.'

The woman turns around, glaring.

Léna flicks the back of her hand under her chin and out, an ancient insult that one of Vera's elderly uncles has taught her. The time she saw him do it, after some retort from his son, she had been thrilled by the effrontery of it. It had the force of a spit. She has to will herself not to laugh at the girl's look of outrage.

Thankfully, that moment of spite has dispelled her guilt.

She looks at her phone. Nine thirty-six. She'd be there in twenty minutes or so. To turn up on time would be ridiculous; he would think such punctuality to be irredeemably puritanical. But was Périclès really a Greek? She knew he had lived in Athens, but he was also Australian, and in her admittedly limited experience of that nation's people they were definitely Anglo-Saxon, whatever their heritage and whatever their colour.

She decided she'd be there close to the agreed hour, wishing she'd brought a book to read in case he proved to be an authentic Hellene. At a kiosk on Ermou Street she purchases a newspaper then heads south of the markets, negotiating narrow alleys to escape the clumps of tourists already beginning to swarm towards the Acropolis. The sun's heat is gathering strength, and she slows her pace. Following a cobbled path that veers away from the main thoroughfare to the Acropolis, she is alert to the bracing scent of pines, the sweet relief of shade.

As Léna walks up Iraklidon Street, the melee of tourist language falls away—the face-masked Chinese, the anxious Germans, the excitable Americans—and the chatter and laughter becomes Greek.

When she first came to live in the city, she had found herself drawn constantly to Thission, that maze of alleys and laneways nestled between the Acropolis and the slopes of Philipapou. Raised on her father's veneration of the ancient world, she had felt a frisson of pleasure having a coffee at a bohemian café with the Parthenon as a backdrop and with glimpses of the temple of the ancient god of fire in front of her. In the first year of the Covid pandemic, she had found solace in walking these hills, the silent streets in lockdown. The audacity of the ancient world's endurance had been fortifying. And with no crowds to block the views, she had also come to appreciate the elegance of the neoclassical villas and manses that had once dominated the area. There had been the long period of neglect in the previous century, but with the new millennium there had begun the reclamation. Even through the economic crisis, Vera had told her, the gentrification of the neighbourhoods around the Acropolis had continued.

Crisis: that ubiquitous word. She had not lived through it, and this was one of the marks of her foreignness. As had been her earlier admiration of Thission. But her favourite neighbourhoods were different now. She was becoming Athenian and she no longer needed the endorsement of the ancients.

Yet, crossing Agion Asomaton Square, walking around the diminutive Byzantine church, determinedly refusing to browse among the trestle tables full of second-hand books on the approach to Psiri, she thinks to herself, I must make the effort to come here more often.

Périclès is already there, at one of the tables in the front court-yard. She is dismayed to see that he isn't alone. A burly bald man is sitting next to him. It must be his partner. He had referred to him, said a name that sounded Russian, Slavic.

They haven't seen her yet.

Physically, they could be Greek. Of course, with Périclès it is his heritage: the strong Anatolian features, those heavy-lidded eyes and the long, proud nose. But on first glance, the other man too could pass for a Greek. In his Balkan masculine stoutness, the strength of his muscular frame, he would not appear out of place in any kafenio in the city.

They are both attractive men still, yet there is something she finds disagreeable about the reserve of their intimacy with each other. And that they are middle-aged men in short pants—that immediately marks them as tourists. But the way Périclès is leaning towards the other man, explaining something on the menu, the tenderness of that other man's smile, it is also clear that they are lovers. Two old fags on tour in Athens.

She is ashamed of the meanness of her thought. She shyly raises her hand in a wave.

The other man spots her first. He says something to Périclès, who looks up, smiles, and stands up.

They greet each other and he introduces her to his partner. Ivan. That's right, she remembers now.

In Greek, rushed, Périclès asks, 'May we please speak in English? Ivan doesn't speak Greek.'

Ivan is now standing. As he extends his hand, Léna leans in to kiss him. He grins, a wide expansive smile that makes her laugh in relief. He returns her kiss.

'It is a pleasure to meet you, Ivan.'

Périclès is signalling to a waiter.

The young woman approaches the table. 'Yes?' she asks in a surly monotone.

'I'll have a double espresso, with some warm milk on the side. Is that possible?'

'It's fine. We can do that.' On hearing Léna's expert Greek the waiter's tone has softened.

'And the gentlemen, will they have more coffee?'

'Yes,' replies Périclès. 'Two more Greek coffees, one sugar each.' He points to a small plate littered with a scattering of dark crumbs. 'And some more *loukoumades* please.'

As she had observed when first speaking to him on the phone, and from meeting him in Pangrati the previous week, the coarseness of his Australian accent is obvious underneath his Greek.

'We're quite hungry,' Périclès explains. 'We spent the morning exploring the Acropolis, and then headed down to the theatre of Dionysus.'

'It was fantastic.' Ivan's enthusiasm is charming. 'I can't believe I was on the steps of the . . .' He is so overwhelmed by the joy of the recollection that his sentence splutters to a nonsensical finish. He inhales, tries again. 'It's like I've seen it all my life, of course, on TV and in books. But to think that I am here, that I could touch it.' His eyes are gleaming; surely, thinks Léna, he isn't going to cry?

Ivan is nodding, as if to himself. 'I'm just really fortunate. I realised this morning how fortunate I am.'

She notices the swiftness of the surreptitious movement. Of how, on saying this, his hand has alighted softly on Périclès's leg under the table before just as quickly being moved away.

She is shocked at herself, appalled and mystified by the jolt of the jealousy that goes through her.

She collects herself. 'Is this your first time in Athens?'

He smiles. 'First time in Europe.' He takes his glass, sips at it, and she notices that two of his fingernails are darkened, the bruising obviously longstanding. He has a working man's hands.

'How long have you been travelling?'

'Three weeks,' Périclès answers. 'We started in Paris. And then we flew to Vienna, caught the train to Zagreb and then on to Belgrade.' He clears his throat. 'Ivan is Serbian.'

'My parents were from the former Yugoslavia.'

There is no rancour evident in Ivan's correction, but his response is immediate and final.

'How was . . . ?' She hesitates, wants to ask him how he had felt on returning to Serbia. Yet that was not quite right; he had never been there before. Her thoughts are rushing to find the correct word and then to settle on the English equivalent. Ivan is looking at her with a keen, benevolent interest.

'Say it in French,' Périclès suggests.

She nods at him gratefully. 'I wanted to know whether he felt a sense of nostalgia for Serbia even though he has never been.'

Périclès turns to Ivan and says in English: 'Léna wants to know whether you felt at home in Belgrade even though you'd never been there before.'

She frowns. Something of the essence of her question has been omitted.

Ivan, beaming, says, 'I loved Belgrade. I fucking loved it!'

The waiter—arriving with the coffees and the plate of sweets just in time to hear Ivan's effusive outburst—scowls. And a young student at the table across from them says to his friends with a mocking laugh, 'It's morning and the Englishman is already drunk.'

Léna, seeing Périclès wince, quickly turns away. Ivan continues to chat away, oblivious.

'Parts of it were dirty and parts of it didn't work and everyone is on the make, but it is so much less neurotic than Australia. People are less scared. Australians are really timid and . . . and . . .' Searching for words, he absent-mindedly starts rubbing at the bald crown of his head. 'And angry. Australians are really angry. It wasn't home. Australia, Melbourne, is home. That's where my life is. My daughter, my grandchild.' She observes the same quick motion beneath the table—that strange admixture of furtiveness and defiance as he quickly squeezes Périclès's leg. 'Where our house is and where our life together is,' he continues, 'that's home.'

He lifts his coffee cup. 'Serbia made me realise I'm not British. And made me realise that Australia *is*—too British.' His smile is warm. 'Yeah, I loved Belgrade, really loved it. Does that answer your question?'

For a moment, and possibly because she still feels that ridiculous sense of betrayal at Ivan's presence, she wonders if he is being sly, if there is a cunning to what he has said, having understood the student's insult and wanting to make it clear he is not English. She immediately rejects that doubt. He is unsophisticated but she is sure his self-possession is genuine. It's evident in his strength, in his bulk and severity, yet also in the patient cast to his eyes, and in the gentleness of his bearing, in how he sips at his coffee with unstudied poise. Léna doesn't despise masculinity. She knows that popular misapprehension is often ascribed to lesbians, but she thinks it a juvenile cliché. There is some truth to it: the haute neighbourhoods and clubs of queer Paris are full of that disparagement for men. It is a bourgeois prejudice; those people are equally unfriendly to working-class *gouines*. She has never found the stolidness of men attractive, but she understands how some might find such strength appealing. And Ivan has that potency.

'It answers it very well,' she replies.

A silence falls among them. One of the students stands up, slings a rucksack over his shoulders, loudly farewells his friends. At that moment, Ivan pushes back his chair, blocking the student from passing.

'Excuse me,' the student exclaims, in precise and brusque English.

Léna watches Ivan get up from his seat. He towers over the young man and, in choppily accented if grammatically scrupulous Greek, he says, 'Yes, please,' and makes way for him. She stifles a giggle at the look of concern that briefly clouds the student's face.

'I'm going to let you two talk,' Ivan says. Then pausing, looking first at Léna then at Périclès, he adds, 'I'm going to take a walk for half an hour and then meet you back here.'

'Are you okay?'

She can't help it, she resents the quiet solicitude in Périclès's voice.

'Yeah, of course I am.' He hesitates once more, then adds, 'This is a big day for both of you. This day is about Gerard.'

Léna looks down at her coffee, embarrassed at the brusqueness of his Australian accent, at the way it makes her father's name sound vulgar.

He continues, 'I want you to know that whatever you two decide is fine with me. I don't have to be there. If you would rather it was just the two of you, I completely understand.'

She glances up at him; his eyes are boring straight into hers. There is only kindness there. 'Thank you,' she whispers.

Périclès's hand reaches out towards Ivan, then drops away. 'Thank you,' he echoes firmly, gratefully, as Ivan walks away.

'He's a very nice man,' Léna observes.

'Yes. He is.'

Alone, they have reverted to French.

'Would you like one more coffee?'

She nods, and watches him signal the waiter, is silent as he orders her espresso. That done, he turns to her, leans across the table and squeezes her hand. 'I want to thank you for inviting me today,' he says, releasing his grip. 'It is very generous of you.'

She senses the tears welling in her eyes, and for a moment wonders if she should excuse herself, find the toilets, to escape the overwhelming force of the sadness she is experiencing. She allows the intensity to course through her. Her crying makes no sound. He sits in silence. When she is done, starts wiping her hand across her eyes, he takes a paper napkin off the table and gives it to her.

The waiter arrives with the coffee and water. She fires a look of concern at Léna and sets down Périclès's glass with a rude bang.

Léna clears her throat, blows her nose into the napkin, scrunches it into a ball and sets it beside the saucer.

'As I said to you last week, my father wrote in his diary that an evening he spent with you at Sounion was the happiest time of his life.' It is her turn to take Périclès's hand, to squeeze it. Her voice is trembling, breaking. 'You made him very happy.'

'You are very like your father. Not physically; you don't have his features or his colouring. Physically, you take after your mother.'

She withdraws her hand.

'It is in your personality. You have his determination. His courage.' Périclès looks at her gravely. 'I need to ask again. Is Mathilde alright with me being with you, with me being there for the scattering of Gerard's ashes?'

'Yes.' Léna makes sure to keep her gaze steady. He is correct in his assessment of her character. Yet there is also a twinge of guilt, because Périclès believes that her mother too has read her father's journals. 'She understands that my father's secret life is something between himself and me, and knowing that he loved you, that he loved men, means I feel that I am not alone.' This is sincerity, not dissembling. She hopes this greater truth cancels out the treachery of the lie of omission she has made in allowing him to think her mother knows everything.

'She is a remarkable woman.'

'How often did you meet her?'

Périclès grimaces. 'Only a few times, at those university soirees that your father would host at your house.' He smiles wryly. 'Where first I met you—when you were still only a child.'

Léna smiles. She does remember him, the diffident young Australian, though her father had been clear in introducing them that Périclès was Greek. He had seemed out of place, nervous, always at the edge of the group. She and her siblings had been drawn to him, because he was closest in age to them, but also because of his outlandish stories: of giant kangaroos that could take you out with one kick of their powerful feet. Or of ocean waters filled with sharks, and dangerous forests where poisonous snakes slithered and lived in enormous pits. The fear had been delicious. He had made her laugh. Now she wonders if it wasn't intuition that had cemented her liking of that timid young man: if she had grasped, within the evasions and silences, what he had meant to her father.

'Mathilde and I only had a few conversations,' he continues. And there is a perceptible shift in his eyes, a sadness in the depths of them. 'My dear Léna, you must understand, I felt a tremendous shame whenever I was around your mother. It was difficult. I detested the dishonesty.'

'She understands.'

'Excuse me?'

She has mumbled; he hasn't heard her. 'She understands,' she repeats.

In English this time, he says, 'She is a remarkable woman.'

He straightens in his seat. His hair is now streaked with silver and white; he is nothing like the young man she met so long ago at the garden parties back home. He has resolve now, she decides, has lost his timidity.

'I remember that trip to Sounion. We had an argument that morning. I almost didn't go.' His glance is shy. 'Are you fine with me talking about this?'

'Please do.' She wants to hear, wants to comprehend. To build a life of her father that belongs to her and only to her. She knows that may be a betrayal of her mother and her siblings, but still she embraces the intimacy of these emotions. She is hungry to know.

'It was very early on in our relationship. I was living in Athens, at an apartment in Nea Smyrni that my cousin Vangelis's parents owned. Vangelis was seeing this girl . . . what was her name?' Périclès rubs at the grey stubble at the point of his chin. He shrugs, shakes his head. 'That doesn't matter,' he continues. 'Vangelis was out with his girlfriend in a car that we were sharing at the time. He was meant to be back at the apartment by ten thirty—which, as I'm sure you know from living here, meant midday.'

Léna nods. She has been musing on the Greek word he had used—γκόμενα—for 'girlfriend', slang that she associates with elderly Greeks. As with its masculine counterpart—γκόμενος—there is something illicit in its casual sexuality, closer to that

English expression 'fuck-buddy'. Périclès's generation, Vera's parents' generation, they still use that term. Léna's friends, colleagues her age, tend not to use it anymore. Or if they do, it is with an ironic smile or the raising of an eyebrow.

Of course! *Une amante* would be the French equivalent.

She orders herself to concentrate on what Périclès is saying. He is painting a portrait of her father.

'It was after one o'clock when Vangelis arrived. He and . . . and . . .' Périclès is drumming his fingers on the edge of the table, then suddenly beams and exclaims: 'Melina. That was her name!' He sits back in the seat, his eyes half-closed, hooded, accentuating the Levantine in his features.

Léna is hushed, waiting. She can see he is now conjuring the past.

'Your father was furious. He had a temper, we both know that. He also had formidable control. It was the coldness that alerted you to his fury. But this afternoon something else had been unleashed. As soon as Vangelis and Melina walked into the apartment he started yelling at them, the most ugly insults . . .'

She has to interrupt. She is remembering another occasion when her father's rage had been unleashed. Anton had taken the car to a party, had returned sodden with drink and reeking of marijuana. The Peugeot's bumper was crumpled; her drunk brother had taken a corner too fast and smashed into a neighbour's gate. There had been three other young men in the vehicle; all were miraculously unharmed. She remembers her father shouting, 'You absolute fool, you idiot, you could have killed yourself and killed your friends! Think of the grief, think of the dishonour!' Yet not once had her father uttered an obscenity.

'Excuse me,' she says firmly, 'I never heard my father swear.'

Périclès looks at her with a certain detachment, and nods. 'You are right. Gerard never used obscenities. That's true. The afternoon I am remembering, his vileness became a different kind of cursing. He called Vangelis degenerate, he called him undependable. Your father was unforgiving that day.'

He has used the Greek words, not the French translations, and she hears the cruelty in them. She can only imagine how humiliated Vangelis would have been. And with his girlfriend there, hearing it all. He would have been furious.

'You must have been mortified.'

'Certainly.' However, he is smiling. The memories must no longer bruise him. 'I was incensed by him treating my cousin in that manner.' He shakes his head and continues in English. 'I was so bloody angry.'

She has noticed this about Périclès from their previous meeting and from their phone calls. He doesn't swear in French. And she is sure, even when she first met him in France, in the garden, he was respectful and polite. Though, of course, she had been an adolescent then and he would have considered her still a child.

'I told him to leave. That I would not be going to Sounion. He was shocked; I saw how that pained him. He pleaded, he begged. But I was firm: I was not going.'

Léna waits for him to continue.

Périclès shrugs. 'He wouldn't accept it. Just would not countenance me not going. By now we were in my bedroom, and I was shouting, and he was imploring me. In the end, I gave in. I had to. Gerard was not very good at taking no for an answer.'

This makes her smile.

'That apartment had the thinnest walls. I was conscious of Melina and Vangelis in the next room, hearing every word.' He frowns. 'It seemed tawdry, melodramatic. I said yes just to get him out of the apartment. But I don't think I said a word to him for all of that long drive south.'

'My father was good with silences.'

'Yes. That's true.'

He makes an abrupt gesture, as if waving away the recollection. 'It was still bright when we got there, with some hours till sunset. I remember walking up to the temple and seeing that astonishing white. It had the aspect of washed bones, as if it were the skeleton of some ancient, dignified beast. And then that drop to the dazzling Aegean—that blue water which is a mirror of the sky. Your father was telling me about the rites associated with Poseidon; how, being the god of the sea, he was the most ancient of the gods, born alongside his sibling Zeus.'

Carefully, lightly, his knuckles brush against her hands.

'He was close to tears. I could see how much he loved this land; I couldn't be angry with him. We sat side by side, awaiting evening. I think it is the most still I have ever been in my life. I think that is why your father wanted to be with me. He loved Greece, adored it. I was part of Greece for him.'

'My father loved *you*.'

His smile is tender, yet she is aware of a sense of disbelief, of challenge, settling over his face. It is this that cements her decision.

'My father loved you,' she repeats, and starts searching her bag. She retrieves the letter. She hands it to him. 'I found this in one of his journals. It belongs to you.'

She stands. 'Excuse me.'

In the tiny basement WC, she carefully wipes the toilet seat clean, and balances over it to urinate. She wipes herself clean, tosses the paper in the overflowing bin, flushes. She washes her hands with care. Has she given Périclès enough time to read the letter?

She spends an age at the mirror, staring at herself with an intense scrutiny. It is important to her that she is not a liar, that she moves through the world rejecting dishonesty and deception. Yet she has lied to Périclès. She has not revealed for how long she has observed him on social media. She has pretended to him that her family knew of her father's secret life. She has to force herself to maintain the gaze of her reflection.

My father was good with silences. She too has had to learn that skill. Those long years of not daring to utter desire or love, fearing opprobrium and disgust and exile. It was an ordeal to become unshackled from those fears.

She glares at her reflection. 'You have done the right thing.'

Léna stands at the doorway of the café. Périclès is sitting still at the table, the letter folded before him. She goes to him, resumes her seat.

'My wanting to bring Ivan along with us troubles you, doesn't it?'

It is not what she was expecting him to say. He is right, though: she doesn't want the other man there. She doesn't begrudge Périclès this new love. Not at all. But she doesn't understand why Ivan has to be part of the day. He has made no mention of her father's letter. He is not being fair.

'But you need to know that it is important to me.' He takes a deep breath. 'Léna, Ivan and I are far from young, and we have found each other after long relationships which were difficult, and which were scarring. That is the nature of love; such wounding is inevitable.'

She is listening intently. She wonders if the wounding he is referring to will one day come to her, will slice through her bond with Vera. It is a terrifying and unimaginable thought.

'Ivan's former partner is alive, and though there are moments when I resent the shadow he casts over our lives and sometimes wish he had never existed, I also know that with the passing of every day, the bonds that have tied him to Ivan are loosening.'

He takes the folded letter, holds it out to her. 'I can't take this. I can deal with shadows. But I think it is unfair for Ivan to compete with a ghost.'

She almost snatches the paper from his hand. He is undeserving of it. Ivan is alive, he will grow old with Périclès. Her father is dead. Her tears are quiet. She doesn't take the letter. 'It's yours,' she says, wiping her eyes. 'It belongs to you.'

She sees he is about to say something, that he swallows his words. He nods sadly. 'I know why he didn't send it.'

She is exhausted. She doesn't want to hear more arguments, more doubt. She wants to honour her father, cast his ashes into the sea he so loved. She was wrong to invite Périclès. His grief is not hers. It has been a ludicrous mistake.

He points to the date heading the letter, the neat cursive script. Her father always spelt out the month, never the mere numerals. The date has no meaning for her.

'This was written just before he found out your sister was pregnant with her first child. A few days before, a week at best.'

It is possible, she thinks. Etienne will be ten this coming November.

'Léna,' he says quietly, yet firmly, 'your father did love me, but he also loved your mother and his family. That hurt me at the time; it nearly destroyed me. But now I understand it. Thank you for showing me this letter, but it doesn't belong to me. It is yours. Gerard's deepest love was for his family.'

The folded note lies between them.

In equal quiet, in equal certainty, she answers him. 'Then I give it to you.'

He draws breath sharply. In the pause that follows, she has to look away. The fatigue that has just come over his features, it has aged him.

He whispers his thanks and pockets the note. 'Ivan has a daughter and a grandchild.' His face has softened and his eyes are smiling once more. 'I think if it wasn't for what I learnt from being with your father about how important those ties are, I might not be with Ivan today. I might have believed that I was competing with them for his love. I know now that is not the case, that love has different forms and different expressions. That was a gift Gerard gave me. I am very grateful for it.'

He will be there, at her side, when she scatters her father's ashes. The small lies can be forgiven. She has done the right thing.

They sit in that silence.

'Have you had enough time?' Ivan stands above them, one of his hands resting gently on Périclès's shoulder. In greeting them he has proffered a bashful, courteous smile. She is determined to return that kindness.

'Where did you walk?'

He sits beside Léna, mops sweat from his brow.

'Along the back of the Acropolis,' he answers her. 'I don't think I'll ever forget it, walking in the shade of the park, and then looking up and seeing the ancient city just floating there above us. It's miraculous.'

He says to Périclès, 'I'm happy to go back to the apartment.' He turns to Léna. 'I understand this is something you two have to do alone.'

'We want you to come.' Périclès checks his phone. 'Should we have lunch in the city or wait till we get to Sounion?'

Ivan is still looking at her searchingly. 'Do you want me to come, Léna?'

The directness of the question is unnerving, and for a moment all thought of charity towards him dissipates. He never knew her father, he doesn't know her.

'If you wish.'

Ivan turns to Périclès. 'I'll walk back. I'll leave you both to it.'

She is hurt to see the disappointment on Périclès's face.

'Please,' she says hastily. 'Please come with us.'

Ivan nods slowly. 'Are you sure? Thank you,' he answers with a blush, so obviously self-conscious in using French. It makes her laugh.

They decide to have lunch out of the city, and she and Périclès discuss the options. She'd assumed that they would take the bus, but he disregards her protestations and is already peering down the street for a cab.

She shakes her head. 'Not here. Let's walk to Akteou Street—it will be easier from there.'

She signals to the waiter, asks for the bill, ignoring Ivan's attempt to pay.

Afterwards, they walk through the narrow lanes. At one point, Périclès moves closer to her, and suddenly they are walking arm in arm, Ivan behind them. The gentle attentiveness of the gesture, the care in it, is tender and fatherly. She blinks back tears, glad that she is wearing her sunglasses.

The cab is only a few years old, a bright red Skoda hatchback with dents along its bumper. The fog light on the passenger side is cracked. Léna is annoyed when Périclès slips into the front passenger seat. Ivan opens the door for her, and she slides in. He settles beside her.

'We're going to Sounion,' Périclès informs the driver. 'Can you take us along the beach road out of Athens?'

He turns around, smiling, and says, still in Greek, 'I want Ivan to enjoy the view.'

Of course. Her disappointment fades. He is thinking of the man he loves—how awkward it would be for Ivan to sit in front, next to the driver, knowing almost no Greek. Périclès is already negotiating with the driver to wait for them for their return journey, and to bring them back to Athens 'off-meter'. Léna still thinks the price exorbitant, especially given the cheapness of the bus fare, but as the car crawls through the horrendous traffic, she rests back on the seat and is glad for the refreshing breeze through the window.

'This looks like an interesting area.'

They are driving along the esplanade of Palaio Faliro.

'In ancient times it was the old port. And more recently it was a very poor working-class neighbourhood. Now it is very hipster, gentrified.' Almost to herself, in French: '*Trés bourgeois.*'

She is aware of the driver, who is glancing at her in the rear-view mirror.

He turns to Périclès. 'Where are you all from?'

'I'm Australian, as is my friend.'

'And I'm French,' Léna interrupts, leaning forward. 'But I have lived in Athens for some time.'

The driver nods approvingly. 'Yeah, your Greek is excellent.'

He turns back to Périclès. 'So is yours. Sometimes I pick up Greeks from Australia or Canada and they don't speak a word of the language.' He shakes his head in furious disbelief. 'You wankers, I think to myself. Make the effort to learn the language. It's your fucking heritage.' His motion is savage as he crunches the gears.

There's a slight flick of his head, indicating the back seat. 'And your friend? He's not Greek.'

'Serbian,' Périclès answers. 'But an Australian like me.'

The driver grins broadly. '*Zdravo!*' he calls out. Then in faltering English, proudly, 'My name is Michaelis, very nice to meet you.'

Ivan leans forward. '*Geia sou*,' he says, and continues shyly in Greek, 'They call me Ivan.'

The traffic increases again as they enter the main avenue leading to Kalamaki Beach. A group of young teenage boys, all in outsize singlets that expose their lithe, tanned bodies, dart across the street. Michaelis slams on the brake and Léna is thrown forward. Ivan's hand immediately reaches out for her.

'Faggots!' Michaelis screams out his car window.

One of the boys, laughing, gestures at his crotch.

'What use are those tiny marbles, wanker?' But Michaelis is laughing as he curses them.

At the other end of the beach, the car picks up pace.

'Are you cousins, brothers-in-law?'

'No,' Périclès answers. 'We're a couple.'

She is holding her breath, awaiting a reaction. For the first time she is aware of how sinewy and strong the driver's naked arms are, and how light the faint sprinkling of hair. There is a small tattoo of an anchor peeping from under the sleeve of his T-shirt. Yet the young man—and this too suddenly enters her consciousness; she has not been aware of it before this moment, that the skin on his lean attractive face is unmarked, smooth, that he can't be older than twenty-four, twenty-five—shows no surprise and certainly no aversion to the older man's response.

The simplicity of the Greek phrase—*Είμαστε ζευγάρι*—sounds old-fashioned, yet it is also perfect, direct and concise, allowing for no misinterpretation. *We're a couple.*

They have passed Vouliagmeni and the urban scapes have fallen away. Ivan's attention is firmly on the calm waters, the soothing sapphire hues of the bay. Léna closes her eyes, lifts her face to the stream of buffeting wind. There are wafts of coastal smells in that breeze; she inhales the odours. It is as if the sudden incursion of those scents has made her aware of something that has been drifting at the edges of her consciousness, of how the small cabin of the taxi has been filled with the scent of men. With her eyes still shut, she turns from the open window, her nostrils flaring. Certainly, there is a corresponding tartness to women, the acerbic whiffs of cunt and menstruation. But there is no denying the odours of the three men, the fruity fragrances and chemical tang of their respective aftershaves unable to conceal the charge of their stink. It is a harsh word; it is both correct and concealing. However Léna is not disgusted; she is fascinated. She inhales deeply, and opens her eyes. Michaelis's large hand is draped casually over the steering wheel. There is the elemental in the smell of men, as there is in the flavour of women; yet they are subtly different essences; she is alert and awake to this, it has a revelatory power, and her mind is busy, attempting to discern and identify the difference. The car speeds up, overtaking on the leeway of the emergency lane, and she smells the sea once again. That is the difference, she is sure of it. Women are water and men are fire. There is something burnt, something smouldering in the smells of men—nothing of the moist and fertile earth. More like what lies deep beneath it, built by conflagration and friction. A memory also intrudes, of when she was very young. Having been rude to her mother, she was made to do the family's laundry for a fortnight as punishment. Sorting through a heap of clothes, she found her brother's soiled underpants—the stench was appalling, it burnt into her lungs. She had been close to nausea.

There is a bottle of water in the pocket of the seat next to Ivan. There is none on her side. She points to the bottle.

'May I?'

He hands her the water. She unscrews the lid and sips; it is satisfyingly cold. She wipes her lips.

'It's very dry land,' Ivan says.

Périclès turns in his seat. 'Yes. But it's a different dry from Australia?'

It's odd, she thinks, how his statements become questions when he speaks in English. It doesn't happen when he's speaking in Greek or French.

Ivan leans forward. 'The difference is that you are never far from the sea here. You don't feel like you are disappearing into the landscape in the same way you do at home.' He sits back. 'There are no trees here.'

He turns to Léna. 'The gum trees in Australia grow very tall. They touch the sky.'

She is charmed by his innocence but also somewhat annoyed by his naivety. There is something juvenile about wanting to compare Greece to home that is unbecoming in a man of his age. Then she remembers that he has not travelled.

'We have big trees here in Greece.' Michaelis's English is crude, and for the first time there is a trace of shyness in his voice. 'Up north,' he continues, jabbing a finger towards the roof of his car. 'Big, big trees up north.'

He swivels with such keen excitement that the car swerves sideways and Léna tumbles into Ivan.

'Up north, near Skopje,' Michaelis continues, his eyes back on the road. 'Near your home.'

The driver turns to Périclès, and in Greek begins to compare the various forests in Greece, from the sweep of mountain pines in Epirus to the verdant beauty of the Ionian islands. His pride in his country is infectious and very soon she has joined in the conversation, good-naturedly arguing with him and Périclès over which is the most beautiful place in Greece. Michaelis disputes her choice of the Ionian islands, and she scoffs at Périclès's assertion that the southern Peloponnese is the most stunning. The three of them find assent in their mutual admiration for the coast and mountains of Crete.

There is a tiny icon of the Virgin and Child attached to the dashboard. The Mother's eyes seem to follow Léna, the gaze stern and mournful. She is aware of Ivan's silence beside her.

'We were agreeing that Crete is one of the loveliest places in the whole of Greece.'

Ivan's half-smile is unreadable. She struggles against her feelings of impatience. Surely he could learn some Greek. It is the most infuriating deficiency of the English-speaking nations, their laziness with languages.

'Périclès told me you are a grandfather. You are very young to be a grandfather.'

No trouble reading his expression now. He is beaming.

Yet his first words surprise her. 'I like how you say Perry's name. In French, I mean.'

There is that awkwardness in his manner, a combination of bluster and shyness. As if the twenty or so years' difference in their ages is reversed and it is she who is older.

'Well,' she answers dryly, 'it is nicer than "Perry".'

Ivan laughs delightedly. He takes his phone out of his pocket, slides his fingers across the screen. 'Here,' he says. 'This is my daughter, Katerina, and my granddaughter, Tasha.'

The photograph is of a woman with a long Slavic face, her features sharp, her straight, fair hair tied back loosely. She is attractive; the lack of make-up, the shaggy old jumper she is wearing, the dash of white paint on the flat plane of her right cheek, give her an air that is close to masculine. It is a handsome face, Léna decides. The woman's daughter is reaching out to the camera, her expression joyous. Her hair is a mass of frizzy black coils and her cheeks are the colour of plums, luminescent. Only the angle of her eyes connects her to her mother.

Léna passes back the phone. 'Your daughter is very attractive. And your granddaughter, she's adorable.'

Ivan smiles proudly. 'Thank you,' he says, jamming the phone back in his pocket.

'I took that photo,' Périclès announces. He turns in his seat. 'Kat and Tash had just moved into their new house. We were all busy painting.' He grins wickedly at Ivan. 'Well, I was trying to look busy. Ivan was not very impressed with my abilities.'

'Home maintenance isn't your strong suit,' Ivan says sarcastically, but there is warmth in his voice.

She is unsettled by the casual domesticity of their banter. And that jarring accent, those shortened Australian vowels, those dropped consonants: she hears no music in it. She shifts in her seat, repositions her bag, seeing the top of the old wooden cigar box.

She concentrates on the view outside the window, the broken stone and yellowing grass, the low shrubs. Occasionally she looks across to Ivan's side, out to the crystalline waters of the sea. Under the high noon sun, the water dazzles with light.

'Are you from Paris?'

Has Michaelis had to repeat the question? Has she dozed off?

'No. I am from Normandy.'

She sees him wink in the rear-view mirror, something that she would have considered flirtatious in her first year of living in Athens but now sees as amicable.

'Have you been to France?' she asks.

'No. My brother went a few years ago. He was lucky—it was just before fucking corona.'

'Did he like it?'

'Yeah, of course, why not?' Michaelis shrugs. 'He said the Metro was dirty. Not like ours.'

Périclès laughs. He turns to her once more. 'That's what Gerard used to say about Paris.' He repeats it in French. 'That Métro is a disgrace, it is filthy.'

He smiles at her before turning back to face the front, and that smile is all she needs to settle her. He has not forgotten her father. Her father is still part of him.

She says to Ivan, 'Many of us French who are not Parisiennes have a—how do you say it?—we have a love and hate relation-ship with our capital.'

'I was knocked out by Paris,' Ivan says, still looking out the window. 'Not that I've seen much of the world,' he adds. He turns to her. 'But I can't imagine a more beautiful city.'

Michaelis pulls up outside a low-set covered brick tavern. Three enormous white tourist buses are parked next to it. He gives Périclès his number, saying to call him half an hour before they want to be picked up. They climb out of the car and the driver punches the car's horn three times in farewell.

Périclès points to one of the tables covered in red-and-white checked cloths. 'Do we want to eat now?' he asks.

Léna is not hungry at all. Though the height of the tourist season has passed, the tavern is doing brisk business, with family groups taking advantage of the mild weather. The air reeks of grilled meats, charred octopus, grease and burnt oil. She can't bear the thought of putting food in her mouth.

'Let's not eat here,' she says to Périclès in French. 'There are better places in Lavrio.' She turns to Ivan and continues in English. 'Lavrio is a beautiful harbour town, and it is not very far from here. I think we should eat there.'

Ivan gestures to a street seller waiting for tourists to alight from a nearby bus. The grizzled old man is unshaven, gaunt, with luxuriant silver hair that he has let grow wild over his shoulders. His thin arms tremble as he carefully rearranges the biscuits and cups of pretzels he has set on his makeshift table.

'Why don't we grab something from him?' Ivan suggests. 'We can come and eat later.'

Léna says, almost under her breath, and in French, 'Thank you.'

It is a climb to the Temple of Poseidon. Léna is grateful that she has brought along her hat. They march silently, Périclès at the front and Ivan in the rear. From time to time they pass tourists making their descent back to the tavern, returning to their buses. Some are breathing heavily, some are wiping perspiration from their brows or their necks, and one unabashed German—she hears the woman groan, complain weakly in her own language: 'My God, it is so hot!'—takes a tissue from her pocket, slips her hand under the collar of her white sodden blouse, wipes assiduously under her armpits.

Then she hears it; she hears Ivan gasp.

She lifts her sunglasses.

She has kept a tight grip on the strap of her bag and has been walking with purpose. Yet during the climb she has felt removed, displaced from the world. She has been watching the dark linen of Périclès's shirt, concentrating on the sturdy tread of his shoes on the path that led to the clifftop. She has been aware of the squawks of the gulls, the occasional burst of language—that of the German woman, and of a young male couple, blithely attractive, in matching tight singlets, speaking in excited Hebrew. She has not been oblivious to sensation. But she has been blind to the world. There has been the murmuring in her head. It is the weight of her responsibility, the duty she feels so acutely. Where do I place my father's ashes? Where in this land he loved is home?

And then she hears Ivan's exclamation of wonder.

The ruined temple is being held by the light of the sun. The carcass of the ancient home of a god gleams in the glare. Léna stops, and realises that Périclès has also done so. Ivan walks slowly past them, oblivious to anything but the sight before him. Then he throws open his arms. In exultation, thinks Léna, as if he were about to sing, or to chant a prayer.

A sense of joy stirs in her belly, rises within her, is at her throat and in her mouth. It is only a passing moment, yet within that delirium she believes that she is witnessing the world through Ivan's eyes, and that in doing so time has been vanquished and she is in eternity. Then she hears a crude click.

Someone behind them, a tourist, has snapped the view with their phone. She returns to herself, to the world.

Ivan turns around. There are tears in his eyes. 'You know, when we first saw it from the road, coming around the bend, it looked so . . .' He falters, grasping for words. 'It looked so fragile, so small.' He smiles wanly. 'And then you come close and the sea is just beyond and the sky is so low.' He stops, heaves, and is quietly sobbing. He drags his palm across his mouth and nose, sniffs, and still with a tremble in his voice, his tone now returning to gruffness, he once more faces the ruins. 'And yeah, then you come up close and it is exactly right. It looks like it has always been here.'

Léna follows the sweep of his gaze as he contemplates a pillar that stretches towards the sun.

'Human hands created this, I know that.' Ivan is still. 'But it makes you believe that gods did live here.'

'It is wondrous,' Périclès says quietly. He walks up to Ivan. The men stand together, their shoulders touching, looking across at the view.

It is the right word, thinks Léna. To describe it as merely beautiful would be to diminish the power of the vista. She marvels at the acumen of the ancients: the expertise, of course, of their architects and builders; at how, even now, the ancient bones of the temple suggest permanence. And at the astonishing rightness of its setting, perched on the sun-drenched rise of scorched land, with the pellucid waters of the bay spreading into the infinite. Today the sea is a benevolent and splendid blue. She had last visited with Vera in winter, and the waters were turbulent and grey. That day had seethed with the violence of the elements, had seemed threatening. She had grabbed on tight to Vera.

Today, it is serene.

Those who'd had the vision for this temple, who had created it out of stone and bare ground and air, had done so to unite earth and sky and sea.

She knows now what she wants to do. She walks up to Périclès. In French, she says, 'I want to scatter my father's ashes on the temple grounds.'

It is as if Ivan has understood her. He points to a bank some distance from the entrance.

'You two go ahead,' he urges. 'I'll wait here for you.'

'You sure?' Périclès asks him. 'You don't want to view the site itself?'

'No,' Ivan says, gazing into the blue, his eyes shining. 'I don't need to. This is more than enough.'

The queue is mercifully short. Léna allows Périclès to nego-tiate the entry fee, to calmy and firmly resist the guides touting for business. Now within the very body of the temple, with tourists seemingly all around, with the monotonous delivery of various guides coming into her consciousness in fragments of German and Japanese and Spanish, she is confused, dazzled by sensation, and unsure of her previous resolve.

Périclès's hand is on her shoulder. 'Follow me,' he says.

A low scaffold rises from the earth: there is restoration work being done in a southern corner of the temple. There are no workers visible, but past the roped-off boundaries of the visiting areas, she can see a group of people in yellow high-vis vests sitting eating lunch.

The murmurs and exclamations and the snapping of cameras surrounds them.

She halts. 'I'm being ridiculous,' she says, indicating the workers. 'Let's go down to the cliff edge. We'll just get in trouble if we do anything here. It's not worth the risk.'

Périclès has his hand up to shade his eyes from the intensity of the sun. In that light, the stubble at his chin is white, not grey. The white of the temple columns.

'Why do you want to scatter Gerard's ashes here?'

'You don't think it's a good idea?'

And his eyes shine with warmth and good humour, which suddenly eradicate the weariness of age from his face. He is kind, she thinks to herself, and Ivan is too. She wonders if kindness is a quality that can be cultivated at any time, or whether it only finds its true expression with age?

'You know, when we first came here,' he says, 'when the marvel of the view and the splendour of the place made us forget our argument, your father turned to me and said, "Périclès, the ancient Greeks knew that God is chaos, and He is symmetry. He created both, but it is in the latter that He dwells. This temple is a devotion to the symmetry of the Lord."'

He has been careful in the elucidation of his French, as if digging for the fragments, familiarising himself with a vocabulary that has long been lost to him.

He looks up to the sky, as if daring the sun. 'Maybe it was in this very spot.'

Still staring up, following the line of the marble columns up into the sky, he asks, now in English: 'Do you believe in God, Léna?'

She shakes her head.

'I too am an unbeliever,' he says, now averting his eyes from the sun. There is sadness in his smile. 'Or maybe it is more true to say I am an agnostic. Ivan believes: he is a Christian, as was your father.' He shrugs. 'Well, Ivan is Orthodox, and Gerard was a Catholic. That is a small difference. You saw Ivan's response to this place. His delight, his adoration. Impossible not to see it in his eyes.' He adds in French: 'I am right, no?'

She nods.

'Your father had that same look of wonder in his eyes when he spoke of the symmetry of God being found in this temple.' He puts an arm around her, draws her close. 'I think we should scatter his ashes here.'

And there is so much to say and so much stirring in her mind: how for a brief instant she had also found herself transported by awe; and that she also, like Périclès, finds herself envying the conviction of believers; and how the proportion that her father exalted—for isn't that the great gift the ancient architects bestowed on the world, the importance of measure and balance?—had been achieved by Ivan being there with them today. She had not wanted him to come with them, but it had been in his awed response that she and Périclès were reminded of her father: his spirit, his memory, his worship of a past world that knew how to seek the stillness within the chaos. Her father's soul had been tortured, afflicted by his desires. That constant pain had been settled in small moments of peace. Cradling a grandchild, embracing Périclès, praying to his God, standing within the skeleton of this temple, contemplating wonder.

So much to say, impossible to collect into words.

She removes the old cedar cigar box from her bag.

There is a shallow drop behind the scaffolding. Carefully, Périclès jumps the short distance, then he assists Léna. They are in a hollow, with the sound of the tourists and guides above them.

Périclès grins at the cigar case in her hands. 'I am almost tempted to have a cigar,' he chuckles. 'For Gerard.' Then he shakes his head. 'I never could stand it.'

'I like the smell of them,' she says. 'It reminds me of my childhood. It's rare to smell a cigar these days.'

She opens the box and a sudden gust of breeze unsettles the grey ash. For a moment she is panicked, but then Périclès says, 'He's eager to be home.' He holds out his hand. 'Wait till the wind dies down.'

Her heart is beating furiously.

Périclès nods.

She doesn't say the words out loud. *I love you, Father.* And then the wind whips past her and she sees her mother's face. There was a peace in the love her parents had shared. She had promised her mother a prayer. 'We loved you, Father,' she says loudly. 'Be with God.' And she raises the box, holds it out from herself, and then upturns it. A cascade of ash, and the dust swirling around their feet, discolouring their shoes.

'Be at peace, Gerard.'

She is grateful that he speaks out loud.

'I loved you, I still miss you,' Périclès whispers. He says it in Greek. He brushes a tear from his cheek. 'Do you have a light?'

Léna places the box on the ground and digs in the front pocket of her bag, pulling out one of Vera's lighters.

'Thank you.' Périclès takes the folded letter from his shirt pocket, unfurls it, then clicks the lighter. The flame appears, vanishes. He hunches over the lighter. The second attempt holds and he brings the flame to the corner of the paper. She watches it burn, watches the black ink shrivel and evaporate from the page. The flame rushes, leaps, and Périclès lets go. They watch it burn as it floats to the ground. When it is nothing but cinder and dust, Périclès steps on it, pushes it into the earth.

Her heart is heavy. More than the scattering of the ashes, the erasure of her father's letter seems to be the final farewell. She stifles a sob. Her father is gone.

'What the devil are you doing!' A young man is running towards them. The casual clothes he is wearing—jeans and a denim shirt—as well as the carefully trimmed black beard, the neatly cut hair, give him the air of a student. She guesses he is one of the archaeologists.

He is breathing heavily when he reaches them. He directs his fury at the older man. 'Are you crazy, you wanker! You could have started a fire.'

She gets between the men.

'We're sorry,' she says quickly to the young man. Feeling foolish, yet not knowing what else to do, she picks up the empty cigar case. 'We were scattering my father's ashes. He adored this place.'

And in the distance, in the haze where the sea mist meets cloud, she believes she can see the soaring of her father's spirit.

The young man is still frowning at Périclès, as if reluctant to let go of his righteous anger. But he steps back, says quickly, 'I'm sorry.' And follows it with a muttered invocation: 'Life to us.'

Léna is hardly conscious of the sightseers as they walk through the temple complex, make their way back to the main path. She is thinking of the young man's graciousness. As always, she is gently amused by the Greek words of commiseration—she mouths the words, translates them, *la vie à nous*—which are both an expression of sympathy and a talisman. As strongly as the disappearing ashes, the words have drawn a veil between the living and the dead.

They approach the meeting spot. Ivan isn't there. She can sense Périclès's agitation as he looks around, searching for him.

It is Léna who spies him first, the sturdy figure slowly climbing back from the bluff. From that distance, she realises he has a slight limp, that he favours his left leg as he trudges up the path.

She points. 'There he is.'

There are dark patches of perspiration on his light blue linen shirt. Sweat glistens on his shaved head too, highlighting the tiny pricks of grey stubble growing back at the side. He is nearly bald, she thinks to herself.

As he approaches them, his breathing is laboured.

Impulsively, she slips her arm through his. 'Thank you for waiting for us, Ivan,' she says. 'Did you go to the edge of the cliffs?'

'Yes.' He grins, sheepish. 'I looked down at the surging waves and for a moment I thought I saw Poseidon's face staring back at me.' His arm is tight around hers. 'The water is crystal clear and so calm. I'm sorry I didn't bring my shorts. I'd love to have a swim.'

'I'm sure you can buy some swimming costumes back at the beach. And towels. You should go swimming.' She spins around to face the bay, and their arms unlink. It is a relief. 'These are my favourite beaches in the Athens region.' She points across to the resort hotel on the nearest cove. 'You should go there. It is always breathtaking to look up to Poseidon's Temple when swimming.'

He makes no reply.

'You won't get Ivan to a private beach,' Périclès says with a wry chuckle. 'He finds it offensive.'

Ivan scowls. 'I just don't understand it. Beaches should be public.'

She is annoyed at the limitations of his thinking. He is a tourist and he is not poor. She thinks his complaint trivial.

Léna walks ahead.

Michaelis is waiting for them, and he expertly navigates the narrow and twisting road to Lavrio. Entering the town, Périclès points to a tavern at the far end of the harbour, the tables covered in blue-and-white checked cloths. Michaelis drops them off at the front of the restaurant, and the waiter escorts them to the table at the far end of the patio. As they settle into their seats, she makes her decision.

'I'm so hungry,' says Périclès. 'Should we share some plates?' He smiles at Léna. 'Are you vegetarian?'

'No, I'm not.' She doesn't open her menu. 'Please, excuse me. I'm going to take the bus back to Athens. I hope you don't mind.'

'You should eat something.'

She shakes her head. 'I'll grab something at the kiosk. I'll be fine.' She takes Périclès's hand. 'Thank you again for coming with me. It means a lot that we could say farewell to my father together.'

'You sure you won't stay?'

Léna stands up, swings her bag over her shoulder. Périclès doesn't move. He is regarding her quizzically.

Ivan scrapes back his chair, and is on his feet. 'It was lovely to meet you,' he says warmly, and he envelops her in an embrace that surprises her with its generosity. As they pull apart, she notices the top of a thick Orthodox cross peeking out from his shirt. She kisses him on both cheeks.

'Thank you for coming, Ivan.' And she means it.

Périclès is now standing, and their farewell is equally affectionate. Unlike the strength of Ivan's clinch, his frame around her seems slight. She kisses him as well, and they promise each other that they will call, and surely it is possible to get together for a lunch or a dinner or at least a coffee before the men leave for Australia, and they would very much like to meet Vera. Before leaving she turns one more time to Ivan and says,

'I know that Australia has a wonderful coast, everyone tells me and I have seen the spectacular photographs, but please, you are here today, go for a swim at Sounion Bay; it is special, something really unique and delightful.' And she taps his shirt pocket, asks for a cigarette. After she has put it in the pocket of her bag, Périclès grasps her hand, and he says, 'Thank you, Léna, for allowing me to say goodbye,' and then she is waving them farewell and she is weaving through the tables and she is out the front of the tavern and waiting for the traffic to slow. And there is relief. She can breathe.

She runs across the street.

There is a bakery in one of the alleys off the main square. A thick-necked elderly woman is clearing the outside tables.

'Are you still serving?'

The woman regards her with suspicion. 'Not table service.'

'That's fine,' Léna says. 'I'll take something to go.'

The shelves at the counter are near empty but she asks for the one remaining *bougatsa* and a slice of spinach pie. She walks down the alley which comes out onto a small square, bordered on three sides by the backs of shops. A garage door is rolled to the top and she can see the stained blue overalls and the frayed sneakers of the mechanic toiling underneath a car. The grass in the square is yellowing and patchy, and the one lone bench under the glorious shade of an enormous poplar is occupied by two old men, one flicking his worry beads, the other sucking on a cigarette. Léna sits on the low wall, at the corner where the dappled comfort from the tree diminishes the ferocity of the sun.

She is ravenous and bites chunks off the pie, finishing it quickly, and then starts on the pastry. That too is soon finished. She brushes the crumbs off her skirt. There is the frenzied cackle of gulls as they swoop to feast.

She takes the cigarette out of her bag. On finding Vera's lighter, she hesitates. She can taste the honeyed tartness of the unlit tobacco. She sees the flicker of the flame, the rushing burning and blackening of the letter in Périclès's hand.

Most probably, she will never see Périclès again.

Léna lights the cigarette.

With the first drag of smoke rushing into her lungs, and with it a sudden sharp awareness—the cooling shade on her shoulders, the clicking of the old man's worry beads, the hideous reek of cat urine in the grass—she realises that she has left the cigar box in the taxi.

It's pleasant under the shifting shadows of the poplar, the soft murmur of the old men chattering in the background. She suppresses a giggle at the leisurely meander of their conversation, their complaints about the current government, followed by long silences, interspersed with good-natured gossip about mutual friends. And every couple of minutes or so, the heavier man with the enormous paunch interjects: 'What are we doing chattering away like two old women, Mr Nikos? And under the midday sun? We should be asleep in our beds.'

She doesn't check her phone; it must be close to three o'clock now. One of the old men has started chatting again but this time old Mr Nikos interrupts: 'You're right, Old Man Giorgio, I'm off to my nap.' Léna watches them. With tender care, Nikos holds out his arm for the other old man to clasp. With a groan, his other hand gripping his cane, the heavier man awkwardly rises to his feet. In slow, shuffling steps, still arm in arm, they walk to the three stairs leading off the square. Léna puts out her cigarette and rushes to assist the elderly men.

Nikos shakes his head, smiles at her kindly. 'Thank you, daughter, you're a good one. But we're fine. Slowly, slowly, we old fools manage.'

She watches Nikos guide his friend to the mechanic's garage. The mechanic has emerged from the car he is working on: he is a dark-haired man, not young, not old, tall and lithe but with a grizzle of grey in the stubble on his chin. He takes the old man's arm from Nikos, guides him to a battered leather sofa that is partly shaded in the corner of the workshop. The mechanic settles the old man on the sofa.

Léna watches Nikos as he walks down the alley, turns right, and disappears from view.

She will ring her mother as soon as she gets home. And with this thought she marches off to find the bus.

The bus shelter is by the kiosk. A sign on the tin shutter, in Greek, English and Russian, announces it will reopen at 4 pm. Léna peers at the timetable stuck to the post. The dirty glass is covered with ugly black and blue slashes of paint, and so the schedule is unreadable. There is only one other person waiting, a teenage girl with her hair shorn on one side of her head, the startling mess cascading from the other side of her scalp dyed a mixture of platinum and cyan. She has pods in her ear, is rolling a cigarette, one foot tapping the ground in time with the music in her head.

From her vantage point in the shelter, Léna can see across the road to the tavern where she left Ivan and Périclès.

She can just make them out at the far table on the patio, the jade waters of the calm harbour behind them. They are eating. She raises her sunglasses, squints.

Ivan's shirt, purchased from some nondescript chain. Périclès's clothes are more expensive, of a finer cut, yet they too are mass-produced. If she wanted to be cruel, if she were a stranger sitting at the table next to the two men, absent-mindedly glancing across at them, she would think they were an ageing middle-class couple. And not think of them again.

She sees that Ivan, who is facing the sea, is pointing to something out in the distance. She can't see what it is but she knows that dolphins are often seen in these waters. What she does notice is that Périclès has put down his cutlery and moved to Ivan's side, also peering into the distance. As he does so, he rests a hand over the bigger man's shoulders. His hand only stays there fleetingly, then almost immediately the two men return to attacking their food. Yet the intimacy, the quiet of it and the care of it—yes, the love of it—banishes all meanness from her observations.

She likes the freedom with which they are clearly enjoying their meals, a facility that she identifies as masculine. Yet Vera also has it, and it is one of the things that first drew her towards Vera, the satisfaction and pleasure in the elemental: eating and making love. There is no pain in seeing the two men in their serene repose together. Her father had chosen another life, and if his happiness and pleasure were compromised, well, that is true for almost every choice in life. Something must be abandoned in order for something to be affirmed.

It isn't just the sea breeze—so restorative after the thick, soupy air of Athens—that is making her breathing easier. *You are not carrying your father any longer, though he is still with you.* She can hear Ivan's rough, deep voice saying those words, though he didn't, of course, and in her head she hears them in French. The man doesn't know her language. Yet it is as if the sentiment has been granted to her by him. Léna's hand rises to her breasts, and she can almost feel the sharp edges of his crucifix on the pads of her fingers.

A quartet, backpackers from Germany, are rushing across the street. The bus rumbles, hisses, stops. The view across the road is blocked. She takes her mask from her bag and puts it on.

The Germans take up the front seats of the bus. Léna wanders nearly to the back. The girl with the half-shaven scalp sits behind her, an elderly woman clutching two large plastic bags sits across from her.

Léna knows that she will never see Périclès again. She will not text and she is almost certain that there will be no message from him before he and Ivan return home. It will be a choice that carries with it no malice or regret.

The hydraulic doors of the bus wheeze and grumble as they lift and close. Léna closes her eyes.

———

The woman across from her, Varvara, has her own eyes clenched while she gingerly massages her right thigh. She is adept now at isolating the pain. Her doctor has told her that the issue is her knees, that the bone there is deteriorating. It's common for women your age, the doctor told her the last time she saw her. It's a deficiency of calcium, you need a new knee, that's all there is to it. Varvara doesn't trust her; she finds her offhand and unsympathetic, one of those young women who are all smugness and impatience, who never imagine they will grow old. You will, my girl, you will, she mutters to herself. Varvara can't afford the time off for a stay in hospital. And she certainly can't afford the extra payment required to grease the hands of the medical staff. It might be her knee that is the problem, but after a morning spent cleaning hotel rooms, she feels a piercing ache along the length of her thigh. She places her palm flat against her leg, wonders if she can feel the flesh there vibrate. It is throbbing. Fuck it! She'll take another pill, that will help with the pain. She searches through her bags, finds the little bottle of pink tablets, puts one in her mouth, swigs some water from her bottle, returns to rubbing gently at her leg. 'Please, Blessed Mother,' she mouths. 'Please help me.'

Her shift finished two hours ago but she always waits for this afternoon bus. The tourists are still down at the beach or tramping through the ruins, and so she can usually find a seat to herself. It will get crowded further on, especially once they pass Koropi.

She can't believe it: she's forgotten most of her German. She had hitched in the back of trucks to Vienna, straight after the regime had fallen. The first time she lasted six months. She was sent back, and then a few months later she returned to Austria. That time she lasted a year and a half before that cunt cop asked for her papers, humiliated her in front of all the staff and customers. It was a lively Serbian restaurant, on the Ottakringer Strasse, not far from where she was living. Kristina, one of the women she worked with, suggested Greece. 'No one checks your papers there,' she had said. 'And we look like them, we blend in. It's the schwartz and the Musselman they pick on there. Go to Greece.'

And she had. And for a while it was good; she liked the climate and there had been plenty of work, cleaning and looking after children, and she had met Pantelis and fallen in love and Stella was born and then Stavros, and they had moved out of the dank apartment in Kypseli and taken out a mortgage in Sepolia and there was even enough to send money back to her mother in Romania. Life had been hard, life was never easy, but she had thought it a good life. She didn't expect anything from the world or from God.

She listens to the German tourists. It is a harsh language. They are true Germans, not Austrians and not easterners. If Pantelis was still alive he'd be cursing them loudly. The idiot, evoking Hitler and the Second World War, the camps and the Occupation. Blaming them for the Crisis. For how the good life had been stolen from them, how the Germans had stolen it.

The pill maybe is working; she releases her hand from her thigh.

She doesn't blame the Germans. What's the point? she'd argue with him. Some of us are born to live in shit.

He lost his job, he fell to grog, and indeed ended up dying in shit, his liver having packed up, pissing and soiling the bed night after night. She had been relieved when he was finally gone. Within days of the funeral she had scrubbed their bedroom, airing it day and night even though it was midwinter, then rented it to three Bangladeshi men, illegals who worked in the markets. And God knows what else they did. She didn't care, she needed the rent, sparse as it was in those awful years when the economy was throttling them all. She had moved into the other bedroom with the children. She was rarely home; she was working, cleaning up the stained sheets, the condoms and ashtrays and tampons in love hotels. At night she cleaned the toilets of a porn cinema off Omonia, being tipped a few euros to let the faggots go off into the cubicles to suck each other off, or to paw at the bodies of the refugee boy-whores. It was dirty, it was degrading, but she had managed to keep the apartment. A year after Pantelis's death, her mother rang from Romania, complaining how Varvara had stopped sending money. What was she meant to do? she begged. Varvara had been brutally honest. 'Fucking survive, Mama, that's all any of us can do.'

She looks across the aisle to the pretty, chestnut-haired woman. Her features—those that are visible and not hidden by that wretched blue medical mask hiding her lower face—are quite soft, and her eyes are winsome. It's clear that she hasn't had to do a hard day's work in her life. Good luck to her. She doesn't blame her any more than she blames the Germans for annihilating her world. Life is fate, that's all there is to it.

She must be timid, that girl, still wearing a mask. Like the Chinese. Varvara has had the coronavirus twice, is vaccinated, what else can you do? It's there in the world. That girl—not really a girl, hard to tell with the mask, but she is a woman in her thirties, Varvara guesses, though youthful still, never had a baby—is soft. Soft people don't believe in fate. The bus is crawling now; they are entering the city and the traffic is abominable. They are passing a church and Varvara quickly crosses herself. The pain in her leg has numbed.

Léna wakes with a start. A long-legged schoolboy has taken a seat next to her. The bus is full, there are people in the aisle. She slides closer to the window, tightens her body, tries to make herself as small as possible. She adjusts her mask. She can no longer glimpse the sea. There is cement and smog and harsh light reflected off the asphalt. She puts on her sunglasses.

At the final stop she waits till all the other passengers have alighted from the bus before she stands. The elderly woman who was there from Sounion, the one with the plastic bags, is the last to take the stairs. She limps, winces as she takes the final step to the ground. Léna is almost ashamed of how she can dismount with such ease.

The city is alive with movement, the symphony of shouts and horns and sirens. Her skin tingles. She could walk through

Pedion Tou Areos, cross the park into Gyzi and soon be home. But the day is still all brightness, the urban sounds and calls too exciting, so instead she crosses the avenue and then skirts the back streets, heading towards Exarcheia. Abruptly she turns off and cuts through the arcades.

Her phone buzzes, and she flips back her sunglasses, reads the text from Vera. Daniele and Leonidas have asked them to dinner. Her fingers tap quickly—*What time?*—and then just as swiftly she erases the question. She is standing outside a small vintage shop, the window festooned with swathes of lace. There is a large mirror, its frame a heavy mahogany, etched with Art Nouveau swirls at each corner. The dark wood is heavily scratched down one side. She checks out her reflection, the blush of sunburn on her cheeks and brow. She takes the small tube of sunscreen from her handbag, applies it to her face, to her neck and arms. She spies a group of three women sitting at a café table behind her, all smartly attired and middle-aged. One of them is staring at her applying the lotion. She smiles at the reflection in the mirror and the woman turns away sharply, with a frown.

Léna is in no mood for company. She is not dismayed by this thought; not at all. She likes Daniele and his new boyfriend is delightful. The conversation will be animated. But she is enjoying her solitude, the sense of having stepped out of the world. It is thrilling, as if she feels less burdened than she has for an age. She continues to admire herself in the mirror: let the older women think her vain. A carnal hunger rises within her. She can trace its course, emerging from deep inside her, as if spawned in her belly and overflowing into her blood. She shivers from the joy of it. The power of it.

There is a free table outside the café. She takes a seat, waits for the waiter, and when he arrives, Léna orders a wine. She takes her phone and texts: *Give the boys kisses. I'll stay home tonight. It's been a long day.*

Within seconds her phone rings loudly, a strident sound under the austere neoclassical shelter of the arcade.

'Is everything okay?' Vera's voice, rushing through the receiver, is strained, concerned. 'I don't have to go out tonight.'

'No, no,' Léna answers quickly. 'I'm fine. You go. I'm a little tired.'

'You sure?'

How does she answer her? How is she to express her contentment? 'My Vera,' Léna says, 'it all went well. I feel so very peaceful.' And as she utters those words, she knows that they are correct, that they give the clearest description of her state. All her previous doubts are no longer important. Her father is dead, and his memories traverse the continent.

Vera, unconvinced, is explaining that she will call Daniele back, cancel the dinner.

'No.' Léna is firm. 'You go. I'll be long asleep when you get home.'

'You sure?'

'I'm sure.'

'I love you.'

The woman who had been staring at her has lit a cigarette, is clearly listening in to the conversation. In the hushed chamber of the high-ceilinged arcade, Vera's voice seems to boom.

'I love you too,' Léna answers.

The waiter arrives with her wine.

She takes a sip, and rings her mother.

'Are you okay?'

Her mother's question, her concern, so mirrors Vera's tone that Léna's reply is brusque.

'I'm fine, Maman.'

She feels guilty. As with Vera, the question is asked out of love. Both women know how important this day has been for her, have been patient with her disquiet.

'It all went well, Maman. It was the right thing to do.'

The relief, the sudden expelling of air that she can hear on the other end of the line, is evident. 'I'm so glad, my child. Is it still a glorious day in Athens?'

'Yes. The water was still. It was beautiful at Sounion.'

'Did you scatter the ashes in the sea?'

The temptation surges to explain that she wasn't alone, to confess the truth: *Périclès was there with me, Maman. Do you remember him? He loved Papa. We scattered the ashes together.*

This is not the right time. There will never be a right time.

'I scattered them in the temple grounds.'

'Perfect.' There is clear delight in her mother's voice. 'Gerard adored that temple. He loved the Aegean, of course, as do all

346

Philhellenes, yet he was invigorated by cold water. He always preferred swimming in the Manche to the sea.'

'That's right,' Léna agrees. 'And he loved the Atlantic. Battling the elements, he used to call it.'

'So unlike Gerard to use military terms. He detested martial language. Except when he was discussing the ancients.'

They both laugh at this, quietly and tenderly, and then they are silent.

'I said a prayer.'

'Thank you, Léna.'

There is a glissando of sound, just audible. Her mother must have the radio on; a classical piano piece is playing.

Léna is about to reply, to say, *You don't need to thank me, it is such a small thing to do, to offer a prayer.* Yet there had been a hesitation in her mother's voice. Words left unsaid. So she waits.

'I know you'll find this a little . . . superstitious . . . however, I will tell you. A few hours ago, I was still in the garden, it was noon and so I was resting on the garden seat, reading my book, when I felt your father there with me. I swear I felt his lips kiss my cheek. It lasted only a second, but I am in no doubt that he was there. I experienced an incredible lightness, Léna. I knew he was at rest.' There is a rasping sound, her mother clearing her throat. 'You think me ridiculous.'

'No. Not at all. I felt him go as well.'

'Ah!' Again, joy in the exclamation. 'My darling, that is exactly it: he was letting go. Thank you, child, I hope you now know that you did the right thing.'

Léna can't answer. The tears are welling, burning.

'I love you,' her mother says.

She calls on all her strength, her resolve, not to sob. There is no reason to make her mother anxious.

'I love you too, Maman.'

Léna ends the call.

The woman at the next table, the one with the haughty glare, is looking at her. Léna turns away, searches her bag, finds a clump of tissues, wipes her eyes, blows her nose. She drinks her wine, stares with ardent determination at the vintage store across the way. She can still feel the woman's eyes on her.

She turns to look at her, ready for a fight.

'Condolences to you and your family,' the woman says in accented yet perfect French. Her dark eyes are not arrogant or fierce; they are kind. 'And forgive me for . . .' She pauses, searching for the apt word, before continuing in Greek: 'Forgive me for eavesdropping.' A long, narrow-wristed hand flutters, twirls, indicating the high curved roof of the arcade. 'Sound carries so well here.'

'Not at all,' Léna answers in French. 'Thank you. It is very kind of you.'

The woman returns to the conversation with her friends. Léna finishes her wine, places a few euros on the plate.

'Thank you,' she says again to the woman, this time in Greek, and wishes the table a good evening. She wonders if they are watching her as she walks to the end of the passage, if they are commenting on her clothes, on her body. She knows her dress is smart, that she is attractive.

The blast of sun, the noise of the crowds and the traffic: she puts on her sunglasses, and walks the length of Asklipiou Street towards home.

Vera has drawn the curtains and the apartment is refreshingly cool. Léna unbuckles her shoes, places them in the rack in the corridor, removes her stockings, unbuttons her dress, unhooks her bra, and tosses the clothes on the bed. She puts on an old threadbare singlet and walks into the kitchen. There is fresh bread on the table, an unopened box of *loukoumades* beside it. She glances at the note on top of the box. Vera has sketched a large heart with blue pen, shaded it in an intricately patterned crosshatch. In equally fine calligraphy, over the circumference of the heart, she has written a note. Léna tilts the torn A4-sheet to read it: the words are in English: *Sweets for my sweetheart, I love you with a love that has no end, that is stronger than Eternity xx.* The 'y' in the final word sits atop a densely scribbled-out letter. Vera had initially ended the word in 'e'. Léna laughs, impulsively grabs the page, kisses it.

She pulls up the blind and sunlight floods into the lower half of the small kitchen. There is a bottle of white wine in the fridge. She pours herself a glass, rips open the plastic covering the box and takes a *loukoumada*. She devours it, her lips coated in icing sugar, then immediately has another. She brushes the sugar from her singlet, her chest. She thinks she could eat the whole box. She takes a Tupperware container, slides the rest of the sweets into it, closes it and puts it in the cupboard. The first sip of wine, after the syrupy glut of the *loukoumada*, tastes bitter. She screws up her face but forces herself to have one further small taste. This time she senses the invigorating dryness of the wine, the fullness of its body.

She wanders into the bedroom and places the wineglass on the floor beside the futon. She sprawls onto the bed. The room is in near darkness, but she doesn't have the energy to wind open the blinds. She appreciates the slight chill in the room, how the sound of the world outside is muted. She closes her eyes.

The jangling of the bells shocks her awake. She lifts herself up, her back against the cool of the wall, counting down the tolling. Six chimes.

Briskly, she gets up off the futon and she unwinds the blinds. The hills of Penteli in the distance are already in shadow, a confirmation of autumn, and a first suggestion of approaching winter. She pours another splash of wine into her glass and is about to head out to the balcony, then she remembers she is still in her underwear. Vera, who was born in this city and to this world, always admonishes Léna for her carefree dismissal of propriety, as when Léna sunbathes topless on the patio. 'Think about the old women downstairs,' she chides. 'What would Madam Toula and Madam Sotiria say if they saw you prancing about in your underwear?' That always makes Léna laugh, as it does now. She likes the two elderly spinster sisters in the apartment below them; they are cheery and ageless, as if by shunning marriage and convention they have defied senescence. There is nothing prudish about them. It is the proximity of the church, just across the narrow street, that worries Vera.

Well, her lover has faith. It is a small and easy negotiation. Léna puts on pyjama bottoms and walks outside.

She leans over the balustrade. Old women in funereal black are entering the church. A young man, tall and lanky, is smoking a cigarette on the corner, one foot on the step of Mr Mavrogiannis's tailor shop. His features are obscured but there is something about him that seems familiar.

He takes another drag from the cigarette, and she remembers: he smokes like her father did, with that furious dragging of the roll-ups Gerard used to smoke when younger. By the time she had started school he had already moved on to those malodorous cigars, that fusty reek which permeated his clothes and his study. But she still has the clearest memory of his hand deftly sprinkling the tobacco onto the paper, licking the side, rolling it into a firm, thin cigarette. She closes her eyes for a second, hears the flick of the lighter, the sound of the burning tobacco, smells its first tart wafts. His eyes flashing, his evident pleasure in his habit.

The youth has butted out his cigarette on the wall, hailing a young woman who is approaching from the opposite corner. Her dress is boyish; a pale blue sweat top with a hood, tight, dark jeans. As if at the limits of his patience, the man weaves among the cars, ignores the shouts and the blasts of the horns. He reaches her and hugs her tightly, joyously. They are insensible to the world: they abandon themselves to a long kiss.

Léna is stunned by the sensual force of remembrance. There is still the linger of tobacco and the familiar musk of her father's smell. As a child she cherished the manifest signs of their difference from one another. His male scent, his hairy arms and chest, the thick fall of his penis that first fascinated her in the change rooms of the gymnasium where she learnt to swim. Yet always she understood that beyond any external variations, she and her father were united in their essence.

She goes back inside to the living room and searches the shelf where she has stored her father's journals. She knows exactly which one to choose: the exercise book with the dog-eared cover and a circular stain where her father must have rested a mug of coffee. She skims the pages, finds the passage—24 May 1999; she was fourteen years old—and begins to read.

> *Mathilde and I had a terrible argument last night. I am mortified by my cowardice, by the awful things I said to her. This morning I made confession, which I have not done for some time now. She was kindness herself after I returned from the confessional, grasped my hand and whispered, 'We have already apologised to each other, Gerard; you know God has forgiven us.' I nodded in agreement, and we walked back home hand in hand, a tenderness that we have not indulged in for many a year. I would like to believe myself forgiven, but I think that would be a delusion. Not that I doubt Mathilde's mercy. I am terrified that I don't have the Lord's absolution.*

Dear Lord, have mercy on me. Here the nib of the pen has pressed so hard that there are tears on the page.

Is my soul different from those of others? And if so, does this 'homosexual' soul banish me from grace? I remember when Jean-François and I were in service together, when we would whisper our thoughts, conduct our ceaseless arguments after lights out, that he would accuse me of having a Protestant's soul. 'Of course, God forgives,' he would declare. 'To believe yourself inexorably damned is the madness of predestination.' I never revealed myself to Jean-François—how could I? I didn't have the words to say it—yet I think he must have been aware of my wretchedness. He was gentle and kind to me. I still wonder what would have occurred if I had reached out to him one of those nights, God forgive me, if I had made my desire for him manifest. In my vainglory, I still fantasise he would have succumbed. In moments of clarity, I know it would have disgusted him.

Was I born in this state? I can't remember a time when I did not love men; that adoration has always been there. Body and soul. I so want to believe that I was created in the perfection of the Lord's image and that part of that perfection is this state of loving men. However, it is also true that every sinner attempts this bargain with God. You made me this way; I am blameless. Doesn't the murderer or the abuser of children not also justify himself in this manner? My Christ, I wish I had been born to that classical age, to the world of the ancients, who affirmed that the soul as much as the body was guided by their desires, that this frenzied love of men and of men's bodies was not a Fall. That would mean I was born to a time that was ignorant of you, my Saviour. Do I really wish that? Can I really wish that?

The next line on the page is scribbled over, violent lines slashing through and obscuring the words. Léna so wishes that she could decipher their meaning. There is evidence that the line her father had written and then obliterated was all capitalised. She believes that she knows what the words were: *I DO WISH THAT!* She will never know for certain. She sips from her wine, continues reading.

Mathilde accused me of no longer loving her last night. I was furious with her. If my soul is corrupted, I have done all I can to make amends by my deeds in this world, my pride in being a good husband and good father. We had gone into town to see a film, an effective thriller by Chabrol called Au coeur du mensonge. *We had both enjoyed it, and we enjoyed discussing it afterwards at dinner at the Vietnamese bistro behind Saint-Ouen. Mathilde had drunk three glasses of wine, which is rare for her, and it was I who drove home. She was in a playful mood, recalling our courtship. When we arrived home, my sweet Léna had fallen asleep on the sofa, the television still playing. I wanted to lift her into my arms, as I did when she was a small child, to inhale her scent, to whisper, 'Goodnight,' as I tucked her in bed. But Mathilde was the one who woke her. I had already started to undress, was about to go to the*

*bathroom and brush my teeth, when Mathilde asked, 'Would
you like a cognac?' I was tired but I felt compelled by a certain
urgency in her voice. The evenings have started to warm up
and we sat on the patio, she with a cigarette and I with a
cigar. I don't think we talked much at all. Maybe we discussed
Anton, how surly he seemed on the phone. I mentioned
how annoyed I was that he was prevaricating about returning
home this coming summer. My mother is ill; it would gladden
her to see him. We finished our drinks, and I went into the
bathroom to brush my teeth. That's when she came up behind
me; she was staring at my face in the mirror. That's when she
asked, 'Gerard, why don't we make love anymore?'*

*I was stunned by the candour of the question. She was
drunk, her words were slurred, yet there was also a cold insistence there. I truly cannot remember what I answered. I was
conscious of Léna asleep down the hall, and I suggested that
we were both tired, that we had both drunk too much and we
should go to bed and sleep.*

*'I don't want to sleep.' She was angry now. 'I want you to
fuck me. Why don't you want to fuck me anymore?'*

*My body was ice. The obscenities added to my shock. This
was out of character for Mathilde. Though I was terrified—
and I do mean this: I was petrified that she was going to ask
me if I was homosexual, that was my immediate thought, my
primal fear—and though I was indeed frozen, I also felt the
old and tired defences assert themselves. My voice was stern
as I said to her, 'You are being melodramatic, Mathilde. You
have drunk too much. Go to bed.'*

She was being overdramatic. She had shut the bathroom door, and when I tried to leave, she wouldn't let me. Now I was furious. I imagined hurting her. She kept asking, in fury and then entreating, 'Why?' Over and over and over again, the same question: 'Why?' I just wanted it to stop.

'Because you are no longer attractive. I don't desire you.' I shouted it to her face. She crumpled, she was broken. She started to cry.

The exercise book in Léna's hand is shaking. She is trembling. Deleting the pornography from her father's computer that morning after his death, reading in his journals the self-loathing words with which he described furtive anonymous sex in parks and in the back rows of adult cinemas, none of that had disturbed her love for her father. Reading this entry had been the closest she had ever come, even more than in the wild vanity of adolescence, to hating him. Yes, she was also her mother's child. Here, he was vile. Here, he was indeed a coward.

She should take them all, all of these self-pitying journals, build a pyre and burn every single one of them. And with that thought she sees Périclès's hand light the letter, she sees it burn.

She finishes the wine, pours a further half-glass, takes the journal and lies across the settee.

I took back the words immediately. I said that I didn't mean them, that they were untrue, words flung in selfish rage. I told her I think her the most beautiful woman in the world, which is true. She was inconsolable. She wouldn't let me touch her.

She was crouching by the door, sobbing, pushing me away if I came anywhere near her. I sat on the bidet, watching her. Finally, finally, the crying stopped. She pointed to the toilet roll and I unrolled a few sheets, handed them to her. She wiped the tears, the snot, blew her nose. She looked destroyed and I couldn't move. At some point she rose, washed her face, and said we should go to bed. We each took a sleeping tablet; we were hushed as we walked to the bedroom. I dearly wanted to hold her, but she wouldn't allow it. She curled into a ball in her corner. Neither of us slept. Or, rather, it was a long abject night in which the borders of dreaming and nightmare and sleep and wakefulness were blurred. I was haunted by my shame and my disgrace. This body and this soul I have been given, they have been the cause of evil.

We must have slept. I awoke and she wasn't there. I found her in the kitchen preparing breakfast. 'Please get dressed,' she said, clearly not wishing to discuss the events of the previous night. 'We are going to church.' It was an order, and I obeyed.

The house was empty when we returned. Marie had left a note to say that she was at the movies with her boyfriend and Léna had gone over to a friend's house. I washed the dishes and, when I was done, I found Mathilde in the living room, curled up on the settee, reading a book. I knelt before her and began making love to her. She was resistant at first; there was the spark of anger again. I was persistent, kissing her feet, her legs, her thighs. Kneeling before her. It was a gentle lovemaking. When we were done and we were getting dressed, as I was clasping the catch to her bra, she suddenly said, 'Do you want a divorce?' The conflict of emotion I experienced was staggering. There was an initial release, as if with that question she had set me free. Suicide has been a resolute friend, a shadow companion for most of my life. I knew in that moment that if we were to part, I could finally submit to that staunch foe. That was the meaning of the liberation she offered me. Yet almost immediately, even though still in that heightened state, which was akin, God help me, to elation, I glanced around the room, at the photographs of our children and families, the well-stocked bookcases, the mementoes of our travels, and I knew that I loved this life. With her, with the children. Not my own life: my own singular and individual life was worth nothing.

She had turned to face me. Her face was unreadable, neither sadness nor kindness there, a strict impassivity. She was waiting for my answer. 'No,' I said, and followed with, 'Do you?'

She didn't respond immediately. She was looking at me, daring my gaze, with that insistent imperturbability. Then her eyes dropped, and she too quickly surveyed the room. I believe, I believe with such fervour that I think it truth, that she had come to a similar understanding to mine. 'No,' she said. 'I love you, Gerard. I love our life.'

I clutched her, my redeemer, and I could not let her go. 'I love you too.'

She was kind then, soothing, patting my hair as if I were a child. Finally, she pushed me away gently. 'I want to return to my book.'

I went to the study and knelt before the icon of the Black Madonna that I had purchased long ago in Crete. I made a promise to the Virgin that, if she were to give me strength, I would be a good and loving husband to Mathilde, a good father to my children, and that I would never again take my wife for granted. I needed this promise to be sincere, so I did not attempt to lie and promise that I would be faithful. This body and this soul I have been burdened with would not allow that. I promised to be safe. I did ask Her for faithfulness. I did beg for that gift.

I will not take Mathilde for granted. I will not take Mathilde for granted. I WILL NOT TAKE MATHILDE FOR GRANTED!

The repeated sentences are underlined. Léna traces them with a finger, as if in feeling the welt of the raised old ink the force of her father's vow is made manifest. She sucks in her breath, preparing herself for the words to come.

I worked in quiet and, at some point, Mathilde came in and asked if I wanted a coffee. I was at the computer, typing up some notes for a coming lecture. She stood over me, her fingers caressing the back of my neck. I knew in that moment I had been forgiven. I took her hand and I kissed it.

Evil has an iron grip. No sooner had Mathilde brought in the coffee and retreated to the living room, closing the door, I saved the document I had been working on and was

exploring the dimness that is the internet. I devoured images
of youth and men, submitted to that perversity, until sated.
As soon as it was done I could smell the stench on me, the
foulness. I had no energy to return to work. I started reading
some emails.

There was one from that rather gauche young man,
Périclès, whom I had met in Thessaloniki in November. He
was writing to thank me for my lecture, and for the books I
had recommended for him. I was surprised by how pleased
I was that he had contacted me. He was very attractive,
a Greek born in Australia, and he had that diffidence that is
characteristic of his countrymen. None of the confidence and
arrogance of a real Greek. His delight in Europe is childlike.
And like a child, he keeps comparing it favourably to home.
He is intelligent, undoubtedly. I answered his email immedi-
ately. It was pleasing to do so; it seemed to unburden me of
the vileness that had come from succumbing to pornography.
I switched off the computer and went to have a shower.

I am writing this sitting across from Mathilde. She has just
raised her head from her book, is smiling at me. It won't be
long before Léna is home. God knows how long Marie will be,
if she returns at all. I will cook dinner tonight.

The entry finishes there and the next one is not till a week
later. Léna shuts the journal, lets it slip off her lap and onto
the floor. She takes the glass, hesitates, and then places it on the
floor again. She will drink more slowly. She doesn't want to
get drunk.

Her anger has been appeased. Though it is impossible not to be annoyed by the superciliousness of much of her father's tone, and with his cavalier assumption that mere prayers and vows could undo the destructiveness of the words he flung at her mother. *Because you are no longer attractive. I don't desire you.* She imagines Vera saying it to her and she shudders.

Léna looks down at the stained cover of the journal. She is grateful for her father's journals, for the insight they have given her into him as a man. Yet, as she had been the first time that she read this passage, she is troubled by the undervaluing of her mother in his life and in his confessions. The events described have no resonance in her memory. She remembers other arguments, but nothing about the night her father has described. She was asleep, metres from the bathroom. She is confident in her resolve to take the journals, not to allow the rest of her family to read them. Especially her mother. Vera has speculated that her mother must have known about her husband's homosexuality. 'Mathilde is a very intelligent woman,' Vera argues. 'I'm sure she must have guessed.' It is possible. However her mother has never intimated anything of it, and even if one day it should arise, even if she were to speculate with her, Léna doubts that any good could come from her mother reading her father's words.

She sits up straight. The flush of her conviction is so strong that she almost dials the number on her phone. Then she puts it away. She wants to sit down with her mother, to record her, to ask her questions of her life and her childhood and her marriage and her education and her desires and her dreams

and her regrets and her love for their father and her children and
grandchildren; and yes, of regrets and misgivings of family as
well. Léna doesn't believe in the soul, not in the sense of her
parents' belief in its material manifestation. She doesn't believe
in a god or gods. Nevertheless, her father's questioning of the
meaning of soul is not something she wants to ignore or ridi-
cule. Like him, she doesn't remember a time when her love
for and fascination with girls and women was not part of her
being in the world. She knows too that not everyone is as she
is. Vera wasn't consciously attracted to women till university.
Léna's first girlfriend, Adelaide, claimed never to have experienced an attraction to girls. And after they had broken up in
their penultimate year at the *lycée*, Adelaide had never slept
with women again, as far as Léna knows.

It's infinitesimal, a tiny knot of pain within her, and as Léna
exhales, it is gone—yet it still lurks within her body, soldered
to her DNA: the jealousy and shame she experienced when
Adelaide left her for Vincent.

She has come to know her father through his words. She has
to do the same with her mother. Foolish to ring her now; her
mother goes to bed early, and it will only concern her, Léna
ringing three times in a day: she will think her daughter is
grieving for her father, after having laid him to rest. When she
visits in the summer, she will ask her questions, she will record
her mother's voice. She will not assume that her mother exists
only in the in-between of Léna and her father.

The bells toll, eight long, lugubrious chimes. She has been
lost in intermediary time herself; two hours have slipped away.

She fluffs her hair, stretches, as if this can return her to the present. As the last peal sounds her phone buzzes. Vera's name in Cyrillic appears across the screen. She grabs it from the coffee table, answers it.

'My love, how are you?'

'I'm fine.'

Léna can hear a melancholy tune, almost in waltz time, in the background. She guesses it is an old Greek song from sometime in the last century. 'I'm having a wine. How are the boys?'

'Leonidas has gone out to get some cigarettes. Daniele is preparing what looks like a feast and he forbids me to help him cook.'

Léna laughs. Vera is impatient in the kitchen.

Daniele's voice suddenly booms in her ear. 'Where are you, doll? Come over. Now. There will be plenty of food.'

'I'm tired, Daniele.'

He makes a rude and exasperated sound.

'Are you okay?' The other sounds fade; Vera has taken the phone into another room. 'I'm happy to come home if you want.'

'No, I'm fine. I've been reading through my father's journals.'

'You sound a little sad.'

'I'm not.' She pauses, then in a rush she says, 'I'm thinking of a fortnight in Rouen next summer. I want to interview my mother. You should come.'

There is a pause. Léna remembers they had talked of going to the southern Peloponnese for their next summer holiday.

'Maybe I'll go for a week.'

'No.' Vera's voice is firm. 'Take as much time as you like. What do you want to interview her about?'

'Her life.'

'What about it?'

The question is too large, unsettling.

'We'll talk about it later.'

'No, tell me.'

Léna takes a pillow off the sofa, places it on the floor. She sits cross-legged on it. 'Reading Papa's diaries, I realised how little I know about my mother's feelings about her marriage. I'm a little angry with my father. I identified with him for so long, sexuality being something we shared, and the journals confirmed it. I was excited about that, and it made me feel less alone. But I realise that I have ignored Maman. Has there been a Périclès in her life? Has there been a grand passion, a big love? She might not answer such questions and I probably won't ask them, not in such a direct way. But there's so much I want to know.'

Vera is silent.

'You think it unwise?'

'My darling Léna, I think it would be wonderful to sit with your mother and to have her open up about her life. It's something I wish I had done with my father before he died. You have your father's words and that is precious. I am enjoying spending time with my mother and hearing her talk about the past.' Vera chuckles. 'She's more patient, and I'm more patient.' Vera's tone is serious again. 'My mother and I are in the same city, it's so much easier for me. You should go to Rouen and spend the whole of the summer vacation there. I'll come for part of it.'

Somehow Léna is aware of something left unsaid. 'Were you going to say something else?'

She hears Vera's breath catch.

'It might be that their marriage wasn't . . . what did you call it? . . . a grand passion.' Vera, too, uses the French phrase. 'But I think you are being unjust to both your parents in not seeing that it was a great love. Your father chose to stay with her, and he was by all accounts kind and loving towards her, as she was to him. That's no small thing, my Léna; many marriages don't have that consideration at all. It was a different time.'

There's a flickering of the light overhead, a moment of darkness, then another sputtering on and off and the light is back; solid.

'Léna?'

'Sorry, I was just contemplating dinner . . .' Her words trail off. And then she knows what she wants to do; the emotion wells up inside her, the longing, and she succumbs to it. She wants to be with the woman she loves.

'Tell the boys I'm coming over.'

She's thankful for the lateness of the Greek dinnertime: she has time to shower. While waiting for the water to heat, she muses on Vera's words. She is not entirely convinced. Léna can't imagine an intimate love devoid of sexual passion. That has been intrinsic to her since she was very young. She knows this is not the same for all women, and maybe not even all men, but it is the truth for her. She can't imagine loving Vera without loving her odours and her skin, her beauty and her cunt, her warmth and her body. She knows that isn't the entirety of love. As she swings the nozzle of the showerhead across her shoulders and her chest and rubs the soap across her body, she is aware of a heaviness in her breasts. Her period will come within the week.

She turns off the water and steps out of the narrow bathtub and onto the mat. She dries herself quickly. Taking advantage of Vera's absence, she wraps the damp towel around her body and walks out to the balcony. The city is now in night. The temperature has dropped, but not too much. Léna puts on a long-sleeved shirt, her favourite pair of Levi's.

In the bathroom she applies lipstick and eyeliner. She then squeezes a large dollop of styling mousse into one palm, rubs her hands together and runs them through her hair. Grabbing a comb rather than a brush, she rakes it across her scalp. Stepping back from the small mirror in the bathroom, she again surveys her reflection. The casual masculine attire and the severity of her slicked-back hair contrasts with the bright scarlet of the lipstick and the heavy lines of the eyeshadow. She is happy with the result.

She turns off the kitchen light and is about to switch off the lights to the living room when her eyes fall on her father's journal, still lying on the floor. Léna picks it up, intending to return it to the shelf with the other notebooks. She examines their broken spines.

The resolve is immediate. There is an empty Apple laptop carton in the cupboard in their bedroom. She has never got around to getting rid of it.

Léna finds the box, brings it to the desk, and carefully places her father's notebooks into it. She then seals the box with tape. She recalls Périclès burning her father's letter at the temple. The thought is immediate: Should I burn it all?

She will never give the notebooks to her family to read. Certainly not her mother. Whatever comfort her father derived from articulating the hidden labyrinths of his desires and yearnings, he would be mortified to think of his wife reading the words. Momentarily, Léna ponders what her brother and her sister would make of the journals. They have their memories; she doesn't want to betray those understandings. She is convinced that, if her father's death had not been sudden, if he had known his life was ending, he would have destroyed the notebooks.

She will not burn them. She thinks of her nieces and nephews. Marie's children, Etienne and Sabine, who are teenagers. And Anton's daughters, Bettina and Tilda, who are still children. Their characters and their personalities are still forming; she doesn't feel an instinctive grasp of who they are and who they are becoming. However, one day they might be curious to read the words of an ancestor who lived in a time and a place and world that they would never know. And there are Vera's nieces and nephews—*our* nieces and nephews, she reminds herself; maybe one day one of them might be curious to glimpse a distant past.

Her father is there, in the words and sentences and marks and erasures on the pages. She has a vision that is pure and solid and true of herself in old age, taking down the box and opening it and reacquainting herself once more with him. In greater understanding and with greater compassion. There's no one in the apartment except herself. She doesn't believe in ghosts. She kisses the top of the box and feels foolish. She teases Vera for her religious faith, which Léna calls superstition. Yet she believes, if only in this moment, that she is kissing her father's shade.

Léna pushes the box to the back of the shelf. She shuts the door.

The boys live in an apartment near the station in Ano Patisia. She considers a cab but decides against it. The night is mild, and she maintains a brisk pace as she walks along the south side of the Field of Ares, along Alexandras Avenue. She ignores the calls of the drug dealers, pays no heed to the shadowy figures inside the park. There is a group of teenagers sitting on the benches just outside the entrance to Victoria Station. A young girl, slender and tall, her short-cropped hair dyed a peroxide blonde, is leaning against an equally tall young man, his long hair braided tightly and falling over his eyes. He is exquisitely beautiful, as is the young woman. They are sharing a set of earphones, one bud each; the youth clutches the phone in his hand. At the foot of the first flight of stairs to the station a Roma woman has an infant in a sling, has her hand out. 'Please, miss'—her voice deliberately forlorn—'have you any money?' Léna shakes her head. She has no change in her pockets. She holds tight to her bag.

Stepping onto the elevator, an elderly couple behind her, she opens her bag and retrieves a mask.

The platform is teeming, and when the train arrives a crowd forms at each door. There are no free seats, but thankfully the carriage is less full towards the rear. The train lurches forward and she grips a strap. She listens to two young students who are gossiping breathlessly about their friends. The boy, his brow and cheeks flushed with acne, has his fingernails painted black and wears a large white T-shirt with an image of the drag-artist, Divine, pointing a gun, the English words YOU THINK YOU'RE A MAN in lurid pink, running across her black-and-white image. The girl has teased black hair, is dressed in black jeans and a black hoodie, and her face is excessively pale, so that the purple of her eyeliner and lipstick are theatrical, confronting. Léna admires the bond of their friendship, how merciless they are in their ruthless dissection of their friends. They are oblivious to anyone else in the carriage. Only their friendship exists.

At Agios Nikolaos, an elderly couple enters and shuffles along the carriage. His sparse hair is silver. His wife, so petite that Léna feels as if she towers above her, is dressed in mourning black. The forward motion of the train makes the old man stumble, and the seated boy reaches out, grabs hold of him. 'Are you alright, sir?' he asks. The old man, blushing, just nods his head. The boy stands up. 'Please,' he insists, 'sit down.' Almost immediately the girl is on her feet, offering her seat to the old woman.

The adolescents continue to speak about school, but now their voices are subdued.

Léna glances down at the old couple. The man shifts in his seat. 'Is there enough room?' he enquires.

The woman pats his hand, whispers, 'There's plenty of room, husband.' She moves her hand away.

The old man notices Léna looking at him. He smiles. She returns the smile, then quickly looks away.

That gesture, that quick and almost furtive touch, is identical to the way Ivan's hand had rested on Périclès's shoulder at the café that morning; and to that moment she had spied them from the bus station, their gentle physical intimacy.

This care, this love that is not possession, that is what Ivan and Périclès have, what she and Vera have, and what her father couldn't offer the man he loved. But he offered that love to her mother. She closes her eyes, and her father's words become concrete in the image of a couple reaching out and holding each other's hand on the way home from church. These small gestures are enormous; they reveal the bonds of love. A further image crystallises, of her buzzing to be let into the apartment, of being greeted by Leonidas, of walking through to the balcony where Vera and Daniele will be sitting and smoking. She will wrap her arms around her lover, she will kiss her neck, she will kiss her mouth.

A robotic female voice announces first in Greek and then in English that the train is arriving at Ano Patisia. The students make their way to the doors. Léna follows.

Daphne and Thimios, for that is the name of the old woman and the old man, are silent all the way to Neo Iraklio. They are exhausted. It is the anniversary of Daphne's brother's burial and they have spent the day with their sister-in-law, Aliki, in Kallithea. Visitors kept turning up throughout the afternoon. Daphne helped with the preparations for lunch, made the coffees and served the sweets and drinks to those who had dropped by. Thimios, who was a carpenter, cleaned and reinserted the exhaust in the bathroom and fixed the door in Aliki's bedroom. The wood had buckled over the years, and it was not shutting properly. Yet it wasn't their labours that had proved most tiring. In fact, Daphne in the kitchen and Thimios unbolting and sanding down the door, screwing it back in place, had found it almost a relief to be working. It was the endless chatter, the conversations and the reminiscences, that had been arduous. Daphne misses her brother; she had been his favourite from when they were children in the village. He indulged her, protected her. When she had moved to Athens as a young girl, she had lived with him and Aliki. She worries about her sister-in-law: Aliki is nearly ninety, and one son is in Frankfurt and another in Thessaloniki. They are good boys. Gerasimos has never married, but whenever he returns from Germany, he seems content. And he has his health. That's really what matters. She thinks of her daughter, of how broken and angry her child has been since her divorce. That fury is no good; Daphne fears it is eating her from the inside out. No life is simple, and no life is without sorrow. No life is perfect.

She looks at her husband. This balding man, his once-strong hands withered from a creeping arthritis, his heavy belly. How good-looking he had been. Lithe and capable and strong and handsome. She shifts in her seat, moving closer to him. She can't bear the thought of losing him; she thinks she will be maddened by the loss.

Terrible, morbid thoughts. She quickly crosses herself, asks for God's forgiveness.

'What's wrong?'

'Nothing,' she says, her tone harder than she meant it to be. 'I was thinking of Pano.'

'Yes.' Thimios sits quietly, then wipes a tear from his eye. He loved his brother-in-law. They had been true friends.

There is loud music in the square at Neo Iraklio. The taverns and cafés are full of young people. No one takes any notice of the two old people walking past. Daphne and Thimios follow the trainline, then turn into their street. There is the odd rumble of a truck from the distant highway, the weak throb of electronic music from the square. But the night encroaches. The old couple walk into the shadows. There is a glimpse of them, side by side, Daphne deliberately slowing her pace, so that her husband won't be humiliated by trying to keep up. They are there, a faint silhouette in the black of the night, impossible to tell where one ends and the other begins. There is that faint impression. Then there is the merging, the disappearing, and the belonging to the night.

Acknowledgements

I have the great fortune to be published by Jane Palfreyman, who is a tireless and magnificent editor and publisher. I have the greater fortune of having her as friend. I am in debt to Ali Lavau and Christa Munns. Thank you both for the splendid, diligent and wise care you have taken in the editing of this book. I am so very grateful—as I am to everyone at Allen & Unwin.

Thank you to Spiro Economopoulos, Fiona Inglis and Angela Savage for their thoughtful responses to earlier drafts of the novel.

This book is dedicated to Chris Brophy. Her love of writing and her love of literature has inspired me for a long time now.

Her wisdom in matters of love and friendship is, I hope, woven into the very fabric of this book.

Wayne van der Stelt has read every draft. His honesty coupled with his unwavering support makes it all possible. Thank you. I love you.